DOWNHILL FROM VIMY

by Christopher Levan

 FriesenPress

Suite 300 - 990 Fort St
Victoria, BC, V8V 3K2
Canada

www.friesenpress.com

Copyright © 2016 by Christopher Levan
First Edition — 2016

All rights reserved.

ISBN
978-1-4602-8114-7 (Hardcover)
978-1-4602-8115-4 (Paperback)
978-1-4602-8116-1 (eBook)

1. FICTION, HISTORICAL

Distributed to the trade by The Ingram Book Company

ACKNOWLEDGMENTS

Fiction is never easy. Didn't Stephen Leacock suggest that he would find it simpler to write the entire *Encyclopaedia Britannica* than fabricate something from inside himself? Fiction, that spinning of a yarn from nothing, drawing together a few suggestive life strands and knitting them into a credible tale requires courage. When you write fiction you are on your own. No hiding. Your wrinkles are visible, your foibles out of the closet.

Who would do it?

Alas, for the writer, there are some stories that cry out for the telling. Indeed, this novel has been waiting in my computer for a dozen years, unpolished and unpublished until this year, the hundred-year anniversary of the events.

Each time I set fingers to the non-fiction keypad, Great-Uncle Gordon hovered at my shoulder and scolded me for cowardice. "Don't shrink from the task, Lad! Get this right! Too many words. Put it out there plain and simple."

I can hear his voice rising on that last word, making his command sound more like a plea.

Thanks to Gordon H. Davis and many others, this story has finally been told.

I am grateful for the help of my uncle Herb Levan, our family's genealogist, and my own father, Victor Levan, the family chaplain— both now passed. They supplied the bulk of the details regarding the protagonist of this drama and did it with a humour and respect that captured both Gordon's life and his dreams. In retrospect, I am also grateful to my paternal grandmother whose kindness only now shows its sweeter dimensions. This novel is written in their honour and that of the Davis family circle to which Gordon belonged.

Apart from the family connections, I owe a debt to my friends. They patiently suffered through the telling of this story when it was in an oral state. Just a wink, a glass of wine and the question, "So what are you writing now?" and I'd be off on the trail of Gordon Davis. To a person, they listened patiently. My gratitude goes to all those have encouraged me to write this work. Thank you for your open hearts. Forgive me if I went on too long.

Ray and Ann, lifelong friends, have been great champions of this work. Ann edited several versions and Ray has been a constant source of great encouragement. Thank you!

And Bronwyn! You're the best!

My children are always long suffering and I am so grateful they continue to join me for meals. Robert with his great heart, Rebecca with her sharp wit and Matthew, always engaged in the world. Griffin, you are such a gift and inspiration. Likewise, I am so grateful to two daughters-in-law: Tia who is so strong and caring and Monica the wise one. Gracias!

A special thanks to my partner, Ellen, who asked me to take this novel seriously again.

to Robert, Rebecca, Matthew and Griffin, my children
" ... the magic never ends."

To Victor, my dad
" ... they shall walk and not faint."

To Ellen, my wife
"... si je t'aime; Prends garde à toi!!"

And men will not understand us ... We will be superfluous even to ourselves, we will grow older, a few will adapt themselves, some others will merely submit, and most will be bewildered—the years will pass by and in the end we shall fall into ruin.

Erich Remarque, *All Quiet on the Western Front*

AUTHOR'S NOTE

I always thought my great-uncle Willie had died in the First World War. I recall my grandmother saying when she pointed to a stained photo in her family album, "That's your Uncle Willie [sic]. He died in the war." She would often continue as we sat together in her tattered rocking chair, "We all thought he would go places and be somebody." When researching an article on Remembrance Day, my father told me that my great-uncle's name was, in fact, "Gordon." Uncle Herb, the family historian, added that Gordon had not died in the war at all, but had been listed as "missing." The official army version, in its understated fashion, listed him as "unavailable for discharge." Nothing more.

In fact, Gordon was wounded in Passchendaele, and a twist of fate disembarked Gordon on Pier 7, in the early morning of December 6, 1917, the fateful day of the Halifax explosion. That's where he went missing.

Eventually, a war medal arrived for my great-grandmother. Too late! She had already died of cancer complicated by a broken heart. With neither torn body nor black-edged telegram as proof of his demise, it was simpler for the family circle to explain that he had died in Flanders rather than to go into the long explanation of how he had mysteriously disappeared in Halifax. He was gone. The "how" did not matter.

Soon after Armistice, his theological college sent a note to the family asking for the particulars of his death as they were preparing a marble war memorial for the chapel. "Should you wish to contribute, the cheque can be made payable to ..." Later, a few pointed enquiries regarding Gordon's whereabouts came from a distant Anglican bishop. Relayed through the local priest, the questions seemed sincere enough, but too vague to credit. There was one final unsigned letter asking for any information about G. Davis to be sent to a postal box in Montreal. Gordon's oldest sister denied to her deathbed ever receiving it. To each and every entreaty the answer was the same. "Gordon died in the war." Full stop.

Not really ....

DOWNHILL
FROM VIMY

CHAPTER ONE

The Call

Worship is not a casual encounter. It begins with a formal call to the people that proclaims, "Now is the time for gathering into God's presence." The Call to Worship begins the service, sets the tone and settles the troubled heart.

Y. Away, *A Guide to Public Worship.*

Saint John, New Brunswick: Centenary-Queen Square United Church
Tuesday, November 17, 1992, 11:04 a.m.

Gordon is dead.

Why did he take so long? For seventy-five years he's been a ghost, a partial name on a nurse's roster. Nothing more. And of all seasons, he waits until the harbour winds blow icebox cold before exhaling one last time. Cantankerous old captain!

Is that snow? Surely, not yet!

By all rights, I should already have started his funeral. But I wait. It's my prerogative, after all. We begin when I say so. Four minutes past the hour and the needle sharp breeze is picking at the undertaker's men waiting by the hearse. A row of overstuffed black suits, standing by the open door, chomping to get this one inside and over. Small pickings. No audience, no tips. I can see their eyes pleading "Come on, padre! Let's start this one down the aisle."

Only professional pride keeps them silent. In their strained patience, I can see the mark of old man Ferguson, the local funeral home owner. None of his men get out of line. Each day before opening, he calls them to attention like a drill sergeant. "By God, a funeral is a funeral if there are two or two thousand people. So you step smartly." They laugh at him behind his back, but they know he's right.

Indeed, there's not a single emotion out of place in their frost-nipped faces. I would be stomping my feet at least, trying to keep them warm. They don't dare even that! "Stand at attention when the hearse door opens!" They're all wearing that permanently fixed, warm funeral parlour smile—affecting a gracious demeanour. Hollywood could do no better.

Their eyes tell a different story. Underneath the mournful veneer lurk bawdy jokes usually involving a minister, his mistresses and a coffin. Black hearse humour is ready at hand to be used once the paying customers are well-seated in their limos, antidotes against exposure to too much grieving.

Once the client approaches, Ferguson rules. It's strictly business and that means dignity at all costs. At the old man's rates, it costs plenty.

At five minutes past the hour, I see that I am testing even their patience. Wiggling fingers ever so slightly to keep them from freezing, they snatch glances at their watches, wondering "What the hell is the minister waiting for?"

What am I waiting for? A message to make it all make sense? A telegram telling me to hold off until Gordon's mystery is solved or maybe a phone call stating that an unknown heir is arriving on the next flight? It's as if I am watching the end of a movie and expecting the final scene that draws it all together: the long-expected dialogue. "I do love you. Forgive me." "You were forgiven long ago." Okay, there's no final embrace. But surely Gordon deserves more. Can't we have a pithy line of text scrolling down the screen, a final assessment of his miseries, giving his life's movie a satisfying "the End"?

Nothing. Just cold breezes freezing our hands.

Gordon's gone. Admit it! He's gone. No deep mystery to be solved. He was just an old war vet who saw too much death, and didn't have the mental stability to come back from the edge. Dead! Let him go.

Yet how could a century of memories be snuffed out and stuffed into a pine box? Where have they gone? Does anyone give a damn? There are no mourners for Gordon. Not a condolence in sight. There's a small bouquet from my dad and his brother, sent in pity. Not they had any real connection, apart from a nostalgic longing for an uncle of the same name.

The flowers came with a card. "Our deepest sympathy." To whom are they sending it—the "sympathy" that is? I'm not sure. There's no family to receive it. I am the only real mourner for Gordon, and I've only known him a little over a year. He's been lost for too long to have any friends.

I breathe deeply. No more waiting!

Giving the lads the high sign, I open the service book to a well-thumbed page and begin Gordon's funeral. "The Call to Worship." Mounting the steps to the sanctuary, the admonitions of my worship teacher, Professor Kelly, ring in my ear, his Scots' brogue giving his advice divine weight. "Read the wards slowly lad. Dunna run doon the aisle. People need time ti mourn."

I am the resurrection and the life and he who believes in me, though he die yet ... (John 11:25)

Toronto, Ontario: Royal Ontario Museum
Friday, April 11, 2014, 5:47 p.m.

"Shit!"

The call came just as I was digging in Jack's diaper bag for a baby wipe. He'd been holding back for a few days, I think. And of course, it's just as he is most delicately balanced on the change table with pants down and poop exposed that my phone rings. With my left hand on my grandson who is quietly waiting for me to clean him up, I reach for my iPhone with my right.

Now you'll think me a cell phone addicted fool, answering a call when I am mid-diaper. I was actually expecting an important call from my son, with final instructions about putting Jack to bed once we'd left his favourite den of dinosaurs at the museum.

"Hi, Rob!" I answer. "Just in the middle of changing Jack ... did you send along his wipes? I can't find them."

"Excuse me?" come a crisp, feminine, very surprised voice. "I am not Rob, and I don't have Jack's wipes." There's a hint of laughter.

"Sorry ... I thought it was my son calling," I cough and start again. "Can I help you?"

"I hope so. Is this Christopher Levan, the minister?"

"The very same, though right now I am Papa, the diaper-changing grandparent." Jack smiled when he heard the nickname he uses for me. He wiggled a bit, stretching out his arms to be lifted up—he didn't care that his male bits were covered in poop.

"Is this a bad time?" This time the laughter was clear and rich.

"Not the best. Sorry I didn't catch your name? Maybe we could ..."

"Oh, excuse me. I am Patricia Patterson. I'm calling about your dead uncle."

"Sorry ... Uncle Herb?" Jack let out a squawk. He was growing impatient ... wanted to get on to the dinosaurs.

"No ...," there was strained pause, "... maybe I should call again later. It is about your Uncle Gordon."

"Gordon? I am afraid ..."

"Yes, Gordon. I believe you buried him in Saint John in ..." (here I heard the sounds of papers being shuffled) "... in 1992. Do you remember?"

A pause, shaking my head out of grandfather mode. "Of course ..." I was searching my mind for the memories of that distant Gordon. "I do recall Gordon of Buttress House, but I did not know he was my uncle. I only had guesses ..."

"I have proof and," here there was an intake of breath, "... and a serious problem ... Can I call you—?"

"Yes, Patricia ... perhaps you could call me later tonight once I have Jack in bed. Are you calling from New Brunswick?"

"Yes. Thank you, pastor. Ah, good luck with the diaper!"

Just as she hung up Jack managed to put his foot into the mess in his diaper.

"Shit!"

Saint John: Centenary-Queen Square United Church
Tuesday, November 17, 1992, 11:06 a.m.

"Shit."

I stop reciting Scripture and swivel around to catch the lead undertaker, Bob Breen, pulling his hand out from between the hearse door and Gordon's coffin.

"Sorry, pastor." He turned red in the face, mortified.

"No worries, Bob." A slight smile and a memory. "Gordon would have said the same thing—or worse. Let's start again. Okay?"

Bob nods and the coffin comes out of the hearse without further incident and four men carry it up the steps. This one is not heavy. Inexpensive, grey muslin covers the simple pine box that will be Gordon's eternal resting place.

Call me cheap. Gordon was out of his mind for three-quarters of a century and living on charity most of his life. He was penniless. I chose the casket, opting for the stripped down, Ferguson's bargain basement special. (They're not on display. You have to go down to the cobweb-encrusted cellar to see them.) Decent, but not stunning. Why bury money? My Uncle Herb was paying, but I was not about to waste his cash on a coffin.

I make a mental note to send off a gift to the War Amps in Gordon's honour. Not that he was ever amputated. I suppose his truncated memory qualifies, since huge chunks were lopped off long ago. Two hundred bucks in their hands would be a more fitting memorial than a polished mahogany casket that will be dispatched almost immediately. Besides, if Gordon's request for a burial at sea is to work, we will be adding a number of lead weights to his wooden container once we set out beyond the harbour. Brushing these details from my mind, I continue the Scripture reading.

The Lord is my shepherd I shall not want.... He leads me beside ...
(Psalm 23:1)

The minister always walks in front. Pressing a polished red button to signal Michael, the organist, we march down the east aisle, lock-step, slowly. "Abide with Me" floats from the pipes.

Silly, isn't it. Who's here to see the ceremony? Yet attention to detail is not lost.

I owe Gordon a good send off.

From several months back, his clergyman's evensong voice rings in my ears: "My son, never pay respects in half measure. Pauper or prince, we all meet the Great Grump in the same dress. Send them forth with due form and dignity." I had been watching an orderly swing another resident into bed, and Gordon had brought me back to his homily, smartly. "Are you listening, son?" I nodded, promising to pay attention. "There's no short cut to grief. Any funeral under an hour is robbery. I recall one time back in my Dundas days there was just me and the undertaker." Gordon took a deep breath, his eyes gazing into the distance, relishing his priestly life. "Poor old lady died without a single soul noticing, but I gave her the whole service, Great Thanksgiving Prayer, word for word." Subtle.

I groan inside, walking past rank on rank of empty pews. "Well, here goes, my long and now lost friend."

> *For I am sure that neither death nor life ... can separate*
> *us from ...love .... (Romans 8:38-39)*

How many times have I uttered those words of late and felt absolutely nothing. I am paid to deliver God's comfort and yet as I stare back at expectant mourners, I have nothing real to offer, only drivel.

I'd like to shout, "I'm sorry to disappoint everyone. My job in this funeral is to remind you, in eloquent tones of course, that we all die! Full stop. It's all bogus! Death wins. We lose." What did Bob say? "Shit!" That about sums it up. Paradise, the great here after, the blessed shore, heaven ... it's all bullshit.

I can't say it. Not now. Do I have too little courage or too much sympathy? I can't tell! In either case, I suppress the straight-talking speech.

The mourners turn their ravaged souls to me. My professional pallbearers deftly swing Gordon into place below the altar, quickly retreating to the sanctuary steps for a smoke. As for me, propriety stills my tongue ... that and a paycheque.

Here at Gordon's last stand, I can hear his sceptical voice: "God gives no quarter."

I arrive at the front of sanctuary and begin the funeral liturgy.

Dearly beloved we are called here today to offer Thanksgiving and blessing for the life of Gordon Davis. We celebrate all that our Maker has done through him—the lives he touched, the souls he saved.

Oh really! Who am I fooling? Gordon was two pickles short of jar for most of his life. If he actually "touched" anyone, they've gone to their reward long ago. No one has been the recipient of Gordon's touch in years. Still, there was once Jo—whoever she was. Did he touch her? "Let us pray."

> *Dear God, healer of every broken heart, stand with us in*
> *this day our day of sorrow. Amen*

The casket rests between communion table and front pews, close to the family for a final viewing if it is requested.

There is no family, no last leave-taking.

The sanctuary is as I expected. The 1100 seats are almost empty. In the east transept, Miss Mary Pringle, the church secretary who attends all funerals on principle. What does she get from them? A morbid sense of decay? Must speak to Mary about pinched, pained demeanour. Who will come to church if the first person they meet looks like Job and whines like Jonah?

Under the west balcony is my theological student. Brian would never miss a chance to watch the "master" as he calls me. He'll want to know why I am taking it so slowly. What happened to Levan's rule #3? "If you can't say it in ten minutes, you can't say it."

Behind me at the organ is Michael Boyd, ever faithful, always hungry for fees that come from extra services. Beside him sits Betsy Hindling, the soloist. She's permanently at his side. (Are they lovers?)

Front and centre, two rows back, sits Joan Simmons, Gordon's nurse for the past few years and a few Buttress Home staff I know by sight only (no doubt they get the whole morning off to attend this one-hour service ... a fair trade in my opinion). And at the rear is the regular quartet of professional church volunteers who have arrived for my benefit. "We're so sorry, pastor. You have been so good to Gordon! A pity really, but then again a blessing as well ... given his age and state of ... well, you know ...."

Oh yes, I know. "Gordon was off his rocker." That's what they didn't say. Their piety won't permit them to voice what we all know: He was certifiable. A nut case. He ate, slept and shat alone, a crazed captive living inside the mouldy prison walls of his own madness.

Only the small box of his final personal affects speaks of the Gordon who lived behind the walls of his isolation. It sat now in my office, given to me by the nursing home staff after he passed. There as an old, dog-eared Bible inscribed with a verse from 1 Corinthians 13 and signed by his sister, Mabel, a packet of yellowed letters and a fountain pen, also inscribed with a verse from St. Paul. An entire life in a shoe box.

Can you blame Gordon really? Any full-brained being would slip over the edge of the abyss after a month or two of any seniors' home routine. Three meals a day, two washroom trips and four walls for company. Human contact came with the daily inspection by an alien nurse. "How are we today, dear?" No answer was ever expected and no time was ever taken to look beyond his jumbled, stripped down world. Who made an effort to befriend him? The first time I met him, I wouldn't have given him a second glance myself except we were both lost in the basement of his nursing home. He was on a voyage charted by his own reckoning. I was looking for the exit. We both needed an orderly to save us. He to his locked ward, me to the street.

Yes, I went back. At first, obligatory pastoral visits brought me around to his bedside. In time, these duties turned into delightful weekly, then twice-weekly, respites from the grind of the parish. Sure, he was on another planet, but I came to see that his self-imposed isolation had a peculiar charm. Once he began to speak (and that took months), I could lose myself in his solitary playfulness. If I arrived before lunch, his captain's voice would call from the bridge, "Ahoy, matey!" He called me his "first mate."

If my visit was closer to dusk, the captain had switched beds with a priest who always seemed to be in his pulpit. "Blessings on your day, my son,"

The seafarer, a bluff-and-bluster friend, shared his tall tales. A wink in his eye and puff of imaginary pipe smoke disarmed my defences. In contrast, the cleric was rigid and aloof, almost brittle, dripping with pious sweetness. The idle listener might assume he was the quintessential vacuous pastor, but I sensed a Doubting Thomas. Like the shoot of bamboo that will not be resisted, his sceptical side broke through all the pastoral platitudes. Glimpses of a divine fool.

I went back for many visits. Each encounter raised more questions regarding Gordon's past. Piecing together the many disparate threads of his life's journey, I was constantly struck by the absurdity of his wasted life. I came to believe his muted state was self-imposed. Why had he remained silent for so long? What had so twisted his heart that he chose muted dementia over salient livelihood? I wasn't the first to wonder what clock was ticking in his soul.

The nursing home staff collected his few belongings in a liquor store box and gave them to me. Who else would want them? I found this war letter on the top.

Feb. 29, 1916

My darling Gordon:

It's too late now to change your mind and I would never call into question your decision to serve the King, but you will admit that it came as a shock to the family. What on earth possessed you? You never uttered a patriotic sentiment in my hearing. Is there really a loyal heart beating beneath that breast of yours, a heart that even your own dear mother never felt? Surely when the dreadful news of our Edward's sacrifice arrived, your zeal for glory and vengeance would have shown itself? But you read the telegram without comment. No revenge, no dedication to fight in his place.

Oh well, let it be.

I don't want to trouble you now. Goodness knows you'll have trouble enough before long. But we have such high hopes for your career. Father especially. I know you've done the right thing. Don't misunderstand. I believe you can do whatever you want and if it's a soldier's uniform you desire, you'll wear it well. But I can't help remembering when you were just a wee-one; you said you could be a priest. Remember dear? It was a Sunday dinner. You stood up in your chair and with scowls like Reverend Jacob, you pointed a finger at each of us saying, "Why haven't you been good?" We all laughed 'til we cried. I don't think that dream of the ministry ever left you from that point onward. And you did go to the interview at the theological college … we were so sure you would sign up … but for ministry. Not for fighting! And when you came home with an enlistment report—the army!— we were so shocked.

Oh my, we miss you, dearest. I still turn, looking for your ragged shirt coming down the stairs for breakfast. The girls are so unruly without their little boy to smother in kisses. They send their love. Mabel says she'll write. Lil told me to convey her disgust (her words not mine). But that's Lil. If she sent love, I'd start to question her sanity.

Father has been getting weaker, as you know. The dust at the forge is bothering his chest so. He tries to put a bright face on it, but I'm worried. He's quiet since you left and keeps mumbling about being "let down." Don't you fret over him! He'll get over his disappointment and when you come home with a rack of medals—he'll bust his britches with pride. He always expected so much from you. Oh, please don't forget to send a note on his birthday. It would mean so much to him. And while I'm at it, your brother Will is going to the West to look for work, so you'd better get a card in the mail to him before he's gone. Heaven knows when we'll have a new address for him. Calgary, he said, was his first stop. Might as well be in China.

I do miss you. Did I tell you that already?

The news of the war is still bad. Of course, the papers never admit defeat, but reading between the lines, we can all smell it. They use such sanitary words to describe the slaughter of hundreds. Last week the headline was "First Canadian Battalion Badly Cut Up." Sounds like all they need is a bandage or two. Do they tell you what's really happening, now that you're one of them?

Sam Jenkins was found, finally. He'd been missing in action for three months now. As neighbours we tried to put a brave face on it. Now it's final. He's dead. I don't suppose the family knows any more details than that simple fact. They say he's buried in a French village with an unpronounceable name. "Ypres." Fred Lewis joined up last week. Little Freddy off to war! He can't be more than sixteen. I wonder if they'll let him sing his hymns like he did in the junior choir. Bill Miller came back on the last hospital ship. He'll never walk again, but he still has that bellowing laugh of his. Says he's going to take up boat building, poor thing.

This war is a ghastly mess.

Did I tell you I was feeling under the weather of late … can't shake it. Probably nothing.

It's been a little less than three weeks and already, I have a chill dread you'll be gone forever. We do miss you. God bless you and grant you long life.

Love,
Mother

P.S. As per you request, I have sent the books by separate post. Please send me the address in Montreal where you will be billeted for that holiday week you mentioned.

She wished him a long life? Little did Gordon's mother know that her prayers for this beloved son would be answered, in spades. Levan's rule #2: "Be careful what you pray for; God might give it to you."

So what *did* you reply to your mother, Gordon? Why did you answer the call? There's nothing I can see that would point in that direction. The motivation for any sane male to sign up for the twentieth century's biggest blood bath boggles the imagination. And, according to your mom, you never showed the least interest in war. Did you fancy the uniform? Probably not! The glamour then? Unlikely. Was it deeper, wanting to dispel the nagging sense of your unworthiness?

Toronto, Ontario: The 7th Regiment (Fusiliers) Headquarters
Thursday, February 10, 1916, 10:20 a.m.

A huge Union Jack trumpeted the presence of a recruiting office. Boldfaced letters etched into the plate glass front window announced: "The 7th Regiment." Britannia's banners hung gracefully on either side. No question. This was a God-Save-the-King establishment. A sandwich board at the curb featured brave men pointing to distant mountains. "The Hills are calling. Will you join us?" Brass buttons all in a row, gunmetal gleaming, unblemished teeth smiling. Who could resist? In small print was written: "Able-bodied men needed to reinforce the ranks. Apply within."

Gordon's mind had been on Calvin's doctrine of double predestination: who was elected to heaven, who to hell? He didn't see the sandwich board coming. It folded itself and fell with a bang as he walked into it. The sound brought his mind back to 1916.

Like a sleeper awakened from a dream, he stared first north, then south. How did he get here? Was it providence that arrested him at this spot? Reaching down to resurrect the flat-on-its-back advertisement, he glanced into the recruiting office and saw men file past the desks inside. Hats held in nervous grips, fingers tracing the inner bands stained by sweat. Why did they go?

Straightening up and taking a deep breath, he wondered at what Principal Cruikshank had said, that his call might be to Flanders fields rather than Wycliffe College.

Just that morning he'd been tempted. Walking down to the Toronto-bound train with his best friend Freddy, the war cry had sounded. His companion had whispered that he was leaving for the front. Freddy? Freddy Lewis?

"God's sake, Freddy, you're crazy. They won't take you! You're underage."

"Yes they will. Pa wrote me a note saying I was eighteen. Signed official-like and everything." Breathless with excitement, Freddy was beaming. "No, mister, I'm going down to the Wentworth regiment and sign up … soon as next week. It will be grand. This is my chance to prove to my pa, to his blessed Almighty God, that I'm worth something … that I can bring back honour to my family."

God and glory—the two bonfires on which people gladly cast away their lives. Gordon was torn. He took a quick step away from the flag-infested storefront, blindly backing into the pedestrian traffic.

Obstacles kept jumping in his path that morning. Hardly had he taken two paces backwards when he slammed into a frock coat laden with parcels. He turned in time to see her falling toward the sidewalk. He grabbed at a flailing arm and held her upright. Fumbling for an explanation and trying to retrieve Eaton's shopping bags, he felt like the goof of the year. She was old enough to be his grandmother and looked as hard as flint.

"What's the matter, boy? Can't get up the fire to go in and enlist?" She snarled as she found her footing and dusted off her beaver-trimmed sleeve. Obviously, she had been watching him from a distance and presumed his hesitation was the sign of a weak heart.

Gordon waved his hand back up Bay Street toward the college he had just left. "Ah, no ma'am … I … just made up mind to …"

"Good man. Don't be a-feared. My son's in beyond those doors somewhere. Came down here last month, walked up to that desk and I ain't seen him since. Brave lad, he was."

"It is a great sacrifice. You must be proud, but I can't …."

"Sure you can. Life's a long journey made up of short steps. That's what my father said." Smelling hesitancy in Gordon's voice, she took matters into her capable hands—as she always did. "Come along." She grasped this reluctant recruit's arm and steered him back toward the recruiting office door. Small though she was, her grip had the force of destiny. Maybe this was it, his real calling.

Facing the door, he could read the army regulations through the street number painted on the leaded panes of the front entrance.

1. All applicants must be 18 years of age (No exceptions!).
2. All applicants must take an oath of allegiance to King George.
3. All applicants agree to submit to a medical examination.
4. All applicants must adhere to army regulations and submit to its discipline.

It was the word "all" that struck him. They wanted everything you had. No secrets, no small hidden pieces overlooked. No extenuating circumstances.

An eager recruit brushed past Gordon, opening the door, carried on the wings of confidence.

Gordon was confused. He let the door swing back into his face. His mind was forming the word "No," but nothing came from his mouth. A glance over his shoulder and his grandmotherly guide smiled back. "Go on in, son. It's your call."

He never knew her name. In the months to come he joked to himself calling her "Saint Mary, the *smother* of all lost souls." How many other green recruits had she helped into a khaki uniform?

Her hand reached around, twisted the doorknob and flung wide the gates of glory. "God bless you … you'll make your mama proud." She stood watching in solemn assurance as Gordon shuffled inside the recruiting centre.

At first, his idea had been to hover on the edge. The door was closing at his back. Maybe he could slip out later—once this war mistress had left her post.

Sweat and shoe polish. He could smell them both in equal measure as the green, chipped door finally clicked shut. Hands still on the latch—as if it was his lifeline to an outside world—he stared blankly from desk to desk. Grim faces did paper work. Smiling jokers jostled each other as they gave their vital statistics.

Beside him a voice barked, "Name?"

Did he jump? He might have. Startled, he looked down to see a gruff scowl sitting at the entry.

A cough to clear his throat; only a whisper appeared, "Davis, sir."

"Davis or Davies? … Speak up, lad!"

"No 'e'. Gordon Davis." Looking for the escape hatch and suddenly needing to pee, he worked his jaw, stiff with tension. "I just wanted to …"

"Address?"

The commanding voice touched off Gordon's obedience buttons, well-trained reflexes built during his scouting days with a snarling troop leader. "Don't talk back." "Stand at attention when I'm speaking." "Old Crock" they'd called him. Recently returned from the South African campaign, he was bent upon strict military discipline, forgetting most times that this young boys' group was for fun. Gordon recalled dust moles floating in the small rays of sunshine stretching down through window wells of the church basement as the boys marched in formation. Peeling left, circling right, finally all facing forward. "At ease!"

"Address!" Pushing hard on the final "s."

"Ah. 85 Barton Street … in Hamilton, sir. Do you have a …?"

"Age?" No nonsense in this fellow.

"22 … this January."

"Right. My boy, here's your enlistment form." Big stubby fingers pointed to the bottom left. "That's your identification number: 02698. Memorize it. They'll use it to print off a tag like this one I have." The clerk tugged a small cross on a silver chain out of his shirt and showed how his name and number were neatly engraved on the back. Gordon looked closely, feigning interest. At close range he could whisper his request. "Is there a washroom nearby?" Something touched the older man's funny bone and he grinned.

"Happens to the best of us." *Soto voce.* "Down that corridor, third door on the left." A green sleeve pointed north, and Gordon went off in search of relief.

A louder voice growled at his back. "When you're done son, take that paper to the desk sergeant and he'll fix you up." A pause, some ruffling of papers, and the same bark, "Name?"

"Fix me up?" Gordon mumbled to himself at the urinal, eyes forward. Sounded like a blind date. At the wash basin, Gordon pushed his hands into the chilling water and examined his face in the mirror. Was that fear he saw winking from the corner of his eye? This was crazy. How could he be joining the army when he had just concluded an entrance interview to Wycliffe College? The priesthood was his calling, not this military posturing.

"Hurry up in there!"

He wiped his hands on his pants and opened the door. No towel was provided—foreshadowing of a persistent problem: the military asked you to do a job and never provided effective tools for doing it.

Turning right toward the waiting desks, another directing arm pointed south to the waiting enlistment officers and a line of civilians. "You can take your oath with those other lads."

Gordon tried to protest. He got a "No" out … but it was lost in the shouting of an officious enlistment officer. "Right, you lot, get in a straight line, on the double. Attention!" Gordon edged his way back towards to the front door. "You there … no loitering about. Get your sorry ass over here." The hard voice and a glare that matched were directed at Gordon. "Get over here now! You sorry excuse for a soldier! Wimp!"

Gordon's pride was piqued. He was no wimp! He walked straight to the line of men, took his place at attention and waited.

That was it. It wasn't like he'd said "Yes" to God and country and marched off to prove his patriotism. In fact, he had gone in search of a washroom and been too embarrassed to say "No." He didn't follow orders blindly or out of fear. Gordon just had trouble denying people what they asked—the fate of a youngest child. A near fatal flaw in the trenches of Ypres.

"I, Gordon Davis, do pledge allegiance to …"

Montreal, Quebec: Thelma Lint's Gentlemen's Parlour
Saturday, December 8, 1917, 6:30 p.m.

"Who are you?" A sharp retort. Sally, the maid, was not disposed to be polite to strangers who hammered on the door without invitation. Firm fingers clasped the door ready to slam it shut at the slightest provocation. Her eyes flashed resolution. No beggars, no hobos!

"I'm … I'm Gordon Davis." He took a breath to steady his nerves, shivers and chills creeping up his legs. A winter rainstorm had plastered his hair flat. What was left of his uniform was blood stained and tattered. The woman's cape he had found on the street in Halifax hung limply from his left shoulder. Gazing down, a faint smile traced over his lips. His odd pair of boots were still there, now covered in so much mud that they could have been mistaken for a matching set. A limp handkerchief dangled around his neck—a simple knot keeping it in place. From the look on the child who barred the door, Gordon realized he was a frightful sight—a washed up and lost cat.

In his prime Gordon was a strapping six-footer, dark hair and clean-shaven. His charm, if he ever admitted it to himself, was not in good looks, though he was passable. Rather it was his gentle heart and open, clear eyes. He had an inviting expression that was magical—when, like I said, he was in his prime. Now bruises covered his highbrow. His beard was a four-day stubble and his lips were swollen from the bruising of the fistfight on the freight train into the city. He'd won the battle and kept his place near the door, but it had been costly. He looked a wreck.

Memories float in and out of his mind. His sister's letter that, against all odds, had come to his hand so quickly. "Mother's gone!" The broken wreckage of the Halifax train station. A baby crushed by a beam … so much death.

Periodic shakes came without warning, and snivels were constant now. Gordon watched his hands move, as if without bidding, to wipe away the drivel from his nose. How had he arrived at this doorstep? The march up countless streets was a blur of melting slush and coughing jags.

"I'm looking for Jo. Could you please tell her that I'm waiting for her?"

"She don't see anyone, no more. Now she's got Samuel, that is." The door started to inch shut.

"Please … I …."

"She don't got time for no young fellas. So you'd best be off." Sally's hand was moving to the deadbolt, ready to throw it home.

She had seen it too many times before. Men! Always ready for the pleasure, but they ain't never ready for the pain. Soldiers were the worst. Love you and leave you. This one ain't no different.

"Please, can't you just …" Gordon took a step forward to press his point. He could feel the war anger building as he pleaded through the fast closing crack in the doorway. "Just … Please … I'm at my wits' end!" These last words were thick with frustration.

Sally saw the fire rising in Gordon's eyes. She'd seen that before, too. Night before last even. Got beat up badly by that soldier fella, when she wouldn't … meet his every need. Bastards … everyone of 'em! Bastards!

Sally hesitated. Thelma always said to them, "Remember ladies, business is business. Don't refuse a good client's money." Times were very hard and maybe this fella had a few extra dollars he wouldn't mind losing in a gentleman's parlour, laughing to herself. Opening the gap wide enough to allow her full face to become visible. "Look, mister, if you want some company, there's plenty of other girls here will do you up fine—even get you a wash beforehand." The door was now almost completely open. "You might even fancy me." This last offer was punctuated by suggestive tongue stroking lip action.

If she had swung a rifle butt at his head, Gordon would have been less surprised. "Is this a ... a whorehouse?" He was reeling at the possibilities.

"Whorehouse?" Sally spit her derision. "Get off with you. This here is a respectable establishment—Mrs. Lint wouldn't have it any other way. A 'Gentlemen's Parlour' is what we are. Now be off. Find yourself some tart down on St. Catherine's Street if you're looking for a quick blow."

"Jo is living here?"

"What's it to you?" Sally began to close the door again.

"Please don't ..."

"Look, Jo was to meet me in Halifax and ... Well ... she didn't or ... I couldn't find her ..." Sally looked blank—she wasn't following him, and so Gordon backed up a bit. "I'm a soldier returned from the front. I got into Halifax just a few days ago. You may have heard that there was an explosion in the harbour there?" He paused hoping for some sign that she was aware of it.

A slight nod of recognition. "I heard of it, yeah. So?"

Gordon tried again, "Well, it was so messy ... I mean ... there was utter chaos ... no one knew where to turn to get information. I just thought she might have missed my boat or been caught in the fires. Who knows?" Misery began to spill out after days of being bottled inside. "For twelve hours I searched for her in the rubble of a train station, under beams down by the wharf, but I found nothing. Then I spent the night walking down rows of hospital beds. Still nothing. I was getting desperate and couldn't stand still. Finally, I jumped a freight train. If she went back home or never left Montreal, then I knew I had to come and find her here. You see, don't you? I've been looking for her in all her old haunts. I don't know where else to turn. Can't you see I'm at my wits' end?"

Gordon paused for breath. "She wrote me ... See! He dug into his right pant leg pocket to retrieve a few crumpled envelopes. His hand pushed itself forward clutching as evidence. "She wrote me in France and said ...." Frozen fingers tried to unravel the top letter. "She said she'd be there! Where is it?" Pointing to the line, "Right here ... here it is. 'Pier

7, December 6th.' And I ... after the blow up ... well ... she wasn't there so I came ... I came here to find her."

It wasn't making sense. Gordon could see Sally's troubled look deepen. "No one's home down in the Pointe where her father lives and I ... well ... one of her notes mentioned this address so I naturally thought. Please ... is she here? I just want to ..." It seemed ludicrous to pour out his soul to a mere child and Gordon's voice finally lost its footing and halted.

"What a load of bullshit!" Sally thought bitterly. "I've heard some stories even in my short life, but this one beats 'em all. Even if this Davis fella is her prince charming, why should she have 'im?" Sally never got anything given to her. Why should Miss Fancy Pants Jo get a man for herself ... and one who loved her enough to crawl over an acre of broken glass to find her. Why should Jo be happy in this shit-hole of a world, when I ain't?

"She ain't here, you deaf or something!"

Gordon visibly shrank. His back went limp and his shoulders slumped down in despair. "She works here does she?" It was barely a whisper.

Sally was losing her patience again. The wind was blowing rain into the vestibule. She'd have to mop it up, if this interview lasted much longer. "Now, either come in and get another woman for your pleasure, or leave." Gordon simply stood there.

"Be off with ya, Bastard, or I'll call a policeman!" Sally threw the door shut with a bang.

Gordon seemed fixed to the wooden planks of the front step as Sally slowly shut the door and pushed the bolt into place. She didn't want this maniac coming back at her unawares. So shut him out. Patting her apron, shaking off the raindrops. Before turning to go back to the needs of her mistress and her "guests" she took a quick glance out the window just to be sure.

Gordon hadn't moved. In the porch light, the shadows of his face were exaggerated. He had a well-worn and wearied countenance. Here's one who had seen far too much. Under the fatigue lurked a handsome face: eyes that could shine and sparkle no doubt. A pity he was broken.

His uniform was almost non-existent. There was the red maple leaf on his shoulder, but some fitful hands had ripped off all the other insignia. It was only the rough cut and the colour that betrayed its origins. Water dripped down from his nose and clenched jaw. He seemed unaware of anything. Shut down, lights off.

"Men! One minute they're fucking monsters and the next helpless puppies! Fuck'em all!"

Thelma, her full-length skirt whisking at the hardwood, passed the living room. Seeing her parlour maid staring out the window, she asked Sally what was keeping her from her chores.

Sally murmured, "Just some daft soldier lookin' for a cheap lay."

The fastidious Mrs. Lint shooed Sally back to her scrubbing of the front hall. "Mop up that water. Who brought that in anyway?"

The boisterous patron in Celine's room shouted again. He was a regular and potentially violent. "More beer." His voice shook the house, and Thelma, always aware of bottom line issues, hurried off to supply the drunken sot with another tankard. The significance of a rain-drenched soldier was washed from her mind, only to be revived much later and much too late to be of any use.

For the time being, Thelma dealt in sorrow, sex, greed and gluttony. They were all actors on the stage of her playhouse. She had come to accept each for its own value and not pass moral judgment. As she said to herself often, "In the end, death takes all comers no matter their virtue or lack thereof."

Saint John: Centenary-Queen Square United Church
Tuesday, Nov. 17, 1992, 11:14 a.m.

"Friends … death catches us all unaware."

There's a bit of vaudeville in all ministers. We love to act. Just look at us. Any Sunday morning finds us dressed up in flowing gowns, pretending to wield the power of the Almighty as we perform before our pious audiences. The best mask our theatrical inclinations in self-deprecating smiles. The worst strut about on high heels of self-importance.

Funerals bring out the best and worst. God must hate us, when, at times of death, we feign deep compassion. We mouth our deepest sorrow, all the while thinking of next week's holiday by the lake! Mercy, we're a pitiful lot.

At this point in the funeral, a touch of the theatre is helpful. Mourners need to know who's in charge, and feel that God is present. So I use my preacher's voice and profess my faith with Luther-like boldness. Slowly. Let the words roll over the crowd like a comforting blanket of hope:

"Friends, death catches us all unaware ... but listen again to the promises of our Saviour in Scripture:

> *Let not your hearts be troubled; believe in God; believe also in me! In my Father's house are many rooms; if it were not so, would I have told you that I go to prepare a place for you. And when I go and prepare a place for you, I will come again and take you to myself.... Thomas said to him, "Lord we do not know where you are going, how can we know the way?"*
>
> *Jesus said to him, "I am the way, and the truth, and the life ... I will not leave you desolate; I will come to you. Yet a little while and the world will see me no more, but you will see me; because I live, you will live also.*
>
> *Let not your hearts be troubled, neither let them be afraid." (John 14: 1-6, 18-19)*

Brian is wincing. He'll correct me later. True. That reading was a tad long. I usually do a shorter excerpt, but these verses from John were obviously important to Gordon. That page in his Bible had been thumbed frequently—whether by conscious choice or the result of an obsessive short circuit, who can tell?

One more reading and I can wheel behind the altar for prayers. The service book lists a number from which to choose, but I reserve a special one for vets. It works well for the militarily mind that is always surveying the horizon for reinforcements. Given that the people of Israel often hid their extra troops in the hills above a battle, this psalm makes eminent sense.

> I will lift up my eyes unto the hills
> From whence comes my help.

> My help comes from the Lord who made heaven and earth. (Psalm 121:1)

Vimy Ridge, France: Forward Observation Trench
Sunday, February 11, 1917, 1:30 p.m.

"Fucking hills."

The curse woke Gordon. He rolled over and exposed his mud-caked stomach to the sky. Time to wet his back. Opening one eye, squinting at the ragged ridge of clouds blocking the sun, he yawned. "What hills? You mean the ridge."

"Not 'hill' hills, you idiot." Gordon's companion, Jack the Snake, paused, blew a wad of snot from his nose. "The sandbag mounds on the opposite side. Each night after 'Stand Down,' we shell the hell out them, sweep them level. Every day Fritz builds them back, making fucking higher hills than the night before. I can see the little bastards have been busy, but I can't catch them at it."

"You've been sleeping again."

"No bloody way. Think I want to get crucified like Fred?"

Gordon was still groggy. "Fred?"

"You know the guy, that sentry, nodded off for a few minutes. Last week sometime. His captain catches him. Jesus—21 days of standing for two hours strapped to a cartwheel back at the billets. Christ, it was fucking shameful. No I'll stay awake until it kills me."

"Jackie boy, how long you been out here?"

Sniper fire forced their heads into the mud. For ten minutes they hugged their knees and waited. Fear was a tight knot in their bellies; German darts whizzed past their dugout.

When it had petered out, Jack was back up to the fire step, watching his section of crater holes. Wiping sweat from his brow, and licking away tension, tasting salt. Eyes always forward—the cardinal rule. Watching, waiting for death to pour over the facing ridge. How long had he watched those few yards of poisoned turf?

"Hear anything about an attack tonight? 'Course we'd be the last to know." Jack spat in disgust. It landed on the mud wall beside Gordon. "Always the last to know … Fucking five-star assholes! Shit for brains. Pass me the shovel will you, Gordie boy. I need to clean off the top here."

Up came a spade. Gordon hardly moved, didn't care!

Careful not to expose any piece of his uniform, and flinging the worn handle full in front, Jack dislodged a clump of grass in his line of vision. Behind it, a human hand stretched skyward still clutching a can of bully beef.

"Shit. It's Gregory. I thought you lads dragged him off last week." The stench of rotting flesh wafted back into the trench. "Christ, I thought he stank in life!"

Rolling to his stomach and inching upward, Gordon peered over the top. "I was off duty. They said they took him back to the pits. You sure it's Black-ass Gregory?"

Jack grunted. "The very same—look at that wart on his thumb—not a second like it on God's good earth."

Gordon regarded the hand as if peering at a quaint church relic. Dying was empty out here beyond sanity and civilization. "This line was cleared after Wednesday's counterattack, but I guess they pitched a few over the front. What happened to him?"

"Caught at daybreak with his breakfast," Jack sighed. "Little fuckers across the way clipped him as he was digging into his iron meat."

"'Iron meat?' That's a new one."

"Emergency rations, dolt." Jack grunted again—a persistent root was jabbing his ribs. He shifted slightly. "Now, I ask you. Where's the decency in this fucking place? Really! The Huns have no place killing a man while he's filling his gut. And at dawn of all times! Makes me want to quit this mess and go farming. Now what was it you asked?"

"How long you been here, at the front?"

"Too bloody long. Came in August of '15." Jack snapped his rifle butt into place and peered down the sights. "Come on you little fucker …

show me some skin! ... Gordie boy, I'm the closest you'll ever come to an 'original.' Only old Bill has been here longer. I arrived in time to be part of the bloody mess at Loos. We took the blasted village. For what? Who knows? So they could shoot at us from three sides, rather than one. Oh, that was a pretty piece of work."

Gordon was still idly staring at the dead hand—all that remained of an interrupted breakfast ritual.

"Me son, I've been here too long. Say, did you hear the one about the soldier who comes to enlist? The sergeant asks him how long he put in for and the blockhead replies, 'A seven-year stint.'"

"So?"

"'So,' the Sarge replies, 'You're fucking lucky. I put in for the duration of the war.'"

Laughter trickled down the trench.

"Quiet there!" An officer's crisp whisper stilled the troops.

"Thinks he's a bloody redcap general," Gordon moaned. No one liked the current captain of their platoon. But since officers came and went with regularity—they were the first targets of snipers on all sides when battle was joined—no one got too excited about their foibles. All part of the slimy insanity of war.

Gordon squinted over the gravel and muck of no man's land. His mind turned to their day's assignment. "Are there many over there?"

"Some."

A feeble moan wafted over the rain-soaked craters.

"Mmaaaa."

Was it a call for water, a sigh of agony or a plea for the Virgin to come with aid?

"What was that?" Gordon's eyes turned toward the animal sound.

"Isn't he dead yet? I'll shoot himself, the fucking fool." Jack had little patience for dying men. "Get it over with and leave us to fight in peace."

"MMMMaaaaa." This time the groan was laced with agony.

"Who is he?" Gordon strained, searching for the wounded man.

"I dunno." Jack spat again, this time over the sandbags in front. "Some loonie down the line. Broke loose screaming about a rat eating his toes and scrambled over the top. Got half way across before snipers clipped his leg." Jack guessed, "He's been lying there for three hours at least. Hasn't said anything for some time. I thought he was dead or sleeping. Listen, you're a stretcher-bearer. Go save the bastard."

"Not my section," Gordon sighed, as a coil of cowardice wrapped itself around his stomach.

"Maaa mmmummma!"

Jack lowered his rifle and leaned his forehead against the barrel, eyes always forward. "Looks like he's not going to die out there, not for some time. Not with only couple of leg wounds. The rats will have him first. Better to shoot him, if we could!"

Gordon could think of no response. He knew his duty. "Damn Saint Mary—she got me into this mess. She can bloody well get me out." Rolling back into the trench and crouching with his back to the parapet, he looked for some likely assistants. He could see a number of men slumped in their funk holes, eyes downcast. No one wanted to risk his skin for a half-dead crazy man. Too many brave souls had been sacrificed working the business end of a stretcher in no man's land.

In past weeks, Gordon discovered he was never a welcome visitor to the fire trench. He was the last of his company and now he depended entirely on volunteers to do his job.

"Too late for that bugger," someone mumbled.

Gordon knew it was hopeless. "Captain."

"Quiet, you bloody oaf."

Whispering, "Captain ... there's a man out there needs a stretcher party." Gordon still could muster an urgent edge to his voice. How could he even care after so many close calls, the long nights crawling on his knees only to find the downed soldier was already stiff, crawling with half-starved maggots?

"Not now, Gordie—Fritz is too blinking close."

"Mmaaaa!"

"Captain ... I can't just leave him there."

"Like hell you can't. It's suicide going out there in broad daylight. That's why that bloody fool is out there in the first place."

"MMUMMMM!"

They say the loudest cry comes just prior to death.

Grunts broke out along the trench. "Can't get any sleep with him whining." "How's a body supposed to rest with a talking corpse next to his ear." "Just in the way if we do attack!" The captain could feel his command slipping as his men's bottled-up frustration mounted.

"All right, Gordie. It's you alone. Your call. Over the top and see if he's worth saving."

Satisfied, Gordon pushed up to stand on the fire step beside Jack. He scanned the terrain again. "Which way is he lying?"

"Downwind about 20 yards, off by that roll of wire near John's barn." No movement from Jack, just his eyes directed Gordon's gaze. John's barn was actually just the remnant of a brick foundation. The roof, walls and floor had been blown away by shells or carted off for trench building. Each side had used it as a safe haven and machine gun nest. No one could remember who John was or why his barn was getting in the way of the war. "Don't think he's down in the basement. Maybe beside it. Get him out if you can. His groaning will wake someone soon. But mind … they'll get a bead on anyone who gets close to him. Watch you don't stick that pretty head up too high."

Without thinking—thinking makes you stop—Gordon belly-flopped onto the wet sandbags that formed the top of the trench.

"Watch, you don't stick that pretty head up too high!" Gordon mimicked, as he crawled forward. He had done this too often to make that silly mistake. "Why is it always 'my call'? Doesn't everyone, from generals to privates, have a duty to save human life?" The army seemed prepared to sit on its hands and waste the finest sons of its country, the first betrayal Gordon knew in that season of carnage.

Not his last.

"It's my call!" he mumbled to himself as he wiggled his way forward. Ten yards into the muck beyond the front line and he could feel the mud squeeze between the buttons on his tunic and under his waistband. God, the smell! Urine laced with the reek of a slaughterhouse and rotten eggs.

"It's my call." His right hand brushed aside a rotting, half-buried uniform in his path. German grey. A fearful duty pushed his body onward, while his mind disengaged and flew to safer havens. When danger loomed large, his mind went back to another "call."

Montreal, Quebec: 27 Sebastopol Street
Monday, March 20, 1916, 1:30 p.m.

"39, 37, 35," Gordon mumbled to himself and counted the doors down to his destination, half-hoping N°. 27 was missing, bombed-out or hidden. He walked through the bluster of a March storm. The wind whipped pinpricks into his face. Cold? It was January all over again on the day before spring! Everything was topsy-turvy in these blood-drenched years.

Squashed between an access archway leading to the back alley and the corner pub, 27 Sebastopol Street was distinguished from its neighbours by a fresh coat of paint and evenly hung shutters. The street whispered poverty. In contrast, N°. 27 spoke of affluence. Someone had money.

Gordon turned in the short walk and faced his doom: The home of the Very Reverend Douglas Samuel Hinks, the Bishop of the Diocese of Montreal.

The entryway was neat and well maintained. A small stained glass transom topped the doorway. Bevelled wooden trim outlined the door and a small oval window graced its upper portion. Below the window, polished and proud, was the brass front door knocker shaped as a lion's claw clutching a maple leaf. Gripping it with a bare hand, Gordon could feel the frost. The tingling metal conjured up the memory of when he had touched a curious tongue to the white frost on the iron knocker of his Barton Street home. "How I howled when Mother poured on hot water to dislodge my stuck tongue. Dumb kid."

The doubt bubbled up again. "Am I any better now?" he wondered. Gordon had trouble loving that silly little boy, tongue stuck to his own front door. Too full of mistakes! He let the brass paw drop. Its heavy thud shook the glass of the oval window.

No one appeared at the entrance. Rapping at the door a second time, he thought gladly, "Maybe they're not home." Relief began to flow. He could discharge his duty with a card, something brief. "Your Grace, I came to bring greetings from the principal of Wycliffe College. He sends his warmest regards. As I am on the way to Europe, I could not tarry long …."

Gordon was reaching for his pocket diary and pencil when he heard distant, muffled footsteps. He froze. Then came the crisp rasping of metal on metal—the lock. Someone was opening the inner door.

There was still time to beat a retreat. A courtesy call on the local Anglican bishop made no sense to his young mind, but Principal Cruikshank argued in its favour. "Let him know you're in town and going overseas. He'll help you around," read the message on the card responding to Gordon's explanation of his enlistment. The good principal and churchman had waxed eloquently about Gordon's choice. "How brave it is for you to see a higher calling within this call to arms. Of course a place will be kept waiting for your glorious return. You'll serve your Lord in France, too!" Gordon winced, at this last line. It didn't ring true.

In the trenches he would be blunter: "theological bullshit." It was served up each Sunday to the men at the front. Gordon thought of it as religious slop, as tasteless and useless as the swill that canteens served when they ran out of meat. In those first few weeks in uniform, his ability to taste duplicity was still untrained. Cruikshank's words were just "preachy." Betrayal was, as yet, a totally foreign flavour.

In a postscript, the good doctor had instructed his soon-to-be-student to visit the bishop of the diocese of Montreal, The Very Reverend Douglas Samuel Hinks. "A great friend—27 Sebastopol Street." And in a curious turn of phrase, "… living among the poor Irish."

It was only as Gordon alighted from the tram on Wellington Street that he understood this. This was certainly not the neighbourhood for a bishop. Houses crowded right to the sidewalk, the air filled with rank odours from overflowing outhouses, mixed with the railyard smoke and a sweet stench from the sugar refinery down by the canal.

Gordon turned around to look down Sebastopol Street. This was not even a rustic haven of quaint walk-up flats. It was a string of tenements constructed in the last century, built to last, but not for comfort or beauty. Bishop Hinks lives here?

Why on earth would anyone choose this hovel over the bishop's palace behind the cathedral on St. Catherine Street?

Before a reply came to mind, a diminutive beauty opened the door. "Yes?"

That voice was imprinted on his brain immediately. It had a husky depth, with luscious softness in the lower register. Quite exceptional, and somehow out of keeping with the small frame from which it came. One would expect such a delicate being to produce a soprano-like sweetness. Not so. In the months at the front, the hardy texture of that one word, "yes", would float to him out of the night, sailing effortlessly across the barren fields of rot.

This woman had an electric charm. Blue eyes, set wide apart, direct and piercing. Dark red lips were a contrast to a faint complexion. Finely combed blond hair fell around her shoulders and disappeared over her back. Not a classic beauty, but a stunning picture, nonetheless.

Gordon opened his mouth. Nothing came out but a half-croak. "I … I have…." A glance at his feet!

"Yes?" This time it was accompanied by a gentle smile. Gordon could feel his cheeks flush as he searched for a dignified way to introduce his mission. "Hellos" had never been easy for a boy who had a blustery exterior and retiring interior. "I … I have come to introduce myself to the bishop." What a pompous start!

Gordon pulled out Cruikshank's card. He offered it as proof of his intentions. Not a peddler or an errant soldier, he had a place—even if a distant one, in this household of God. "Is he home?"

"Come this way." No explanation, no hesitation. Was she always so trusting of stray uniforms? She must be accustomed to strangers—Anglican lads showing up at this door on the way to the trenches. No doubt, seeking one last bit of assurance. A prayer for protection before sailing.

"Johanna," not turning.

"Pardon me?" Gordon was still watching her back as they threaded down a hallway lined with books. Long hair flowing to her hips, hips that moved like music.

"Johanna, my name is Johanna." Spoken with experience and layered with just the right thickness of warmth. "And you?"

Gordon groped about for his manners and drew breath for his introduction. "I'm sorry, Miss Johanna, forgive me for being so tongue-tied. My name is Gordon Davis. I'm a ministry student from Wycliffe College in Toronto. The principal of the college suggested that I visit Bishop Hinks when in Montreal." Once the dike was breached, the flood of words wouldn't stop. "I don't want to bother his Lordship, if he is occupied, but I was in the area and felt that it would only be … ah … fitting … I mean … I don't mean to intrude on his very busy schedule, but …"

"Not at all." There was laughter in her tone as she looked over her shoulder and stared directly at him. "Come this way."

Her eyes were brilliant, direct and somehow daring him. Did she wink or did he imagine it?

He wasn't sure.

Saint John: Centenary-Queen Square United Church
Friday, Nov. 13, 1992, 10:20 a.m.

"Are you sure?" My mind was racing down the list of possible ailments. "He often goes silent, shuts down and looks for all the world like a corpse."

"Yes, we're sure. Gordon's dead."

The call had come when my right hand was trying to shake dry coffee-drenched fingers. It's the damn half-door locks. Never fails. I'd gone for my morning caffeine fix and Mary had locked the bottom half of the office Dutch door behind me. So I fiddled with keys, papers under my arm. Next week's board meeting was running through my mind while my-not-so free hand was clutching a mug of java in mid-air. Of course, it dribbled down my hand. Mary could see me juggling paper, keys and coffee, but she sat resolutely at her post, slitting incoming envelopes.

She likes that part of the job best. Slitting envelopes. It gave her an emotional rush, opening other people's secrets, being derisive about it at the same time.

I found the latch, set the mug on a coaster by my computer, reached for a Kleenex and the phone rang in the outer office. After a few perfunctory comments, Mary shouted, "Undertaker's on line 2!"

The call!

As I wiped down my fingers, I thought, not for the first time, that my secretary was never one for delicacy. Lifting the receiver, I pondered how, at some distant date, she might be taught to say something more professional: "Could you please answer line 2? I believe it's Samuel Ferguson," or maybe a simple: "The Funeral Home is calling with an urgent message."

As always, when the undertaker calls, I run through the list of close cases. I see hospital beds, folk on the brink. Who is dead this time?

"Yes?"

A smoke-scarred voice scratches back, "Morning, pastor. I have bad news, I'm afraid. It's Gordon, Gordon at the Buttress Home. He died just this morning."

"Dead? Are you sure? He often goes silent, shuts down and looks for all the world like a corpse."

"Yes, we're sure. Gordon's dead." Old man Ferguson paused. "Sorry about this, Chris. Gordon. He was close to you ... ah ...." He was reading his client form, scanning for the connection.

"He's just a friend, a close friend."

"Not a relation?" I could hear more papers been shuffled. "He had you listed as next of kin. Sure you're not related?"

"No," still trying to fathom that Gordon had finally died. Funny thoughts push their way in. I always assumed such bad news would arrive in a more sacred moment. Doesn't the dreaded call always come at midnight? Drowsy with sleep you grope for the phone, only to hear the curt, final words, "He's gone." Then you fall back and sigh. Or why not on a Saturday morning when you're sitting at the breakfast table planning another foray into the garden, juice glass poised to expectant lips, and then, "the Call." Setting down the glass awkwardly, it tumbles, juice spills. The grim message.

But not now and not like this.

"Gordon is dead?" I parrot the words, still unbelieving. "When? I mean? Thank you, Sam. I wasn't expecting ...."

"Of course, Chris, it always takes us with such surprise. Please accept my deepest sympathies."

"Sure. Listen could I just ..."

"Take all the time you need." The undertaker was patient. We'd worked together often enough. I'd never been on the client side of his well-oiled manners.

I peer out the window toward the harbour. High winds were blowing the white caps—mist rising from the far shore.

"Sam, we have it all arranged. Right? I mean ... how did it happen?"

"He passed away less than fifteen minutes ago. Well, that's when they found him. He was okay at breakfast and when the nurse came to dress him for his morning shave, he was gone. Your line was busy, so I got the call. They didn't say much but believe it was his heart. Do you still want to follow the instructions you left with me?"

My wits were coming back. "To the letter, just as he wanted."

"Okay," with resigned affirmation. "As you wish."

"No, I told you before. It's as Gordon wished."

"Right. We'll get started. It will take some time to arrange the boat. The high seas over the past few days won't make it any easier. Are you sure you don't want any visiting?"

"Sam, we've been over this. You know Gordon had no friends or family left."

"You're the boss."

"I only wish I was." There something about Gordon that made me think he was really in charge. His madness was too purposeful.

"What was that?"

"Nothing ... thanks again." Replacing the receiver, I draw out the funeral prayers and orders of service. This one had better come out of the book. I don't think I could keep a lid on my feelings otherwise.

Toronto, Ontario: Wycliffe College
Thursday, February 10, 1916, 9:10 a.m.

Gordon balanced from one foot to the other, trying to control his thoughts, focus on the pending interview. The conviction that fired his soul was flickering erratically. Maybe this isn't what God intended after all.

Pictures on the wall portrayed the "Greats" of the Wycliffe College, two deans and five principals. Both deans challenged the viewer with dominating, what-do-you-want stares, keepers of the academic keys. In contrast, the first principal had a kindly countenance, a yes-my-dear-child pastoral smile. The last principal but one seems to have had a crick in his neck, for his head was tilted well to one side, as if looking for something under a stack of papers on his desk.

Perhaps, it would be better to go home before the current principal arrived. He tried standing still, but his inner agitation seemed to make his feet all the more uncertain where to place them. Heels clicked together, then one shoe crossed over the other in a gesture of supposed repose. Then his feet stood wide apart as if they were soldiers "at ease." "Can't you be still?" he asked himself.

His feet didn't reply.

He paced down the row of portraits again—this time reading dates. *Dean White, 1894-97; Dean Whiston, 1897-1904.* Is this the final sum of countless years of scholarship? A couple of vague dates in a dusty hall that few ever visit? Where is Dean White now? Sweating in an Indian market place converting the masses to Christ? Is he valiantly dodging bullets in France, bringing comfort to the fallen and fearful? More than likely, he's upstairs parsing Greek verbs, as he has done, lo these three-score-and-five years, to neither his own credit nor anyone's benefit. "Every man's labour in the vineyard is rewarded." Or so said Gramma Alice.

Taking a seat next to the exit, Gordon tried to quell his uncertainty. "It's only an interview." He repeated it to himself twice more. "It's only an interview. It's only an interview," but his stomach wasn't taking the hint. With Damascus road flair, he told himself that this was the rest of his life. In this oak-panelled room his career would be carved in stone. He could be so pompous, especially when writing his own script and using the template of too many pious sermons.

More soberly, his dad had said, "They'll take you, in a second, boy. A simple thing, given your marks." "If it's so simple why don't you do it?" Gordon had wanted to reply. But he never talked back to his father, not out loud at any rate. He did what he was told and had gone off to Toronto to do this "simple thing" by himself.

"This must be the first time that Dad isn't here to give the right answer for my life's question and punctuate his reply with a story to drive home his point. Is Dad actually manipulating me, living out his lost dreams?"

Gordon reprimanded this hint of distrust for his father almost before it arose. "It's not as if God's call is orchestrated by Dad! This is my idea and I'm certainly not trying to live out his ambitions."

No one seriously expected old man Davis to be a preacher. "Swears too Goddamn much," joked his fellows at the shop. But they all saw it in Gordon. The ministry was his vocation, always had been. He would be God's instrument. Years ago inside his prayer book, he'd penned a solemn pledge:

> Show me the cross and I'll bear it.
> Smooth shirt or rough, I'll wear it,
> No wall too tall,
> No promise too small
> With Christ at my side, I'll swear it.

Alas, poetry was never Gordon's strength, and he knew it. Naive and pious though it sounded now at age twenty-two, it still expressed his heart's desire.

It was actually three years since he first felt a guiding hand shaping his life. The local priest, Reverend Hawthorne, was quick to encourage Gordon in his call to Christ's ministry. "No time like it, lad. Frontiers for evangelism abound. 'The world for Christ in this next generation.' That's what they're predicting." Special catechetical lessons were arranged for young Gordie. Sunday afternoons in the vestry. "How many sacraments?

Who's the primate of the church? How do you address a bishop?" The wardens made exceptions to the reading roster so that he could test his skill during worship. Finally, this interview would settle it all. If Jesus wanted him as a soldier of the cross, Principal Cruikshank would know it.

Gordon waited, eyes down.

He'd walked about the college before seeking out the principal's office. His first impression was musty smells, oiled furniture and cracked leather chairs. On second thought, he sensed how years of earnest piety had been poured into this building. The classrooms were scrubbed white, evidence of the moral fastidiousness of dark-faced professors. The chapel floor creaked, no doubt, weary from bearing the load of ceaseless prayers poured out by youthful hearts. The surroundings left an imprint on Gordon: an implicit message of faithfulness. It's as if the entire building said "Faith matters!" Indeed. Gordon could see it. Faith, once applied with vigour and devotion, does not rub off easily.

Satisfied, even awed, by the look of the college, Gordon had found the administrative office that served as the anteroom to the principal's office and asked about his appointment. Several secretaries, busy at their stations, all looked up. As if on cue, they all spoke ... eager to assist. Gordon was too young to realize that a young man attracts attention just by virtue of being handsome. He was shown to the common room, offered coffee and reading material. He declined and decided to walk about the room a bit.

Now seated, he could hear them driving away at their typewriters; the tap, tap of wisdom. "Lectures of great import, no doubt!" Gordon let the excitement of higher learning boil over in his mind. "Here I will come to see God." Now and again students passed by the doorway. Vigilant in their purpose, Bibles under their arms. "Soon I will be one of them. Drawing strength from my professors and colleagues. Virtuous all. Not a crack of doubt, no blemish of indecision." Only while sitting long hours in the trenches could Gordon laugh at how naive and silly he once was!

The old building's floorboards cracked as feet scurried from chapel to class. Gordon waited.

The principal did say 9:15—sharp. "Just after morning prayers." Gordon came early, wanting to make the best impression.

Hoisting his grandfather's pocket watch from its small pouch on his waistband, he glanced at the hands. 9:14. One minute to go. What to do when one waits for the Almighty? Without thinking, he found himself standing again, too nervous to remain anywhere for very long. Opposite the deans' portraits were those of smiling rows of graduating classes. Row after row of grinning students ready to meet their Maker and earn the right to preach God's everlasting word to the heathens. His pride burst at the thought. Since he could remember, China was Christ's mission, millions of souls lost to damnation, if no one would take them the Word. "Whom shall I send?" The hymn echoed in his mind.

"Here am I, Lord," his heart cried. Gordon Davis would be a disciple for Christ. Just three years in seminary and then off to that distant land.

"How many of those smiling faces are prepared to make the supreme sacrifice?" a deep voice boomed.

Gordon whirled round to face the man himself, The Reverend Doctor Harold Cruikshank.

"Davis?"

"Yes sir."

"Look at those faces carefully Davis. These are God's elect, now serving in the ultimate battle for truth."

"In China, sir?" His voice had an expectant glow.

"No. Flanders, man! Most of our alumni are in the fields of combat fighting the evils of imperial aggression. Brave lads all."

"Flanders? As Chaplains?"

"Some." Cruikshank scanned the line of photos like a company of warriors. "Here's Henderson—chaplain to the First Hussars." His finger touched another smiling face. "That's Pentland, he's with the Deer Park irregulars as their padre. But not all wear the cloth." Cruikshank warmed to the task of boasting. It was a common speech. "This is not a school for weak souls, Davis. Many have enlisted as fighting men. Here's Douglas, and that's Joshing. They joined together. Another, MacBride, he's with the gunners I believe." His confident forefinger kept picking out students. "There's Goodings, he's some sort of river scout—always got a unique posting that boy." Looking off, the principal continued his well-greased speech. "Does my heart proud to know that they left these halls and signed up for their duty without flinching. Drive the devil back to his black hole in Berlin."

"What about China, sir?" Gordon was unschooled in encounters with principals. One did not interject when the homily was only half-delivered.

"China? Ah. No. There's no fighting in China. Not yet." A spark of anger flared as Cruikshank stared hard at his new recruit and he pondered, not for first time, what manner of men were now presenting themselves to his college. "China? Don't you read the papers, Davis? The battle to be joined is in Flanders. That is where your glorious crown lies."

"Sir?"

"Sit down, Davis." Cruikshank took an armchair and he propped open a crisp file folder. "Born Hamilton ... attended St. Giles ... good little church ... Father Anglican ... Mother ... Baptist?", this last with a little surprise. Leafing through documents and letters of reference, Cruikshank grunted a few times, whistled once. (Over the mark of 95% in English, no doubt.) His free hand twirled in the air—as if grasping an unseen chalice.

Gordon sat, wincing with every sound or gesture. Would he pass muster?

"Why here? Why now?" The principal came to the point, penetrating eyes fixed the questions to their mark.

Gordon swallowed his anxiety in a gulp and began his testimony, each word memorized, little recognizing that this was not the time for Sunday school recitations. "Sir, I have walked with my Lord all my life, but was grasped by the Saviour three years ago. It was on a Christmas Eve as I was contemplating the Virgin Mary's—"

"Yes, of course," the principal was paternal, but not disposed to being patient. "But why Wycliffe? We all have faith. Why did you not turn to Trinity across the street? They'd snatch you up in a minute with marks like this," holding the file folder.

Gordon had never thought of any other institution. "It's the name, sir."

"Wycliffe?"

"Yes ... I mean ... not just the name, but what he stood for. The open mind, the challenging spirit that defied the authorities with respect to Christ's teaching."

"Are you a rebel, Davis?" There was anger under the question.

Blushing, Gordon stumbled over his zeal. "No sir. Not at all. Having the desire to serve and knowing of Wycliffe's courage, I naturally assumed this would be the appropriate college for me."

Mollified, the principal slipped back into his regular routine. "Right! Well, you can start next term. My secretary will send you all the paperwork. In the meantime, start reading in Greek and Latin. Brush up a bit on your biblical studies. There's a dandy course in biblical evangelism that might interest you ... Offered to lay people on weekends during Lent ..."

"Yes sir!" It was actually going to happen!

"Oh, yes, and get enrolled in a militia unit back in Hamilton." Closing the file, the interview finished, he rose to go.

"Militia, sir?" Gordon's voice rose with his body as he politely stood before his superior.

"Yes, militia." Cruikshank despaired of the calibre of hearts that Christ was now bending to do his will. How can we ever win the Kingdom with such untested wits? "Makes for good discipline. Church baptism's not enough. We all need discipline, lad ... holds us together when we have our baptism of fire." With that parting shot, he marched out of the room.

Sauble Beach, Ontario
Monday, September 7, 1908 (Labour Day)

"You must have discipline." Scanning the clutch of faces, Gordon's among them, James Davis knew it was time for his story. For the start of a new church year, he had brought this young teens' class to his aunt's shack by the beach. After a swim and meal, it was time for the lesson, and James never missed an opportunity to tell a tale.

"Long ago ... almost eighty years now, a great Christian missionary named Matthew Cunningham came to these parts, working hard among the last few Algonquin Indians that lived by the shores of Lake Huron. He was trying to establish a foothold for the Lord. Ministering to one clan, he eventually persuaded the male chief to convert ... to be baptized.

The chief in question had a funny name, 'Starlight.' Can you imagine?"   Snickers flitted round the circle and James continued. "'That's gotta change,' thought the black-robed priest as he took Starlight down to the lake shore, just over there by that rotting stump."

All eyes went to the stump. History danced into life.

"Here?" Young Ferguson was amazed.

"Yes sir! They probably stood right here gazing out at the afternoon ripples. Baptized right here ..."

Halifax Harbour, Nova Scotia: close to the Narrows
Thursday, December 6, 1917, 9:09 a.m.

Was this his baptism of fire? Gordon's mind was fogged over. "Why so much water?" He slipped beneath the waves. Salt touched his eyes and he woke with a start, splashing to the surface.

The explosion. Where had it come from? Was it an air attack? The whole harbour had erupted.

Treading water, trying to get his bearings, the morning's events came back in bits and pieces. He could recall the tingling of excitement as his foot touched Canadian soil. Pier 7. At first they were alone, a couple dozen men waiting by their packs for a lift to the train station. Was it an hour ... more like three? Then the word must have spread that vets had arrived. Soon the dock was crowded with well-wishers.

Gordon had scanned the crowd for his Jo. She promised to be waiting, but he arrived early. He felt sure she would be present with these initial greeters. Hurried glances for her face in the crowd that surged forward to meet them left him hopeful, but uncertain. General laughter and hugging had been brief—the fire on a harbour ship was distracting everyone. In twos and threes they were leaving the pier, arms locked, never to be broken by war again. So they hoped. A few souls were still milling about the pier, when his world was drenched in sound and spray.

It would later be called the Halifax Explosion, but at the time Gordon only saw water, flames and smoke. From the perspective of history, it was momentous. At his eye level, it was nothing but flotsam and flame. No order. The headlines that would give structure to the brutality were yet to be written. He drifted in confusion.

Then a weak plea. "Help … please someone … I can't see."

Was that her voice? He couldn't find the dock, but knew it was just beyond the curl of the smoke to his left. Blood streamed into his eyes as he made several futile hand-over-hand strokes, slapping the water but not moving toward the shore with any speed.

"God … please! Someone!"

It had to be Johanna. Gordon grew more certain as his mind cleared. She must be trapped! Yes, the dock had been almost vacant. He had been staring out to the burning vessel when it blew up. Anyone could have crept up quietly behind him. That's it. She had held back from the throng, wanting to catch him off guard and now she was burning alive!

A torched barrel blocked his view of Pier 7—whatever was left. He was among the pilings before he realized that the deck boards had been wiped out.

"Please … someone!" Definitely a feminine voice, bent with agony.

It must be her.

"I'm coming! Hold on." Shouting above the crackle of fire, his hands began to flail at the water.

She promised to be waiting when he arrived. It must be her.

Montreal
Nov. 09, 1917

Gordon:

Thank God you're alive.

Father and I make a daily trek to the Rushbrooke Street post office and read the list of casualties.

There's always a clutch of folks scanning the names. We knew you were in heavy fighting. My heart was in my throat as I ran trembling fingers down the list. Faint sighs of content or sharp intakes of breath punctuate the air as we all tally up the cost of this horrible war.

Last Tuesday I saw what I had always dreaded. "Dain, M., killed in action, Dateman, F. wounded, Davis, G., missing in action." I fainted into Father's arms.

When I regained consciousness, returned vets tried to persuade me that "missing" didn't necessarily mean "dead." "Why I went missing for two weeks—on leave in Paris," said one. The others nodded.

They guided me back to the list and showed me where there was a line for corrections. "Keep your eye on that line, lassie. If he's really dead, his name will show up above again, but if he's alive, they'll list him under corrections."

For five days I watched that line and then, miracle of miracles, there you were. "Wounded." Please don't think me harsh if I say that the day I discovered you were wounded my heart was soaring. I thought nothing could make me happier. But it did. Your letter arrived telling me that all was well and you were coming home ... to Halifax.

I am writing hurriedly because I want you to get this before your ship sails—what a curious name, "The Imo."

Please rest my Joseph-of-many-colours. I will be on
the dock to receive you home. I will check about
disembarkation. You mentioned a projected time
of arrival around the 6th of December—an auspi-
cious day: the feast of St. Nicolas. How I recall the
chocolates that waited outside my door on the last
St. Nick's day—silly man—I still don't know how
you arranged it.

I must stop—I feel like I could write forever—I want
to talk your ear off.

Safe passage. I'll be there. I promise.

Jo

P.S. I love you

P.P.S. I have a great surprise for you!

Saint John: The Buttress Home
Friday, September 11, 1992, 11:05 a.m.

I bounded up the steps to Gordon's floor. The morning had been a
waste—the church deficit. Again. Eyes had glazed over as the salary
figures were repeated. No one wanted to say it, but they couldn't afford
to keep me much longer.

"How about cutting back the janitor?" No takers for that idea.

"Maybe we could reduce the music budget?" Silence. After an hour
we gave up. I hate those meetings.

Rather than visit Gordon as promised yesterday, I had an emergency
call. The stranger claimed I was his pastor and died soon after I arrived.
A bad week all round. Now a funeral to arrange, the sermon not yet
complete and this overdue visit.

Gordon always cheered me up. One of Gordon's great gifts to me
was the conversations I had with his two "masks" as I came to call them;
in the morning he was Captain Jims and in the evening he was Reverend

Inkling. Coming to his room before the sun was over the yardarm, I knew who would be lying in his bed. Gordon himself may have been a blank, but these two characters were full of life.

"First mate reporting for duty sir," I announced before I sat down.

"You're late, matey."

"Couldn't be helped sir. Crew member died and I had to conduct the funeral." That was close to true.

"Never keep your captain waiting. Do you understand?" A determined chin thrust forward, part stubble, part clean-shaven. "Never."

"Aye, aye, Captain."

He winked. "Wind blows hard from the south. Storm's a-coming. Batten down all the hatches and get those barrels below. There's nothing like the high sea to rock a man's nerves—'specially if his freight isn't lashed to."

I looked about his bed for anything that might be a barrel. A few scattered washcloths would have to do. I began folding them, readying to stow them in the ship's hold. "You worried, Captain?"

"About what?"

"About the freight shifting on your deck, about going down."

"Never! Never worry about going down son. It happens to every blessed thing alive. More certain than the tides. Can't be helped." His gaze was fixed on a distant shore and I lost Jims for a few minutes. But like the sudden shift in wind direction, he was back with me and shouted, "No, my mate, spend your energy on something worthy, like keeping your promises. A man's no better than his pledged word. Bend that, even a little, and you're done in. Mark me, matey."

"Sir?"

"Keep your promises."

"I will, Captain."

"So you say, so you say. But you won't grow up 'til you don't, 'til you let someone down in a big way. We all begin a voyage swearing we'll be true and then it happens. Leave some poor sailor crossbeam to the tempest. That's when you know you're a godforsaken creature of God."

"Sir ... you mean?"

"I mean ... I mean, matey ... you ain't worth a seal's flipper until you break a few good promises and discover what it costs you."

Toronto: 20 Mountalan Ave.
Friday, April 11, 2014, 7:46 p.m.

"I promised I would call, Reverend Levan."

Still drowsy from falling asleep on the couch with Jack, I had picked up the phone. He was still nestled into the crook of my arm, out like a light. The movie "Cars," his favourite, was still running.

"Hello, Chris Levan speaking."

"This is Patricia Patterson."

"Patricia?"

"I promised I would call, Reverend Levan."

"Oh yes ... it was about my ... you called him my Uncle Gordon. I must confess I often thought he might be my relative, but I could never ... er ..."

"Never prove it. I understand, but I am calling to inform you of two facts," Patricia's voice was crisp, all business.

"Yes?"

"Perhaps I should explain. I am retiring as the regional under-secretary to the minister of veterans' affairs. Clearing out the files, I came across an old dossier on Gordon. Seems he was quite an enigma. His file reads like a who-done-it with all the names and places left out. However, inter-governmental exchange protocols now make it very easy to trace identities across many jurisdictions. There seems little doubt. Fact #1: Gordon of the Buttress Home was your Great-Uncle Gordon Davis."

"Ah! That is a comfort. I wish I could tell my dad ... oh, and my uncle would have been pleased."

"They are gone?"

"All of that generation, I am afraid."

"A pity ... we could use corroboration."

"Corroboration? You just confirmed he was my uncle."

Patricia sighed. "The second fact: You are named as the next-of-kin."

"Yes," I explained, "Gordon insisted on it at the time, though I was unsure what the point might be. He named me as his heir … It was a kind gesture."

"It was done legally," Patricia was reading the document. "Signed by several witnesses."

"He insisted on it—like a benediction. Maybe he was bequeathing to me all the promises of his life … the ones he kept and the ones he didn't. I don't know. They were kind words."

"Actually, Reverend, he left you more than words."

"Pardon?"

"He left you an envelope. It says clearly, 'For my pastor … I leave my worldly goods.' It turns out he had some."

"What? Is this a joke … Are you certain?"

"I am in earnest. Our current com-stat interchange allows for matches between black file trusts and retired dossiers and—"

"Patricia, I really appreciate all the work you have done and it is reassuring to know Gordon was indeed my great-uncle. But you're losing me with 'Black file trusts and ….' What did you call them … 'retired dossiers'? Gordon had nothing to leave me but good wishes. I was there. I know."

"That's actually not the case."

"Really?"

Patricia was all business. "I think you should come to New Brunswick. I would like to settle this account in person if possible. I didn't read everything that is on Gordon's envelope. It ends with 'He is an answer to my prayers.'"

Distracted, looking for my pen, I respond, "Curious … I never felt he was listening to me. How can I be an answer to his prayers?"

Seeing the old fountain pen under a bill from the bank, I pull it out. "Can I get your phone number … or e-mail address … I suppose you already know that I worked in Fredericton for seven years just recently … so I am aware of what is happening there."

As Patricia gives me her coordinates I am struck by the fact that this, my favourite pen, was, in fact, Gordon's. Given long usage and habit, I had long ago forgotten its origin.

Smiling I continue, "Tell me … does it really say that I am an answer to his prayers."

Saint John: Centenary-Queen Square United Church
Tuesday, Nov. 17, 1992, 11:15 a.m.

One final word from Scripture and then we can pray.

"Friends, *'The promises of the Lord are sure, comforting the weak.'* So let us take comfort as we turn to our God, the Source and Life of all things. Let us pray."

CHAPTER TWO

THE APPROACH

God is present in all of creation. No one needs a special invitation to
come into the Almighty's presence. "Stand in the open meadow and
breathe deeply." This may have some salutary effect upon one's respira-
tory system. It does little for one's spiritual well-being.

I am dismayed at the recent rise of mindless informality in church.
More thought is applied to a telephone conversation than modern
ministers put into their approach to God.

J.R. Miah, *Hints for Holy Communion with God*

Ypres, France: Canadian Corps Forward Observation Trench
Sunday February 11, 1917, 2:30 p.m.

It had taken an hour of belly crawling to make a scant fifteen yards. A
fool's gamble to go out into the muck of no man's land under cover of
darkness. In the light of day, it was an invitation to get dead. Snipers on
either side shot at anything that stirred, checking the colour of uniform
after the smoke cleared. Lives had been wasted by friendly fire, sacrificed
on the altar of rattled nerves!

Twice in the past thirty minutes bullets had dug into the ground at
his feet, the second much nearer than the first. Someone was watching.
That someone was getting closer. Gordon plotted his course from covering to covering. Ahead was a crater they called "Bertha," caused by artillery blasts. She was like two huge eyes joined at the bridge of the nose

by a rather broad trench. He slithered onto the lip of the western-most socket, and rolled to the bottom. Too fast. An overhead shot hurried him down.

It wasn't exactly Christmas, but each crater held a surprise. You never knew what you would discover until you slithered into it. Some were filled with forgotten comrades, long dead but stirred to the surface by shelling. Others held pools of poisoned water, fever in every drop. Still others were just mud, a clinging, sucking morass that could be a death sentence. This time Bertha was empty of bodies.

"Thank God for small favours." Gordon was sick of finding half-rotted comrades—the bright flower of Canada—caked in dirt, limbs torn, bellies gaping, rats chewing at eyes and ears.

No cadavers, but Bertha had her share of mud, chilled to near freezing at this time of year. In his haste, Gordon had slid down into the slime at the bottom, a fetid pool of pestilence—water welled up through cotton and leather until he was soaked to his knees.

"Damn, I just got a new issue of socks this morning." Dragging himself free of the scum to lie on his back, he tried to shake off the worst sludge. Thinking of the past month when trench foot had threatened to turn his limbs green, he struggled to control his fear. It wasn't just the bloody bullets, the night raids and the enemy shells. Watching your body disintegrate under the relentless pressure of water, lice and boredom was the greatest terror. A fierce battle against insanity.

The whiz of bullets continued to fly over the lip of the crater and "plip" into the mud on the Allied side of his little valley. Gordon went stone still. "Breathe," came Jo's voice. "Breathe, my love." After a deep sigh, his tentative hands groped down his chest, around the small of his back, to his groin. Nothing showed. No telltale rips in his clothing, no sticky splotches of blood. He was still whole. The snipers had missed their mark.

"Maammmmmmm." The cry of the wounded soldier drifted past.

"Shit. He's still alive." Gordon thought about waiting out the next five hours until dark. "Gordon my son, don't you budge your sorry ass," a small coward's voice whispered in his mind. "You could stay here in safety until nightfall—maybe survive until the next leave." A soldier's life was measured by relief from combat and the incessant pressure of preparing for or resting from it. The constant prayer of the firing line: "Please God protect me until my next furlough, until I get a decent meal, clean bed and warm embrace." Gordon joked that it was the only "prayer of approach" worth reciting in this godforsaken land.

"Maammmmm." Gordon's wounded man, obviously sustained by that desperate hope, was unwilling to give up the ghost.

"Why me, Lord?" Gordon rolled to his stomach and inched ever so slowly to the east bank of the crater and began to belly walk through the bridge between Bertha's eyes.

"Plop."

Looking over his shoulder he saw the widening rings on the sluggish pool behind him. Some damn fool had fired a grenade into his hiding hole. Working knees and elbows frantically, he scrambled into the second eye socket and cowered beside a stump sticking out of the bank.

The blast, when it actually came, was more like a gusher of thick water than a fiery blast. "Thank you, Jesus, for mud." No man's land had been so churned up by shell-fire, it was like a great soup of half-congealed cement. If shells went in deep enough, they simply turned themselves into fountains.

The grenade blast had stirred the waters and exhumed a tin helmet, head still strapped in place, and a severed blue sleeve from a French uniform, sergeant's stripes running down the arm. Did helmet and sleeve belong together?

"Mmmmaaaaa."

"What a mess!" He ached to return to safety, but each cry was a whip to Gordon's conscience. It had his father's tone: "Get moving, Gordie!" Duty, obedience, the right thing, no matter the cost! The "shoulds" of his father's determination were breathing over his shoulder. No place to hide.

In the end, it wasn't Gordon's virtue that moved his body forward. It was the fact that the Hun had found his range and just a matter of minutes before they had cracked off a hit. "Move forward or die." The next landmark to offer any cover at all was the "Rum Barrel," a broad but shallow indentation directly in front of platoon 13's line. It was named after the deadening German shell that all Tommies came to hate and fear

"Mmmmmaammmamm."

The cries for help were indeed coming from "John's Barn." Jack was always accurate in his co-ordinates. It was a scant five yards, just at the far edge of the Rum Barrel, but it might as well have been a hundred. The German snipers would be watching his hiding hole, hoping for a piece of tunic, a scrap of flesh into which to empty a dozen rounds.

To stay was to wait for another grenade to end it all. Gordon plotted his approach. A quick dash? They'd be expecting a slow crawl.

On the stump beside his head there was a single shoot missed by shelling. Slowly, not to make any sound, Gordon wiggled it back and forth until it came loose. He slithered back to the helmet provided by the last blast, removed the strap so that the head could slide back into the slime—"Poor bugger won't need it now"—and returned to his post.

Fixing helmet to branch and jabbing the thick end into the mud, he levered his decoy up above the lip of the crater. Shots rang out almost immediately—cross hairs on the helmet. It began to spin and Gordon dove over the side and half-ran, half-swam to the Rum Barrel's safety.

His trick worked and he whistled slowly as his hands automatically moved down his body. Again, no bullet wounds. The legging on his right shin was torn by a piece of stray wire as he made his entry into this new crater, but that was a small thing now. He'd join the medical parade this evening and see that it was stitched. Any bodily orifice was a welcome mat for gangrene and typhus.

"MMMMMAAAAAA!"

Louder now. Close by. Looking left and right, Gordon plotted the direction of the sound. "He must be just on the other side of that blasted wall." Gordon whispered his co-ordinates out loud, as if to reassure himself of their accuracy. A roll of wire was messing up his line of sight and distance was always a bugger in the faceless mud. "Maybe five more yards. Not much to go."

"MMMMMaaaaa." What *was* he crying about? His mother? "I'll fix his mouth when I get there." It wouldn't be the first time he'd used a handkerchief in the mouth to stifle wounded moans as he carried soldiers out.

The foundation wall would offer some protection. It was in a slight indentation and the Rum Barrel's eastern slope touched one line of the bricks. He could reach his wounded man if he just went slowly and watched the noise level.

It took another hour to move across the saucer-like crater. But his patience paid dividends. No sniper fire was drawn to his position. A few well-placed shots from his own side had dampened their ardour. Gordon reached the groans and lowered his head for a deep prayer— no words or identifiable feeling, just a creaturely sigh—he examined his patient.

"Mmmmmmmaaaaaaa." Whispers now. His man was in a bad way. Lying too long in the chilling mud, with blood oozing from a wound on his right side and a bad shot to his lower left ankle. Threads of skin held his boot to his body.

There could be no words. Not now. Gordon deftly took the rag he called a handkerchief and squelched a cry from his patient. Eyes darted in terror until Gordon lifted his own tunic enough to show the medic's cross. Relief flooded into the wounded man's gaze and his body relaxed. Gordon leaned down to his ear and whispered, "The cavalry has arrived." He started on the leg. Experience had taught him to attend to what was fixable. Gaping abdomen wounds were usually fatal. This guy's was a question mark. But the dangling foot he could fix—well not fix, but at least bandage up. Cutting off the final strands of sinew with his trench knife, he wrapped the stump in a roll of gauze from his first aid pouch. This caused a slight shudder, but Gordon was pretty sure this guy was floating somewhere beyond pain.

Reaching in his pouch for gauze, he also withdrew his "healing oil:" a flask of whiskey, sometimes the only sedative in the field. Removing the rag that corked his patient's mouth, he poured in half the contents. A cough, sputter and gulp, told him that the liquid had gotten past his tonsils. "That'll slur your mind. At least keep it off a telltale itch in the foot that is now missing." The hankie went back into the gaping mouth before another cry could disturb their peace.

One job done, he went to the stomach. Peeling back the tunic and releasing the frayed belt, he watched as a small flesh crater emerged. Blacked at the edges and caked with blood and bits of uniform. It looked horrid. An acrid biting smell of intestinal fluid.

"Is this guy even worth saving?" he wondered.

It was not a rhetorical question. If Gordon could even get him back to his own trench line, there was the problem of transport back to the dressing bunker. A half-dead man might cause any number of fatalities as he was carried to medical attention. The communication trenches in this chalky soil were not deep. Cut quite narrow so as to offer as few targets to snipers as possible as troops advanced to the firing trench. Any stretcher party pushed soldiers up out of the zig-zagging slits to let the wounded man pass. It was the perfect opportunity to be picked off by an enemy shooter.

"A man who was going to die had best do it at the front." So said the instructor of their squad when they first arrived in France. "We've lost hundreds of good men because they were exposed by working the stretcher or making way for one to get to the rear. If that stretcher is carrying a man who is dead or going to die, what's the point?" At that stage in his lecture, the burly Brit they nicknamed "Whiskers," in honour of his handle-bar moustache, pointed at his small audience of green recruits. "You make bloody sure anyone you bring back is worth it."

Gordon went through a quick inventory of his wounded man's injuries. Not dead and not yet dying. Apart from the slashed abdomen, there were no other serious problems. The leg would heal by itself. Yes, he might be worth the chance of a run back through the trench system. His eyes had closed—either from the whiskey or the wound. "Let him sleep." Drifting between eternity and mortality, there was little movement or sound now that his moans where stifled.

Gordon decided to wait. "There's no point taking a bullet for someone who can wait another two hours for darkness." Apart from a very well-placed artillery shell, they were as safe here as back in the trench. Moving directly south, he would come to his own line in fifteen yards, twenty at the most. He could lift this fellow that distance once his strength returned and the night masked his actions.

To pass time, he looked at his fallen comrade. It had been his practice never to ask names.

Whiskers was sharp on that point too. "Don't get personal. Each piece of man-flesh you drag off this bloody dung heap has a mother and a lover somewhere. You start digging around in their intimate details (he spat out the word "intimate" with distaste as if he were describing some form of illicit sexual congress), and you'll lose perspective. Keep your eyes open for whoever needs the medic most. I don't want any buddy-buddy feelings to get in the way."

It became a joke with the regular stretcher teams. "No intimacy please," would ring out as they passed each other back and forth to the field hospital.

But Whiskers was right. This battleground was no place for friendship, at least not in the traditional sense. Dreams of going home were kept close to the heart. In the trenches, it was raw humour, and a shared hunger that kept comrades close, but they were not friends in an ordinary way.

For those who survived, these few months would later be venerated as the time when they were truly alive. Linked as they were in this brotherhood of blood, after it was over, trench rats were always seeking out the haunted face of a fellow "Tommy". It was an unspoken, yet widely acknowledged dictum, that "those who have not seen the trenches would never understand." Civilians who huddled safe in their jobs back in Canada were roundly and regularly scorned for their ignorance of "what this war is really like!"

So soldiers on both sides were close but not intimate. Each day replacements came forward for lost members of the platoon. In an hour they were sized up, given their space, christened with a nickname and made part of the circle. In a day, they were kindred. But a bullet could just as easily take them down. They'd be gone. No tears were shed. They were just gone. The cycle continued and life, of sorts, continued. In a strange way, the proximity of death made men closer than friendship and at the same time made friendship a shallow affair. Common suffering was their bond.

Gordon knew the day when he broke off trying to make friends of his comrades. It was an idle conversation really. Bob, a recruit who had joined the unit three months before Gordon had arrived, took him under his wing and showed him the ropes. Without Bob's guidance, he would have been blown apart several times and he would have been robbed by the canteen workers even more often.

Bob always knew where to find the best rations, how to dodge the grunt work and yet how to step smartly when the battle was joined. Once, to get something better than hardtack to eat, they had broken the lock on the YMCA dugout. It had been closed due to lack of personnel, and Bob had led Gordon to their well-stocked larder when no one was looking. After that escapade and having been reprimanded twice for insubordination, they became "intimate." They exchanged love letters from home. Filled the idle hours with stories of family history. They came to know each other's dreams and fears.

It had been several hours that Gordon and Bob had been half-standing, half- crouching on the fire step, a small elevation on the forward side of trench from which soldiers fired their guns. As was the rule when you stood in that position, all eyes were fixed forward. Bob was on sentry duty. Gordon was waiting for the call. Whenever someone was hit, the first thing out of his mouth was, "Stretcher!" It was still that afternoon. Bob was from Peterborough, Ontario, and he was telling Gordon about the magic of the lift locks in that city. On the Trent canal system, they moved small craft up a sixty-five-foot rise by hoisting the entire ship and the water in which it floated in a huge cement shoebox-shaped container.

Gordon was having trouble picturing it.

"Look," Bob said with a touch of annoyance at Gordon's inability to catch what he meant. "It's like this ...." Standing up and turning sideways to look directly at Gordon, a bullet sliced across his face and he slumped to the trench floor in agony, clutching the space where his eyes had been. Bob died before they got him back to the medic. With him went any of Gordon's desire for friendship.

"No more friends." He'd written it on the top of his paybook. For the intervening months, he'd lived by that slogan.

Why on that day, when he was slouched beside a brick wall in no man's land, he had decided to rummage through a wounded man's affects, Gordon could never say. Was it to pass time? Were his fantasies of a return home to family, and to Jo, becoming too predictable or unreal to be satisfying? Maybe he was just bored.

Whatever the reason, Gordon began by looking at the now calm, very pale face. Blond hair protruded out from under a helmet of drying mud. A strong chin and straight nose gave the lad a handsome look.

Feeling his right pocket, Gordon came up with a few scraps of paper that looked like torn pages of a Bible and a "before the battle" postcard issued by the army to men who were going over the top. Filled out by the infantry before combat and left with the commanding officer for safekeeping. Any cards not retrieved would be sent home. "Dear_____ : If you receive this card I am gone ..."

The left pocket, as usual, contained his paybook. This guy's was fat, precious letters squeezed between the pages. "Private Terrance Hinks, Canadian Corps." The last name ... a coincidence? The ledger's notations were brief, marking Terrance as a relative newcomer. "Bloody fool." Looking back at his face, Gordon guessed him to be just under 20-years-old. "Bloody young fool."

While flicking through the pages a letter fell out into the mud. Gingerly retrieving it, Gordon noticed a familiar hand. The penmanship was immediately recognizable. "It can't be the same family, surely?" He unfolded the pages—three in all and scanned for the signature. There it was.

"Know that your sister always loves you! Jo."

That changed everything.

Montreal: Corner of Peel and Sherbrooke Streets
Thursday, March 23, 1916, 2:00 a.m.

It was the first brush of their lips that changed everything.

Gordon was slow, a bit shy and not sure how to follow her lead in physical contact. His heart was a novice. Jo's was leaping ahead, eager and vital.

They'd been walking, aimlessly, speaking of little things: his gifted, unhappy father, her lost, and much missed mother, the dark skyline of the city. Anything but the raging storm going on inside, the delicious anxiety of feeling close.

The snow had stopped hours back. They hadn't gone home as they promised they would. It was too early to quit and too late for excuses.

Their hands had been linked for several hours playfully, exploratory, charged as if by electric current. Now and again, she would tug his body into hers. Once she thought he might actually bend down and kiss her, but he retreated, diverted at the last moment by a shop window in the Ritz Hotel.

Empty streets. Two lovers. A city of snow.

Finally, came the corner. Neither started to cross. Where next? On a whim, Johanna jumped up on a block used to hold a gas lamppost. Gordon stood looking up and she rested two hands on his shoulders, looked long and hard into his eyes. No flinching. She traced a finger down his chin. No words now, just the current crackling between them.

She could see his desire, confusion and finally horror as she leaned close. No aunt-like peck on the cheek, she planted a firm and suggestive kiss on his waiting lips.

Was she falling? It wasn't a desperate plunge, but like a slow tidal flow, she could feel herself descend into him, her arms ran around his neck, down his shoulders. His hands were on the small of her back. A single kiss, sweet and moist. A kiss like no other, Johanna could feel her heart pounding.

They parted, looked into each other's amazement and knew with frightening assurance that everything had changed. Everything!

Saint John, New Brunswick: Centenary-Queen Square United Church
Tuesday, Nov. 17, 1992, 11:16 a.m.

In ministry some things never change. Over fifteen years of funerals, I had not altered a single word in this introductory prayer of approach.

It suited most grieving situations and the prayer's content was largely irrelevant. Speech is just a vehicle to soothe the troubled heart. "This prayer's like knocking on the front door of the temple." My mentor, the Reverend Robin Wilks, comes back each time I recite this portion of the funeral service. "You wouldn't present yourself to your girlfriend's house with shirt-tails hanging out or zipper at half-mast. (He could be a bit sacrilegious as a pastor.) So also at the beginning of a funeral. The prayer of approach helps people straighten out their spiritual attire. You get them ready to meet their Maker in their Sunday best."

So I begin as I have always begun:

"Let us pray:

Dear God, Comfort to the heart heavy with grief and light to the eyes blinded by sorrow, sustain us now as we gather one last time with our brother, Gordon Davis. May your words speak to us and ..."

My mouth works the syllables long since memorized, my lips move, but my mind is wandering. Words! A few hollow phrases when you're born. And repeat them when you're dead. Words!

"It is with longing that we turn our souls to you. Death stands as such a barrier, and we seek your ...."

I shouldn't be so cavalier. After all, I live by words. If I were unable to speak, I'd be on the dole. Yet there are times when I hate them. Our church is nothing but words; empty, deceiving, masquerading words. We're drowning in rhetoric.

Montreal: Crossing the Victoria Bridge
Saturday, December 8, 1917, 7:30 a.m.

The train snaked forward across the trestles toward Montreal. Gordon felt dead, empty. His body rocked back and forth with the see-saw motion of the train car. Bleeding from a broken lip that wouldn't heal, he could hardly get two words out without tasting blood. At first nearly drowning in it, he now had a rag to stop the flow. "Damn bastard," he swore and spat out the open door watching the city come into view through the steel girders of the bridge.

It hadn't been a pretty fist fight; over, of all things, who got to sit closest to the door. When he jumped the freight in Halifax, Gordon had assumed that position, hoping to spot Jo on the side of the track. Though there was some jostling for Gordon's spot as other men hopped on, he held onto it until a regular on the rails tried to assert his authority just past Drummondville. An ugly face, broken nose and greasy beard shouted above the noise of wheels, "Move over, shit face."

It was a short confrontation.

Ugly-face struck first and fast, clubbing Gordon in the mouth and head. Gordon's senses slurred into a blur for a moment and then rising from his crouch by the door, his teeth found his opponent's forearm. He bit hard! While the bully reared back in agony, Gordon snapped a kick to his balls, followed by a fist to his right ear and the ugly brute crumpled, crawling back into the shadows of the boxcar.

On most nights, Gordon was a gentle sort, but trench warfare had taught him something no vagrant man on the rails in Canada could ever know—the driving imperative of violence. Gordon had seen it so often. There were moments in battle when his otherwise calm comrades lurched at the enemy with incredible force. No holds barred. No hesitation! Thrust and slash with a bayonet 'til entrails splattered the ground. Club with a nail-studded bat until blood ran down the handle. This was war and no one was going to call foul or interrupt the play or assign penalties. Kill or be killed. Once you saw that the battle was joined, you bloody well finished it. It was a potent drug, unrestrained violence, stripping away inhibitions and leaving raw anger in its place. It was freedom, a demented sort to be sure, but freedom nonetheless.

Gordon licked his lip. He was cold. Frost from the metal plates of the car door he was holding bit into his hand. The cape he had picked up from the cluttered alley on the edge of the Halifax railway station was stiff with sweat. He looked down at it and wondered what woman had lost it on that day when the harbour exploded. There was a splotch of blood on it. He imagined a wounded nurse struggling away from the collapsing glass building, only to be struck by flying glass. Who was she? It was too large to be Jo's, that much he knew for certain.

He'd paid to keep his spot by the door, but his vigil had been fruitless. No Jo—not in the station nor by the tracks. There'd been a few close calls. His longing had played tricks on his otherwise clear eyes. He thought a dark-robed figure in Rivière-du-Loup was his Jo—until she turned. Too young. Later, he'd actually shouted out her name outside St. Jean-Port Joli—the woman by a milk wagon waiting at a crossing looked so much like her. But he was embarrassed to see she wasn't. And there was the angel by the siding near Quebec City. A hallucination— induced by blood loss no doubt. But he sent her a kiss anyway.

The train cleared the bridge and was pulling to the west, slowing and moving past the main lines that ran toward the centre of town. It was time to jump. "Now or never," he shouted to the wind as his feet lurched from their place and he hurtled into space toward a patch of grass beside the tracks.

It wasn't Gordon's fault he knocked himself out. The train was moving too quickly and the grass was a small covering over a cement block. More blood, more pain, but this time he slept through the rougher parts of it.

Saint John, N.B.: The Buttress Home
Tuesday October 6, 1992, 9:15 p.m.

I've never fallen asleep at the pulpit, but I might as well have done it. In fact, I had been sleeping through many of my Sunday services. Not during this year's World Wide Communion service, though. After the Sacrament had been passed to the faithful ones at the kneeling rail, I was commissioned to take it to the shut-ins, a collection of elderly saints who were housebound. The final station on this way of the cross was Gordon's bed. It was late in the day, so I knew that the Reverend Inkling was in residence.

Before turning into his ward, I shouted, "Bless me, Father, for I have sinned."

"My child, is that you?" It didn't take Gordon more than a couple of visits before he recognized my voice.

"With the Sacrament."

"Communion? So soon again?" Gordon had no sense of time. "You brought the bread and wine last time."

"Gordon ... I mean Father Inkling. It's a custom at this season of the year."

"Hold your tongue, my child. There is no need for comment. God sees all and knows all. If the Almighty ordained you to attend to me this evening with the blessed gift of his Son, who am I to argue?" The priest, played with the top of his pyjama jacket, arranging it like his surplice.

Clerical lace in good order, he took a minute to adjust the hospital issue blanket, straightening wrinkles in the black alb which only he and God could see. His dress now presentable to the Lord, he was ready. Hoisting two withered hands into a prayerful attitude and arching his head back ever so slightly, he closed his eyes, bent his soul heavenward and waited.

I placed the portable communion set on his bedside table and began the prayers.

"The Lord be with you." I always gave Gordon the full measure of the service. No quick or informal entries into this meal, known to some as the medicine of immorality.

"And also with you." Gordon may be nuts, but he forgets nothing from the *Book of Common Prayer*.

"Lift up your hearts."

"Your *farts*? What are you saying child?" His shocked countenance withdrew from his communion with God to stare indignantly at me.

"I said 'hearts', Father."

"You did not. How could you spoil such a sublime moment with your vulgar references to bodily functions? Start again."

I tried not to laugh. Each time the good Father Inkling was in residence, he never failed to insert an irreverent comment into the conversation. At first, I thought it was the slipped gears in an old codger's mental engine. But it happened too regularly for me to ignore. Gordon was making a point, heretical dissent disguised as piety. It would do no good to confront him. He'd deny any ill will toward "mother church."

"The Lord be with you."

"And also with you."

"Lift up your *hearts*." I pause. Did he hear me this time?

"We lift them up unto the Lord," came his reply and with that the Reverend Inkling was lost to the world and I droned on. He only came down from heaven as I began the actual prayer of consecration.

"So we do as our Lord Jesus Christ did. On the night he was betrayed we take .... "

"Hold it there, son."

"Father?"

"Best part of the entire service." The old priest was rolling the words around in his mouth silently. His tongue bulged out one cheek, then ran around his gums ending at the opposite cheek. Tasting every syllable.

There was no further explanation coming from Father Inkling, so I didn't know if I dared continue. It was not wise ... ignoring his pronouncements or interfering in his spiritual reveries. What to do? Levan's rule number eight, "When in doubt, fudge it!"

"Ah ... (whispering) I didn't quite hear you. Which part is the best part?"

He woke from his trance with a start. "The damned betrayal." His eyes flashed disapproval. "Don't they teach you young people anything at theological college? This is where we admit what we did and still do. We betray. That's our primary function as God's children—to let him down.

"Surely, that's a bit .... "

Inkling was not to be interrupted. "All this religious stuff—the pretty words we recite; it all boils down to that one hellish phrase: 'On the night he was betrayed ...'"

There seemed no more to be said so I took up where I left off. "He took bread, blessed it and—"

"See!" He threw a satisfied smirk my direction and then went back to his prayerful posture.

"See what?"

"You couldn't leave it be, could you? You had to trundle along, not stopping to ponder the words you speak." His face changed hue and he gazed at me with pastoral concern. "But ... maybe I am too harsh!"

"No. Father you're right. Ah, I should take more time to ...."

"Will you be silent child and listen?" His rasping voice was weakening. It was getting past his bedtime and exhaustion always showed first in his speech. He coughed and continued, "God has not granted me much more time among you. (Oh no! The I-will-be-going-to-my-Maker-soon speech!) But please listen carefully." Long pause. "Listen to your own words or more precisely to what falls between them. You speak of great betrayal and hardly give a downbeat before you're off to find a solution." He worked his mouth again as if he had bitten into a raw lemon. He took full measure of my presence. Up one side and down the other, his eyes flickered over my black suit, matching tie. Not a stitch out of place. Shoes polished.

"Jesus Christ! You're so young." Father Inkling never swore, but he would call upon the Lord at such peculiar moments and leave it a question whether the invocation was intended as exultation or profanity. "Look child, you go out and do some serious sinning before you do another communion service."

"Sir?"

"Why don't you do something worth confessing before you ask for absolution in the Sacrament?" He closed his eyes and his attention to the divine presence seemed to fade. The service was over. From high priest, he seemed to slump and shrink down into a frail and very old man.

I was at a loss what to do. "Do you want me to finish the Eucharist?"

"It is finished."

"But the bread and wine!"

"Oh, for heaven's sake." He was almost asleep. "Say the 'Our Father' if it will make you feel better."

"*Our Father who art in heaven, hallowed be thy name. Thy kingdom ....*"

"'Hallowed be thy *shame*?' What are you talking about? 'Hallowed be thy shame', indeed."

"I said *name*." But he wasn't listening.

"That's about right. You go away and eat a little shame young man. Get a belly full of it before you come back here. Now let an old man rest in peace."

Almost before I snapped the communion set closed, he was snoring.

Hamilton, Ontario: St. Giles Anglican Church
Monday, September 29, 1913, 11:02 a.m.

Gordon stifled a third yawn behind the cross he was carrying. He was not always so tired, but it had been a late evening. His oldest sister, Lil, had brought home a stranger, Frank by name. Her fiancé. She said the word with such pride. From Toronto, no less. The family had been up past midnight with an impromptu party—always great times in the Davis household. Mom conjured up a magical feast from what she confessed were "leftovers in the ice box." James broke out the vintage tales and his children all played along. Later there was singing and a few mandatory jokes at Lil's expense. A classic night.

Gordon shook off his weariness as he tried to concentrate on what Father Hawthorne had said. "Walk with dignity child. You are approaching the Lord's table. Imagine how God must feel. A lowly little sinner coming before him."

Gordon balked, "Am I a sinner?"

"Indeed ... we all are."

"How?"

"How what, my child?"

Gordon ignored the "my child." At 19 he could hardly be classified with the kids that ran round the lower hall on Sunday mornings. "How could I be such a great sinner? I haven't done anything wrong yet."

"Hah ... I told you."

That seemed to end the debate. The priest went on to explain the mechanics of a funeral service. Old man Gates had died and they were rushing to get things in order. Hawthorne didn't have time to pursue any theological issues to their conclusions. Not now. The relativity of sinning would have to wait for another time. There were candles to light and Bibles to open.

"A funeral is our best service, often the only time we'll see certain folk in church. We don't want to disappoint them." Hawthorne spoke like a circus ringmaster preparing for the crowds. "Make sure that cross is well cleaned. I want it glowing with God's fire."

Holding his burden in one hand, Gordon was reaching for a towel, when the priest stopped him. "Mind that you never smile. Not the time for mirth. A good wholesome sombre countenance." At that, Hawthorne gripped Gordon's chin gently. "Here, let's see your best consoling face." Gordon tensed, but tried to don a suitable manner. He was unpractised in the use of liturgical masks, so his effort came off rather badly.

"That'll have to do. And don't yawn for heaven's sake. The last thing people want to see is a bored attendant at the farewell celebration of their beloved."

"Yes, sir."

"Do try to move with reverence."

"Yes, sir."

The priest had hurried to the vestry closet to put on his best black gown. When Gordon had his back turned, the old cleric peeked around the edge of the door, appraising his new acolyte with a knowing eye. "A bit old," he thought, "but oh-so-delicious." Out loud he called to Gordon, "I think it's time we undertook some personal devotions, my son."

Gordon turned around, smiling at the prospect of special attention. "What's that, Father?" Expectant and eager.

Hawthorne mumbled into his alb, "What an easy mark this one will be."

"Pardon, Father?"

"I said, 'You'll see.'" Unthinking, his hands moved down the buttons on his robe. His dressing complete, Hawthorne strode up to the boy, proud and powerful in the young man's eyes. "We'll discuss the matter after this service. Now mind that you keep your eyes on me and what I do! No slacking and for heaven's sake don't ever look bored."

Heaven smiled down that day, for no yawns disturbed the novice acolyte as he processed down into the sanctuary. The coffin arrived without mishap, and Gordon was able to assist his superior with all the minor acts of service that made the liturgy such an impressive show.

He watched with a mixture of awe and trepidation as Hawthorne proclaimed absolution, consecrated bread and wine, and offered prayers for the bereaved. Could he ever hope to be so comfortable in a priestly role? So comforting to those who mourn?

But it was the homily that sparked a real flutter of terror. To speak to so many people at a time like this, in the very valley of the shadow of death. His heart both swelled at and shrank from the prospect. Hawthorne had a well-oiled funeral homily. It began in mediocrity and ended with banalities. "Life, my friends, is like a locked silver chest. We're all looking for the key. And, you may ask, 'Where is it to be found?' I will tell you. It is found in Jesus of Nazareth, that bountiful shepherd who knows our needs even before they are spoken. Yes, he is the key, the way, the truth and the life. Oh how we must cling to his strength at times like these...."

The sermon ran its course, comparing dear departed Mr. Gates with one beast in a team of oxen (Jesus being the other) and with "a broken bell that needed mending," Christ being the glue. Finally, the dear departed soul was a blade of wheat, God being the industrious harvester. There were references to his saint-like virtue and heroic charity. The congregation sighed and cried in turn and left the church with a religious glow.

There was no internment and the cleric wished each mourner "The peace that passes all understanding," as they filed past him at the back door. A bell was pealing.

Gordon was hoping for just a tad bit more understanding. When they were alone, he blurted out, "But what did it all mean?" He had no idea how blunt he could be, and at precisely the wrong time.

"Mean?"

"Calling Mr. Gates a pillar of the church. He never came except on Easter morning when Mrs. Gates made him."

"Oh ... that! It was just a little white lie to keep the family coming to morning vespers."

"Ah." Gordon was unclear why a falsehood was inspiring enough to encourage a family to attend church, but then he was, as yet, unschooled in the dynamics of guilt.

Father Hawthorne was fussing in his vestments' closet as "the child" stewed on theological dilemmas. Reaching for the flask of consecrated wine that sat on a shelf above his clothes, he continued his lecture. "It's just part of the craft, Gordon. You'll see soon enough." He took a quick swig from the flask and continued, "People don't want to think at times like this. They're all tears and sobs."

"Yes, sir. But do we allow them to .... "

Hawthorne took a second, deep swallow; hot rum coursed down his parched throat. (The wine had been replaced long ago for something with kick.) Gordon's persistent voice was slightly muffled by the closet door. "Do we allow them to leave without any hints of understanding? Ah ... May I ask another question?"

"Yes, my son." Another nip and the bottle was back in place. The Father had little time for the earnestness of Gordon's queries, but he emerged from the closet prepared to be patient.

Gordon tried to get it right. "For example, what did you mean when you said that Mrs. Gates should not mourn for her husband?"

"Ah, that. Well, if our Saviour said that we should not let our hearts be troubled, as it states in John's Gospel, then, it would be a sin to mourn for those who are not dead, but alive in Christ."

"Alive in Christ? But Mr. Gates *is* dead."

"Dead only to our eyes. But he has put on the robe of immortality and has passed onto the blessed realm. As Paul declared, 'We see through a glass dimly'" Hawthorne was into the groove again. "Then— meaning after death—'we shall see face to face.' 1 *Corinthians*, chapter 13: verse 12. Memorize it, lad. Handy little ditty. At any rate the understanding part is this: God's grace will sustain Mrs. Gates until she, too, joins him in that world beyond our sight."

Gordon was not entirely sure. "Why are religious ideas always beyond us, our understanding and sight, I mean?"

The priest looked patronizingly at this young student and feigned an interest he had long lost. "My child, be patient. God's grace will show you the way. If you become a priest you will realize that all mourners ever want to hear is that their beloved is with God, waiting for their arrival."

While Gordon digested this bit of wisdom, Hawthorne wondered if this untested youth knew what it would be like: lonely days and nights, endless cups of tea with matrons who were too old to stimulate any decent conversation. What a waste of this lively child! So tender and desirable. The fine features, the lean physique!

The priest blocked the natural course of his thoughts. "Soon. Not now. Soon," he promised himself.

With the funeral behind him, Hawthorne suddenly felt hungry. "Let's get out of here and see if Mrs. Hawthorne has baked those apple pies yet." With that, he laid a heavy arm on Gordon's shoulder and steered him toward the door. His fingers burning to reach lower on the young man's back, but not daring to do so, not yet.

For Gordon, his doubting was back. Why did he always feel so small and stupid? He was never able to shake it, but closing the vestry door he could remember when it began.

Sauble Beach, Ontario
Monday, July 10, 1899, 4:20 p.m.

"You stink."

Gordon was approaching the dinner table with the untarnished joy of a hungry stomach. His sister, Lil, who took great delight in controlling the seven other children, was the guardian of the dinner purity code. Being the youngest, he had been allowed to play for the afternoon. It had been cloudy and cold so the lake was out. "Too chilly for you, Gordie." His mother had pushed him off to the little brook that ran by their summer residence. The brook, like the residence, was really a small affair, hardly deserving its name. But to a child of five, it was a mighty river. Its pools contained endless mysteries—most of which were mired in mud and swamp weeds. A rusted paint bucket, two discarded rubber tracks from a broken wagon wheel, and a rotten racoon fur. It was from these objects that Gordon gained his smell. Three hours of hauling his treasures about in the water, chasing tadpoles and building dams of muck had left their mark.

"You stink!" Lil said it a second time, pinching her nose to underline her disgust.

Gordon tried to defend himself. "Do not."

"You certainly do. You stink." Holding her nose and now wagging a finger as if to make the point even clearer, Lil repeated her charge loudly so the whole table could hear. "You stink of dead fish and slime, and you won't get any supper until you clean up."

Of course, he did stink and while he couldn't make fine distinctions between the reporting of his nose, mouth or ears, he knew that something was amiss. In consequence, Lil's obvious scorn planted a seed that day. As he grew older and became aware of hygiene, Gordon always supposed that he smelled too much. There was never enough soap to lather away his stench.

It went deeper though. Gordon heard Lil's assessment as a judgment on his body. His thoughts, feelings and actions. In his mind, she had labelled him, given him a slogan—his corporate image. "You stink." No amount of scrubbing would ever wash away his smell—the odour of a stupid little boy covered in mud.

The unbridled joy of a 5-year-old swept from his face at her words, never to return. Gordon spent the next 94 years of his life trying to get it back.

Neuville-St.-Vaast, France
Wednesday, May 10, 1916, 10:15 a.m.

The stench was beyond words. Gordon and his mates tried to ignore it. Flies buzzed. Not a whiff of wind to scatter the thick smell of butchery.

The non-commissioned officers always set the new guys to the worst tasks, sandbagging muck for the trench walls, rolling coils of barbed wire up from the railhead for eventual deployment in no man's land, and hefting "bath mats" for lining trench floors. After arriving at the front Gordon had tasted three weeks of this back-breaking ten-hour-a-day tedium.

Like the others, Gordon was worried that he'd never see any action. He came to France to put his courage to the test. He could have joined the war effort at home, if it meant menial labour.

His group of three, Eric, a man they called "Boomer," and Gordon, had just finished another row of sandbags for a second line trench, when the sergeant called them to a new section of the line.

"Bad shelling in the night. You three clean up this mess." He pointed vaguely to a bomb-blasted foundation that had served as a billet for four or five men. Giving it a once over, Gordon realized he had been in this shelter once or twice in the constant shifting of men between front line trenches and auxiliary units in the rear. Raw, untested recruits got bumped from the better spots as the "originals" came back for a rest.

There was a reek that floated on the air near the crumbled walls that was new and hideous to Gordon. Death!

When he joined the corps, his nose had been the first casualty. Unimaginable smells assailed it daily. The acrid stench of urine was everywhere. Men relieved themselves at any convenient point. They pissed on their guns if there was nothing else available for cleaning weapons. Some mixed urine and mud and smeared it on their legs—a cure against the cooties, they claimed. The week-long stints at the front with only the shallow latrines, no showers or laundry gave everyone a urine-like fragrance. *Eau de piss.*

Gordon was used to fighting his own smells—polished his skin raw at every turn. He had always been the first to exchange his uniform whenever a clean one was offered. He was careful to handwash his body parts each day before bed. Even with all these efforts, efforts that some-times gained him the nickname of "Sweetie," he was unable to escape the build-up of odour.

On top of the defecating flavours, there was the mud—poisoned by gas and turned to gunpowder pudding by exploding shells. It oozed with stench. Like a piece of gangrenous ground, it smelled of unnatu-ral decay.

Gordon thought, in his few short weeks of duty, he had tasted every possible fragrance, but stooping to "clean up" that bombed shelter, a terrible aroma assaulted his senses: roasted, blasted human flesh. The foundation was filled with body parts. It must have been a direct hit, no survivors and no bodies without some grotesque amputation. The buzzing flies added to the chaos.

It was grizzly work. A wheelbarrow was found. They pieced soldiers together as best they could and trundled them down to the cemetery outside the hospital tent. The shock of dismemberment was numbing, but the stink of decaying bodies, that smell would never leave him.

The mopping up after battle carried the same foulness. Bodies from past raids or present assaults had to be collected whenever possible. Gordon's squad always got the nod. In time, he grew accustomed to every manner of death. But he never could get used to the smell. His only way to cope with it was to classify the reek. In mock sophistication, Gordon and his stretcher buddy, Eric, offered their expert opinions on the many variants of human stench. Two-day old bodies were milder than four. *Obsession #2 or #4.* Someone encased in mud had a different fragrance than someone who rotted in the sun: *L'air de Boue.* Bringing the stretcher forward, he and Eric would speculate on the vintage they would be picking up on that trip. Sniffing the air, Gordon would suggest: "Three days in water." "No, I thinks it was mud," Eric replied. Black humour, the only antidote to sanity.

Then Eric took a sniper's dart in the head. Gordon was alone with his jokes and smells.

Halifax, Nova Scotia: Halifax Harbour, Pier 7
Thursday, December 6, 1917, 9:16 a.m.

"Ice must be forming on my feet," Gordon mind's reeled. He tried to kick them furiously to shake the clinging weights from his limbs but they responded as if in slow motion. His arms still worked and he flailed forward. A smoking gangway was just within reach—salvation.

"Help ... please!" Wisps of anguish came from small pieces of the decking that had not been blown away.

Struggling with fingers that would not grasp the railings tightly, Gordon sloshed his way upward, lurching his body out of the waves onto the rough slats of the gangway. He felt leaden and alone, but his training was operating without conscious effort. Cold hands ran down his body, searching for injuries. He could feel warm blood on his right trouser leg. He dug into the several holes in his pants. No breaks met his touch. He felt his forehead and came back with blood. "Must be a flesh would." Then his fingers felt around for his pack and found it still slung over his back. His first aid pouch made the journey safely as well, attached to his waistband.

"Help ...." Softer now. Gordon strained an ear toward the sound. He knew that plaintive tone. It signalled the coming of the night. Life was losing the battle. Was it Jo?

"Help! Please ... someone ..."

Rising on trembling limbs he struggled upward. His feet could still hold his weight. One step ... still limping from his battle wound, but he could walk. That's something. Another step. He half-walked, half-dragged his chilled stiffened legs to the small bit of pier 7 that was still standing.

"Where was she?" He thought she might be further back along the wall of a semi-collapsed warehouse. Had she been standing inside or outside? "Hello?" His voice was swallowed up by billowing smoke and snapping flames. "Hello?"

"Please ... help me!"

He pitched forward toward the voice, each step more urgent as he imagined his Jo in pain.

"Ahhhhh ... I can't move ... help! Please!"

Closer now. It did sound like Jo's voice! He dragged his way through splintered timbers and found her under a broken beam. Black hair smeared in blood, her chest crushed under the weight of its death-dealing burden. Shards of glass stuck from her left cheek.

A broken stranger, it wasn't Jo after all.

Gordon thought he had seen it all, but this pitiful wretch turned his stomach. He'd seen many, many men cut to shreds, but never a woman. His knees buckled involuntarily and he found himself leaning close to her searching eyes.

"Please ... help me!"

Gordon knew there wasn't much to help, but he had to try. Gripping the beam with both hands he offered what reassurance he could. "This may hurt ..." He heaved upward, but the beam didn't budge. Who was he kidding? A team of horses would have trouble moving the timber, twelve inches square.

"Please ... my baby ...."

"Baby?" Gordon frantically looked through the rubble.

"He's in my arms. Help him!"

There was no sign of her arms. They were buried under the wood. What was left of the baby was there as well. Gordon's mind wanted to burst; his stomach was rolling over. "Not a baby!" He stifled a lurch that brought bile to his mouth. He heaved again on the beam. This time to the point of fainting. Nothing moved.

What energy he had been able muster seemed to dribble away and Gordon slunk down beside the dying woman. His hand found her forehead and stroked her brow. Human touch was all he could offer.

"Help my baby ... please." It was half-gurgle, half-whisper.

"Hush now, he's in good hands."

Montreal: 27 Sebastopol Street
Tuesday, March 21, 1916, 6:00 p.m.

Holding the dish with both hands, Johanna placed the mashed potatoes on the table and slid into her place at the table. Steam was rising from several platters and candle smoke created a mist that enveloped their dinner. In a rare irreligious moment, Gordon thought of an ancient altar strewn with smoking offerings to the gods.

They were just three people around the table. The Bishop presided. His wife had died of cancer in the distant past and he was left in charge of two children, a son and daughter. On this evening, the boy was absent. "Rehearsing some variation on Mozart with that quartet of his. I wish he would devote his mind to other, more holy pursuits."

"Father, you love music." The daughter, Johanna, had taken on the motherly role in their home. Sitting as she did in the place closest to the kitchen door, she accepted many of the tasks that would normally have fallen to the matron of the house. She was also quick to correct the extravagances of her father's wit.

"Yes, well, organ music certainly. Bach, most definitely. But these new atonal arrangements leave me cold. Are we ready?" A glance at Gordon by way of welcome. "Let us offer thanks."

Hinks reached out and flapped open his serviette, placing it carefully in his lap. Back to the prayer. "Dear God, lighten our darkness that we might see, feed our bodies that we might serve, open our hearts that we might love. Amen."

Brief though it was, the blessing gave Gordon a chance to glance at the table. Silver glistened from every corner. Candlesticks were finely tooled. Every place had its own collection of silverware, many of which Gordon had never seen before. Food was nestled in matching serving dishes and wine was poured into crystal goblets. "Is this how the other half lives?" he mused.

Coming down to earth, he wondered, "Did he stink?" It was the perpetual worry. He'd washed well after accepting the invitation for dinner. He wanted to make a good impression. Had he been clear enough that his initial visit was not to mooch a meal? "Surely, I would be pleased, but I pray you, don't go to any trouble on my account, for my visit was simply to convey greetings. I would not wish to inconvenience you."

The bishop had cast aside Gordon's polite protestations with a wave of his hand. "Nonsense, Johanna here is always looking for an excuse to bring out the finery. Isn't that right, dear?"

Johanna had smiled. "Indeed, Father." Turning to her uncomfortable visitor; the impish smile was back. "Gordon ... Mr. Davis, you are most welcome. Please be our guest tomorrow evening. At five-thirty if that is to your liking?"

So here he was, feeling out of his depth, and yet longing for the evening to last 'til eternity.

Grace offered, the meal conversation took off in all directions at once. Hinks was well-read and was always looking for new fields in which to expand his understanding. Having regard for his guest he began with a question of the Hamilton region. "They say there's a fine beach at that end of the lake. I am such a fan of swimming, builds character."

"You think everything, save atonal music perhaps, builds character." Johanna was never shy with her remarks.

"Yes, but the water refreshes at the same time as it exercises. A nice metaphor don't you think? No wonder our Lord chose water for baptism. Have you been there, at Hamilton Beach, I mean?" Hinks directed his gaze toward his guest, raised bushy eyebrows entreating a response.

"Yes," Gordon was about to explain how his great-aunt had a house there, but he was too slow for this crowd.

"Jesus didn't choose water, Father. Surely it was just *there*." Johanna pointed to the ground to make her point.

The bishop had been waiting with a reply. "Oil, dear daughter. Oil was 'there' and often used for special anointing: kings, prophets, or messianic figures. We certainly have evidence that it was used for other, shall we say more pleasurable, purposes, but I am of the opinion that our Lord chose the simple, more abundant substance of water. Part of his proletarian attitude."

"Mr. Davis," Johanna, remembering her hosting responsibilities, interrupted what she knew would have been a long lecture on the benefits of water over oil for liturgical purposes, and turned to Gordon. "What inspired you to enter the ministry? I dare say it wasn't a debate over oil versus water for baptism."

Gordon winced inside. He had no place here. His skill was too meagre. "I ... well ... it was just an inner conviction really."

"Do tell." She made it sound like the most unique experience ever recounted and passed Gordon the steaming carrots.

"Thank you." Gordon began to fill his plate. "Well, it wasn't much more than a queer warmth in my heart."

"My God, Johanna, he's a Wesleyan."

"My Lord?" Gordon was not sure how to take the bishop.

The bishop was smiling as he ladled mounds of potatoes onto his plate. "It's a joke, Gordon. Let out that belt of yours a notch or two. Here have some potatoes—they're my favourite dish and Johanna does them to a turn." Hinks scooped a mountain of mashed potatoes onto the young man's plate. "John Wesley tells us that he was converted to a greater and more fervent grasp of the faith at Aldershot, in England, where upon listening to Martin Luther's commentary on Paul's letter to the Romans, he felt, and I quote, 'a strange warming in my heart.' You're in good company lad."

"How do we know that it wasn't just indigestion?" Johanna had an ironic glint in her eyes as she glanced at Gordon.

"Indeed, it may well have been. Being a bishop in the church that Wesley sought to reform, I might be constrained to claim that it was. However, I have never been able to shake the feeling that dear old John was right after all."

"Right, sir?" Gordon was warming to the table talk. "I always thought the Wesleyans were a little too emotional." He took a mouthful of potatoes to squelch his nervous tongue.

"Yes, well, you can never have too much emotion. Our society has grown up thinking the best thing to do with grief, sadness or animosity is to bury it. Never touch on the pain in your heart. A lot of rubbish, I say. This war is a direct result of too much suppressed emotion. All that blocked resentment and anger has to emerge somewhere."

"Now you sound like a mind reader, Father. Have you been inside the heads of statesmen and generals who push this glorious battle on us?"

"A point well taken, my dear." Hinks was not used to losing an argument, but he conceded his daughter's point and changed the subject. "Yes, well ... be that as it may, Wesley was preaching for a revitalized institution. Could you pass the roast beef please?" He always ate too much when his logic was questioned. "Wesley knew that we had become too hierarchical in structure and conversely too flat in spirit. We'd become a fat and lazy collection of moralists. Contrary to what you might suppose, your average disciple wants to be called on for extraordinary service. The cross is not an icon to be rubbed bright for Sunday service, it is an invitation to die for Christ's sake. It's not that we ask too much of people, we ask too little."

"Too little?" Gordon was trying to keep up.

"Father means that the church has let people off the hook of discipleship too easily. Am I right?" Johanna rose to fetch more potatoes from the kitchen and gave a reassuring squeeze to Gordon's shoulder as a signal to push back against the bishop's arguments.

Hinks continued to preach to the congregation he had before him. "Of course, God's gift of grace is ... "

"Grace is free to all, is it not?" Gordon had taken the hint from Johanna and offered his best argument first. "Therefore, how can we let people off too easily?" Gordon lifted his wine goblet to his lips unconsciously hiding behind it like a boy who had fired a snowball and then crouched low while he watched it land.

"Indeed. God's grace is free, but it's not cheap!" Hinks gave Gordon a knowing look and thought there must be more to this fellow than good looks and a down-home charm. "You see, when we made Christianity a religion for the nation, we reduced its obligations. Anyone could and should join the club. Grace was offered for everyone at wholesale prices. We now sell it too cheaply. As any of my good business associates will tell you, you can't make a business run if you give away your best articles at bargain basement prices, so to speak." Hinks was on a roll and even the return of his daughter couldn't slow his pace. "God's grace is not like some warm blanket that you cuddle with when it's convenient. 'Bless me, Father, for I have sinned.' Nonsense!" Here the bishop's voice hardened and his hand flashed into a fist. "Grace doesn't stroke. It grabs you and thrusts you into the world."

"How is that, my Lord?" Gordon could feel a flame flickering in his heart. Was this a revival meeting?

Hinks, whose voice was as versatile as a well-tuned violin, took on a rich timber. "Do you think God cares about our petty little souls and how we weasel our way into heaven? What does John 3:16 say?"

"That God so loved the world, he gave ...." Gordon knew his Gospels.

"Exactly. 'That God so loved the world.' Is there any mention of our spirits or our heaven-bent souls? No!" The lecture was rolling. "It reads: 'That God so loved the world.' It's this world that is God's eternal concern. Not heaven. Not spiritual salvation ... all these religious trappings," here the bishop flicked the golden cross that hung around his omnipresent dog collar, "are rubbish." A long pause, fire in his eyes, fixed Gordon in his place, fork halfway between plate and mouth. "Trash, they're so much trash, unless they're put to the purposes of God's love for this world. We serve God by loving his world."

Johanna broke the bishop's spell as she placed a fresh bowl of potatoes at his side. "Ah. Thank you, my dear."

Gordon's tongue seemed to be stuck to the roof of his mouth. His mind was racing. Here was someone who understood his questions, seemed to invite inquiry. Maybe this was his chance, but how to approach the issue that had been plaguing him for the past month. "Sir, my Lord, …"

Johanna coughed. "Really … Mr. Davis … Gordon … he may be a bishop, but he's also my father and much as he would wish to deny it, a mere mortal. We do not stand on ceremony here. Please, a simple 'Mr. Hinks' or even 'Douglas' would be acceptable." It wasn't a rebuff. The smile in her eyes told Gordon it was closer to an invitation. To what, he wasn't sure.

"Mr. Hinks," he'd try again. "Ah … recently a … ah … church leader suggested that I could best serve the Lord by fighting in France. Is that what you mean when God has a regard for this world? Could you tell me how best a soldier joins battle for—"

"Was that Cruikshank who said that?" Steel in the bishop's voice.

"Ah … yes, sir. I believe you know him well."

"Bah. We were at Oxford together. Silly ass."

Gordon nearly dropped through the floor, shocked a leader of the church could be so blunt.

"I didn't think he had much critical thought back then, and with the war every halfwit theologian is clamouring for blood. Makes me sick."

"He's a fool, Gordon." The words were out of Johanna's mouth before she could think. Her wine glass hovered in mid-air.

"You're always so subtle, Johanna. Comes from your mother's side, I imagine. But in this case, I believe you're right."

Johanna was not finished. "It makes my blood boil. These overweight, empty-headed churchmen, who equate their own silly ambitions with the providence of the Almighty. Is murder God's design? Can an entire generation be butchered for our Maker's pleasure? There is no glory and no 'Lord's service' in France. It's lunacy and anyone who suggests that God wants or needs this present slaughter is a complete fool." She had inherited her father's spirit, it appeared, and plunked her wine glass down to punctuate her indignation.

The table fell silent as they each worked through the main course and their own thoughts.

Le Touquet, France
Monday, May 8, 1916, 6:15 p.m.

Each man stood at attention. Keeping thoughts hidden behind squared shoulders and a tight-to-the-chest chin, each listened to the crisp, chilling words of their new commanding officer, Major Ryan. There had been many speeches on their approach toward the front—mostly light affairs: bits of military discipline, battle tactics, morale boosters, bawdy jokes. This talk was less eloquent than usual. Low on humour, high on obedience. Ryan's intent, as far as Gordon surmised, was to harden the troops for the trench warfare that lay just over the next few hills.

Major C. F. Ryan, D.S.C., M.C., was a hard-nosed graduate of the British Army. Duty was his highest virtue, spit and polish came a close second and compassion was a *non sequitur*. He enjoyed giving the troops his "Just Before the Battle Speech." Toughen them up to the real world. Looking down their ranks, he could see how green they were, still smiling at the prospect of combat. Between phrases he wondered where the Canadians were digging up their recruits. "They look like lumberjacks for Christ's sake!"

Though he never mentioned it to a soul, he loathed being seconded to the Canadian Corps. Passed over for higher commands, he was shifted sideways. He often wondered if he had unwittingly been a pawn in a political game. But orders were orders, so he'd make the best of it. Once saddled with the Canuck troops, he vowed he would whip their sorry, undisciplined backsides into shape.

Though he'd been with this battalion since its departure from Salisbury Plain, it was just yesterday the word came down for him to take charge. Crossing the Channel together gave him a chance to size up fellow officers. After three weeks of close quarters he had a pretty fair idea of each one's metal. He knew that he was their superior in discipline. Now he was also their superior in command.

A day from the front, Ryan's job was to put the fear of God into them. All the information about combat readiness had been delivered, they had marched their boot soles thin and crawled over every muddy, godforsaken patch of ground he could find. Now he had to lay down the law. Make sure there were no pansies or layabouts in the ranks.

"Men, you have been equipped, trained and hardened for a single purpose. Do you know what that is?" Ryan paused, raking the lines of eager faces with his most officious, some of his subordinates would say most pompous, stare. One eyebrow tightened around his eyeglass while the other rose slightly. He was tapping his leather boot top with his riding whip, ever so slightly.

"Do they know the punch line?" he wondered, allowing the silence to thicken a bit before giving it to them.

"Men," Ryan shouted loudly, "you're here to kill the enemy." He paused again to allow the message to echo around the parade ground and into their heads. "This is not a bloody party, some limp-dick fairy tale." The major knew that there was nothing more piercing than the combination of hard talk and dirty language. "Three miles from this spot are seasoned Jerries who would like nothing better than to drive a saw-edged bayonet through your flabby belly and watch you bleed to death slowly as they piss on your fallen comrades. Your job is to kill the Huns before they have any such chance to do that to you." Long pause. "Make no mistake, the other side is cruel beyond measure. Last year they tried to smoke us out with gas. It burns your lungs, eyes—any flesh it touches. Twenty miles north of this very spot, I watched as my entire brigade was blinded by mustard gas. Half died, bleeding from their ears, noses, assholes. The other half of them still can't see."

More than one soldier gave a silent gasp at the prospect of facing gas.

"It will happen to you, too. Make no mistake. The odds are that one in every ten of you will not return from this war. A full half of you will suffer some casualty. This is not a fucking picnic! I didn't get these metals," here Ryan tapped the row of ribbons on his chest, "because I look pretty in a uniform. I got them for killing Germans, sometimes with my bare hands."

"Never forget. Your first and last job is to kill the enemy."

Ryan consulted his notes, but it was only for show, since he knew his lines by heart. Looking up, he eyed them carefully and began at a low pitch. "Now, you might be asking yourself how you're going to do your duty and make it out alive. There are certainly ways to do it right. Here are the rules of this dangerous game we are about to play.

"First, there will be no quarter given to the enemy. Don't hesitate. Kill him before he kills you. Period. No exceptions, no pity. Last week we lost two-dozen Aussies because they believed that a company of Germans was surrendering. They let down their guard when they saw grey uniforms walking across no man's land with their hands in the air. No sooner than these bastards were within throwing range, they lobbed a dozen grenades into our trench works and killed twenty-four men outright, buried twelve more alive, and critically wounded another sixteen. No mercy. Kill first. Ask questions later. A dead Jerry can always apply for prisoner status once the shooting is over."

A few ripples of laughter greeted this first point.

"Second, no running from duty or leaving the trenches without permission. Any unwillingness to follow orders, especially during an attack will be considered an act of mutiny and will be met with the severest of penalties."

Ryan took a deep breath, and seemed to grow in stature at this point, ready to play his trump card, as he slowly unfolded a single sheet of paper. The rows of men fell into a deep silence as they each contemplated their fear of cowardice. Ryan watched a tightness grow in their eyes. "Good," he thought, "scare the silly buggers into obedience." To drive home his point he read aloud the names of twenty-three soldiers who had been caught in some dereliction of duty. Along with each name came the specific misdemeanour, the date of the court martial, its verdict and the exact time when the punishment was carried out.

"Here's what happens to men who don't follow this second rule:

Private C. Cossman, desertion, court martialled March 10, the verdict death by firing squad, carried out 14:45 the same day.

Private M. Farmer, unlawful retreat, court martialled April 1, the verdict death by firing squad carried out 5:17 the same day.... "

Each name was like a nail pounded into a coffin. Gordon could feel his stomach rolling over. He dared not look down the line of men, but wondered how many others were probing their own conscience. Would he ever be that derelict or frightened?

Ryan read out all twenty-three names and their punishment with a deliberate, quiet tone. "Don't be a bloody coward" was made all the more menacing, since it was delivered as an understatement.

While he found the actions of these useless cretins distasteful, Ryan actually enjoyed this part of his speech very much. It highlighted the stiff metal from which a good soldier and army is made. It was like the ultimate badge of courage: "See, we're even willing to cut off rotten limbs to save the whole body."

There were five other laws, later to be recalled in the trenches "Ryan's Commandments," but none struck the same note of fear in the hearts of the men as the list of executed comrades. Each solider pulled his inner doubts into line, locked them away, along with all the desires to see home again, and carried on.

Saint John: The Buttress Home
Tuesday, October 13, 1992, 11:00 a.m.

"Pull! Put your ass into it, lad!" Gordon, dressed in the mannerisms of Captain Jims, was waving me forward with a tongue depressor. "You think you can approach a schooner with idle strokes like that. The seas are high, matey. Pull! Puuullll!"

The nursing home staff were amazed at how Gordon had come alive. For years beyond memory, he had slouched, eyes open, mouth gaping. Not a hint of humanity in him. That was how he first looked to me. Days of coaxing had finally broken through his shell. There wasn't much small talk left behind the masks, but the two voices came clearer with each visit. Neither Captain Jims nor Father Inkling would interact directly with anyone but me and then only through role-play.

On this visit, the captain was sitting up straight at the stern of the bed while I rowed from the bow using my multi-coloured umbrella as a prop. How did I ever agree to this? The things they never teach you in theological college—like how to help old men with their delusions by pretending to be an oarsman on the Atlantic while perched on their pillows.

I shouted over my shoulder (fortunately the rest of the ward was empty due to an impromptu bingo game organized by the Loyalist Lioness Club), "Ship ahoy!" Maybe that would put an end to the charade.

"'Ship Ahoy?' Where the hell did you get that from—a cereal box? You call her by name. Let's sail in closer and come abeam."

I pulled for a full minute and then declared, "We're in tight. (Was that a nautical term? Sounded more like sexual foreplay.) Hold fast to the lines." I threw him a worn sock that he gripped intently, leaning back to steady our craft as it ground into the hull of the larger vessel. "All secure, Captain."

"Hoist the oars!"

"Aye, aye, Captain."

"Move smartly." Gordon was impatient as a seaman.

I raised my umbrella.

"That's better. At ease, men." I looked around for the men. Gordon had the capacity to people his dreams with quite a cast of characters. "Well done. I didn't think you young bucks had it in you."

"Thank you, sir. We're learning. But it was a long trek."

"That little bit? It was nothing. Try four days, pulling with all your might and coming up on a deserted shore. That takes balls of iron and a fair bit of heave-ho, I tell you."

"Four days?" It was the first time the captain had ever hinted at anything specific. Was his history breaking through?

"Four lonely, long days at the oars. All my shipmates gone. None escaped the fire. I did, blast my cursed little soul. Worked for a day trying to pick up pieces before I went off to find her ... four eternal days searching."

"Her?" He needed little prompting. Just as well, since I had no idea where we were. I thought we were rowing to a favourite ship of the old captain, but it seemed we had sailed into another plot entirely.

"My beauty. Oh, she was a fair looking rig, decked out in long tresses and with a bow that could cut through the thickest sea. Yes, I went after her, tried to catch up to her. But she was too fast for me. Ran in another league, she did. But I tried, nonetheless. The ache of muscles is nothing compared to ache in your heart." Captain Jims gave a quick look at his first mate who was obviously too young to understand grief. "Most likely lost on you youngsters. When you don't know which way to go and the winds seem to shift with every watch, you'll taste failure and want to give up, let me tell you."

Even though the first mate didn't know what to reply, Captain Jims fell back into his story. "She wasn't at her home port nor in her close waters. Knowing that she's out there, not knowing where to find her, knowing that you can't keep going forever and knowing that you have to. That'll drive any man mad."

Wherever Captain Jims had taken us, we were in deep waters. "Is that what drove you crazy?"

The captain bristled. The spell was broken. "Me crazy? Whose side are you on? Are you my first mate or not?"

"Aye, aye Captain. Yes sir. I'm you're first mate."

"Don't put words in me mouth. I wasn't driven crazy, lad. I'm tougher than a boiled owl. Them four days didn't sink me. It weren't the high seas nor the gales neither. When I couldn't find my beauty, I sank myself. Yes indeed. I sank myself."

Gordon fell silent. No amount of prompting or play-acting brought back the captain's voice. He closed his eyes, curled up in the stern and shut himself down. In a few minutes he was asleep and I was left holding my umbrella, my dripping imaginary oar, at the other end of his bed.

Most of his seafarer episodes were fictitious—whaling expeditions off Grand Manan Island or rum-running to Bar Harbour, but this last tale had the flavour of fact. Who was his beauty and what was the four-day search all about? There was a depth of anguish in that captain's voice that I was too frightened to touch.

Saint John: Centenary-Queen Square United Church
Tuesday, Nov. 17, 1992, 11:17 a.m.

I allow the prayer's pause to linger. Words cannot speak like silence. It's as much for me as the mourners ... trying to sort out my doubts, find the strength to be honest and yet comforting.

My head bowed slightly, halfway through the silence, I take a quick glance around the sanctuary. All heads are bowed ... reverence reigns. Just as I turn the page to begin speaking again, a stranger ... attractive, a woman ... slips through the east transept door and quietly takes a place.

I refocus on the hymn book in my hand. The silence had gone on long enough. Time to announce the hymn, travelling music for the minister to leave the table and get to the pulpit.

"Friends, lift up your hearts. We shall sing hymn #1 found in the green book in your pews, 'O for a Thousand Tongues to Sing.'" With barely ten voices in the church, I know Reverend Inkling would enjoy the irony.

As the organ plays a few introductory bars, I watch the congregation rise. Who is that stranger?

Monday, January 1, 1917

Dear Gordon:

I don't want you to become a stranger to us. The letters you write are so vague about your life in France that we don't know what to think. It's not like you to be evasive. Father says it's because things are indescribable. I wonder if you're hiding something. Are you sick? Have you been receiving my parcels? They're not much really. Just a few treats from home. I know you like the Scotch cakes and the candied grapefruit peel. There's been no news of your regiment for some time. I keep scanning the papers for any mention of it. Let us know where you are and what they have you do. Please. It would help mother so much.

It's another new year and I wanted to be the first
to wish you all the best. Pray to God that this
war is over before we turn another 12 months.
I am beginning to wonder at its usefulness. The
papers keep telling us we're winning and that it's
a glorious fight. But the men who come home are
so quiet. They don't seem at all flush with victory.
Nevertheless, I wish you the best of the season.
Did you keep up our custom of banging pots at the
stroke of midnight? We had a jolly time last night.
Mr. Lewis and Mr. Oar came by to celebrate with
Mum and Dad. They sang "Auld Lang Syne" with
such gusto, it made Mother laugh.

Mum is no better. I am worried. She is weaker each
day it seems. Your last note asked about her health.
It's not good. It wasn't your fault of course, but
since you left last February, she's been declining.
Her spirits were certainly low, but by summer her
body was showing signs of illness. We couldn't
afford much and she wasn't in any pain so we let
it go until September. When she finally saw the
doctor, it was too late. They say Mum has cancer.
I am sorry to blurt it out like this, but someone has
to tell you. The other girls were all for keeping you
in the dark, but I think you should know. According
to the doctor, it's early yet and with bedrest and
care she may well enjoy many more New Year's
celebrations. Please don't fret. There's nothing much
any of us can do. She's trying to keep up her spirits
and tells me as I write to say that she rejoices you
are still with us, if only in spirit at this point. I know
she lives for your letters.

There's little other news. Lil will be married next
month, as you know. Edna has her eye on a beau.

He's not much to look at, but he has lots of money they say. They've been on a few dates and she says he dances well. Bully for him! I've been sticking to my Albert. He was about to sign up when his boss told him to stay and run the foundry. "You can fight the war best from these four walls." A raise in pay, lots of pleading on my part and mother's illness have kept him home ... for now.

Fred Lewis was awarded the Military Medal. (We're not sure what he did. The news arrived with Mr. Lewis last night.) Eva's boyfriend, Jack Pierce, was wounded. Nothing serious and he'll be home soon.

I finished school last month. My final class is behind me. Now I'm off to work in a millinery shop. It's not much and the pay is minimal, but in these hard times, the family can use every penny we get. Father is always reminding me to thank you for sending back what you can.

We did receive your request for a Bible. It was blessed by Reverend Hawthorne and is winging its way to France. The inscription was my idea, but I'll let that be a surprise.

I must go now. Mother needs some help.

Your loving sister,
Mabel

P.S. Who is "Jo?" You mentioned him a couple of times in your last note but didn't explain. Someone you met in Montreal, I believe.

Montreal: 27 Sebastopol Street
Tuesday, March 21, 1916, 8:00 p.m.

"It's called redaction criticism, a new biblical hermeneutic. I haven't discussed it seriously until this evening, but enough of my work. Tell me, Gordon, this is your first time in Montreal. How do you like it?" Hinks was feeling that his evening was not a waste after all. So much of the hosting function of a bishop was filled with delicate and often empty conversation. This caller was a notch above the average.

"It is a fine city, sir. A bit crowded in places. There is a charm evident here that my hometown lacks. I believe it is the French influence."

"You've felt it?" Johanna was taken with their guest and his observations, straight and ungarnished. This last one touched her as she had a passionate affinity for the sense of life and immediacy found in French Canada.

"Yes, ah ... it's only a few days that I've been here, but wandering the streets in the old city there seems to be more colour than Hamilton. Parties spill out of most doorways. On the walk here this evening, I counted a number of houses where the lights blazed and laughter drifted out onto the sidewalk. In spite of the weather, people seemed to be warm and welcoming."

Hinks chuckled. "I, too, was born in Ontario, Gordon, near your hometown, and each time I go back it always seems so threadbare and so tightly knotted."

Gordon could think of nothing to reply and smiled instead.

"But we have not allowed you the opportunity to answer our first question." Johanna wanted to know more of this gentle, timid soul. She suspected there was something tougher underneath the soft exterior. "How is that you chose the ministry?"

"It was a story that did it, really."

"A story? I love stories." Johanna's tone was solidly sincere. "But shall we retire to the drawing room? It's much more comfortable there."

The bishop rose and gestured. "Do help yourself to the wine. Telling tales properly takes a good deal of spirit."

Once settled with comfortable ease in the adjoining room, Johanna urged Gordon, "Go on!" She was not going to allow the conversation to stray from her purpose. A quick glance at her father kept him from starting off on a new path.

Gordon coughed. Was he really going to tell them? It had been a secret he kept to himself, afraid of ridicule. In the past he'd fudged the details and claimed he had been called of God. "It's a rather simple affair."

"Good, the simpler the better," said the bishop. Though he loved his own voice, Hinks was also a good listener.

"It was at a Sunday school picnic. Three, four years ago now. They're grand affairs: foot races, ice cream and swimming in the river—that sort of thing. Actually I believe it was at Hamilton Beach."

"Indeed." There were smiles around the room. Speaking here was a joy, they were so attentive. Gordon coughed. "The highlight of the day came when the invited guest spoke. At such gatherings, it was acceptable for the speaker to tell tall tales, use humour and laughter. On this occasion, the man was a missionary from the Western Territories and he regaled us with stories of sod huts and whitewashed winters. I don't recall the first two points of his sermon, but the third has remained with me. He preached from the story of the talents and suggested that the chief point in the parable was the invitation for disciples to risk what they had been given. I can still recall his words. 'Take what the master has bequeathed to you and take a chance with, it for Christ's sake.' I was listening to every word. I felt he was speaking to my soul. 'The Gospel is not a relic. It is a thing to be risked.' He concluded, 'Don't bury your heart until the master returns. Give it freely to those around you.' So many such stirring phrases, but he ended with a story that I have kept dear. It changed my life."

"Do tell us." Johanna was herself enthralled.

"I am sure you've heard it before."

Hinks was interested, not only in the tale, but also in his daughter's attentiveness. "A good story bears repeating."

Gordon took a swallow of wine and began. "I won't do justice to it, but here goes .... Ah. The missionary was explaining his first charge. It was at the turn of the century when railways were pushing across the prairies, criss-crossing every valley and plain as they tried to keep up with the rapid expansion of settlements.

"Farmers had gone ahead of their families, staked out their claims, built sod huts and begun the work of breaking the land. Rail companies laid track through these new farms. At regular intervals of about ten miles, the distance a team of horses could travel in one day with a load of grain, an elevator and watering station were built beside the line. These installations attracted a few other amenities—a general store, schoolhouse, RCMP office. Before long, little villages were growing along the railways.

"The churches had been sending missionaries to the West for years; rugged men who on outward appearance looked more like trappers than pastors. But when towns began to appear, it was clear that a new wave of ministers was needed to build the faith among the small white communities.

"The preacher at our picnic explained how he had been assigned to build a church in Kindersley, a village on the southwest border of the Saskatchewan Territory. It was located on a feeder line out of Saskatoon, and he jumped at the chance to strike a blow for the Anglican Church and convert the whole town to the true faith. You see, it was the custom in that race for the West that each denomination would send out its zealots, hoping to capture an entire town for their church. I guess we all did it. If you could be the first flavour of Christianity to arrive, chances were good that no matter what faith people had once held, they'd join your church since it was the only show in town."

Hinks laughed, "So our knight went out to capture Kindersley for the Anglicans?"

"He did. But fortune was not smiling on him that day, for when he mounted the steps for his train ride to this promising mission-field, he spied a Presbyterian minister at the other end of the passenger car. There was little doubt as they exchanged looks that they were both headed for the same location. It was the last town on this particular branch line to be won. My missionary was beside himself. How could he ever hope to win the town for Anglicanism, if this heathen was going to run competition?

"As they sat watching the prairies go by, the perplexed Anglican formed a plan. After the stop at Rosetown, the closest settlement to Kindersley, he went to the door of the passenger car and stood on the stairs. It was a rocky ride, prairie winds blowing dust and smoke in his face, but this way he knew he would be the first off the train when it stopped. His idea was to jump quickly to the platform, utter a brief prayer of consecration and declare the town Anglican. Then he would turn and welcome his brother in the faith to a village steeped in the traditions of the Church of England.

"It was a good plan. As he stood there waiting for his chance, he noticed the Presbyterian go forward toward the dining car. 'Typical of the Presbyterians! When the battle is joined, they're looking for lunch!' The Anglican smiled at his joke and went on dreaming about the little white chapel he would build to God's glory among the unsuspecting citizens of Kindersley.

"As they approached the town, the brakes began to squeal. Seeing the platform through the steam pouring from the engine, he made his leap of faith ... right into the arms of the Presbyterian pastor who welcomed him to a good Presbyterian town."

"Touché!" Hinks loved the irony. "An Anglican plot foiled again."

"You see the Presbyterian had not gone to lunch, but to the front of the train where he sat on the cowcatcher. He was going to be sure to be the first one to the village.

"The missionary laughed at himself and said that the Christian on the cowcatcher of a train was a modern parable of discipleship. 'You young people (I knew he was talking directly to me), you get out there ... out where the sparks are flying and the wheels are pounding. Oh sure, the risk is great, but the vision ... ah the vision is out of this world.'"

Gordon was silent, caught by his own rhetoric he could feel his face flush with embarrassment. "It's just a story, but I ...."

"Just a story? It's marvellous." Johanna was adamant and reassuring. "Don't ever say otherwise."

Hinks smiled again. "Don't cast away your pearls, son. That's a great tale. Keep it close. May it be a caution to your pride."

"Thank you, my Lord." Gordon paused. "It actually speaks to me of hope."

"Hope ... how interesting! Say more."

Gordon took a moment to select the right words. "Well, ... it has to do with the imagination of the Presbyterian, I believe. Many men would risk their lives for a great cause. This present war is evidence enough. But only a few have the creative minds to imagine what a worthy cause *might* be. It gives me hope that a Christian could possess that sort of intellectual flexibility."

"And courage." Johanna looked so directly at Gordon that he began to blush. "Wouldn't you agree, Father?"

"Yes, of course. Christianity lived properly takes abundant courage."

"That," thought Gordon, "is just what I lack." And he was relieved when the good bishop took the conversation out of his hands.

CHAPTER THREE

The Hymn

Make your music roll with the thunder of justice; its notes played out through acts of mercy, tuned to the demands of the powerless! Only then can we knowingly sing about "Amazing Grace".

A. Moss, *Tending the Sheep, a Guide to Just Worship*

Toronto: 20 Mountalan Ave.
Friday, April 11, 2014, 7:47 p.m.

"No wait ... Patricia, I am sorry ... You may be wasting your time. I knew a Gordon from the Buttress Home and I am certain he is ... I mean, *was*, penniless when he died. No fortune. It's very impressive that you would dig up this piece of history and track me down, but I am not going to send you my bank information ... and maybe ... well, I'll just hang up now and not waste your time any longer."

As I pull back from my iPhone to hit the end button, I can hear that there's a pause at the other end ... the silence of a magician who has had her trick unceremoniously exposed.

"Pastor Levan, I am going to ask you to hang up and dial your friend Richard Dundas. I believe you have his number ...."

"Richard, of course." My oldest and closest friend draws me back. "What does Richard have—"

"I approached him to find you. I believe he will vouch for my authenticity. If you are satisfied, call me back."

The line goes dead.

Montreal: Down the Street from Thelma Lint's
Gentlemen's Parlour
Saturday, December 8, 1917, 7:10 p.m.

Gordon was dead, lost to misery. Neither rain nor reason waking him. Limbs worked without his knowledge or command. Where his feet took him, he could not have cared less.

Thelma Lint's had been a long shot and Jo wasn't there. She was out! "Busy now with Samuel." How could one be so close yet so heartless? Had their encounters meant nothing, so easily cast aside? Flashes of her smile mingled with the moments of their love. He could see her lips, almost taste her kisses; the gentle way her hand caressed the small of his back, unbidden and casual. It set his heart ablaze. He could smell her hair, taste the soft silken texture of her breast.

Each recollection was but a brief impression, precious as an icon, preserved through the sweat and sacrifice of the trenches. Holy and untouchable, each one had been wrapped and unwrapped countless times over the past year. Now a dark hand crushed them into dust.

Breathing came harder as his trust collapsed.

Grasping at straws, Gordon remembered all their communications. Was there not a steady stream of assurances? What of the many protestations of "all my love?" How could she?

Strangers break promises. On the battlefield, even across the pew, such reversals are common, and, for the most part, we shed them with a curse and a shrug. But between lovers? Surely, there was no deeper betrayal! Was she able to cut herself off from the fire of their passion?

"You're sick, lad," Gordon whispered to himself. "Pity is taking hold. You're wallowing in it." Through his anguish, he reminded himself how he always grew pathetic when he pitied himself. Better to be silent than to whimper like a crestfallen poet. Yet his inner voice could not block the questions.

How could she find another man so easily and not tell him? Who was Samuel anyway? Where was Jo this very moment? Did she die in Halifax? Maybe she never intended to meet him?

It was not until this last question was formed that Gordon realized he had been punctuating each query by stamping his feet in a water-filled pothole in the middle of Sherbrooke Street. Traffic buzzed around him. Passers-by were giving him warning looks. Lights flickered. Horns blared warnings that only now he heard. A beat cop was weaving his way down the sidewalk, arrest written on his face. Gordon realized this was no time to lose his mind, did an about-face and promptly ploughed into an umbrella-wielding pedestrian.

"Watch where you're headed, young man!" The voice, churlish and crisp, had a faintly familiar sound.

Gordon bent slightly to look under the edge of the dripping umbrella. "Principal Cruikshank? Is that you?"

The umbrella paused mid-street. "Yes ... who is asking?" There was hesitancy hiding behind the assertive tones.

Gordon knew his appearance was far too haggard for the cleric to recall the once innocent youth trembling in his college lounge. Cars still rushed past, splashing the two of them and so he gestured to the edge of the road.

"I do look a fright, and I am sorry to bother you. You won't recall my visit, but I applied to your college for admission a few years back now."

Cruikshank was feeling cold and curt. "Name?"

"Davis, sir. Gordon Davis."

"Indeed. Davis you say?"

Cruikshank thought to himself that there was something about the name that he should remember. Something urgent, something tragic. What was it? The principal regarded his companion more closely, noting his torn uniform and washed out expression. It wasn't his custom to talk with students outside of his classroom. It lowered academic standards. But a flicker of compassion won out. "Actually, this is going to sound strange, but I have a message for you. It's slipped my mind for the moment. Not like me really." He gestured down the street, "Why don't we get out this rain? I'll recall it, if we walk." He set off down the Sherbrooke Street toward St. Lawrence with determination. "'Gordon' you said."

"Yes, sir." Gordon nodded, rain dripping from his nose. He made a few futile gestures to clear his face of water. Hair matted to his forehead and blood still showing on his uniform, he wasn't the most presentable companion. He tried to match his step to that of the principal, but was having trouble keeping up.

As they walked Cruikshank gave Gordon a few side-glances and sniffed his distaste over the obvious disarray. "You look like you need a dry spell to calm your nerves." Glancing up and down the street for a suitable shelter, Cruikshank said, "Let's drop into that café. Perhaps I can buy you a cup of tea."

To Gordon, those words so unexpected, so warm and welcoming, were as if the principal had said, "Let me offer you a place in my home!"

They made their way quickly, and a pair of ancient creaking hinges announced their arrival.

Cruikshank motioned to a booth close to the door. Candle lights flickered with the wind that blew in the door each time it opened. A bored waiter took the order for two cups of Earl Grey. They sat looking at each other, one dry and composed, the other soaked and hanging onto reality by the frayed ends of a very thin thread.

Cruikshank snapped his fingers and blurted out, "That's it. It was about your father." Used to the authority of his own words, he continued without the slightest thought to their impact or impropriety. "I am so sorry to hear he committed suicide. It must have been a shock for you and your family. A humiliation to all concerned."

Gordon's heart stopped, his jaw dropped and tongue froze. He didn't even know his dad was dead, let alone by his own hand. His father could not commit suicide … surely not! His mind was reeling. Excuses mingled with denial.

Death surprises yet another victim!

Saint John: Centenary-Queen Square United Church
Tuesday, Nov. 17, 1992, 11:17 a.m.

There's no surprise here. No miracle resurrections. We're just a small band of mourners singing our farewell to a man few of us knew.

O for a thousand tongues to sing …

As our dozen frail voices lift praises to the Maker of earth and sky, I marvel at the human species. How baffling we can be! Very few of us here would sing anything in the course of a day, certainly not a hymn. At best, a campfire song or hit tune. Most will listen to others, on disc or radio. Yet, when we gather in this sacred space, there is an expectation that we must sing. It's like the eleventh commandment.

"Make a joyful noise unto the Lord." Isn't that the first Psalm any Sunday school child is asked to memorize?

I suppose we sing at a funeral because we dare not remain silent too long.

Did I say that words were cumbersome? In this hymn the entire fourth verse lights up my imagination now.

Hear him, ye deaf: His praise, ye voiceless ones,
Your loosened tongues employ:
Ye blind, behold your Saviour comes,
And leap, ye lame for Joy.

Who or what loosened your tongue after so many years, Gordon?

Saint John: The Buttress Home
Tuesday, December 17, 1991, 11:45 a.m.

"Look, Mary … I'm not sure you hear me …." I was on edge that morning, so it came out more harshly than intended. Squelching the urgency, I try again. "Sorry. It's the season. I still have four Christmas services to plan, which means three sermons and a pageant for the fourth. All the shut-ins deserve a visit and I am only halfway through the list. The last thing I need is to spend a hopeless fifteen minutes with Gordon at the Buttress Home."

"Don't get high and mighty with me." Mary was never one to take abuse. "Just because you're overbooked. I warned you."

"Yes, you did." With a sigh I sat down by her desk.

"They called twice yesterday and once this morning." Mary liked to count my sins. I try to ignore them. "It's not much to ask. The poor guy has no visitors. You're his one and only, Freddy." My secretary delighted in calling me by strange names. "So what if he never talks. The nurse said that after you've been to call, he's better, more co-operative. And as they're having a terrible time with him this week. Just pop by!"

"Any other messages?" Mary had been dutifully taking my calls. She hated to be shut out of my business and considered the minister's agenda her own to control and invade at will. She consulted her ink blotter, a catch-all for phone messages and memos. Holding one aloft and sniffing in displeasure, she read, "Melody wants to hold a prayer meeting at the Lions Nursing Home." Mary let the note drop to the desk, consigned to wastebasket status.

Melody is my "Sunshine". Every church has one: the elderly matron who makes it her sworn duty to meddle in the spiritual lives of every member of the congregation. Each day she calls to check out what I am doing. Chinese water torture can't hold a candle to Sunshine.

Mary wasn't done. She lifted another note. "Michael returned your call and said Friday at 1:00 is fine for a music meeting." Another item to add to the list.

"Oh … and Jessie phoned to say Mrs. Fetterley hadn't received a Christmas visit yet."

Jessie is my "Rosebud". She is alive and "well" in every church community. "Wellness" is a concept beyond her. A perpetually sick soul, Rosebud is never happy with anyone, particularly the paid staff. She could moonlight as a bookie, never forgetting even the most insignificant misdemeanour. Once she complained that I had visited her twice for tea, whereas I'd been three times to Ethel's for lunch. Ethel lived down the hall in their apartment building and the implication was clear.

Mary smiled. "I think that's about all, chief." She began to fold worship bulletins again with a smug assurance that she had ruined my holly, jolly spirit.   "Right. Another morning at the sheep fold." I grumbled off to my study, hoping to find some way to escape my duty. Picking up Sunday worship files I pretended to be thinking deep liturgical thoughts. Nothing came.

Flicking on the computer, I tried focussing on the *Telegraph Journal* article for that week. High season was always hard to write about. My mind could not focus. The silence in the next room was distracting. Mary was still waiting for an answer.

"All right, I'm going. I can't concentrate anyway." I grabbed my coat, slipped a few bulletin covers under my arm and left my fresh coffee unattended. As I whirled out the door, I couldn't help noticing the satisfied look on Mary's face. She loved the thrill of being in my driver's seat.

Icicle edged winds greeted me as I ran to the car. "Why did God invent snow and why did it have to be cold?" I complained as I tried to wedge open my car door. The drive gave me a chance to breathe deeply. Last night had seen this winter's first slush storm and the slippery conditions kept my speed down. Ruts of half frozen water wanted to grip the wheels and throw me into the oncoming traffic. I pushed the cassette back into its groove. A smooth southern accent: "Be good to yourself, make room for recreation." Jackson Jeremiah was the latest guru in clergy self-care. Hah!

I tuned out the spiritual fix-it-man's drivel. The slick streets demanded my full attention. I took a right onto Spencer Street to get to the nursing home driveway. The street wasn't ploughed yet. "Perfect!" Five minutes of skidding and rubber burning brought me into the parking lot. The building's usual gloom was lightened by its crown of snow. Red bricks covered with a thin coating of ice shone as if painted with shellac.

I made a promise as I opened the oak front doors. "This will be a quickie."

As always, Gordon was sitting stone-still in a chair I'd scrounged from the basement of a wealthy and willing church-goer. A worn blue blanket covered his limbs. No sound. His parchment thin hands, knuckles white with determination, seemed driven into his lap, wedged into his crotch—hard!

He registered not the slightest degree of change, in the month I had begun to pay regular visits. A drop of drool was always waiting at the corner of his mouth. His eyes were constantly open, unseeing. On "good" days, he would move when asked, a pliable plaything—a wrinkled Ken doll with no will of his own. On the "bad" days, he got progressively stiffer and less biddable until he was like an ancient, crusted beam, inflexible and stubborn. I could tell this was a "bad" morning.

Good day or bad, his hands never gestured on their own.

"Hi, Gordon." No movement.

"It's a rotten, slimy day outside, snow turning to mush as its lands." I don't think he ever looked out the window. Why bother? But a weather report was a way to keep my side of the conversation going, since I knew nothing, as yet, of his life story. Levan's rule #12: "Talk weather." Like a worn slipper, when conversation was tough, I slid into comfortable superlatives about too much cold or hot or rain or snow.

"Looks like Christmas will be white and wet."

If Gordon heard me, he gave no indication. Not that the vicissitudes of the Christmas season were of any importance. According to the Buttress Home records, there had never been a single invitation that arrived for Gordon. No reason to worry over snow-plugged streets. Never a parcel. Not even a card sent to him to mark the festive day. An island surrounded by a sea of indifference. Outside the four walls of his room, he wasn't. There were moments when I doubted Gordon's existence, until I arrived at his ward.

Of late, I had taken to reading the Bible. In some cases that would have seemed too pious for me, but I was a pastoral visitor, after all. Let the orderlies read him the sports page. Besides, the Scripture recital gave structure to our time together and assuaged the "Sunshine" part of my personality.

I dropped into the chair beside Gordon, rooted through his nightstand and found his dog-eared Bible, the only book he possessed. "I've just stopped by to read a bit more Scripture. Why not take a look at our Advent stories?" God, I sound like an evangelical idiot! I have to get my cheery voice replaced. It can sound so pathetically empty. "Let's look at Matthew, Chapter two. It's not the beginning of Matthew's birth narrative because he opens with the genealogy of Jesus. Most folk prefer the wise men story that comes a bit later."

I could be quite chatty in my Gordon monologues. The temptation, to which thankfully I never descended totally, was to get cute and slip in a few off-colour remarks. No one's listening right? Gordon's on his own continent. As later events unfolded, I blessed myself that I had never taken that liberty. It would have mocked his intelligence which was not gone, just buried.

From the radio down the hall came the voice of the announcer counting down the top ten 'White Christmas' hits. 'Jingle Bell Rock,' number eleven ..."

Save me!

Rubbing my hand over the opened Bible, I began: "Matthew, Chapter two, verse ..."

"Jonah!"

A clear voice.

I looked up to see who had come into the room, but there was no one around. I looked over my shoulder and was tempted to peek under the bed. "Who's there?" Gordon kept up his stony face, knuckles still white.

"Matthew, Chapter two, verse ...." I had my head up this time.

Encrusted with age, the voice spoke again, "Jonah." It was Gordon! Though his lips hardly moved, a word came from behind the high walls of his dementia.

"Gordon?"

No response. "Gordon, shall I read the story of Jonah?" There wasn't even a flicker of comprehension in his eyes. I sat still. There was someone inside him after all, at least a voice and one word. Faint strains of "Joy to the World" echoed from the nursing station. "Number ten, folks."

I tried again to reach Gordon. "Yes, Jonah was a man who ran from God and was swallowed by a whale." I decided to tell the tale. "It all began with an encounter between God and the prophet. They were discussing the sins of Nineveh, a distant gentile city. No knows what the sins were exactly, though there have been speculations." Gordon began to sway slightly, no more than a hair's breadth, backward and forward.

Over the next twenty minutes, he uttered not a word. Not even a grunt of satisfaction, when the fish swallowed the backsliding prophet. But now I knew he was listening. Careful to avoid banalities or idle questions to which I expected no reply, I spoke to his still, small voice.

After a time, I thought I might have been dreaming. Did he really speak? Rising from my place, I put my hand over his. "Gordon, I'll be back tomorrow. Think of another story you'd like to hear." I felt a tremor in his fingers. His pinkie moved ever so slightly and then went still. But no more words.

I must have been dreaming. He didn't really say anything.

Turning to leave, I noticed a bent man coming into the ward, guided by the nurse. He occupied the bed opposite Gordon; maybe he had heard Gordon speak on some occasion. Sensing my stare, his nurse looked across at me and wrinkled her forehead into a question mark.

"Have you ever heard Gordon speak?"

She smiled in a kindly condescending way, professional caregiver to a lay person. "No dear, he's stone deaf as far as I can tell. Never a peep." She returned to her charge, a slight smile curling her lip. No doubt I seemed foolish to her.

"I think … I mean … I heard Gordon utter a name this morning."

" … that so?" The nurse wasn't convinced.

"Yes …" I looked closer at her name tag. "Miss Law … could you just give him extra attention today … in case … I mean I wouldn't want to miss anything else he might say."

She smiled again, this time broadly. "Oh, I'll write down every word." She was playing with me and I didn't mind.

"Yes … well … I know it sounds crazy and I'm no doctor. But I know he did speak, at least once."

She now gazed at me more closely. "You're the minister fellow who comes for services now an' again, aren't you?"

"Yes."

Something convinced her. Maybe it was the title. Whatever it was, she was now ready to take me seriously. "I'll call you if we hear anything. You just leave your number at the nursing station down the hall to the left." She pointed vaguely toward the exit door. "I'll tell the other girls to take special care. Who knows, he might be waking up after seventy years?"

"Thank you. I … we appreciate it." Turning to Gordon I touched his hand again. "Now remember, you find another tale you'd like. I'll be waiting for your suggestions."

At that I placed his Bible back on the stand by his bed and it fell open to the front leaf. "To my Gordon," it read. "Though I speak with the tongues of angels, if I have not love, I am nothing." There was no signature.

Passchendaele, France: Forward Dressing Station
Thursday, October 11, 1917, 11:11 A.M.

"Though I speak with the tongues of angels, if I have not love, I am nothing." Gordon's sister's voice ... reading the inscription in his Bible. Where is she?

The last letters on a ferry from France: "J" and "O." Bright red on the funnel. A street sign: Montreal Street. Jo was everywhere.

"Jo ... is that you? Come to me!"

"Hold on ... I'm coming ..." An unshaved waiter paused by Gordon's table. "Was there sommmick more you wanted?" He waited while Gordon collected his thoughts and fussed with a napkin.

Gordon tried to focus on the waiter's question. "Ah ... more? No thank you. But it was delicious." Gordon looked down at his second plate of eggs and chips, the long promised meal he told his buddies he would enjoy on leave. Rather than canned bully beef saved from the Crimean war or biscuits that would stop a bullet, he was eating real food.

As if from a distance, Gordon heard his own greedy voice ... loud now ...."Ah ... on second thought, another pint of beer would be great ... and maybe a piece of that pie I see warming by the counter. More food!"

Thunder rolled over the waiter's response, blinding light flashed through the window ... then silence, a female voice spoke softly, "Take it easy, dear ... you'll be right as rain soon ...."

The light passed. A clutch of patrons burst into shouts and the waiter turned to check, "Bloody fools smash up more beer steins when they gets into their cups." He turned back slowly having determined it was just a rude story and not the beginnings of a brawl. "What'll it be then, mate?" "Want a little spotted dick to go with it all? Best my Martha's made in weeks, and all the fellows on leave rave about it."

"Sure. Great! Bring it on." The waiter nodded approval and cleared away his first course plates.

Gordon's mind moved in a haze. He had no idea what he'd just ordered. "Spotted dick?" Was it fowl, fish or fruit? No matter. "God, leave is great!" he murmured. The Bull and Bear pub was like a dream come true: a workingman's haunt. Oak beams covered in the tar of generations of pipe smoke gave testimony to its clientele's loyalty and a polished bar spoke of its worth. This was the place for his idyllic meal: Chips and eggs! Hardly a feast, but he was looking for comfort food … something close to the fried eggs, cream corn, bacon and potatoes that his father loved. It was a peculiar taste that the elder Davis passed down to the younger Davis.

Gordon raised a hand to order yet a third plate, when a machine gun burst strafed the wall behind him. His table was covered in blood as he dove for the floor—feverish with fear. Momentarily, a gentle hand touched his shivering side.

"Peace, peace there my son," said a voice.

There was his father, sitting at his table eating his own plate. "Best meal on God's green earth, and it's sitting right here in front of me." With a wink, he stuck out a hand to lift Gordon from the floor.

Jo's voice called out of the fog, clear resolute: "No."

Gordon looked up to see flags waving over a crowded pier. The band was playing marching music and he stood in his crisp uniform, a rank of medals on his chest, scanning the throng for Jo. As if on cue, she emerges from behind a kettle drum and they embrace, hold tight. Tight.

Over his should Harry Lauder starts singing his big hit, "When the War is over."

> When the fighting is over, and the war is won,
> And the flags are waving free,
> When the bells are ringing,
> And the boys are singing
> Songs of victory,
> When we all gather round the fireside,
> And the old mother kisses her son,

A' the lassies will be loving a' the laddies,
The laddies who fought and won.

"When the war was over?" Fat chance. Glancing left, Gordon sees a recruiting banner: "1967… the Year to Win the War!" and below it, he sees a boy and knows him to be his grandson, dressed in uniform, hefting a rifle to march back to the trenches that his grandfather had dug.

The voice grows louder. Gordon joins in.
When the fighting is over, and the war is won,
And the flags are waving free.

Now he's standing outside the marquee of a London Theatre where *The Maid of the Mountain* is playing. Its 200th performance.

He's about to enter when a firm grip holds him back.

"Don't go in!" a gruff voice warned him. Don't! … Listen to me boy." It was John, his sergeant. John whose dead brother, Mark, had saved all their lives. Mark was cut down in the early days of the Somme. A rum barrel blast, they said. 'Never found his body.' But Mark came back several months ago. Late at night he appears to John in a dream, starts shaking his arm, all nervous-like and warning everyone to get up. John tried to roll over and ignore him, but Mark would have none of that. He kept telling John to leave this piece of the line. "Get your company up!" Gordon could see them again … middle of night, grumbling … everyone stumbling out of their section of earth works 'because John's dead brother Mark told us so.' And just as the last man clears the corner of an abandoned communication trench, the section of the trench we'd just left took a direct hit. No survivors!

Gordon cried in terror as he did that night and a soft female voice spoke in his ear, "Private Davis … are you awake?"

Gordon tried to answer … tried so hard to break through the mist.

"Jo … Jo … is that you?"

Another voice, another song flooded his mind.

At Seventeen he falls in love quite madly,
With eyes of tender blue.
At twenty-four he gets it rather badly

With eyes of a different hue.
At thirty-five you'll see him flirting sadly
With two or three or more
When he fancies he is past love,
It is then he meets his last love,
And he loves her as he's never loved before.

"My son, let me teach you as one who knows about love." Gordon knew the voice immediately and went cold. Rev. Hawthorne grabbed his shoulders and spun him around. He was naked. Hawthorne was reaching a hand down ….

"No," Gordon shouted, "Leave me alone … don't you touch her!" "Hush my love, Jo's hand touches his arm as she rises to find her

robe."Just sleep now … you're safe."

Gordon called out, "Don't go … Wait for me …."

"Who's that you waiting for mate?" The waiter plunked down a pint of ale and shook his head. "Poor bugger…did you leave half your head over in France?"

Gordon looked at the waiter, at the smiling faces round the tavern. They had no idea what a bullet sounds like when it bursts through the tin hat of an unsuspecting soldier. Could they imagine the agony of hearing shells blow apart a trench full of men, burying the survivors in mud? Was there really any winner when the screams floated across from the battlefield, English and German mingled together into an anthem of agony?

Resentment over waste and carnage rose in his stomach as he thought of his return—twelve days off. Sod them all—the generals, the politicians, the flag waving crowds! He pushed down his bitterness. It ain't worth the energy! "We're here because we're here because we're here, because we're here." Cynicism is the only antidote to patriotism.

The tavern walls shrink and buckle into the mud walls of his trench. Gordon is wet again, shivering in his funk hole and he watches with terror as a German bowie knife snakes it way down the trench, plunging itself up to the hilt into every soldier caught in its path. It's slowly, painfully looking for him ... Sweat is dripping from his forehead as he shouts "Help, Help, Help!"

Gordon wakes with a start as gentle hands lower him back down into bed, "You've been dreaming soldier!" A no-nonsense nurse wipes his brow with a cold cloth and smiles, "Had a touch of trench fever, I'd say."

Toronto: 20 Mountalan Ave.
Friday, April 12, 2014, 7:52 p.m.

Richard called me right away ... before I could dial his number. Patricia Patterson was proving herself to be very insistent. She must have hung up and dialled him directly.

"Hi, Guy ... I hear you've been talking with Patricia ... you think she's a con artist, haha! Not so!"

I could feel my denials slipping away as Richard took the conversation in his own hands. "You may have found your uncle after all ... be patient with Patricia."

Toronto: Wycliffe College
Friday, May 14, 1915, 4:35 p.m.

Patient? It's not in Ryan's nature. He stood erect, as was his custom when in the public eye. He was not pleased at the long wait, but this interview might prove to be beneficial so he suppressed his frustrations. Looking at the graduation photos on the wall. "Do priests get drunk like army officers when they finish their studies?" he wondered. "Don't imagine they get laid on graduation night."

Truth be told, Major Ryan thought religion was a hoax, sometimes useful to propel men into battle, but largely a pastime for idle housewives. He would never have given a theological college a second glance at his current posting in the department of recruitment, had it not been for the intriguing letter from an Anglican professor/principal.

Ryan looked at his diary to recall the name, humming the national anthem as he thumbed the pages. "Ah, here it is. 'Cruikshank.' Sounds English enough." When alone, he often spoke out loud. "Ryan will make short order of this fellow." It was also his custom to speak of himself in the third person. It lent a certain historical prominence to his actions, as if he was reciting from his own memoirs.

The letter had been discarded by his superiors as nonsense, but had come to his desk for a reply. Ryan was arrested by the possibilities. The writer had made a very interesting pitch. "With mother church as a springboard, I believe we could double the recruiting efforts from within Christian ranks. Using Wycliffe College as a hub, we would be able to co-ordinate a parish-by-parish campaign for new recruits."

Ryan usually was preoccupied with bigger fish: farming unions, Orange Lodges and sporting clubs. They were natural locations for his posters and parades. But it was a slow Friday and it didn't hurt to follow up on all the leads he was given in this godforsaken country. Anything to build numbers so he would be recognized by the upper echelons of the Army establishment, maybe gaining a posting at the front where promotion was swift.

"Where is that little man?" Ryan asked the rows of pictures.

"He is right here," replied a dignified, English voice.

Whirling around, Ryan was presented with a much different picture of his correspondent than he had imagined. The word "principal" had conjured up images of a wizened apple with a cracked voice. Spectacles hovering at the end of a nose, ready to fall to the floor. Instead, Cruikshank was a robust gentleman, straight shoulders, broad, intelligent face and clear eyes. No glasses. A man to be counted.

"Excuse me, sir," Ryan coughed. "I ... sometimes ... let my impatience get the better of my tongue." He let it go at that, leaving the introductions to Cruikshank. It was an old army trick. Make your enemy ask the first questions.

"Yes ... indeed. I imagine it is a vocational hazard within the military." Cruikshank looked about his lounge, pleased. It was neat as a pin. Every volume on the bookshelves was dusted regularly; the pictures were cleaned each week. No stains on the carpet. Sherry was served each day at three, but the glasses from that day's "tea" had already been cleared.

"Please sit down."

"Thank you." Ryan found a comfortable chair and waited again.

"How is that I can help you, Major ...," Cruikshank searched his memory for the name and found it, "Ryan. I believe you have come in response to my letter to the General Staff."

Ryan cleared his throat and produced his best officer's voice. "Yes, indeed, I was initially quite sceptical of your idea, as was my superior."

"Oh," A pause to regroup. "Well ... that is not surprising. The church has rarely had much contact with the military of late, at least in Canada." Cruikshank had an ironic smile on his lips. He, too, was cautious, not wanting to play his hand too quickly. Let this man prove his metal before he laid out the entire plan.

"Yes, well ... I am not well acquainted with this nation, having just been assigned here." Ryan was a quick study of character. This principal was hiding a good deal more than he was revealing. Something in his personal bearing and the ease with which he guided a conversation told Ryan that a direct approach might work well. "Sir, I'll be frank. I can't really see how a church banner could drum up more recruits for the army than a country's flag. We are reaching more men through our town hall rallies than your prayer meetings." There was the bait—a simple frontal attack. Would the principal rise to the occasion?

He did. "Nonsense, young man. You obviously have little under-standing of what motivates individuals. There is no more potent force for action than a spiritual entreaty. Tell men this is the King's war and they line up dutifully to do their homage. Yes?"

Ryan admitted the point. "I suppose so."

Cruikshank was not finished. "But tell them this is God's war, and they'll rip pickets from their pretty little fences and rush off in white hatred to impale the foe face-to-face. If no such weapon is in reach, they'll kill him with their bare hands." The principal smiled as Ryan began to appreciate this cleric's understanding of human nature. "You see ... there is no war fought more ferociously than a 'holy' war."

"The Crusades being a fine example," Ryan replied, his mind churn-ing with possibilities. A 'holy' war! The potential was enormous.

"Now you've got it." Cruikshank was impressed with this fellow's perception, but even more so with his obvious, though understated, eagerness for results, no doubt stemming from his own ambitions. "Can you picture what would happen if the men of this land began to see our fight with Germany as a crusade, taking up the cross and rifle together? Can you see the potential?"

Ryan could. It would have an enormous edge on any other scheme his office had thought to initiate. "But … forgive me for being naive. How does one get a war declared 'holy?' Is there an authority within the church that can make such a determination?" Ryan was pragmatic. "After all, you are Anglican and not able to invoke the power of the pope like the Catholics."

Cruikshank was silent for a moment. "There are ways. While the Church of England does not have a designated committee, the house of bishops could make such a claim. Indeed, if our primate was persuaded, we could move forward."

"And what will that take? To influence the primate, I mean." Ryan's mind was working overtime. There was something in this for the principal, an angle he couldn't see yet. What was his side of the bargain? No doubt Cruikshank wanted something for his efforts—power, money, fame. It had to one of three. Maybe all of them.

"The current primate is due to retire in a year, so he would be of little use to us. But …," here Cruikshank took a deep breath, "but a new man might be groomed now, given the right word before he ascends to that exalted position."

Ryan didn't flinch at this obvious allusion to corruption. "And that new man might be you, perhaps?" He smiled wickedly.

"No. I have no interest in that position."

"No?" Ryan was taken aback.

"No! I have only the interests of the country at heart." Cruikshank could appear guileless, an expert at hiding his ambitions. His goal was much higher than being the lowly primate of a colonial outpost. "I believe we can work together on this, providing you give me three things."

Ryan smiled. "Here comes the negotiation," he thought. "And what are those three things?"

"First, I want to go to the front, see for myself what is happening. Bolster the troops and know the situation first hand. There is no position stronger than that of someone who has seen what is happening.

Reading between the lines in the paper, it appears that this war will not be over quickly, so we have time to prepare the ground."

"Done." Ryan would have to find a reason for such an exception to the rule of no civilians in the trenches, but he could already imagine a few gambits that would do the trick. "Second?"

"Second, I want a military position, preferably with the rank of colonel." Seeing the doubt in Ryan's eyes, he explained. "Make me a chaplain general of the Canadian troops. It can't be all that difficult. I know you're looking for a way to co-ordinate the many chaplains who are enlisting. What better person than a principal of a theological college—well-schooled, used to authority, able to direct large numbers of young men."

Ryan smiled. He could tell when he was being manipulated, but as long as things were going his way, he would play along. "All right, it can be arranged. Third?"

"Third, when this war is won, and it will be, I want a knighthood for my efforts."

Ryan gasped. "You can't be serious?"

Cruikshank smiled. "Deadly serious. I never joke about my ambitions. Major, I have laid out before you my hopes. I've been frank. If this scheme works, you'll have thousands of willing, able-bodied men at your door. Men that you desperately need." Cruikshank could see agreement in Ryan's eyes. "Just a helpful word from your superiors, once I have delivered these thousands of men will be all that it takes. Make sure I am recognized, invited to the best circles. That kind of thing. Nothing too overt."

Ryan was hooked. He would take a chance on this man. There seemed little to lose. "And what do I get?"

"You?" Cruikshank held his hands, fingertips touching. "You, meaning the army, will get the full backing of the Church of England in Canada to support your recruiting efforts, declare this war against Germany to be God's sacred mission and consequently supply you with an endless stream of glowing hearts and ready hands. We'll find recruits in confirmation classes and summer camps, places the army hasn't even touched and never will." The principal stopped for a moment, a brief smile tugging at the corners of his mouth. "Now ... what's it in for you, meaning you personally, there will no doubt be an eagerness within military circles to promote the young buck who built the bridges for this wildly successful enlistment drive. Perhaps this officer would receive the command he has always deserved. I'll leave the details to your imagination."

Ryan was uncomfortable with being read so openly, but he smiled. Extending a hand, he muttered in a low voice, "We have a deal, Dr. Cruikshank. You get me a 'holy' war, and I'll get you a knighthood."

Cruikshank took the hand and smiled. "A deal." He really wanted more than the title "sir" before his name, but that was a step on the journey.

Ryan rose to leave. "When do we start?"

Cruikshank smiled. "We already have. Why don't you join me for tea next Friday? You can meet a few of my friends, and we'll explain how the plans are coming together."

St. Lawrence River, Passing Grosse Île
Tuesday, March 28, 1916, 1:15 a.m.

Each hour took Gordon closer to France and further from Montreal. "Montreal! Montreal," he whispered with faint longing. He missed Jo unbearably already.

Gordon waited until the ship was truly at sea, no chance of steaming back for repairs or docking to retrieve a tardy soldier. Only when its course was set, irrevocable, did he turn to the note Jo had slipped into his hand at dockside.

Before embarking, there had been much confusion, smiling troops finding their company commanders, hastily arranged farewells, much backslapping and hand holding. Kisses and jokes exchanged with equal feeling and tension. Mingled with the laughter, Gordon could hear sober pronouncements offered to reassure the listener: "Once I'm there, it'll end soon enough." "Be back by Christmas at the latest." They were sailing off boldly, and, yet, underneath brave talk they were all frightened they might never return.

Gordon's family had been unable to see him off. Money was tight. Father's daily wage at the foundry could hardly fill his own mouth, let alone a family of eight. Turning back toward the city, he saw his six-day old friends, Johanna and Dr. Hinks snaking their way through the crowd.

Gordon stepped around a gaggle of kilted pipers, unable to reach Bishop Hinks and his daughter on account of the clutter of drums and duffle bags that separated them. A pipe band was first to embark, hefting their burdens up the ramp. Gordon watched the pair on the opposite side of the pile of baggage as it was slowly carried on board. He could see them, but they had not yet found him. Hinks and his daughter were standing in the midst of dancing hankies. Jo was trying to be bright, even cheerful, craning her neck to catch sight of Gordon. Looking behind, along the ship's lines. Nothing yet.

The bishop was calm, stiff. His crimson vest and collar were visible, the gold chain of his cross catching a few glints of sunlight. As he waited, an over-excited girl whirled around and embraced him before she realized he wasn't her Uncle Harry. She blurted out her embarrassment. "Oh my gosh, I'm sorry ... I thought you were ...." Hinks smiled back at her, placed a hand on her shoulder in blessing and she turned to find her party, blushing.

The bishop waited, a tranquil point in a frenzied sea. He was a patient man and said to himself that he was not bothered that this Gordon fellow had not yet made his appearance. While he had been down to the ships a dozen times to send off hopeful farm lads or eager chaplains, he was unable to explain his emotions over this particular leave-taking. "Why so heavy-hearted?" he wondered. "The man's only been here for a week. I'll probably never see him again. It's silly and quite unpredictable, but I feel warmly disposed to him." He looked down at Johanna. "Quite clearly my daughter has even stronger feelings. But she is such a passionate creature." A sigh came to his lips. "Is that it—just an over-protective father watching out for a potential son-in-law? There's no question she is attracted." Hinks never failed to marvel at the freshness, the life that radiated from her face. She was now straining to see someone off to their left. Following his daughter's eyes, he saw Gordon striding in their direction.

For a brief moment no one spoke. The threesome just looked at each other, heavy hearts all round. Finally, wanting to break what was becoming a disconcerting spell, Hinks took his young soldiers's hand, and offered a simple farewell. "Safe journey, Gordon. Don't neglect your reading, if it's possible. A little more Bible wouldn't hurt." He smiled and inwardly rebuked himself. "Could he ever speak without attaching a moral?" The bishop gave him a knowing wink as if to take back what he had just said and held Gordon's glance for a moment to register his real concern. Then he turned to Johanna, sure she would have deeper feelings to relate.

Johanna was caught off guard by the throng pressing close and her father's pious propriety. She fumed inside, "Why did he have to come and crowd our last minutes with his little sermons?" When it came her turn to say farewell, it was stilted and impersonal. "Gordon, I have so much appreciated your visits!" "God," she thought, "I sound like he was a visiting cousin." She tried again, but the words caught in her throat. How to say what can't be said? Faltering, she extended a hand.

There was a rising colour in her cheeks, and, if Gordon had been more experienced, he might have known its meaning. Grasping her hand as courteously as possible, he felt a folded paper pass from her fingers to his. Their eyes locked, an electric current flowing. How long they stood staring, saying what didn't need to be said, he couldn't tell. It was an eternity, and it was over before it started. As if by signal, the wind picked up considerably, flags snapping on the deck of his ship. The crack of cloth and the ringing of guy wires broke their connection. The moment passed.

Gordon had to say something. He could feel her letter hot in his hand. "Miss Johanna, thank you for all … ah …" Gordon was about to say "love" or "passion," but moderated his tone and found "hospitality," immediately regretting his choice. What a ridiculous thing to say! But it was out. Her eyebrows lifted at the word "hospitality" and he could see a smile creep into her eyes. "Indeed. Travel well, Gordon."

Time to leave. Looking down to his waiting pack as if discovering it for the first time, he smiled, "There we go then." Lifting his duffle to waist height, he noticed Johanna leaning forward. Without thinking, ignoring any inhibitions, even forgetting the bishop-father at his side, Gordon gripped Johanna fiercely and kissed her for all eternity. How long did it last? Who knows!

Finally, when Gordon and Johanna separated, he gave a sheepish smile to the bishop and sighed, "Well, farewell, then and thank you again for everything." A quick glance at Johanna, now hugging herself, and he swung his bag over his left shoulder, slipped his right hand, paper and all, into his pocket and made for the gangway, pushing clasping couples aside with as much gentleness as he could.

At the brink of entering the ship, Gordon turned to wave. Dr. Hinks was already moving off, but Johanna was rooted to the pier. Gordon waved. One hand clasped over her mouth, she tried to lift an arm in reply but could not muster it. Gordon thought she might be crying and would have leapt down the gangway and held her fiercely, soothing away her distress, but the line of soldiers behind him swept him forward into the dim interior of his destiny.

Once inside, a ship's steward directed him to deck five, far below. After a few false turns, he found his bunk and stowed his gear. He had not taken to the mid-ships bar as so many others did. Rather, he walked to the upper deck and to the stern. He stood silently, watching the receding dock. At first, he could make her out. A small dot of resolution swaying at quayside. She no longer tried to cover her anguish. She was too distant to see, but he could feel the tears streaming down her cheeks.

In time, the crowd became an indistinguishable mass of colours and shouting. Once the ship turned into the main channel, even that spectacle was lost.

For five hours he had been rooted to his place by the railing. Sparks of light on the shore signalled a passing farmhouse. When they gathered into a swarm, Gordon knew they were steaming past a slumbering village.

Now, it was time. Reaching into his trouser pocket, he drew out her note. By the running lights of his ship, he could just barely make out the words. But he was determined to read her note in the thick night air. It reminded him of their encounters on that mountain park bench. Two pages unfolded into his shaking hands and a dried maple leaf drifted down to the deck. He reached for the leaf, and, holding it tenderly in one hand, he read her letter.

> My dear, my love:
>
> I know Father will come with me to see you off. This will be my only way to speak what is in my heart. Has it only been a week? No ... much longer. I'd say years, even centuries that we have known one another—two souls moving toward eachother. Remember our walk up the mountain? I said there are old souls that have long been together. They migrate from age to age and in every new incarnation they seek each other out. So you and I found one another ... again. Just in time. I don't want to lose you! Not now.
>
> How did I realize you were the one? It was the first day you stumbled into the house looking for "the bishop." I could hardly contain myself. "This is he." That's all I could think about. And you wouldn't even tell me your name! Rotter.
>
> You left that night and I went up to my bedroom, sat on the edge of my bed and couldn't stop crying. I was telling my mother about you, how you were the one and how I wished she could have met you ...
>
> You were so quiet at first, but our days dissolved your natural reserve (maybe it was my charm?) and I came to see the gentle courage that lay beneath that shy exterior. We must never let a barrier come between us.

I will wait for your return.

Here's my litany of wishes for you, Gordon, for the one who has come to mean so much to me. My ten commandments:

First, stay safe! My God! I shudder when I think of where you are going.

Second, keep your mind free of the filth that passes for virtue in battlefields. Vain acts of bravado are useless to me. Charging up hills of glory stirs me not in the least. I want you back! I will admire that feat above all else.

Third, watch out for your comrades. There is no bond greater than the one forged in companion-ship. They will help you in my stead and in a strange way they are your link to me.

Fourth, stay well.

Fifth, sing! I love to hear you sing the campfire songs from summer camp. What was it your father used to sing? "Give me oil in my lamp, keep me burning?"

Sixth, stay whole.

Seventh, keep your head down. The long journey up the hill of life is hard enough without looking up to see how much farther we must climb. I counsel patience, but I already burn in anticipation of your return.

Eighth, come home to me!

Ninth, don't steel your heart against pain and suffering. As soon as we lose our passion, or refuse to be enraged by injustice, we are a lost species.

Tenth, stay calm. I will be with you always and if I am not, God will take my place.

Time is getting short. Know that I will be waiting when you get back. A union such as ours can never be broken.

Love, Jo

P.S. If we are ever separated from each other, the memory of our love on Sisson Ridge ... on that mountaintop bench will lead us home. The enclosed leaf is proof that we can never really get lost once we have been loved.

Saint John: The Buttress Home
Wednesday, December 18, 1991, 10:13 A.m.

"He's like a man come back from the grave, Reverend!" Those were the words of the attending nurse, Joan Simmons, a largish elderly woman who watched over her flock jealously.

Did she have first-hand experience with resurrection? We were making our way past the ten-foot Christmas spruce that adorned the front stairs.

She was telling of Gordon's revival. "We don't know what you put in that communion juice of yours, but we'd all like to try some when you're done with Gordon."

Clutching a small present from the church women's unit #2, I tell myself not to rush. Joan, who was already huffing after a few steps, would be left behind.

"He's ... ah ... awake then?" I didn't know how to put it.

The nurse paused and gave me a knowing look. "This has been like Easter morning for Gordon—out of the tomb and into the light."

"Remarkable." I wanted to run, but instead I matched the nurse's gait. Late afternoon shadows fell across our path as we took the stairs at half-speed.

"What you got there, Reverend?" The matron asked between deep breaths as we plodded upward. Her gaze had settled on my wrapped box. "Oh, it's the church's annual Christmas gift to the elderly." I shook it a bit. "This one's for Gordon—sugary treats probably." The women's group, mostly widows now, for several decades had prided themselves on packaging a small "something" from their Yuletide lunch meeting for all the shut-ins of the congregation. I often joked that they were working out of self-interest since many of them would soon be needing a box of treats as a sign they were not forgotten.

"Oh! Nothing too hard I hope. Gordon's teeth ain't too strong."

"No, I thought about that when they gathered up the treats and cookies from today's tea—nothing too hard to hold or eat." I pause at the top of the stairs waiting for Joan to catch her breath. "Is he talking, then?"

"No, not exactly. Oh, maybe a word or two, but it's more his face. It's come alive. Spooky. Gladys and I were talking about him just this morning." As she spoke, we headed down the narrow corridor to D ward. "It's like that movie 'Awakening,' when Robin Williams brings Robert De Niro to life again after so many years of being a vegetable. Spooky, that's what I say. Anyway, see for yourself." She opened the ward door for me.

In the chair where a previously comatose patient had sat was a lively rocking spirit. Gordon's face was relaxed; a slight smile curled the ends of his mouth. No drool. His eyes stared with a knowing consciousness. His hair had been combed in a much different style. Prior to this visit, it was the industrial part—down the left side—applied to all inmates without discretion by the local "hair" volunteer, Fred Angles, a butcher in his day job. Today, Gordon's hair was parted in the middle and obviously some care had been taken to tame the curls that had hitherto been unruly.

"Gordon! You look great!"

No response. Maybe the rocking slowed a touch.

"May I sit down? It's close to Christmas and I brought you some …." looking down at the box I was uncertain exactly what I had brought him, but I made a guess. "Some … fudge from the ladies' tea." I could hear an intake of breath behind me. Nurse Simmons disapproved of fudge as well as hard candy. "Would you like to try some?" I opened the box gingerly. Pulling back the white tissue paper, sure enough, there were small squares of fudge waiting. I offered the box to Gordon, all the while expecting a policing grip to intervene, but it didn't. Nurse Simmons let it pass. "Peanut butter and honey, my favourite." I tried to keep any condescension out of my voice as I extended the box right beneath his gaze. "Have one, they're delicious!"

Slowly, a parchment covered hand, old beyond time, lifted from the armrest and fiddled with a small square. His aging fingers, claw-like and uncertain, finally caught the corners of one piece and it rose toward his mouth. Dead ahead slow. A flash of afternoon sunlight caught his hand and the fudge in a picture-perfect frame. Just a flash, but it felt like a signal, an intervention of light in his world. Gordon looked down at the approaching candy, but never increased his speed. It finally came home to port, docking on the waiting tongue. His mouth closed and I could hear the mild crunching of ancient teeth as they bit into fresh butter and sugar.

"FFFruuummm!" The words were mumbled, rounded into vague sounds by the interfering fudge.

"Fun? Did you say 'Fun' Gordon? Sure fudge is fun." I turned quickly to the nurse to see if she had caught his meaning. A shirk of her padded shoulders told me she hadn't understood either.

"Rum!" More insistent and clearer now.

"Rum! An excellent idea for this time of year. But do you have any eggnog?" It was a pretty feeble joke. Thank God I'm not being marked on the eloquence.

"Bah!" Was there a twinkle in his eye? Maybe he didn't like eggnog or maybe it was me? His jaw stopped working, and he swallowed the fudge. With it went his all words, for coax as I might, he continued to rock silently.

I tried reading Scripture. This time we turned to Luke's gospel. Nurse Simons sat beside me and tried to animate the readings. "Isn't that so beautiful?" "My, I love that verse!" "Imagine, so long ago!" But no suggestion of hers nor reading on my part could pry anything else from Gordon's lips. Although he did seem like he was actually listening to the story, he made no comment whatsoever.

Nurse Simmons rose. It was clearly a dismissal. "The Reverend will visit again soon, Gordon. Maybe then you'll say more?" It was meant as a kindly remark but came out more like an ultimatum. She took a few steps toward the door. Obviously, I was being ushered out.

Frustrated with the nurse, but having nothing further I could say or do, I decided to leave. Laying my hand firmly over his, I leaned in close and whispered. "I'll bring the rum next time."

"You do that, matey!" Quiet as a summer breeze, his words floated back. We were bound by a conspiracy. That was how the dead came to life again. Actually, it was Captain Jims who was resurrected that morning, like the sun rising in the east. A little fudge and the promise of a dram and the old sea dog strode out onto the stage—what an actor he would turn out to be.

Ypres: Canadian Corps Forward Observation Trench
Sunday, February 11, 1917, 7:30 p.m.

The light was dying in the west.

Gordon rolled on to his stomach, whispering to the shadows as they fell around him, "What an actor I have been all my life!" He'd spent the past hour rehearsing his faults, a traditional pastime. The "if only" chorus. If only he'd known Jo's brother was wounded, he might have come out more rapidly, taken a few more risks to reach him! How could he know that the bishop's beloved son had joined the army or been so close? If only he had known! He might have given the kid a few pointers. Shown him how to ward off the demons. If only he'd had more medical training, he might stop young Terry's bleeding belly.

Shit, this war is a monster, tormenting poor souls like Terrance. He should be home playing in his band, not out here covered in blood and slime. If only it hadn't begun! If only it would be over!

Johanna would be beside herself with agony. She loved her brother more than any other being. There was no music like Terry's, no smile to equal his. No hair so blond, no sibling so understanding.

If only he'd known. He would have gone out directly.

Or would he? Initially Gordon had leapt at the chance to save a dying voice. His team prided themselves on saving every last soul. But as the slaughter continued, day after day, he felt his virtue slipping, sliding into the mire of indifference, the carnage slowly corroding his courage. He didn't want to end up like one of his own cases, a mangled body on a stretcher.

In spite of a growing disquiet over his shrinking determination, Gordon beat his brains with imperatives that December night. No matter who it was, the first time he heard the cry he should have been over the top to the rescue. He should have taken more bandages. He should have called in a barrage to cover a hasty retreat back to his own lines.

The litany of errors continued. If only he could learn to be strong when common sense required it. His sins rose up and stood in the mud before him like a cast from a bad morality play. A farce titled "Gordon's Betrayal," since he felt he had always let down his side.

His doubts notwithstanding, along the trench, Gordon was commonly believed to be the bravest soldier of the line. No one would tell him straight up. But his selflessness and valour were taken as rock solid. Some even used his courage as the metaphor of assurance. "I swear on Gordie's balls" they'd say when they wanted their statements to be accepted as Gospel Truth.

Terry stirred beside him, bringing down the curtain on self-pity. Gordon snuggled in closer and looked at his ashen face. Terry's eyes were open and knowing. They darted about, struggling to find meaning in the pain, the wet rag inhibiting speech. Gordon could see that his wounds were awakening, biting back.

Terry could only feel stabs and stings. It came in sharp thrusts down his left side; then mind numbing, sharp-edged, it travelled over his belly. While he could feel his hands, there was no sensation below his waist. Nothing moved. Staring up, panic rolled over him just as the dark clouds curled and buckled overhead. Snow was coming. Needles of fear pricked at every thought. The stench of urine washed in from some distance shore. "Was this hell?" His mind began to wander, lethargic now in its uncertainty. "Maybe I've been sent to purgatory!" Mists slurred his thoughts as sensations came and went—slices of pain, chill in his fingers, the noxious catch at his nostrils. His mind slipped into the fog.

Gordon grew apprehensive. He knew the wounded man needed explanations—"the wounded man." For Christ's sake … this is Terry—her brother. He had to save him.

He mouthed a brief prayer. "Dear God, if You pull anyone back from the brink, let it be Terry."

Terry stirred again, eyes flashing. Gordon knew he yearned to see his sister or some other comforting agent, but this was no time for a long conversation. Jerry was too close. So he whispered what solace he could offer. "Hold on to her, Terry. We'll have you fixed up and well, once the night falls completely. I'll heft you back to the medical trench. Hold on tight."

Eyes edged with anguish, turned toward the words. There was no smile or hope in them, just a dull plodding agony. Gordon tried again, "You'll be fine, don't fret now. Fritz is too close for talk."

Having assured his charge of a long life, he now had to set about obtaining it. Looking along the length of his body and beyond, he thought he knew where their trench line lay. Back past a charred wagon, he thought he could make out the head of a sap trench. That might be their salvation.

Each side had dug shallow ditches out into no man's land called "saps." They were used for listening to enemy movements, watching for wire parties, and guesstimating potential attack points. In this case, the sap would provide a protected route back to his own line.

Another fifteen minutes and he would make a run for it. Terry would not be easy to carry, being a few inches taller than Gordon and he wasn't lean. It would be a risky few yards to cover, since the beginning of nightfall was signalled with a particular alertness of the troops on both sides. Sharpshooters were primed to fire on any movement.

They'd have to wait until the required firing of the "stand to" order was finished. "Stand to" was a quirk of the quiet times in the trenches. Each side went through a mock battle as night fell. It was more like a pantomime reminding them why they were there. "We're here because we're here, because we're here."

At the command of "stand to" tired limbs, both khaki and grey, stretched as men stepped onto the firing shelf. Once the soldiers on both sides settled into an upright position, their weapons were flung in unison over the parapet to offer a few random shots at the enemy, an exorcism of the passing day's tedium. The other side returned fire. Darts of anger and frustration. It didn't matter that there were no targets worthy of the waste of ammunition, shooting was a reminder that the war was not yet over. The show of force never lasted long, but it could be deadly for any who took this charade lightly.

Once this ritual was complete, Gordon would have to work quickly. He prayed neither side had work parties venturing out. Any noise would bring out the Very lights, and the silhouettes these flares cast were the favourite target for snipers.

Gordon felt down to his waist to check his gear. The first aid satchel was closed and clipped. His trousers were free of snags. When he leapt up, he didn't want any hesitation caused by catching his clothing on a stray piece of wire. All was ready. He waited, marshalling his energies.

Gordon closed his eyes to rest, knowing his daydreaming always took him to their first date. This was especially true after watching the daylight fade, for he had first seen her special smile as it was reflecting the dying rays of sunlight strained through stained glass.

Westmount (Montreal): St. Matthias Anglican Church
Wednesday, March 22, 1917, 6:35 p.m.

The day Thou gavest Lord, is ended …

The packed church took to their feet and chanted in unison. Johanna and Gordon were near the back. They had arrived late. The tram on Atwater street had skipped a rail, and they were forced to walk the final blocks to the church on St. Anthony's Street.

Who would ever bring his girl to a hymn-sing and call it a date?

Well, to be perfectly honest, Johanna wasn't "his" girl. Not yet … probably not ever! And this wasn't a date. Gordon wasn't bringing her anywhere. This was just a gesture of hospitality on her part. No meaning past a mild kindness. They were each in their own minds attending a choral evening out of duty to God and country.

He looked across at her face as they sang side by side. There was a fresh and clean delight in her manner. And, yet, behind her decorum lurked a wild wench spirit, waiting to burst the bounds of propriety. Nothing was done by half measures, not love or music. She sang at full throttle, hair swept into a neat ponytail, eyes fixed on the altar. She seemed to be enjoying each syllable. The lyrics certainly appealed to the romantic side of her personality, boasting of an unending providential care. Gordon wasn't even paying attention. The words slipped from his lips unattended.

Johanna, sensing Gordon's regard, turned a bit. There was a mixture of joy and sorrow on her lips. The final rays of late winter sunset glanced off her cheeks and forehead—red, streaked with blue from the west transept window. The longer they looked at each other, the broader grew her smile, ending in such a portrait of joy, it took his breath away.

It wasn't appropriate to fall in love at this stage in his courting, was it? "Besides," he thought, "I'm not really courting her. Not really." The stirring that Gordon felt in his loins went deeper than a physical desire. Unpractised as he was, this feeling had a novel ambiguity to it. There was a flush of sensual desire mingled with heart-breaking doubt.

It was more than attraction that confused his heart. He found equally appealing the sensation of being appreciated. He was no expert, but thought she also felt something for him. There was no empirical evidence, just the assurance of his intuition. Okay, maybe it was just her way or a common courtesy, but he knew that on some level, albeit superficial, she liked him and that small measure of attraction was intoxicating. The night before she had praised him—his stories. "Imagine that!" Gordon was ready to accept whatever perceived merits Johanna might want to assign to him. In fact, it thrilled him greatly. She seemed to want to ask him deeper and deeper questions.

But … Gordon always had a "but" close at hand to squelch any self-esteem … but while her feminine attention excited him, he was sure that, if she really knew him, she would find him quite unacceptable. To be known well and still loved, this form of intimacy was beyond his ken.

Nevertheless, to discover each other's best kept secrets was an arousing prospect. Gordon held love to be an exalted affair, not an emotion to be applied to a three-day acquaintance, yet there was something potent that was stirring directed toward this young woman with soft as silk hair and razor-edged wit. Propriety kept his thoughts above the waist. He called his feelings deep esteem, for he did not want to presume any further.

Jo was curious and, yes, flattered. Gordon was a good-looking man, sensitive and intelligent and she enjoyed the feel of his fixed gaze, delighting in the delicious awareness that he was drawn to her. Of course, it had happened before. But she had rarely felt her body stir in response. On the surface, a decent man-child going off to war. But underneath, Jo could sense a mixture of simple virtue and unbridled love. He was a neophyte and innocent but capable of great courage.

It was this latter quality that endeared Gordon to her. She had known many boasting buffoons who blustered about their bravery, precisely because they lacked it. This quiet soul standing beside her never mentioned his courage and yet had it in abundance. That was the single memory she had from the previous evening's encounter. Even the bishop mentioned it before retiring. "That fellow has a special clarity about his heart." She agreed quickly, perhaps too quickly, and she saw her father pause at her retort. He kissed her forehead and said tenderly, "Watch your heart, Johanna!"

Gordon's bravery, the kind that mattered to Jo, was not only the ability to run at drawn bayonets without flinching. That was important, but there was also a courage that related to the inner life. It was the capacity to see oneself without pretence. To live without self-deception was her great goal. The man who looked so lovingly at her now was a living example of what she wanted to become.

So two lovers searched each other's gaze as the lyrics to an evening hymn rolled on. Eventually, the moment passed and they turned back to the music. Hymns were safe.

Glancing at her again as they closed in on the final stanza, Gordon could see she was wrapped in obvious pleasure. Was she happy with him or this hymn? Full lips formed an oval that was open and inviting as she offered praise to God's faithfulness. Surely it was the melody that made her so happy. Perhaps she was pleased to offer this gesture of hospitality to a stranger, a lost soldier? She flicked him a quick glance. He smiled back his gratitude.

While mouthing words of the last line, their eyes strayed again to each other. It was a long interval lasting well into the priest's hallowed invitation for the congregation to remain standing while the opening prayer was offered. As they looked into each other's eyes an unspoken agreement was made, the content of which Gordon could not fathom, but it was solid and lasting nonetheless.

If only he could let go of his own apprehensions—the "You stink" qualms about his acceptability—he would admit that there *was* something deeper in their communion, something that words could not touch. She moved a hand closer to where his rested on the pew ahead. The brush of her palm was enough to send his heart into his throat. Whatever else happened, Gordon knew this was not to be a casual evening of devotion.

The prayer began.

> *"Most glorious God, the keeper of every soul, and the giver of every gift. Look down on us this day as we remember the men and women who have answered your call and dedicated their lives in service to you in France...."*

He had two sons in the army and wasn't going to miss his chance to boast.

Johanna sighed in disgust at every suggestion of God's desire for the patriotic pursuit of the war.

As they stood, Gordon could feel her body close at hand. Was she leaning toward him? How immoral, to have hands tingling with sensual pleasures, while the priest intoned God's glorious love. Distracting, inappropriate and delicious.

"Please be seated."

A red-faced senior plodded to the lectern, old battle medals clinking in tune to his step. Again Johanna sighed. He read a brief passage from Isaiah about comforting the chosen people and announced a hymn. This one was more patriotic. "Oh God our Help in Ages Past." It had become the standard lifted high for battle-weary communities. The organ carried the tune for a few bars before the gates of anguish burst and voices choked with the loss of loved ones boomed forth. Maybe the boys would hear it in France.

> Oh God our Help in ages past,
> Our hope for years to come.
> A shelter from the stormy blast
> And our eternal home.

For a moment, Gordon was caught in the tide of feelings. He too would be seeking God's shelter before too long. War was not yet real, but he would soon know it first-hand. A shiver went through his voice. Would he die?

Johanna leaned close and whispered, "God, you will be in it soon. I can't bear to think of it." This time her whole hand squeezed his.

Gordon's head was swimming. He had not had many girlfriends. No relationships of note. He took a few turns on the dance floor at the school prom, but that was hardly preparation for anything like a love affair. The proximity of this open and opposite sex was enough to boil his brain, and her unsolicited physical touch scrambled his wits. She did feel something for him—whether brotherly affection or something greater, he could not distinguish. But emboldened by whatever he represented to her, his voice took on a timbre and force that he had not intended as he joined in the hymn.

It was as he was taking his leave from their dinner party, that his excitement first awoke. Johanna had mentioned the evensong service earlier, and, as he had a hand on doorknob, she inquired if Gordon would like to go.

"Would you care to accompany me? It begins at 6:30, so if you drop by an hour earlier we could go together." It was offered with such ease. Gordon would have taken an hour to compose such simple elegance. He stammered an affirmative and the date was set.

But he could not leave. He stood on the doorstep, she in the vestibule, silent. Then on impulse, she had taken both his hands and fixed his gaze. "I did enjoy your stories, Gordon. Please don't see so little in them. They speak of a great spirit."

Again he was too tongue-tied to speak.

"Until tomorrow, then." It had a wistful tone when Johanna uttered the phrase.

Gordon, unwilling to let go, but feeling the blood rising in his cheeks, tried to command the trembling in his spirit. "Miss Johanna, it would be an honour to accompany you and …" That was too stiff, and he could see the rebuke in her eyes so he added. "Please forgive my awkward words. Really, I would be delighted. I love music and I love …." He was going to say "you" –not really "you", but more "your rich and freeing spirit." Nevertheless, he tacked on another word. "Hymns. I love hymns." A lift of her eyebrows brought laughter to them both and they parted in the glow of a promising fire. It was certainly fortunate that she had been so bold as to make the first gesture. He never would have found the courage to ask her to join him in anything.

Now as they sang the final verses of God's providential care, Gordon took his turn at conveying a quiet message. Placing his mouth next to her ear, he told her how they sang this hymn at church camp, gathered at the chapel on the pine-decked hillside. "It has the power to take me back to that golden time when God's promise flowed so easily."

"Indeed."

Anthems followed upon songs of praise. The night passed.

There is potency that thrives in pent-up feelings, shared furtively in public places. As the service continued, Gordon knew its force as each hymn brought more gestures of love—a whispered joke: "Whenever they sing about God being a firm foundation, I think of garments." That was Johanna. Gordon turned beet red. At some point they had dispensed with two hymn books and now held a single text, fingers touching underneath.

The final benediction took them to the peace beyond understanding. It was clear that neither wanted to leave. They sat down in the custom of the day and bowed their heads for personal devotion. Eyes closed, Gordon tried to force time to a standstill. "Let it not end." Slowly he allowed the moment to slide, raised his eyes and saw that the church was almost empty.

Struggling to his feet, he extended a hand to the awakening Johanna without thinking. She took it. If the floor had opened up and swallowed Gordon, he would not have been more surprised at himself than at that moment. He asked himself, "Does love always happen so innocently and yet have so much weight poured into every simple gesture?"

They walked back up the aisle, a short distance to the door. "My father and mother were married here." Johanna played with the words, teasing Gordon into smiles and light. "Love doesn't have to be so ponderous," she continued.

Gordon stuttered, "Pardon me?" Does she read minds too?

"Gordon, didn't you feel it? The hymns all spoke about a love for God as if it would take a saint or a century to formulate anything decent. Surely love of the Creator is much less work than we think! Just feel." With that she gave him an extra squeeze of his hand.

He released her hand as he pulled mittens from his pocket. She buttoned her coat and together they tripped out the door into the cold. Gordon thought she was hurrying to get home and followed after her. Johanna knew she had to run before her heart took her too far.

So they trundled down the steps at double time and headed back towards Sherbrooke Street and transportation home. Even muffled by woollen mittens, their hands found each other again. They cleared the church precincts and left off speaking. Gordon's gut ached, a pleasure that he had never known before. They smiled into the mounting wind, puffs of snow still swirling from the weekend's storm.

"I want to show you my favourite park."

"Tonight?'

"No, silly, it's too late now. It's called Sisson Ridge—well that's what I call it. Everyone else calls it the mountain. How about tomorrow afternoon? Are you free?"

Gordon had nothing to do at all, for four more days. "Why don't we have a winter picnic?" His Boy Scout training leapt into action. "I know where to find the army's supply of outdoor utensils. I'll arrange it and we'll …." He stopped for she was almost laughing. "What is it?"

"I love it. You're the first person who thinks the way I do and wants to do something more than sip tea in a polite parlour. Sure let's do it."

The pact was made and they walked on clinging to each.

Ypres: Several yards in front of the Can. Corps Forward Observation Trench
Sunday, February 11, 1917, 7:45 p.m.

Gordon could see the vision of that huddled, happy couple from the distance of France. They leaned into the wind, the gusts lashing at the warmth that was blossoming between them.

The touch of a snowflake broke the spell. A night storm was brewing. It was time to go before the weather broke in earnest. The day's intermittent sunshine had thawed out shallow puddles, but the ground was cooling to winter's embrace. How many men died for lack of warmth while waiting in the field?

Sporadic shooting echoed down the line at some distance. Directly behind him nothing was stirring. He couldn't recall any orders for raids in this sector, but he was not an officer. Things happened to the enlisted men often without forewarning.

Darkness was complete. What starlight might have betrayed them was shrouded in the thick and threatening storm clouds. The odd snowflake fluttered to earth. Should he wait until the storm hit? Blizzards offered excellent cover, but it might take hours or days. No, it was better to take the chance now. Wounded bellies cannot hold out forever. A final check of his gear, some manoeuvring to get Terry ready for a quick lift onto Gordon's shoulders and a few seconds of absolute silence to check once again for any movement.

"Not a creature was stirring." Christmas jingles rattled in Gordon's brains. It was deadly to be distracted, so he focused his efforts on his planned route to the sap.

Rolling to hands and knees, Gordon could feel the wet slime through his mud-caked clothing. Trying to control his breathing, keeping his movements fluid and simple, he reached under Terry's arms and rocked backed into a squat, pulling his limp body across his shoulders. Dead and dying men weigh so much more. "Do our souls keep us light?"

Knowing that he could not remain crouched and carry his burden, Gordon slowly eased into a shallow stoop, legs almost straight. From this vantage point he saw that the sap was filled with a few bullet riddled bodies. Blocked. Useless for protection. He'd have to run straight to the line without the advantage of much cover.

He went to move and discovered that Terry's good leg was caught on a piece of protruding wire. "Damn this war," Gordon muttered as he tried to wiggle the wounded leg free, caught by the thick yarn of his military issue stocking. Brute force took over from clever twitching and the knot finally let go.

"Twang." The wire had vibrated back into its natural spool. Gordon froze. Did anyone hear it? Moments passed and it looked like he was lucky, when a flash exploded from behind the German lines. It was followed by a muffled thud. A flare was spluttering upward.

Gordon knew he should freeze and wait, but he was uncertain if he could hold still. Once the flare exploded, they'd be easy targets. No matter that Gordon was obviously helping a casualty back to medical care. Wounded men and medics were fair game. He sprang into a full gallop. Secrecy discarded, splashing puddles signalled their hasty retreat. Gordon could see the hunched line of trenches only a dozen yards ahead. "Please, God, Keep them from firing too."

Every footfall echoed across no man's land and he waited, his back itching, knowing that the bullets would fly toward any noise.

For a second or two there was no gunfire. But finally the darts came, a shower of shots rang out as snipers focused on the hunched burden splashing through the craters to safety. The flare burst and the night turned to day.

"Now they have me in their crosshairs. Now they pull the trigger," dismay was shouting in his head. He heard the close zip of bullets as he fell forward into the arms of a waiting comrade at his own trench line.

Safe and panting, he smiled his relief at the soldiers who reached to shoulder him down to the duckboards. Bullets continued to ping overhead. "Shit, buddy, I've never seen anyone run so fast." Hands proffered water bottles. Someone lifted the burden off Gordon's shoulders and slung Terry gently to a cleared and clean blanket.

"This one's off to Blightey."

"Sure enough," Gordon moaned. "He's got a wound in the gut and you can see his foot was blown off. But with some steady care, he might make it." Gordon gave his patient a quick look, patted Terry's unmoving shoulder and then leaned back against the trench wall, drenched in released anxiety.

"No, you don't get it, pal." A concerned face stared back at Gordon. Sergeant Brooks from St. Catherines, Ontario. "He's been shot through the back. Must have happened as you came over the sandbags. Caught one of those fucking sniper darts. Silly bugger." A pause as Gordon looked blank. The sergeant thought maybe Gordon was shell-shocked. "You okay, Gordie? Sorry to say your friend here isn't doing too well. Got himself dead, he did." He stooped down to look into Terry's face. "Say … Isn't this the one who ran off a while back? Bloody idiot got what he deserved, though I guess he saved your sorry ass."

"He's dead?" Gordon lurched forward, awakened from weariness by the shock. "It can't be! I know him! It can't be."

"Shot while you ran, but kept you alive … no doubt about it."

"He's dead?" Gordon's mouth couldn't fashion any other question.

"Looks pretty much like that me to me! Poor bugger made it back in time to be buried. Bloody fool causes me another sleepless night of filling in forms. 'Dear Mrs….'" Brooks stooped down and ripped Terry' tags from his pale neck. Reading the inscription in the sparkle of flares,

"Dear Mrs. ... Mrs. Hinks, I am sorry to inform you that your son ... Terrance was ..." Looking around the circle in the trench, he smirked, "Say guys, how do I say 'yellow-bellied coward' in God's good English?" Laughing, the soldier turned in search of likely candidates for burial detail. "Harris, Smithson. It's your lucky day."

Gordon shouted at the sergeant's back, "She's dead!"

Brooks turned around. "Who's she?"

"His mother. She's dead—been dead for years. If you're going to write to his family, write to Bishop Douglas Hinks or his daughter, Johanna." Gordon glared. "Get it straight!"

"Yeah ... okay. I get it, and I'll make damn sure his record reads the truth no matter what I say in a letter. And make no mistake you'll have your name in the official account. Good enough for you?"

"Fine!"

Brooks started back to his dugout. Gordon reached out quickly and grabbed his tunic. "He's so young ... just a kid ... be kind to his dad ... say he died saving the life of a medic ... that much is true."

Brooks turned to face Gordon. "He mean that much to you?"

"Yes ... I know his family ... sister and father ... they'll be crushed ... No need to drive them deeper with this kid's cowardice.... Please ...."

Brooks relented, "Okay, I'll do it for your sake, not for his for sure ... for you Gordie boy ... You're the boldest one in this entire outfit, so I'll do it for you!"

"Swear!"

"I swear," Brooks agreed and then chuckled. "I swear on Gordie's balls!"

With that assurance Gordon let go of his sergeant's coat and slumped onto a frozen lump of mud—not even smiling at the joke. For a time, all he could feel was failure. He'd let Johanna down. Promising to protect all that was precious and keeping to the spirit of her admonition about compassion, he'd tried his best, but it wasn't enough. Oh God, if she found out, she'd never speak to him again. He couldn't explain how he came to be helping Terry. That would be cruel, and in the circumstances might appear self-serving. His death would cut off their relationship as neatly as her brother's severed foot.

Gordon awoke from his nightmarish musings just as Harris and Smithson were dragging Terry down the trench, one at the arms, the other at the feet.

"Wait." Gordon struggled to his knees and half-crawled, half-walked to the inert body, now pale with death. No stench yet. The burial detail had removed his identification tags, a wallet and pocket watch—all to be sent home. "There was a letter from his sister." The two gravediggers looked blank. "In his paybook. I thought I'd write to her and tell her what happened." One man let an arm drop into the mud, fished in the dead man's pocket and came up with the paybook. He passed it to Gordon who fumbled with it until the folded pages were in his hand.

"Thanks lads!" They grunted their satisfaction and took up their burden again. This time, they both took an arm. Less mess, quicker.

Gordon flopped back into his funk and opened the letter for a second time. "Was it decent to read her correspondence?" He wondered. "Would it help at all, when he tried to write back?"

Mortar shells were landing down the line. The battle was joined. He could hear the crump as shells hit the sandbags. Bodies were running past him on the way to reinforce the line. Gordon ignored all the action and carefully unfolded the worn pages. Seeing her writing brought back a wave of peace and desire and he laid down the pages with a sigh. Where was she now?

He gave her letter a second try. "Dear Terrance:" She loved her brother deeply. What would she do without him?

The opening line jumped at him from the paper. "His name is Samuel and I love him with all my heart, with a passion I did not know was in me." Gordon could go no further. Samuel? Who ...? Had she found another lover? There was a stabbing thrust under his belt. His breath was cut short.

"Move it Davis, this place is too small for bystanders." Gordon looked up into the sergeant's eyes. "We'll call you if we need you. Looks like we're in for a raid from Fritz tonight. We'll want all the room we can get to use this." He held up his persuader, a two-foot club with spikes arrayed at its tip. With a sneer, he walked on.

Gordon stumbled in the mud, wiping Terry's blood from his tunic, making the mess worse. He opened and read the first line again. Samuel? The name was burnt into his heart. Samuel!

Anger and dismay warred within him. He could hardly breathe. "Can she betray me so selfishly—never even mentioning a word to him? What happened to her promise of marriage?" Her letters had been all sweetness and light. In a fit of anger he later regretted, Gordon ground the pages into a ball and threw them into the puddle of mud. He watched her letter sink into the muck as he turned down the trench toward his billet.

Let them fight the bloody war without him.

Saint John: Centenary-Queen Square United Church
Friday, December 20, 1991, 1:30 p.m.

God, there's no fight like a church fight and no mud thicker than that which is thrown around a ladies' parlour.

"Jeff, you're a silly busybody."

"You're a hopeless ingrate, Michael."

Not pausing to reflect on that jab, Michael pushed his point home. "You stick your nose into everyone's business, especially my music! I'm sick of your petty conniving! I have worked damn hard to know what I'm talking about and I'm tired of your whining about the hymns."

My mind is drifting. A Friday evening movie is beckoning and my thoughts stray to my last visit with Gordon. So he can talk and is thirsty for some good rum. I have fantasies of smuggling in a nip of good cheer. Nurse Simons would ban me from the premises if she ever found out. It would be delicious.

Even though I'd heard only a few words, I am sure there is someone inside the crusty shell. What might he reveal about himself when I go back? There must have been a tremendous trauma to cork up his conversation for well over seventy years. I make a mental note to look at his files more closely. Perhaps there is a clue from his past. I resolve to make another visit before Christmas. Maybe Monday.

I wake from my daydream to see everyone staring at me. "Pardon me?"

"The communion hymn. You will have communion won't you?"
"Yes, yes of course …"

Montreal: Sebastopol Street
Sunday, February 11, 1917, 1:47 p.m.

Jo was still humming the communion hymn as she walked toward
home. "Break thou the Bread of Life." She couldn't get the second verse
lyrics out of her mind:

> *Bless Thou the truth, dear Lord, to me, to me,*
> *As Thou didst bless the bread by Galilee;*
> *Then shall all bondage cease, all fetters fall;*
> *And I shall find my peace, my all in all.*

What was the truth Jo needed? Surely it was her love for Private
Gordon Davis. When she turned her heart toward him, she felt capable
of loosing the daily fetters of fear, breaking the bondage of the war.
Indeed, in his embrace she had felt a peace that passes understanding.

The small local parish held a noon-hour Sunday service. It was an
easy stroll … good for her to get out of the house. She could set the
table, arrange the greens, put the Sunday roast into the oven and have
it ready at 2:00 when the good bishop came home from his cathedral
duties. It was a bit more difficult now with Samuel in her life … but the
joy she received from him was more than just compensation.

As was her custom since Gordon left, Jo said a silent prayer for his
safety at every corner of her walk home. Even though he was across the
ocean, she could still feel him close, his spirit against her side as she
walked. Silly man, always running himself into the gutter and never
seeing how he was a rock for so many. His self-pity was disgusting. And
yet she had never met someone so selfless. Oh she loved him … his
warts and wrinkles along with his shining moments.

Jo reached her front gate and unconsciously turned to look east
across the CN train yards. Beyond the constant screeching of train
wheels, the smoke of the harbour, down the river and across the endless
waves of the Atlantic … to France. And in her mind she traced the miles

across green countryside before she arrived at his dugout. Was he safe? Was he feeling what she felt? If only she could touch his hand, hold him tight.

Jo turned to open the gate when she felt a deep stab of pain. In shock she looked down at her abdomen for the knife. There was none. It wasn't physical. It was a spiritual wound … so deep, so poignant that she doubled over. Breathing came hard. Her head was swimming. Something had happened. Something very serious. Horror filled her mind. Gordon? Gordon is in trouble! She was certain of it.

As Jo slowly straightened up, she imagined Gordon clearly. There was blood on his chest, he was crumpled in a heap. His head was down. Was he dead? There was a shadow of dying about the vision and she couldn't shake it. She had no power to move or think. Only prayer helped. Her spirit was furtively tracing her steps to Gordon, willing him to live, wanting to take him in her arms. Did she cry out loud? "He's so young. My God! So alone. Dear God, you can take so easily. Give him back!" Tears were flowing down her cheeks as she repeated her lament: "Give him back!"

How long her spirit was in France, she could not tell. It was only when Bishop Hinks rounded the corner that she came back to Canada.

"What happened my dear?" her father asked immediately shocked at his daughter's shaken countenance. He took her face in his warm hands.

"Death … oh, Father, death has touched us."

Halifax Harbour: Pier 7
Thursday, December 6, 1917, 9:25 a.m.

Death's touch is chilling, numbing our minds.

Slowly, Gordon shook off the trance. He had been lost to the misery of dying, caught in this whirlpool of smoke and blood. How long had he sat beside the dying woman, stroking her forehead, picking hairs from the blood now sluggishly flowing over her temples?

Coming back from his dazed state, he saw that her eyes were still open, the fixed stare that marked the flight of the soul. There was no hope here, at least not on this side of the great divide.

Fire was creeping up fast. Gordon could do no more, even mourning seemed futile. France had beaten grief from his repertoire of emotions.

Looking about he saw only flames and rubble. He knew the city rose up to his left and he began to scrabble over the ruins of the warehouse, searching for fresh air. The entire pier must be burning. Sheets of fire barred most directions. What had caused the attack? There was no time for reflection. He had to find Jo.

Images of her torn body lying beneath a broken beam or collapsed wall haunted every step. He glanced to the left and right in the crumbling building searching for bodies. A few males were caught in grotesque postures—one crushed beneath a toppled bale of hardwood, another impaled on a bent and rusting steel beam. No more women.

Did he cry out to her? He couldn't remember those first panic-swamped moments, when later he roamed through the streets looking into dark corners and deserted alleys. Perhaps he shouted her name out loud, but the smoke swallowed whatever anyone cried out.

"Jo!"

No response.

Glass covered everything, crunched underfoot as he clambered over bits of brick and stone. Gordon found himself on the street that ran parallel to the harbour. What was left of walkways fed off this street down to loading docks. She should be here. Close at hand.

Gordon never doubted her sincerity. If she promised to be here, she was here, somewhere. But did she wait for him as a lover or a close friend? The perpetual round of questions.

He had written about the arrival of his ship. It had been a rather unconventional trans-Atlantic route, but it was the quickest way back after the hospital stay at Saint-Omer.

Across the street in a company warehouse office, he found a shipper's waiting room. The door was ajar. Gordon pushed aside some fallen plaster and lathes that blocked his entry. Dust rose to choke his nostrils. He thought no man's land was dangerous! Jagged glass and upturned nails waited to catch any unprotected part.

She promised to be here. Must be here somewhere or in some other warehouse. Maybe she had been waiting at the train station or gotten lost coming down to the harbour. Could she have mistakenly arrived at another pier? Maybe she got the date wrong?

Gordon had promised to wait until she arrived. "I won't forget." She had responded. "I will wait for you, if it takes years." Promises, both broken; at least suspended.

Gordon left the warehouse. Every building on the street was demolished. He walked south toward the citadel. Howls of disaster began to emerge from the wrecks that had once been houses. Two blood-soaked children crawled out of a basement window. He dashed over to aid them up the last few steps, drew them a safe distance from their burning home and sat them down on a crumbled piece of masonry.

They couldn't speak. Their faces were a mass of cuts and he reached for his first aid kit, drew out some gauze and began to wrap what was visible. "It will be okay, laddies. I'll have you right as rain. Just a little wait and we'll have you over to the hospital trench … I mean … the emergency station." They sat whimpering, too numb to feel much of anything. Did one say something close to "Mummy?"

"Is your mother inside?"

Blank looks.

A little louder, "Is your mother inside?"

Fear grew on the face of one child, but the other nodded sullenly, tears flowing down his cheeks.

Gordon looked back to the collapsed structure from which they had come and knew there was no hope. It was a ball of fire, the wood licked by huge tongues of yellow and orange.

Looking for assistance, Gordon realized he had no idea where help might be found. No rescue squads were in sight and precious little at hand to protect these small waifs from the cold. Where was the bloody hospital? How could he get two children some first aid?

No vehicle was at hand. In war, you at least knew where to find a medical trench. Looking down, he saw his charges shiver. He slid down to hold them in his arms while he thought of a plan. Cold wind whipped at their backs. They cuddled in close, safe in his arms. He searched his mind for a solution.

None came.

There was no point waiting to freeze to death. Gordon hoisted them in his arms and began to walk south again. He thought he could see some undamaged buildings through the smoke up ahead.

It was only after walking a few paces that he felt the pain in his right leg. Looking down he thought he could see blood. With the children in his arms it was hard to see clearly. It must be a deep cut.

There was no time to examine it more carefully.

Saint John: Centenary-Queen Square United Church
Tuesday, Nov. 17, 1992, 11:19 a.m.

I close my hymn book as the last verse ends and begin to mount the stairs to the pulpit.

> *My gracious Master and my God,*
> *assist me to proclaim,*
> *to spread through all the world abroad*
> *The honours of thy name.*

From here I can see the stranger has likewise placed her hymnal in the book rack. In her late forties, she's taller than I imagined and sings the final verse off by heart, staring forward. A professional? A black shawl covers neatly cut blond hair. In the half-light under the balcony, I catch her eye and there is some message written there. But it's too distant to gauge. Grief probably.

Who is she and why is she here?

CHAPTER FOUR

The Confession

I once argued with a friend, "Let us sin boldly," then added, "and trust our Saviour even more boldly." No more milk toast confessions. Let's do battle with the Devil where the war is waging and not in some sentimental sideshow.

Martin Luther, *On Prayer*

Toronto: 20 Mountalan Ave.
Friday, April 11, 2014, 7:54 p.m.

My fingers punch in the numbers returning Patricia Patterson's call. Imagine … Gordon, my real uncle! Family. What had he left me? I often joked with my grown children that I had no inheritance to offer unless a long-lost uncle came through with our fortune. We'd all laugh. My daughter especially would rib me, "Dad, it would useless even if you did have a rich relative. You'd give it all away."

The connection gets through … a busy signal! I'll try again in a few minutes.

I hear Jack in the next room. He's still awake. Maybe I should try another lullaby. "Edelweiss." It easily takes a dozen repetitions to lull him to sleep. Grandparents have all the time in the world.

Hamilton: St. Giles Anglican Church
Thursday, October 14, 1915, 7:45 p.m.

"Forgive me, Father, for I have sinned in thought and word and deed against thy divine majesty. I have ...." Gordon paused and opening one eye toward his confessor said, "What do I say next?" Private confession was optional in Anglican circles. For the Reverend Hawthorne, it was an absolute necessity for anyone presenting themselves for ministry. Consequently, Gordon had been called to the vestry after the junior choir practice.

"Just list those sins which have most burdened your heart." Hawthorne did not look up, but held his hands together, head bowed, ready to dissect each misdemeanour and pronounce a cure. The clock on his desk ticked away the silence.

Gordon bowed his head and searched those evil sides of his personality. "Forgive me, Father, for I have been insulting to my sister, Lillian, when she criticizes me about the mess in my room. I should not have left my bedclothes on the floor. Forgive me, for I have harboured evil thoughts against my teacher, wishing to be free from school and believing her ...."

Gordon looked up, "Should I confess that I called her 'stupid'?" Hawthorne nodded his head and mumbled something that sounded wisely affirmative. "Forgive me, Father, for calling my teacher 'stupid,' and ... ah ... forgive me for I have allowed my heart to drift when listening to the sermon at church." A cough from Hawthorne reminded Gordon who preached that sermon. Some sins are better left unconfessed. Gordon went through the other minor betrayals—a forgotten word of gratitude, an angry remark. It was becoming more difficult to imagine a decent sin. Then his mind cast upon the bigger issues, the wet dreams, the urges he could not control. "Forgive me, Father, for I have touched myself in the morning when I felt a lust-filled desire. Forgive me for ...."

"What?" Hawthorne, the soul physician, was suddenly alert. "You touched yourself?"

"Yes, Father." Gordon felt his blood rising on a tide of humiliation. "Yes .... I'd rather not .... I feel ashamed of ...."

"Shame. Don't stop on the brink of admitting your crimes, boy. Spit it out. Be done with it once and for all. Let me help you! Was it your male member that you touched?"

"Yes."

"Was it hard and standing erect?"

"Yes."

There was a long pause in the room. Only the clock spoke. Was it counting out his punishment? Gordon felt that a heavy burden had fallen on the shoulders of his confessor and was uncertain what to do. Could he take it back? Was it permissible to continue with a prayer of confession, citing other minor sins, when such an obviously great sin was waiting for absolution?

Hawthorne stirred in his seat. "Show me."

"Father?" Gordon looked about the room thinking someone else had spoken.

"Show me your sin, my son." It was spoken with such grace and care. "It is the best way to rid yourself of the desire. You do want to be free of sin, don't you?"

Gordon could hardly disagree. "If it is at all possible."

"Oh, it's possible all right." Hawthorne paused, pursing his lips and taking a deep breath. "Let us exorcise your lust before it grows any deeper, spreading its filthy roots into your very soul. Show me what you did."

Gordon was confused. He had never heard of such a practice. "Is this the prescribed penitence for …."

"Do you want to enter the priesthood, Gordon?" Hawthorne's voice was urgent, though his body did not move at all. There was a poised tension in his countenance and touching fingers, as if he were on the point of grasping the devil with his bare hands.

Gordon could feel the wrath of God pressing forward. "Indeed, sir I do. It is my fondest wish."

Hawthorne resumed an inviting and sweet tone. He broke from his penitent posture and looked lovingly at the boy, eyes languid. "You will make a great priest, but you must rid yourself of all shame. You're sure you want to enter the ministry?"

"Of course, Father." There was no doubt in the young man's mind. He would do anything to be a priest. Anything.

"Then show me what you did. It will lift your guilt, I assure you." The old priest could massage the very air in an interview. He had spent years perfecting his cunning craft. "Let me take your sin upon me. The medicine of the heart is my expertise. It may not make sense to you now, but I assure you this is necessary to purify your desires of the flesh. Stand up and show me."

The logic was lost on Gordon, but Hawthorne knew how to press home his point. "Don't let Christ down, my son. Discipleship is costly."

"Do you have 'desires of the flesh'?" Gordon asked his confessor as he was fumbling with his belt buckle and zipper.

"None, my son." The priest was watching intently as Gordon worked his pants down to his knees. "What did you do? Be specific so that I may know the extent of your sinfulness and make full absolution."

Gordon moved a hand under his shorts and touched his penis. "Only played with it like this, Father." A hand flipped the flaccid member back and forth beneath white cotton.

"Did it excite you, my son?" Hawthorne's voice was still solicitous, honey-coated.

"Yes, but I knew it was wrong, really I did. I tried to stop, but then it began to grow and feel hard. I was frightened that I had done something wrong. But at the same time, it felt so firm." Gordon could feel his penis hardening again and was ashamed and frightened. "Is that all Father? I have to get home to do homework and …."

"Pull down your pants and let me see for myself. Then you can go home." It sounded like a prescription for a flu bug. Gordon did as he was told and stood with his growing erection in full view. Hawthorne seemed to take a special interest in it. Shifting forward in his seat, he made knowing sounds as if measuring Gordon's sin. His hands were lifted up slightly—as if in blessing over the naked penis.

Gordon was feeling dizzy and uncertain. His words rushed forward. "Forgive me, Father, for I have sinned. I do want to become a priest. I do earnestly wish that my soul becomes pure." His hands slid down and jerked his cotton underwear up over his stiff penis. The pants followed with the same speed.

His abruptness broke the trance into which Hawthorne had descended. He jumped and fell back into the prayerful stance, finger tips touching again. "Yes, my son. In the name of the Father, Son and Holy Spirit, I absolve you of all your sins. Know that you live as a forgiven child of God."

Pulling up his zipper and fixing his belt, Gordon offered his thanks, and bowed his way out of the room. Why did his cheeks burn so?

Watching the door close behind the retreating postulant, Hawthorne, reached below his padded chair for his sacrament. Uncorking a bottle, he took a swig of last Sunday's communion wine and wiped his lips with linen from the ladies parlour.

"Christ!"

Saint John: Centenary-Queen Square United Church
Tuesday, Nov. 17, 1992, 11:20 a.m.

"Christ calls all his disciples to this place." I was standing on the top step of the chancel to the left of the pulpit. Looking down, I tried to inject some at-your-own-home feeling. "This is our haven, built to hold our worries. Everyone has a place here and in a spirit of compassion, we offer up our confessions to God even as we mourn the loss of Gordon from our circle."

In actual fact, Gordon had never really been part of any circle in Saint John. He floated like a ghost ship through many institutional waters. Through his file, I was able to chart his journey from one dusty hall to another.

Arriving here in a fog of confusion from Montreal where he was found wandering the streets, he was shipped off to a facility for people with mental difficulties. His uniform gave no indication of his military affiliation since all badges and tags had been ripped off. He was army, and that's all anyone ever knew. During the war years, individuals passed through many doors unnoticed. No paper trail. It seems no one took time to investigate his background. Casualties were common in those days. He was sent to a large wing of the local Catholic hospital which dedicated three floors entirely to veterans. Medical officials could find no label for his disorder apart from prolonged shell-shock. After a brief flurry of interest, they suspended his treatment. Bigger, more immediate fish to fry.

Eventually the hospital was used entirely for the battle torn of Flanders. Gordon disappeared in the crowd. For many years he languished like a discarded toy, moving from bed to bed at the whim of whatever reigning management held power.

As the memory of the war receded, its victims lost prestige. Money available for rehabilitation diminished and a "wait and see" policy dominated decisions about extended care. As the number of vets dwindled it no longer seemed necessary to have a separate facility devoted to their care.

Then came another "Great War," with even more conflict and slaughter. Fresh wounds to heal! The younger generation of vets began demanding the time of doctors and nurses. The staff was only too eager to drop everything to attend to the new war-wounded. So the three dozen remaining Great War vets were transferred to three long and narrow wards in a small and unused hospital on the west side of the city. It was to be the last placement of these ancient vets who didn't have the decency to get over their diseases and live or to succumb to them and die.

For thirty years that windowless room was Gordon's home. In the end, Gordon was the last of two vets. The others had finally succeeded in doing the right thing, going to their heavenly reward.

With so few patients, the bureaucracy in Fredericton decided to change the focus of what had become known as the "Vets Hospital." In a revised plan, it would now house an out-patient clinic for diabetes and hold the offices of the West-Side Public Health Authority.

Gordon was shipped to the basement of the big general hospital on the hill. There, apart from sporadic visits by bright-eyed medical students who wanted to see a "special" case of what experts began calling "post-traumatic stress disorder," he was forgotten. Food arrived every day, orderlies and nurses were dutiful in walking down the long corridor to his isolated room, but, otherwise, he sat alone.

Gordon wouldn't, couldn't, die.

There was one flurry of activity when he was "discovered" to be the oldest veteran of the Great War living in the province of New Brunswick. A ceremony was organized to award him a pin for his valour in a Remembrance Day performance orchestrated for the hometown crowd. The local MP, Jake Harris, wanted to regain some of his voter popularity. He had been painted as a dove and this little show of war-linked patriotism would play well in the press. Gordon sat through the exercise unmoving. His hand was raised by a helpful orderly, so that the politician could shake it while the cameras flashed. The crowd left immediately afterward, and, if it weren't for a janitor stacking chairs, Gordon might have been left to sit in an empty room all day. The custodian, who was himself long in the tooth, found a wheelchair and took the old, but now decorated, veteran back to his bunk.

Gordon was filed away and forgotten.

When the General Hospital, in its turn, was abandoned in favour of a new regional facility, he became the subject of concern. The administrators didn't want to ship this "old" patient into their state-of-the-art, shining hospital. Where to put Gordon?

It just so happened, that at that same time, the Buttress Home was mounting a financial campaign. Costs for geriatric care were skyrocketing. They would take Gordon for a price. "After all, 24-hour care is expensive." A deal was struck. The Buttress Home would get a number of upscale hospital beds, an automated dishwasher recently shipped to the old hospital but not needed in the new one, and new bed linens for the entire home. In return, they would also take Gordon.

Done.

How could seventy-five years pass so easily? Gordon rocked his way through each hour of every day, a separate being without contacts.

I bow my head and invite the congregation into God's presence. "Let us now offer our words of confession. Let us pray."

January 15th, 1917

Dear Gordon:

I have a confession to make. We've been snooping about to uncover the identity of this friend you keep mentioning: "Jo." Lil thinks it must be Joseph Breecher who went off about the same time as you did. He was in Montreal when you had your leave and took the same troop ship to France. But I think it's a woman. Am I right?

Dr. Cruikshank preached at our church last week. He and Mr. Hawthorne are great friends. So I asked him if he knew who Jo was. He was uncertain.

I'm betting Jo is a "she." She's your girlfriend. You may not notice it, but you mention her (him?) quite often in your cards. I haven't whispered a word of this to your sisters. They'd tear you apart to get the truth. I am happy for you if Jo is a woman. We all need a companion. I have been blessed by your father ... so blessed.

Did you receive the parcel we sent? It is so hard to know what will be of most use. I packed some medical supplies in with the fruitcake. The military people here say that you need powder for lice and other varmints. How horrible. Anyway I sent them all off—actually Lil took them to the post. As you know I am unable to get around much.

Please don't fret about me. The family makes me as comfortable as possible. My little aches are nothing compared to the stresses that you must endure. I catch glimpses of the agony when I get visits from returning vets. Fred Lewis was over to say that he'd go back in a minute. The fact he has no legs notwithstanding. But I can see there's a lot that is left out. You're not telling me all that has happened, are you? It must be horrendous.

The doctors say I must rest. They never express any hope that I will get better, so I assume I am dying. My fondest wish is to hold out until you return. I do so want to see your face again. You're my special boy, my bonus baby. I recall when you were born. How small and helpless you looked. Why don't babies stay young forever? I loved to play with your chunky feet. You would gurgle and laugh. What a time we had.

To the present. Times are hard. When will this war be over? It hangs like a weight on everyone. Father is well, though increasingly tired. Working hard with his boys at the church. Now he's doing badminton with them. The children are happy. Lil's marriage is just a few weeks off now. She thunders about the house. Thank God I am bedridden or I would be bone-tired carrying out her commands. When did the child become so willful? Anyway, her dress is adorable. Mabel and Eva helped her sew it. We will host a small party here after the service. Just close friends. She and her new husband (it sounds so strange to speak of my eldest as a married woman) will live in the upstairs guest room for the time being. He's talking of going out West in the spring. Something about taking horse teams to farmers in Winnipeg.

Oh, I almost forgot. Dr. Cruikshank said he would keep a place open for you until you return. "Always

room for our brave men at arms, the favoured
of Christ's disciples." Those were his words. He
said he would be down to Montreal for next
Christmas season—some sort of conference—and
would consult with Bishop Hinks of the Diocese of
Montreal about your proper training. Apparently
the good bishop had written him praising you and
your courage.

Gordon, I have a confession to make. It is not easy
to tell you this when I can't see your eyes, but the
sickness makes me rush into things fearing I won't
have another chance. I wanted to tell you so that
you would be able to act after I am gone. Your
Great Uncle Adam, my mother's brother, was, as
you know, an Anglican priest and professor of
church history. He wrote three books, I believe, on
the Council of Chalcedon—beyond me, though
I did try to read each one. I'm straying from my
confession. It is this: I never told you of his last
will and testament. When he died he left a large
portion of his estate in a trust for any of his rela-
tives who might join the priesthood. I thought it a
silly idea at the time. But he was insistent. As you
know, you're the first of any of our clan to take to
the cloth and so this money is yours to use for your
education and also to set yourself up after you
graduate. In fact, the trust was signed over to you
the day you were accepted into Wycliffe College.
Don't misunderstand, you're not rich, but ... well ...
let's put it this way: you won't have to work full-time
if you don't want to. There's just one stipulation.
Adam was funny that way. In your lifetime the
money can be given away, donated to a worthy
cause or shared with a wife or child, if you so

desire, but if you commit suicide the entire amount reverts to the theological college from which you graduated. What a curious condition … but there you have it. Uncle Adam was always a queer duck. No surprise!

Dearest, I may not see you again, so think of this information and my uncle's inheritance as my final blessing to you. The cash now sits in an account in your name—number 00451. The account is held by the Bank of Montreal. You can cable a Mr. Tompkins at their downtown Montreal branch if you want more information.

I must finish off, for my arm grows tired. Eat and sleep, that's all I do.

Please keep me in your prayers as I do you. I am so proud of you and yet so frightened on your behalf.

Love,
Mother

Toronto: Wycliffe College, Tea Time
Friday May 21, 1915, 3:15 p.m.

Ryan had been sitting for an hour and still no mention of the project he had been promised by Cruikshank. No recruiting slogans, no banners, not even a single suggestion of a Holy War. Just endless bickering and gossip.

"He's close to a heretic!"

"Self-righteous prig!"

"I'd love to find some way to pin his feathers."

"I dare say that would be a good thing for mother church. But how?"

"Every armour has its chinks. That's it. 'Hinks has chinks' … what a slogan!"

Every voice was attacking the bishop of Montreal who was apparently making a stir with his declarations about Jesus. Ryan watched and listened. He could sense a brewing crisis. Looked like it was coming to a head in a conference two years hence. Inwardly he laughed, "And I thought the army was dense. All this heat and light over a few inconsequential doctrines. Don't they know that we're at war?"

Ryan shifted in his chair, trying to keep his impatience from showing. His hope began to flag. Maybe it was a dead idea after all. His mind started to drift to the coming evening, when he hoped for a winning time with that gorgeous blond from the typing pool. Could he excuse himself, clean up early and find a flower shop before closing? Maybe she'd like a bottle of perfume or a romantic ….

"It's the war, gentlemen. For heaven's sake! Let's stay focused." Cruikshank broke into Ryan's daydreams with his own loud impatience.

All eyes turned to the principal. "Hinks is a scandal. You're right, but not on account of his outrageous attitude toward Jesus." Here Cruikshank pounded his fist on the armrest of his chair. "No, that's not his heresy. It's his cavalier and traitorous response to the war that troubles me." Sympathetic grumbles were exchanged round the circle. For the first time in the past sixty minutes, Ryan felt a flicker of interest. The principal was not finished. "The war calls every son of mother church to obedience, and if this sorry excuse for a bishop doesn't support our work to have this great conflict declared 'holy,' we'll have to neutralize him and his influence."

Ryan sat up. "Now they're talking," he thought.

"If we are to achieve glory for this land and our Maker, we must not take Hinks lightly. Two years is not a long time to plan and prepare. Although God will inspire hearts with our message, there is nothing the matter with assisting the work of providence."

A voice from the circle asked in an idle tone, "Does he have any kids in the army?" Half-laughing ensued.

Cruikshank turned to the speaker, "Good idea Hawthorne, but I think his son is a musician. Not yet old enough to enlist. However, …" Cruikshank stroked his chin. "However, it's something to watch.

Hawthorne, can you keep an eye on the enlistment records? Like I said, we have a few years to plan and things might change."

Hawthorn agreed. "I'll look into it. Who knows? Hinks may have the kind of rebellious son who would run off to war to spite the old man."

More laughter.

Finally, Ryan coughed and spoke, hoping to move things along more quickly. "So this Holy War *thing* is really going to happen?" Though he tried to mask it, an edge was still lingering in his voice.

The principal turned to his ally and smiled. "We appreciate your patience. All these petty matters of church politics need to be addressed. One bishop, especially a powerful one like the bishop of Montreal, could upset the entire 'thing' as you call it."

Ryan wanted to be helpful, "Anything I can do?"

"For the time being, no. But there may be a moment when information about certain clerics' children's activities in or out of the army might be useful." Cruikshank smiled and Ryan took note.

Saint John: The Buttress Home
Monday, December 23, 1991, 4:10 p.m.

Why couldn't I print a sign? "Take note ... I'm off duty!" Maybe wear it around my neck. It was Monday. Monday was usually my day off. I normally tried to avoid those stops and streets where parishioners might greet me. It's not that I'm anti-social. I just need time alone.

That morning, I took a chance on my favourite restaurant, a popular spot with many Saint John residents called "Reggie's" named after the omnipresent owner, Reginald Baxter. I'd crawled out of bed at 10:00. Surely most customers would be off at their office desks. I nipped down to the deli just in time to get the breakfast special. Reggie's eggs and ham with hash browns were not to be missed. But you had to be prompt. The cook switched the grill over to a luncheon menu on the dot of 10:30. No exceptions.

After polite greetings of the season and a nod to the owner, I was left alone. I dragged with me a stack of library books on the First World War. Most featured glossy fronts showing memorial crosses, rolls of barbwire and men charging over mounds of mud with bayonets drawn. They had obviously been popular, for their jackets were well worn. Prior to meeting Gordon, these graphic war books always seemed too ghoulish for my tastes. Surely in these pages there was a clue to awaken his tongue.

At this point, I had heard just two distinct words from Gordon's mouth. "Jonah" and "rum." The former gave me no clue at all to his state of mind. The latter came with a brief hint. In a whispered, almost confessional tone, he called me his "matey." Something about the navy? Then I recalled the file note that explicitly stated he was wearing an army uniform—albeit badly torn and stripped of insignia—when he was found wandering the streets without sense or sensibility.

Maybe in the well-thumbed pages of war books, I would find some key to unlock Gordon's mystery. If he came back in the fall of 1917, he was more than likely in the third battle of Ypres, the one which historians called Passchendaele. A bloody, muddy mess, a morass where tens of thousands of lives were wasted to capture a few miles of swamp from German defenders. It was a largely useless stretch of land, subsequently lost to the Huns in their 1918 offensive. Passchendaele was to become synonymous with bloodshed and lunacy for it marked the costliest battle ever fought between two opposing armies.

Reggie himself brought my breakfast special to my "office." Setting down the plate, he turned one book to read the title. "Keep reading books like that and you'll have indigestion. What's with the war books? You writing another hot article to upset my wife?" Reggie laughed. "I got a real kick out of it. She was ready to come down here and chew you out over that piece on homosexuality."

I winced. My column for the local paper excites more unwelcome responses than I care to admit. "No, this is just a little research for a visit this afternoon."

"A visit?"

"There's a guy down in the Buttress Home, a World War I vet. I thought some of these ideas might spark his imagination—maybe he'd talk some more."

"Hum ... well, eat hearty, my son." Reggie left me to my books, sure that he would never quite understand the work of a minister. "Better stick to fried eggs," he said to himself.

I pushed aside the ham and hash browns for a moment and closed the books. Who wouldn't go crazy living through that mess? I drank three cups of coffee while watching the passers-by. Gordon, you were right to choose the path of insanity. The war-to-end-all-wars didn't, and the country you swore to defend sold itself for a cheap imitation of well-being. Look at us. Madly spending our hard-earned cash to make up for the fact we don't spend our time as we want, because we are too busy making money to live as we feel we deserve. Who is crazy here? Gordon or the rest of the rat pack?

I turned back to my breakfast—at least some things have lasting quality.

After breakfast, I spent time shopping for a few items for my mother and father. It wasn't until 4:00 that I was free to head toward the Buttress Home.

Once parked beside the building, I fiddled with the communion set. Normally, my small glass vial held grape juice. It was customary to fill the small shot glasses from this flask and then pass them to the penitents in a home or hospital ward. For this visit I had substituted rum for the grape juice. I may be daring, but I'm not stupid. Nurse Simons would catch any underhanded sipping by her patients. No bottles in brown paper bags. I never made a vow of honesty, so I was prepared to camouflage the rum in a communion service, if it would grant Gordon an early Christmas wish. Surely, no one would object to a minister performing his duty?

"Let's see if he remembers his request."

The inside of the home smelt of gingerbread. The cooks were working their way into a festive menu. I mounted the stairs and made my way to Gordon's bed. No one was in sight on ward D. (Does the "D" stand for "demanding" or "deranged"?) A burst of laughter rose up from the stairwell. There must be a party in the main floor parlour.

Gordon sat at his post, rocking. There was a shade of light colouring to his cheeks. His feet seemed to be pushing off from the floor with a bit more purpose.

"Gordon, I've come for a visit before Christmas."

No response.

"I brought Holy Communion."

No response.

"I'll just get set up here, if you don't mind. Okay if I use your night table?" I sat on his bed and opened my case. Six small glasses lay on black velvet, a sterling wafer tin balanced on top. "This is the feast of our Lord, there is none unworthy, none forgotten." I usually offered the service by heart. Reading from the service book didn't seem to make much sense, when it was just the two or three in a circle. Gordon's face was a graven image giving no indication he knew what I was about.

"Let us join in a meal for our benefit." I looked across at Gordon. His rocking was slowing down. The gentle cadence that was his daily grind was now uncertain.

"Peace be with you." Silence fell. Gordon's chair continued to slow down. It was hardly moving. I added the congregational side of the communion litany. "And also with you."

"Lift up your hearts." I waited for the liturgical reply. Gordon's chair was now silent. His mouth moved, but no words came out.

I helped him a bit. "We lift them up to the Lord."

Gordon turned and gave me a dark look as if I had trespassed on his territory.

I resumed the litany. "Let us give thanks to the Lord."

Then weak and frail, like tissue paper rustling, I heard him reply, "It is right to give God thanks and praise."

I tried not to react—a smile broadened over my face as we continued through the Great Prayer of Thanksgiving. It was an ancient collection of entreaties, but Gordon offered no other assistance and did not join in the *Sanctus* nor the final amen.

I consecrated the little dabs of bread and the dribbles of rum (a.k.a. communion grape juice). Handing him a piece of bread, I intoned the well-worn words. "On the night he was betrayed, Jesus took bread, gave thanks and gave it to his disciples saying, 'Take, eat, this is my body broken for you.'"

Frail fingers with long unclipped fingernails gripped the morsel of bread and brought it to waiting lips. His jaws moved slowly as he mashed his bread and swallowed. Then his mouth opened again. "Amen." It sounded sweet and delicate on his lips.

I continued. "In the same manner, once the supper was ended, he took the cup saying, 'This is the new covenant written in my blood, drink this in memory of me.'" I handed him the shot glass of rum and waited.

Again his fingers held the glass, with a slight tremor this time, and then the liquid passed to his lips.

There was cough and a sputter. Most of the rum ran down his front and onto his white undershirt, leaving a red splotch.

"Pew ... ugh ... is that wine, my son?" Gordon didn't move much, but I knew he was angry. His eyes were on fire as were his lips, no doubt.

I whispered, "You asked for rum. The last time I was here. Remember?" I searched his eyes for acknowledgement, but they were blank.

"Nonsense! How dare you corrupt the Lord's meal with a common liquor. Pew ..." He spat on the floor, twice. I hoped Nurse Simmons' attention to detail did not extend to the analysis of telltale spittle beside her patients' beds.

What to do now? "Would you like me to continue?" I was looking for help, confused and little disappointed. Obviously, he was still muddled inside or lacking in memory.

"No."

"All right." I felt a bit ashamed and began to buckle up the communion kit. I took the glass that was still in Gordon's hand, but he resisted.

"Didn't get my wine, yet." He seemed adamant, gripping his glass tightly. His knuckles showed white, when I tried to pry it from his grasp.

I whispered again. "Gordon, all I have is rum. You asked for it last time and I brought it to you. But I don't have wine with me today."

There was a long pause. I thought he hadn't understood and I was ready to leave it with him, when a frail voice sputtered into life.

"Rum then." His voice had a slightly pious tone. He would condescend to my foolishness, just this once. I had an inkling that the man who begged for rum in our previous visit had been replaced by someone else—a more religious fellow, but they both would accept a wee drop, one willingly, the other under duress.

I filled his glass with rum and it went to his lips, he looking down at the liquid with deep concentration. Once it arrived at his mouth it was taken in one great gulp. With a smile on his lips, eyes closed, he concluded our service: "Amen."

Ypres: Canadian Corps Relief Billets behind the front Line
Tuesday, February 13, 1917, 7:12 p.m.

It was the rum ration that ignited Gordon's rage.

For two days after discovering Jo's betrayal, he had been unable to think or breathe. As if in a drugged sleep, he had gone about the chores of a stretcher bearer without comment: dragging men back from the edge, ducking bullets to bring bandages and carrying booze to the forward saps. Not that he was careless. He just lost that cautious edge that had kept him alive so long. His mind was fogged by humiliation. Had he been played the fool?

Luckily the front was quiet. Twice he was tempted to follow Terrance Hinks in his suicide run across no man's land. "Better to end in a hail of bullets." But the fear of only being wounded kept him from going any further than climbing up to the first row of sandbags.

The second evening after "saving" Terry, the mess detail had missed Gordon's outfit because they were huddled off on the west side of a burned-out farmhouse. In the dark, the tattered canvas shelter was almost invisible. Gordon was indifferent, so John Fraser was sent out to beg enough soup for the entire squad. After a few well-chosen words, John persuaded the kitchen to send some rations to their small tent. Stew in a rusted milk tin, nail-hard biscuits, several cans of bully beef and a precious double-sized bottle of rum; the latter, an unspoken apology for the kitchen's negligence.

Gordon was in the corner crouched on his cot and took no notice of the newly-arrived vitals. He was focused on his shirt and the lice that seemed to be permanent tenants in his clothing.

Lice. First you find them. Then you burn them alive using the army issue matches. His search for these bothersome insects blocked out the sounds of his comrades. While the others dug into their meal, he went about his lice-killing. The first match broke in his hands. Trying to light a second match, he cursed the weather. His matches were soggy. "Damn rain. Can't keep anything dry." With his shirt off, Gordon was shivering in the cold as he tried for a third time to light the stubborn matches.

A spark struck and the match leapt into flames. Gordon held the tiny fire close to his shirt's collar.

"The seams you bloody idiot." John had turned from his meal to catch Gordon trying to light his shirt on fire. "The cooties lay their eggs in the seams. That's where you have to catch them."

Gordon adjusted his aim and scorched a number of nests found in an around the armpit area. God, it stank! "Do they ever leave you?"

John was munching on a hard biscuit. It cut into his gums, but it was food. "Hell, no! You just keep their numbers down. Say, Gordie boy, why not have a try at this food? It ain't your ma's, but it's better than nothing." Gordon mumbled a refusal, but John pressed. "Well try some rum then."

Gordon had never used his rum ration, always giving it to the others or storing it in his emergency flask for easing the pain of those he carried. At this moment, he had two full jars waiting for that purpose. Tonight his normal reserve was breaking down. The seething uncertainty over Jo was shut up tight, but it took a tremendous toll on Gordon's energy. "Damn you, Samuel, whoever you are." He could see them touching, lying together, and it made his guts wrench.

The dike would hold no longer. In a flash of un-Anglican zeal, he pulled a cracked cup off the shelf by his head. "Maybe I will take a drop of my ration." John obliged by pouring him a brim-full.

Gordon took a deep swallow and could feel it burn all the way down. His eyes watered, cheeks went scarlet and he fell back into his bunk, smothering a cough. When he spoke it was more like a croak. "Jesus ...."

"Feel better now, matey?" John smiled at Gordon, who was turning a bright red and then turned to joke with his buddies. "Gordie's taken to the bottle, silly bugger. No stopping him now."

They chuckled for they knew Gordon to be a tee-totaller. Rising, John winked at them. "Last night, in his sleep, I hear him raging about some chump named Joe. If only he could get so ticked off at Fritz." John went and sat beside Gordon on his bunk. "We'll make a soldier of you yet, Gordie, my son. Just store up the anger you feel about that Joe fellow for a real battle." John slapped his shoulder and his mates laughed.

The lads were turning to their stew, when an angry snarl came from Gordon's lips, in a voice even he didn't recognize. Stopped them cold. "Johanna! Her name's Johanna and she's a bloody liar and cheat. The little bitch betrayed me. Fuck her." The air hung heavy in the tent—wet and dank. Gordon stood up, looking for somewhere to run. A restless bear. They'd never heard him raise his voice before, let alone swear so pointedly. The group fell silent. Gordon with a lover? It seemed unthinkable.

Unable to stay and explain, unable to talk, breathe or think, Gordon grabbed his overcoat, flung the first aid kit over his shoulder and stomped out. Humiliation burned in his heart. Even at several yards from his billet, he could still hear the excited banter of his mates. "Been stung bad that one! ... Anybody know this Johanna? ... Sounds like a tart to me."

Their voices drifted into faint mumbles as Gordon half-ran toward no place in particular. The February sky was overcast, no stars. His broken spirit pushed his body into a quick march. He brushed past a wire party, rolling their spools toward the front, and kicked over a paint tin of spikes. Someone to his right was snoring loudly. An officer came forward and told Gordon to be more careful. "Noise attracts snipers, son." Gordon nodded politely, but carried on in his breakneck manner. He didn't give a shit who heard him or shot him! His life was over.

He still held a half-filled cup of rum. Taking another swig, he emptied the cup. That took away the chills nibbling at his fingers. This time it went down without a cough. Gordon let the cup drop into a mud puddle. It gave a soft splutter and was gone. In minutes, his quick strides had brought him to the edge of his camp; nowhere to go but out.

Reaching into the first aid kit, Gordon drew out the first of his two emergency flasks of rum. "Bloody good stuff." He shook the bottle to discover it was full and ready for business. "Now, aren't you grand?" he addressed his bottle. "Hey, sister, how about you and me passing the night together?" The flask made no reply and Gordon took a quick nip and then stumbled up a small rise in the plain.

It was an hour before he ceased his wanderings. The night was deeper and the sounds of battle snipers' shots and artillery fire were now distant. He could rest. Slumping down beside a broken fence post he took a swig from his second emergency flask—the first having been discarded a few swallows back. "Nectar of the gods. Don't know why I didn't drink it before." The drink was blurring his mind. "No, I don't."

The anger inside burst like thunder on the half-drunken soul. "Jesus-fucking-Christ ... what did I do to deserve this?" Gordon took another swallow of rum and on its heat he lashed out, "I'll fix her wagon. I'll write the little witch and tell her how her brother really died."

So he composed his venom-slurred message.

> Dear Jo:
>
> Your brother died like a little fucking fool; a coward
> he ran from his post and got himself shot.
>
> Best regards,
> Gordon
>
> P.S. Who the fuck is Samuel?

Gordon laughed at his letter. "She'll shit bricks when she gets it. Hope she pukes until she turns white. Bloody bitch." He took a deep draught of rum and set about revising his invective.

> Dear Miss Hinks:
>
> I have the regrettable duty of informing you that
> your brother is a yellow-bellied bastard who got
> his sorry ass shot off because he ran away, and
> deserted his post. I hope this doesn't distress

you too much. The army gave him a posthumous
dishonourable discharge.

Yours sincerely,
Mr. G. Davis.

P.S. I hope Samuel, whoever he is, goes blind
with syphilis.

Drunken laughter spilled out of his mouth and dribbled down his
bare chest. He couldn't help it. It began as small chuckle but developed
into a hysterical and unbounded wail. Soon it turned to tears and he
wept until he was hoarse. Hugging the bottle to his chest he rocked
back and forth, a single word coming from his lips.

"Jo .... Jo .... Jo ...."

Fate was not with Private Gordon Davis on that night, for his crumpled, slumbering body was found by Major C. Ryan, D.S.C., M.C. who
was returning to the front after a brief encounter with a French mistress
he used for his pleasure.

Whistling a marching tune, Ryan's quick eye spotted the khaki in
the grass by the side of the road and immediately thought the worst.
Gordon was snoring. His greatcoat draped over one shoulder, leaving
the other bare. The second emergency bottle, now three-quarters empty,
still in his hand, the picture of a deserter.

"Blast, another bloody coward," the Major muttered as he climbed
down into the ditch to shake this man to his senses. "Makes sixteen this
week alone."

Applying the steel tip of his riding boot to Gordon's ribs, he cursed
his luck, at being stuck with such undisciplined, backwoods men like
these Canadians. After several kicks, his efforts produced a grunt. Eyes
began to open in the drunken mess at his feet.

"Wake up, soldier," Ryan shouted, his venom thick. "You're in deep
shit now."

Groggy, startled by the command and uncertain of his surroundings,
Gordon tumbled to his feet. He wiped a dew-drenched sleeve across his
eyes, leaving a long smudge of dirt. Not a pretty sight.

Through the blur of a pressing headache he recognized his commanding officer. "Sir!" He gave a respectable salute and managed to look like he was at attention, even though his mind was still half-asleep.

"What's the matter with you, private? Why aren't you with your outfit?" Ryan didn't really expect nor want a reply. He enjoyed chewing out a lowly subordinate. "You look a mess. You've been drinking and have deserted your company." There was an unmistakable sneer in his voice. "Grounds for a court-martial, I'd say."

Gordon tried to keep his fear from showing. His knees were unable to withstand the strain and he folded back down onto the roadside.

Pleased that his bark still struck like thunder, Ryan marched off to find the provosts. Over his shoulder he commanded the private to "wait right there." If he were lucky he'd have the military police back in a flash to escort this deserter to his just punishment.

It surprised no one, least of all Gordon, that he was thrown into detention for seventeen days. In fact, the authorities were being lenient. His sergeant pleaded his case to a quickly assembled panel of inquiry, "Silly sod lost his girl back in Canada. Everyone's entitled to one good piss-up after being jilted."

Even though Ryan lodged a formal complaint with his superiors, the Canadian military judiciary was not prone to punish one of its own just because a Brit was ticked off. Didn't matter how many stripes he wore on his cuff.

Their judgment was final. "Undue duress in soldier's personal life" was what was written in his record—a footnote mentioning Major Ryan's protest was all that his frustration achieved.

Montreal: Mount Royal Park (Sisson Ridge)
Thursday, March 23, 1916, 12:35 p.m.

Though the air between them was tingling with intoxicating emotions, Johanna wanted to keep sober, for the moment.

"I have a confession to make." Jo's hand was resting firmly on Gordon's knee. Sitting on a park bench near the lookout, a blanket was laid out on the grass before them. The sun warmed the hillside; the snow was almost gone. Gordon was gazing at a small green shoot poking its head above the winter-burned grass. Slender and fragile, easily ground under by a passing foot. Oddly, it reminded him of himself; a small sapling trying to reach the sun, the sun being Johanna Hinks.

Jo gripped his knee firmly. "Are you listening?"

Gordon came back from his dreams and looked at her. She wasn't kidding this time. "All right, I am sorry. I was just thinking about what our child would look like."

"What? Our child? Don't be so silly. We've know each other— what—four days and nights and you have us married with children."

"Who said anything about marriage?"

"Aren't you a man of the world?" Jo laughed. "You're a fine postulant for the priesthood. Having a young maiden's children before wedlock." She slid to the blanket, reached down and plucked a bit of dry turf and threw it his way, a gesture almost as intimate as the touch of her hand. He joined her on the blanket.

There was a silence as each looked at the other. The electricity that passed between them was constant, a current not to be resisted. Frighteningly close.

Gordon searched his mind for something to say. "You said this is Sisson Ridge?"

Lunch was spread and waiting. A few chunks of cheddar, a round of sourdough bread and three precious oranges. It was a meagre feast, but in their eyes, it sparkled with Solomon's grandeur.

"Yes. Officially they call it 'Parc de la Montagne Royale,' but I've always preferred my family's name."

They shifted to sit side by side. Hands moved closer and touched. Gordon felt like he was melting. Johanna knew she was flying. The food waited as their hands intertwined.

"Listen." Johanna gripped his knee again. "I said I had a confession to make and I want to get it out of the way so that we can spend the afternoon in peace." She picked up a small piece of cheese and began to nibble.

"I'm listening." A snake was coiling in his stomach. Was she going to tell him there is someone else or that she'd was going to take religious vows? Maybe she had a fatal disease?

"I've had another man before you, Gordon."

Gordon gulped and didn't know how to reply. Apparently, there was no need for she wasn't pausing. Taking a deep breath, reconciling her past with the present, she continued: "You see before you a very nice girl. Some say I'm pretty—" Gordon made to interrupt her, but she cut him short. "No, let me get this all out and then I'll feel better."

Jo paused and then pushed onward. "If I can't say it all now, I might never have the courage again … Ah. Some say I have good looks and a quick wit— I guess it's true—there were always plenty of young men buzzing about the house, especially after Mother died. One was more attractive than most and I fell for him, hard. Maybe it was misplaced grief over Mum's passing or loneliness. I don't know how it happened, but I was in love before you came along. How silly, 'before you came along.' Sounds like we've been together forever. In a way I think we have. Anyway this other fellow was alive and funny. He tickled my fantasies and I believed I was joined to him. Gordon, you'll think me terribly loose, but I kissed him often and lay beside him as well."

Gordon gulped again. Jo's stature was strangely rising and falling at the same time.

"We were young." Jo broke her stride, reflecting on the intervening time. "That's over-stating my case. It was only a year ago, but I was much younger back then …. Really I was. I felt that if I didn't give my body to some male, I wasn't really in love." She cast her eyes down and did not see Gordon's dismay. "Steven, that's his name, he was my knight." She looked up suddenly and stared directly at Gordon. She would let no pretense of shame mar her confession. "I was willing. Of course, he pushed and pried until finally I agreed. But I also wanted it to happen."

Gordon swallowed hard, made as if to speak and then realized he had nothing to say.

Trying to inject lightness she didn't feel into her voice, Jo added, "After it was all over, and there wasn't much to it, I was disappointed and ashamed. It was the first time, but not at all my dreams come true."

Gordon was trying to conjure up exactly what the "it" looked like, but couldn't. He finally found his footing on a more familiar path and supplied a simple absolution. "Jo, you have a clean heart, I know that." Gordon shook his head. "No, that sounds like a pious Sunday school moralism." He snatched at a piece of cheese, chewed it hastily. "What I want to say is that I know you are honest in your dealing with people. You have no reason to be ashamed."

Jo smiled her thanks. "I didn't want you to picture me as the virtuous maiden who held out until she was forced. I went willing to his bed, but it wasn't what I had expected. Anyway, to put it bluntly, I am not a virgin and if that is important to you …. You'd better …."

"Jo …. I …." Gordon could feel his morals slipping onto thin ice, but he couldn't let her punish herself further. "I would never think any less of you."

Jo bowed her head and let go of his knee. It was all out. He could walk away or stay. Which would it be?

"I don't think any less of you," Gordon continued. "*It* is not something I know anything about, so I don't feel I have any place to make a judgment. I'm sure you were caught in the moment. And I don't see you as a loose woman. You're a delight to be with … rather like a beacon to me."

"You're too kind and a bit dishonest." Jo was a very keen judge of men and she could see Gordon was torn and uncertain. "It is never easy to accept that our ideals are a bit tarnished."

Gordon thought back to his dismay over the behaviour of his hometown priest. "I know what you mean." But he was still too young and green to understand the conflicting torrents of erotica and passion. What else could he add?

Finding nothing else to say, he bent close to her face and brushed his lips against hers. It wasn't really a kiss, not a lover's caress, not yet. But it had an intoxicating sweetness. He closed his eyes and could feel her hand reach around behind his neck. Her full lips came back to his with a fierce urgency and he was swimming in light. He would dissolve into the hillside if she kept up. He wanted the moment never to end.

Jo was lost. There was no hillside. There was no picnic. No confession or confusion. Only the ocean's depth of connection. "Kiss me forever," she thought. His touch was so slight and yet so blinding.

Sisson Ridge lodged itself in their souls' memories as a place of deep delight.

They pulled apart and looked at each again—long and hard. The promise was made. It was clear and firm.

"Are you upset with me?" Jo asked without flinching. "I don't want you to lie, not now."

Gordon mumbled his truth. "I would be less than honest if I didn't say I was a bit dismayed. But ... but ... I am new to love and have been fed dreams of virginity. I ... I mean ... you will be able to teach me and that does excite me."

"Really?"

"Really!"

She kissed him again. God it was heavenly! Gordon could feel his stomach turning somersaults, his body moving into the kiss, deeper and deeper.

Johanna finally pushed herself free, smiling and fresh. "Not now ... soon, very soon ... but not like this. I have a plan." Gordon was left with a delicious sensation in his groin. "Soon?"

"Soon!" Johanna rose to her feet. "Let's walk off our passion, shall we?" When she was happy, all the candles inside were lit. Who could resist that fire? She extended a hand to Gordon and pointed up the hill. "Maybe we'll see our dreams from up there." Jo led the way.

Gordon followed along willingly. "What was her plan?" he wondered. He had no idea where she was heading. He only knew that he didn't want to fall behind. As they headed toward the summit observation platform, he knew that the real challenge was emotional, not physical. She had an honesty and self-assurance that it was hard for him to match. Would she desert him, when she knew who he really was—the frightened boy wanting above all else to be loved?

They found a bench at the summit and sat as one body entwined. In months to come he would take that Sisson Ridge walk again and again and sit with her on the park bench. Each forced march, every

6

night patrol was kept bearable by that first lover's walk. And the kiss? In the freezing cold slime of France, he could still feel her hot lips pressing against his own.

"If we ever get lost," Jo said finally, "Come to this bench ... the memory of love will guide you."

Saint John: Centenary-Queen Square United Church
Tuesday, Nov. 17, 1992, 11:20 a.m.

> *Creator, Father and Mother of us all, hear us now as we offer our words of confession to you. It is at times of death that we feel our failings most deeply. The grave shuts off all possibility for apology or reconciliation. Comfort us now, dear God, for we know we have broken our word....*

I keep reading the prayer of confession but my mind strays. How we wish we could change. Our script has been written for ages gone by. It is only the exceptional man or woman who can rewrite their part in this unending play.

Confession is our only outlet—the place where we admit that we are trapped.

My thoughts wander to the weekly article, which, of all things, had been written about confessions. Then I am on to the growing to-do list. Finally, I rehearse my missed visits ... my personal confessions.

I push back these nagging thoughts and return my concentration to the confession at hand—Gordon's.

> *Oh Ancient of Days, protect us from ourselves, shield us from our best intentions and forgive us our high ideals ... We ask these things through him who knew betrayal and fear, abandonment and temptation, Jesus Christ your son.*

And the few scattered voices reply, "Amen."

Montreal: Thelma Lint's Gentlemen's Parlour
Monday, April 9, 1916, 11:57 p.m.

"Was this the temptation into which I pray regularly *not* to be led?" Bishop Hinks paused on Aylmer Street outside a four-storey Georgian mansion. Yellow-and-white striped awnings covered the windows. Wind chimes fluttered in the breeze sending soft notes cascading down the street. A neat hedge lined the walk. A brass doorknob and eagle-head knocker gleamed on the oak front door. It was the kind of stately home that might well receive the likes of an Anglican bishop.

Thelma called it a "parlour," and, indeed, there was a polished plaque in the main hall that read "Gentlemen's Parlour." It sounded like a club filled with leather couches, cigar smoke, old grumpy men and sherry. There were couches, and old grumpy men and Thelma could supply any liquid the heart desired. But no smoke. She said it was bad for her girls.

It looked so decent and above-board, but Bishop Hinks knew it was really just a lace-lined and oh-so-discrete whorehouse.

He came once every few months. All pre-arranged, a streamlined entry with no questions asked. A short visit to relieve his tensions. Thelma knew his special needs and had become a friend and confidant. After his wife's death, he came to her with all the pains of raising stubborn children and a lost church. In a curious way, Hinks' dual functions, father and cleric, were not dissimilar: enforcing good table manners and keeping the night demons at bay.

The soft aroma of sandalwood greeted him. A maid came forward, to offer assistance. As he handed over his umbrella and gloves, he snagged the silver chain of his ever-present cross in a finger of the umbrella's cloth. "Damn thing always gets in the way." Hinks absent-mindedly stuffed the cross into his right vest pocket. "Enough of Jesus for tonight," he thought. Dusting off his shoulders, he tried to slick back the sides of his head. His curls became unrulier as he grew older.

Gazing around at the familiar surroundings, Hinks wondered how often he had found the peace that passes understanding in this place rather than his own church.

The maid broke into his thoughts. "Is there anyone you wish to meet?" She had returned from disposing of his outer garments and winked at him with a knowing smile.

"Yes ... thank you ... I have a regular appointment with Thelma." Hinks gave a brief smile.

"Mrs. Lint? Are you sure?" The front door maid was puzzled. She had only been at her post for a few days, but she knew that no one asked for Mrs. Lint. Not anymore. She was past the game. "Sir, I can call her, but perhaps you would like to sit with one of our more ... our more versatile matrons."

Hinks was getting impatient. The longer he stood in the vestibule the greater the chance of running into one of his own priests. Heaven forbid that any should be here—they'd bankrupt themselves with Thelma's prices. Hinks had a personal fortune to call on. It would be damned embarrassing and he shouldn't have to stand for it. "Miss ... ah ...."

"Blushlips!"

Hinks couldn't help a wry smile. "Miss Blushlips, it has all been arranged. I am a regular ... guest ... with Mrs. Lint and I only need you to announce my presence. She is waiting for me. So ... please lead the way."

"Sir ... yes ... of course." The maid scolded herself, "How stupid of me! Of course the old girl still has her regulars. What they see in her, who knows, but the world's a queer place." She led the way and said evenly, "Mrs. Lint is in her sitting room."

They went through an oak-paneled hallway and ascended a curving staircase. Mrs. Lint's chambers took up the front rooms of the second floor. At Thelma's door, he waited as the maid went forward to announce him. He studied the exquisite watercolours that graced the walls in the upper hallway. He couldn't place the artist, but the scenes of Montreal came alive under his or her hand.

"Mrs. Lint will receive you now, my Lord." Obviously the young, Miss Blushlips, whose real name was "Grace," had been informed of his rank and position. Thelma was a harsh matron on that account. This was a "gentlemen's" parlour and that meant respect, titles and deference to the patrons whenever possible. Her foundational rule—the line the girls recited jokingly to each other after their sexual encounters—was: "You can never say 'thank you' too often."

"Douglas, get in here." A husky, inviting voice at his ear. "Stop sizing up my art collection. It's all willed to the Diocese when I die, so you'll get it soon enough." Thelma was leaning suggestively close, a few steps from her boudoir.

The maid was dismissed with a nod from Thelma. The matron of this whorehouse was hardly built for the job. She boasted a small, trim frame. Narrow hips, and a thin waist. Short legs, slender feet. These things Hinks knew by heart. Thelma had a warm and intelligent face. Not stunning, but bright in its inflections. The jaw was angular, a dimple setting it off well. Her high cheekbones and broad forehead were not classically beautiful, but intriguing. Thelma's lips were now lined in bright red rouge. Waiting and wonderful. But it was actually her piercing blue eyes that worked the magic. They shone brilliantly and clearly, missed nothing and overlooked much.

Her deep, lustrous voice was quick to laugh, slow in deceit. Most men couldn't say why, but there was little question Thelma was extremely attractive. Even at her seven-and-forty years, she was a woman to be desired—not only physically, but also as a mental, perhaps even spiritual partner. She was the most attractive woman Hinks had ever met, including his now deceased wife. She had a beguiling spirit that was beyond his resistance.

Hinks took her kidding in stride and held out an arm to escort her further into her chambers.

"My lady."

"My Lord." Thelma took his arm and they waltzed into her sitting room.

"Is your name really 'Thelma' or did you pick it with an eye to your clientele?"

"Thelma Margaret-Ann Lint. I never want to deceive. The world can take me as I am or not at all." Thelma sat on a red brocade *chaise longue*. Swinging her legs onto a well-placed cushion at her feet, her white silk kimono fell open to reveal well-sculpted legs.

Hinks couldn't help notice the art with which she plied her trade. "What a gift God gave you in that body." He paused to undo a tab and pull off his clerical collar. "Let me rephrase that. What a gift God gave you in the *movement* of that body. I would wonder what our world would be like if we were all so graceful."

"There'd still be a need for my business. Men tire of beauty as quickly as ugliness."

"Really?" Hinks loved her mind, the grasp of common sense wisdom that was uniquely Thelma's.

"Come, come, my Lord. You're not that dense. Men come here like fireflies to a mirror. It's not the sex they crave. It's the idea of being seen and adored by someone new. To parade your wares before a fresh face. That's what sex trading is all about. Sure men want to prove to themselves that they can still seduce a lovely lady. That's part of it. But mostly they crave the thrill of being known *one* dimensionally. Marital affairs are about living the lie of perfection. To be an Adonis without wrinkles or farts, even if it's only for one night," she chuckled. "That's close to immortality for most men."

"If that's the case why do I always come back to you?" Hinks was ready for a battle of wits.

"But you don't always call for me, do you?"

Hinks winced. How did she know about the other women? They were just a few flings to keep his mind off work. Damn the women's network. "You know?"

"I have a friend who makes it her business to keep tabs on the big players. You should be proud you made it into her league. She's never indiscrete. Don't look so shocked. We women of the world need our own weapons to protect ourselves. How do you think I stay in business? Because I buy savings bonds and give to the mayor's favourite charity?" Laughter winked at him from her eyes. "Give me more credit. We use a system of gentle reminders to keep the wheels of justice from turning in our direction. Simple and effective. No one gets hurt and we keep up our labours in this essential industry during war times." There was mirth in her words. "Oh, sit down, Douglas, and stop looking so surprised." Thelma shifted her legs to make room, allowing the front of her gown to fall open. "I believe I have something in here," she tugged slightly on the tie that held her silk gown in place, "that you would like."

"You know how to seduce a man, Thelma. That I grant you. None of the others can give me the shakes as you do."

"Honey-tongued Bishop." Thelma used two hands to undo her gown, letting its sides fall around her body. She gave him a few seconds to adore her wonders and then pulled him onto her. "I've missed you." Thelma had grown a thick shell around her heart and had but a few clients now, but Douglas was her favourite—would she call him a "lover"? It wasn't so much his body that she craved, though he was in good nick for a sedentary older man. It was his mind and heart that touched her.

Hinks allowed himself to let go of the natural propriety of his office as his hands hungrily found her breasts, beginning a delicately slow massage. "God, I've wanted to come to you for a month, but life has been too busy. That damned synod meeting went on for …."

"Hush now. Lord Bishop, be gone. I want Douglas, the man, to make love to me. Now … come, Douglas. Let the church go for a few hours." She fumbled with his clerical vest, lifted the cross out of his pocket for it was cutting into her breast. "What will we do with Jesus?"

Douglas laughed and rose to his feet. She watched him as he undid his buttons and zippers, folded and fixed his clothes. She half-rose and slipped a hand on either side of silk undershorts. A quick tug and he was free. Naked, they looked at each other. She muttered again "I've missed you. 'Come into my bedroom, said the spider to the fly.'" She reached out a hand.

With that invitation they walked together into her holy of holies. They never kissed. That was beyond the boundaries, but all the other pleasures were explored fully.

Did they sleep? Douglas couldn't remember. He had enjoyed the dreamy state of half-waking. Stroking her breasts and thighs, he could remain enmeshed with her slender body for a lifetime.

He rolled to his side so he could enjoy her curves. A deep sigh escaped his lips.

"It's Johanna, isn't it?"

"What?" Douglas' daydreaming was cracked open. "Johanna?"

"You're worried about your daughter. Am I right?" Thelma moved onto her side and propped herself up on one elbow and watched his face.

"Damn you woman, how do you read my mind?"

"It's your body that I read, Douglas. You came here because you were tense. I could see the worry in your eyes. And we haven't made love that fiercely since you were elected bishop. What is it? Have you just discovered your daughter is a woman?"

"Well, yes ... I suppose I have. I mean ... she has always been mature for her age. But with this Gordon fellow .... I mean. Well, there's no point in denying it. She's fallen head-over-heels for a postulant, Gordon Davis by name, a young man preparing for the priesthood under the bishop of Hamilton." Hinks began to rub his temples with two fingers of each hand to help with tension, but only made matters worse.

Thelma gently removed his clumsy fingers. It looked like he was trying to polish his skin; he was rubbing so harshly. She began more soothingly. "So? Is it all that bad? At least he'll carry on the family business," Thelma chuckled.

"It's no laughing matter, Thelma!" The bishop flopped his head back with a groan and closed his eyes in ecstasy. "How do you do that so well?"

"C'est mon metier."

"I see. As preaching is mine," Hinks laughed.

"Exactly." Thelma was not to be side-tracked for long. "So what's the matter with this young man? Does he have two heads, no brains? Too pious for you?"

"No, no and no," Hinks responded too quickly. He was obviously more than a bit defensive on Gordon's behalf.

Thelma's eyebrows rose slightly. "You like him, too?"

"Not really I ... well ... maybe a bit."

The matron smiled. "So what's the problem?"

"He's a god-damned soldier and he has just arrived in France. That's the problem!" Hinks could spit he was so upset. "He was passing through Montreal with his unit when he visited my home and the two of them met. Their relationship was like a forest fire it spread so fast. Now the blighter is off to the trenches of this bloody war leaving Johanna at home in complete desolation."

Thelma's fingers stopped mid-stroke. "Oh shit. Douglas, why didn't you stop them? Is she truly in love?"

"To the first question, I couldn't and to the second, I believe she is. Yes." He paused waiting for some reply, but Thelma was thinking. Hinks continued "I am surprised at her in a way. This fellow is a quiet type. Lots of gentleness, no outward pizzazz! I can never understand Johanna's tastes."

"Is she mothering him? Maybe he has a wounded wing she wants to mend."

"Oh saints save us. I hope not. Her first fellow was a hopeless mess of welts and whimpers." Douglas gave further thought to the strange lad, Gordon Davis. "Damn it. He's gotten to me too. I can't comprehend it, but I feel lonely without him underfoot." He grimaced at the notion. "Ridiculous, really. He was only at the house a handful of times. But he had a sparkle that endeared him quickly. Imagine, each day I scan the lists for his name, dreading I'll find it."

"What does she do?"

"The same thing, though with her special brand of enthusiasm. Nothing by fractions. Johanna writes once a week without fail. He's equally faithful. It's a hot little romance. Of course, the flames are fanned by distance and danger."

"This may be her One, Douglas. Don't discount it, whatever you do." Thelma let her fingers go back to work on his temples. "Maybe you're a wee bit jealous because she's found a decent man, perhaps a keeper, and her attention is divided."

Douglas winced for the second time that evening. "You're cutting too close to the bone, Thelma. I suppose I am jealous. He's handsome enough, cuts a fine figure in his uniform. And there are signs, a hint, that given some time and the hard knocks of a battlefield, he'll give her a run for her money."

"Sounds promising. I'd say you have nothing to worry about. If he's killed, she's off the hook. If he lives, she's got herself a running mate. Does he really have the intellectual strength to stand up to Johanna?"

"Indeed. I received a note from the principal of his college. Cruikshank's the fellow's name. We studied together once. I find the man obnoxious, but he mentioned that Gordon entered with the highest standing in the history of his institution. The kid's got brains, not that you'd ever notice. Hmm ... I suppose it is a bit of grief. My little girl is growing up."

"Is he in any danger over there? What's his unit?"

"Oh ... that's the one bright spot. He's pretty safe. He joined the medical corps as a stretcher bearer."

Thelma sat bolt upright. "No danger! Douglas, do you know nothing about war?"

"No ... what is it?" Hinks saw fear in Thelma's eyes. "He'll be safe surely, just taking wounded men out of harm's way. Simple."

Thelma looked down at her naive lover with dismay. "It's one of the most dangerous jobs in the army right now. With both sides locked in their trenches all day, who do you think they take shots at to relieve the tension?"

Hinks paled. "You can't be serious? He's a neutral, a medical officer .... Surely, they wouldn't ...."

"Sometimes you church people are so damned naive." Thelma cast about in her frustration. "This is war, Douglas. How many returned men have taken up their leave in this very house boasting of the German red crosses they have buried? And while all the bullets are flying about, what do you suppose Gordon uses to defend himself? A canvas stretcher?"

"Jesus, Mary and Joseph ...." Hinks was deep in thought. "Do you think Johanna knows all this?"

"I wouldn't tell her, if I were you."

"Me? Never. Apart from her brother Terrance, this Gordon chap is the rising sun of her life."

"How is Terry?" Thelma was looking for a more comforting topic and pulled him up off his back and worked around behind him. Her expert hands worked the doubts from his shoulders as knotted muscles began to unravel.

"He's still loving music. What a reckless kid. He's just fine, but the war will get him too before long. I can feel him working up to answer the call. He hasn't said anything, but I know he's been down to the recruiting office. God help Johanna, if he joins up too!"

"Don't think about that now. Let me take your mind off your burdens. Isn't that why you came?" She ran a hand down over his chest and could feel him stirring again.

Douglas smiled and let the time and magic flow. "My angel of mercy."

Ypres: Canadian Corps Detention Cell Block
Thursday, March 1, 1917, 6:30 a.m.

The time plodded heavily from behind prison walls. He had only a few more hours until he was released back to his duties at the front line. Seventeen days. The world could disappear in that time, though the word from the guards was that it hadn't. In fact, aside from exchanging a few hundred yards this way or that, the battle lines were pretty much as he had left them.

Apart from a loose-tongued corporal who brought the bread and water each morning and evening, with extra helpings of gossip, he had seen no one. He had no idea what had happened to his squad or his buddies at the front. They were due for leave. Did they get it? "Isolation must be part of the punishment," he whispered to the four walls. No response came.

The floor was greasy with damp mould and what light there was came through a hole by the cell door. He could see very little about his small chamber, even after his eyes adjusted. He found out, upon his release, that he had been thrown into a converted barn cellar. His own wastes were taken out each day in a bucket—the same corporal acting as agent of the chamber pots, but the urine smell lingered, clogging his senses.

Regaining some sense of balance on his first sober day, he set about the grueling task of writing to Jo about her brother. It would be three weeks before he could send a note. He had nursed his pity, but Jo's smiling face came back to him, the sunshine on her smile at St. Matthias Church. She deserved better of him than recrimination. He had no pen or paper, but after several hours of false starts, he had composed a reasonable note. The empty days that followed were time enough to polish away any rough ridges of resentment. In the end, he had it memorized perfectly. Rehearsing it daily along with his prayers was the only way to stay sane.

He pictured her. She was opening his letter. He could see her delicate fingers tearing off the end and sliding out his one page. Would she cry? Was Terry's memorial service a fading memory by this time? Or maybe Gordon's message would be the first indication of anything going awry with her brother.

With a head made cooler by days of solitary confinement, he hoped that, whatever the circumstance, his words would bring the solace and comfort that she and her father deserved. A few white lies and a certain amount of fudging, and it worked well.

Dear Johanna:

I confess I am a coward. Did you know that already?

It has been a month since I pledged to write to you about Terry. I suspect the army has already conveyed its regrets over his death, but they can be so nondescript. Could I be more personal? I was with him when he died and each time I took up a pen to express my sympathy, I have been overcome with both remorse and longing. Remorse over his death, longing for you. So I was unable to begin for I could picture your tears. It is only with a deep desire to help lighten your burden that I send my condolences along with a few details of his final hour. I know how much he meant to you and your father.

He was wounded in no man's land, a desert flowing with mud rather than sand. It's indescribable. I was called out to bring back a fallen man and had no idea it was Terry. (He must have

arrived recently, since I knew most of the boys
down the line.) He was badly hit in the leg and
stomach and I am not sure if he would have made
it beyond a few days. But we were unable to test
his endurance, for as I dragged him back to our
lines, he shielded me from sniper fire and was
himself killed.

It was a courageous act, one for which I owe
a debt of honour that I can never repay. I will
always remember him as the man who saved my
life. Though he is gone, I hope you will be able to
rest more easily, knowing that he did his duty and
gave himself, not only for me, but for many others
as well.

If I get back to Canada, I will be able to explain
the day more completely. For now, I am overwhelmed with gratitude for his sacrifice and sorrow
for his passing.

My love is with you, and you alone,
Gordon

Gordon was pleased with his skill. The last phrase was his promise
to her. She could do whatever she wanted with his affection except
pretend it didn't exist.

For the rest, he hadn't lied about any detail, just carefully shielded
Jo from the harsh realities of this dismal battleground. He hoped he
would never be called upon to make good his promise of more details.
The chances seemed greater as each week passed that he'd never return
to Canada. If he did, he had many months to work up a credible story.

Gordon couldn't imagine anyone who could contradict his tale.
Fortunately, Terry had been so new to the line that none of his trench-
mates knew him enough to meddle. The army would be discrete. The
last thing they wanted was to broadcast the spectre of a new recruit,

driven mad by fear and rats, running amok. Gordon was confident his secret would be safe. The family would never know the whole truth.

As he was pondering the niceties of keeping skeletons in the closet, the door of his cell was banged open. "Get up, Davis. You're a free man." The jailor held the door ajar and pointed to the outside. The prisoner needed no more invitation and leapt to his feet.

Gordon couldn't wait to strip off the ratty clothes he had worn for weeks and find a clean pair of underwear and an open air meal. Even canned bully beef sounded tasty after his dark meals alone.

"Hold it, Davis. Not so fast." The corporal gripped the fleeing bird with an iron grip.

Gordon was momentarily stunned. Was there more punishment yet to be meted out? Had he forgotten to salute or make whatever obscene gesture the rule book required?

"Your mail." A gruff hand pushed forward a single letter. There was no comment, no excuse. According to army protocol, deserters, even if they were love struck, didn't deserve even common courtesies like their letters from home. Mail was withheld until their time was served.

"That's it?" Gordon felt relief. "I can go?"

"See the captain at the front for details of where your unit has been posted."

"Thank you, sir!" Gordon snapped a salute and went off down the dimly lit corridor. He heard the guard push the door closed behind them. "And, Davis ..." Gordon halted in his tracks. "Keep your fucking nose clean."

"Yes, sir!"

It took a few minutes to find his unit. The officers in charge of the detention centre couldn't recall where his squad was stationed. Luckily a messenger who carried new orders to all military police units was able to enlighten them. Gordon's squad had shifted down the line several miles to the south ... they had been denied leave, as it turned out.

He set off at a smart walk, hoping to reach his platoon in time for rations.

The letter burned in his hand, but there were some basic necessities to be remedied first.

When he finally found his chums, they welcomed him with open cans of beef, a few new jokes. He was introduced to the fresh recruits, given their nicknames, and, in fifteen minutes, it was as if he had never been absent.

Snipers fired back and forth; one wounded officer needed his services. It was several hours before he turned to his correspondence. He knew it was a letter from Jo, and he dreaded it what it might contain. His hands were shaking as he opened it.

Halifax Harbour: Durham Street
Thursday, December 6, 1917, 9:25 a.m.

Gordon was shaking. How long he had been walking? It felt like hours as the pain in his leg increased. He feared his mind might be slipping. It happened to many in the trenches—loss of blood meant loss of short-term memory. He shook his head, trying to regain some sense of time and space.

Immediately after the explosion, the air bore ash mixed with the rain, turning the streets and faces black, but now a light snow had replaced it as the temperature dropped. He muttered as he walked, with each footfall, "This is crazy."

Down an alley he saw soldiers hoisting small bodies onto a wagon. Children! The rescuers moved with dignity, and placed each tiny corpse with respect, but the sight of small limbs piled high was more nauseating than anything Gordon had seen in France. Fighting men expected death, but kids?

His own charges whimpered, and he could feel their fear. Everything in the north end of the city was demolished. All their landmarks were gone, and with them the sights and sounds that offered security. "Hush now, we'll have you right as rain, in no time." His gruff voice sounded miles away, choked by his own shock.

Gordon looked about for some sense of direction. Street signs had been buried along with the telegraph wires and masonry walls. He shouted to one of the soldiers, "Which way to the hospital? I've two wounded children here."

The man looked back, sadness, maybe desperation in his eyes. "Mate, they're full up everywhere, but your best bet would be the Victoria General, corner of Robie and South Streets. More than a mile away, past the Citadel and turn right." With those vague instructions he went back to the tomb where so many little lives had been lost.

Gordon had no idea about street names or directions. Obviously, south was the route to safety. He could ask again. The pain in his leg was rising. "Feels like a bullet wound," he thought. His arms ached from hefting the burden of two very frightened children. For the next ten minutes, they whimpered off and on. Slow going. Rubble was everywhere. Walking was a treacherous business. Gordon desperately wanted them to walk on their own, but each time he set them down, they screamed and clutched his neck to the point of strangulation. Their minds were addled by shock and no amount of reassurance could penetrate the fog that gripped them. They hugged his neck, as if it was a lifeline. His rest breaks were becoming more frequent as his arms ached for rest.

As the threesome ventured south, the city looked more like the ruins of Ypres than a bustling and safe Canadian town. People everywhere were lamenting, "Who could do this?" Expletives about the Germans were rife. "Bloody Huns have no decency." "God damn Germany, it's filled with devils." "Did you see the Zeppelin attacking?" "Must have been a secret weapon. God help us!" "Maybe it was a giant submarine torpedo."

The sights of battle met him at every corner. A woman cut in half by a falling timber; a man, his face carved down the middle with a shard of glass; A child's severed head in a gutter; a line of women from a whorehouse were laid out in all their glory—each face dolled-up for business, each body grey in death.

Mangled houses titled in all directions, fire from toppled wood stoves was burning out-of-control. Walls collapsed on innocent and unknowing victims, who, pinned down, were in danger of being burnt alive. Many others were close to frozen as a bitter winter breeze rose up from the harbour.

The further towards the downtown he walked, the more victims of glass attacks came to greet him. To hundreds, the last picture of this earth had been a blinding flash. To Gordon's seasoned eye, many of the walking wounded appeared to be blind. They stumbled over pieces of broken sidewalk, bumped into splintered telegraph posts. Arms stretched out seeking a secure footing that didn't exist. Spirits flagging.

As Gordon stopped frequently to rest his arms, he did what he could for others. Placing the boys on their own feet, he helped a crippled older couple extricate themselves from what was left of their home. The doorway was barricaded by fallen timbers, and it took Gordon several minutes to wedge an opening for them to escape. Blessing him many times, they went off to find grandchildren. Another time, he assisted a child pinned under a piece of crumbled foundation. Gordon had to dig under the boy to ease some of the pressure on his legs, then find a beam light enough to lift but strong enough to lever bits of wall upward. Finally, Gordon found an edge that held and was able to ease the masonry off the small boy long enough for him to pull himself free.

Now there were three in his charge. This new recruit wouldn't leave him any more than the first two. This new boy had one badly damaged leg, but was able to stand. So he hobbled along, clinging to Gordon's tunic.

"Which way to Robie Street?" Gordon asked his new companion. The boy was unable to speak, but a bleeding hand pushed up toward the right. Gordon saw an avenue that took that general direction, and, hoping the young lad was correct, he moved toward it. Taking up the two small kids, he called to the third, "This way troops." They shuffled down the street looking for a Red Cross station, a hospital, any place of comfort.

At one point in their search for a hospital, a team of fire fighters rushed past looking for the leader of their fire brigade asking each pedestrian they encountered about a special brigade truck called "Clarabelle." Gordon was of no help to them, but he did snatch a bit of information as they passed. The hospital was three blocks forward and to the right several more streets. "Can't miss it."

Alas, they did. The confusion of streets, downed wires, sputtering ruins and glass-strewn alleys, made even simple directions difficult to follow. Like many, Gordon found himself going in circles, up an alleyway only to find a dead end, down a cluttered street to discover the exit blocked by fallen wires, still sputtering. Now walking with a decided limp, he could no go no more than a few dozen yards before he had to pause, ease his two charges from his arms and rest.

Fatigued as he was, there was always some energy left to scratch at the rubble in response to buried voices. He had little assistance to offer. His first aid kit was soon depleted of anything useful. Even through these agonizing hours, Gordon never lost sight of his primary goal. To find Jo.

Gordon did learn from a soldier, who, like himself, was looking for a loved one, that a train from Montreal had been warned off. It was waiting outside the city limits until the real damage was assessed. "Can't tell who is waiting out there—no light or heat. They'll freeze in those old rail cars." Apparently, the train station to which it was headed had collapsed in a shower of glass. "Hundreds have perished."

The soldier was able to direct them to an emergency medical station. Finally! The name on the front of the building said "Chebucto Road School." Cars were unloading casualties everywhere. A string of dead bodies lined the sidewalk. Inside, he found a few helpful nurses. They were shocked by the state of his three companions. "Get them over to the General," one shouted, and two helping arms pried the children's arms free of his neck and uniform. A driver appeared with his assistant and the wounded were taken off to waiting car. Gordon never knew their names or saw them again.

Disasters make fast, but very short, friendships.

Looking about in a daze, he was struck by the growing piles of causalities. Looking at an orderly, he asked, "Is this a hospital? A soldier down the street said it was."

"It's the bloody morgue, mate," came the reply. "If you're sick, get over to Camp Hill Hospital. They'll fix you up. We're busy counting the dead. God, I've never seen anything like this." With that understatement, the orderly rushed off to supervise a new truckload of corpses. Gordon whispered, "Neither have I!" and left. Where was Jo? His mind raced with possibilities.

From a driver he discovered that there were two stations that took trains bound for Montreal. "I'd try the North Street Station first. It's been the traditional spot for reunions of soldiers and their families. But folks tell me it's pretty much blown to bits."

Gordon walked along Chebucto Road, passed Robie Street, and asked passers-by the way to the station. Most were unable to answer, lost in their own fog of misery.

As he walked back toward the North end, the destruction mounted. Gordon grew frantic with questions. Was she on that train that was delayed? Maybe she had been waiting in the ill-fated station? Did she escape the blast, only to die in the ensuing fire? Was she still alive, even now, languishing under a steel girder?

Off to his right came a pitiful moan. Someone was trapped beneath a wall of fallen masonry. Hobbling to the spot, Gordon found a bloody mess, an elderly gentleman with a face full of plaster and blood, his body buried under a heap of bricks. "Help me ... please. I can't feel my legs."

Gordon looked about for assistance—none was at hand, so he began stone-by-stone to uncover what was left of this latest victim. "I'll have you right as rain. You'll see, mate." All the while he chanted his comfort, his mind was racing to find Jo. Gordon was itching to strike out into a gallop and find her, but his first call was to get help for this old guy. (Truth be told, Gordon's own wounds precluded any rapid leg movement.) "There must be someone who knows what happened, who's survived." He mumbled his discontent and frustration through gritted teeth. "Surely not everyone in this blasted city is wounded or lost!"

Saint John: The Buttress Home
Thursday, Sept. 3, 1992, 9:28 a.m.

"Lost at sea? Now there's a fix. But, God bless my thick hide, I've never suffered that ill fate." Captain Jims was hoisting a sail for another long conversation. I could tell from the way he held his head, nodding ever so gently to punctuate his phrases. Put a pipe in his hand and the picture would have been complete. "Been in some pretty tight spots, but never lost."

I had come for a morning visit to the nursing home expecting to find the captain in his sea chair. They had called to say he was failing a bit. Nothing too serious, but he wasn't eating as heartily as was his practice. "Could I come to see if there was something wrong?" I was busy with the start-up of Sunday school and Bible studies, but there was always time for Gordon.

Arriving just in time for coffee break at the second floor nursing station, I was able to snag a bit of java for myself before I went on deck. I needed something to fortify my brain and keep it rolling over. A hot day was brewing outside, and Gordon's room always had a gift for holding the humidity longer than most.

"You see, matey," he extended an arm skyward, "there's always the sun and moon to steer by. A seaman's never lost when he's got God's compass to steer by."

I had tried to probe Gordon's past—the four days in Montreal seemed to have been lost. "So, Captain, have you ever been out to sea, I mean really lost without a clue?" He wasn't biting on my proffered suggestions, preferring his own tales.

"Yes, sir, a seaman's never lost when he's got God's compass to steer by. Come to think of it, there was that once."

Taking a sip of my coffee, I debated in mind whether an interruption would close off his story or keep it going. I tried the former option. "Once? You were lost once?"

"Not really lost ... just a bit confused." My gambit had worked. I could feel a long sea story coming. "It was back a number of seasons. I was a young lad like you. Well, not exactly like you. I had more muscle and a bit more guts in my heart than you young people today." I let the dig pass.

"Anyway, I was sailing alone that day—just a shore trip, when a great whale of a storm began to blow from the southwest. She was a nasty one and I knew that I wouldn't be able to make it back to port."

Captain Jims spit over the rail of his imaginary deck. "Round those parts there were shoals and hidden rocks—we called 'em 'sinkers' and a fellow had to watch his course pretty closely. Well, wouldn't you know it! The fog began to roll in with the rain. A nuisance, floating back and forth across my line of sight. In a couple of hours, she was as thick as my grandmother's corn chowder. Couldn't see a thing."

Jims waved his hands in front of his face. "Thick, you bet yer sou'wester, she was. By this time, I had brought down the mainsail and was steering with a storm jig up. Tricky."

"A storm jig?" My knowledge of sailing was limited.

"That's a special rig used to reduce your canvas, but keep you under power." Gordon's explanation didn't help me a bit.

"So there I was. Caught in the middle of dangerous waters, not a beacon nor marker in sight. I was some scared. I could hear the breakers all around. You don't know what you're made of 'til that moment when death looks you square in the eye. Well sir, I discovered I was pretty thin inside. Went all wobbly, I did. It's not that I was a coward. I just couldn't come up with a reason why I should keep on living. There weren't any guiding hand to keep me going. My boy, it was at that pass that I confess I was even more frightened. The waves didn't scare me none, not like the whirling empty feeling in my gut."

Unable to respond, I just nodded as he spoke.

"Lost ain't a matter of geography, it's a matter of the soul. And it sure is easy to give in rather than face your own aloneness. I've seen the strongest brutes give up just at that point. Most do. Most do. Let themselves down, they do." He looked closely at me and smiled slightly. "You don't have a sweet Jesus clue what I'm talking about, do you matey?"

The best I could do was honesty. "Not the foggiest, Captain."

"Let her go, son. You'll come to it soon enough, when the wind blows in your face and the waves overwhelm you. Then you'll know. Leastways, if you're not dead first." There was a long pause in his thought. I could see him reliving a few such encounters with the Grim Reaper. "I saw him yer know. On that foggy day ... Sweet Samuel in the flesh, but she was too late to do anything. Too late, by harf."

"Samuel?"

"A wave, matey, the great mysterious wave we captains call 'Samuel'. Great towering monster that swamps all in its path."

"Samuel—not a person?"

"Ain't you listening? He's a baby wave that grows into a monster. Yep … saw him with my own eyes." A tear fell down his wrinkled cheek. The captain shook his head to rid himself of a trembling memory—one I couldn't fathom. "So death is a matter of the soul not the body. And I made myself a promise that day. Keep the heart well-fed, work as hard at the inner life as the outer. Only safe way to find your home port that I know of."

Hamilton, St. Giles Anglican Church
Sunday, February 15, 1917, 9:37 p.m.

Closing the door to his office carefully, Hawthorne held the two telegrams tightly as he checked that the latch held.

It had been a long day. Too many mourning parents, too few answers. Five services and a baptism. Three homilies, which was three too many at this stage in his career. A single private confession with a young man, Alec, new to the church, had been his only relief. It was promising. Not a great conquest, but something. The real news was in his hand.

As was his habit, he had squirreled away his Sunday paper until the services were finished. Evensong done, duties discharged, he could relax in the relative quiet of his study, sip some well-deserved consecrated wine and read the news.

There was nothing much of note. The war ground on. Flanders was Flanders. Politicians were dismayed over Quebec. He looked over the society column, a good shot of the Mayor. Hawthorne didn't care for the sports page and only read two editorials: one for and one against conscription.

The back section of the *Spectator* was always his final destination. A dreaded chore, he scanned the lists of the wounded, missing in action and killed in battle, looking for the names of his flock. There were two. The first one had been killed in action, the only son of a local banker (it would hit them hard) and the other, an orphan child adopted by the church's custodian. Jake by name. He was "missing, presumed dead." There will be no end of mourning for that boy. He was loved by the entire congregation. It was going to be a very long week.

Hawthorne could feel his energy dipping and decided it was time for sleep. Folding the paper in two, and reaching for a final swallow of his glass, it was only by chance that his eye scanned the list one last time and fell upon a simple notation: "Terrance Hinks, killed in action."

"That's old Hinks' boy, I'll warrant." Hawthorne was wide awake again. "No idea he signed up." He set his wine down, took the paper in both hands and read the line carefully. "That has to be him. Lists 'Montreal' as his hometown! Has to be him."

Hawthorne flung the paper down, went to his desk and withdrew pen and paper. He'd send a telegram this very night. No, better make it two telegrams. One to Cruikshank and the other to that military chap, Major Ryan. Perhaps he can discover more of the boy's death ... something they could use against the good bishop from Montreal. They needed leverage and this might just be the ticket. He scribbled out his notes and left immediately for the closest telegraph office, pulling the church door behind him. Holding the two telegrams tightly, he checked that the latch held. Too many secrets to be left unguarded.

Saint John: Centenary-Queen Square United Church
Tuesday, Nov. 17, 1992, 11:21 a.m.

There ... the door is closed on our sins. All the confessions have been offered and forgiven. That's the theory. Right at this point there should be a collective sigh from the congregation.

It is rare I feel the weight of guilt rise from my shoulders, but I hoped that I had eased the burden for those present. Looking out I didn't see relief anywhere, except on the face of the woman who was sitting to one side.

Our eyes met, she smiled and inclined her head slightly.

I had no recollection of ever meeting her before. The exact features of face were masked by the shadows cast by the overhanging balcony, but its general shape had a familiarity. I was intrigued, but the show must go on. No time for idle thoughts. It was time to read from God's word.

CHAPTER FIVE

The Word

For God's sake, read the Gospel as if it meant something. Give this
miraculous tale the surprising edge it deserves, like a first-time reading
when the humour, surprise and wonder are jostling for prominence.

J. Wes Lee, *Preach to the Back Row*

Montreal: Christ Church Cathedral
Saturday, December 8, 1917, 8:30 p.m.

A recess was called in the proceedings of the National Synod. The
question of Holy War was temporarily suspended. Hawthorne and
Cruikshank were huddled in the church vestibule. The single paper
they held between them had silenced all conversation. The letterhead
was of the Canadian Corps. An army telegraph under the signature of
Lieutenant Colonel Ryan.

Looking up, Cruikshank murmured, "He's moved up."

"Pardon?" Hawthorne's mind was still on the letter.

Cruikshank explained, "Our friend, Mayor Ryan, is now a Colonel.
A smallish step, but progress nonetheless."

"But how will this help us?"

The principal shook his head over his friend's slow political mind.
"See here." His index finger found the line: "It was suspected that the
soldier was attempting to dessert at Vimy Ridge—April 9, before he
was apprehended by the CO (Major Ryan) of the Canadian Corps. No
court martial undertaken at that point. This was the second instance of

suspicion—the first taking place near Ypres, December 7, 1916—court finding was 'undue duress.'"

Hawthorne still didn't get it. "So how can this have anything to do with Hinks?"

"Easy," Cruikshank remarked. "When I met Gordon Davis a few hours back, I knew we had the key to our plan—how to inspire the neutral bishops and neutralize Hinks at the same time. After the stir Ryan made last week, I had half a mind to call him to speak again, but then this Davis fellow crossed my path. So I telegraphed Ryan—he's in Quebec City preparing to return to the front—and he sent this message back. We'll let this Davis fellow speak to synod as Hinks requested, and, when he's done, we bring out the real facts of his cowardice."

Hawthorne scratched his temple. "That takes care of Davis, but what does that do to Hinks?"

"Here, did you read at the bottom? It's a godsend."

Hawthorne mouthed the words in a stage whisper. "Was recommended for a medal of valour for saving one Terrance Hinks who was reported AWOL."

"I don't see …"

Cruikshank snapped, "Think man. Remember you sent me that telegram about Terrance Hinks being 'killed in action.' It wasn't battle. He ran out into no man's land as a coward. Ryan confirmed that with me. It took him several months to track down the CO in that section of the trenches. Then after a long night and couple of bottles of rum, apparently, he finally gave it up. 'Terrance Hinks was a bloody coward.' His very words! We have that on record. And now …. We have just to hint at the association—two deserters. Davis leading Terrance into desertion! Perfect! Who will say anything against us?"

"Davis will deny it."

"No one will believe him once we prove he's a deserter. When we bring out the evidence of the good bishop's son and his cowardice, well, it's all over for him. I doubt Hinks knows what happened to his son. So he'll be blind-sided and keep his mouth shut tight when we vote on the Holy War proposition."

"Did you know about the connection before tonight? Between Davis and Terrance Hinks, I mean?"

"Not until tonight. God bless us. Davis is delivered into our hands ... a perfect example of what we're fighting against. We'll crucify him!" Cruikshank chuckled. "He'll be ruined with any who stand with him. Done! Finished!"

The picture of Gordon's ruin was not lost on Hawthorne. He was smiling for his own reasons. "It seems too perfect."

"Before Ryan's research into what happened, I had my suspicions about a connection between Davis and Bishop Hinks, but it was between Davis and Hinks' daughter Johanna. But a cowardly son ... delicious." The principal looked around the church vestibule for allies. "Let's not let it go to waste! We'll want to orchestrate tomorrow evening's events carefully." Seeing a friend who owed him a favour, the principal called out, "Jacob, a word, please!" Cruikshank steered Hawthorne toward Jacob. "Jacob, have you met the most promising priest in western Ontario?" The threesome smiled as the principal laid out his concerns. "Okay, we may have suffered a small setback, but all is not lost. I was wondering if you could ...."

Halifax Harbour: North Street Train Station
Thursday, December 6, 1917, 1:20 p.m.

How long had Gordon been sitting by the overturned milk truck? From the trail of broken crates and milk bottles, the horse appeared to have raced down the street untended for some distance before slipping its harness and bolting free. Fortunately for Gordon, a few bottles remained unbroken and he was able slack his thirst. "Premium Black's Dairy." The words on the bottle were bold. The liquid inside was salvation for his parched throat.

Though his mind was working at a gallop, his body was strangely shutting down. Fatigue and the constant string of grotesque casualties had numbed his senses. His arms ached beyond measure. His leg throbbed.

His mind was turning over the messages of doom that he had picked up concerning the train station: "Too close to the blast. I don't think anything is left." That was the estimation of a sailor whose jersey read *HMCS Noble*. A passing fireman had said the building was a heap of shattered glass. "Bloody awful."

Gordon asked a clergyman about directions to North Street Station. He had been kneeling down to give last rites to a woman crushed by a wooden beam. Straightening up, groaning a bit, he looked into Gordon's eyes. "There's nothing left there for you, soldier. Nothing but buried bodies and broken steel."

At this grim news, Gordon started to slump toward the ground, legs buckling under him. "I must save her," he moaned.

The clergy grasped Gordon's arm to ease his fall. "Peace there now, my son, it's beyond you now, wherever she is. Do you need a hand back to the hospital?" The cleric made as if to heft this wounded, possibly delirious, soldier onto his back and deliver him to a medical station. Gordon shook his head, thrashed his arms and stumbled to his feet.

When Gordon accepted this last message as truth, he lost hope. Failure. Despair put lead into his feet and brought him to a halt by the overturned cart. "What if she's buried there?" He said it out loud, to no one in particular. Strange at first, hearing his own voice became a soothing reminder that he was still alive and that the devastation his eyes picked up was indeed real. This was not a dream.

Minutes passed, Gordon staring alternately at the milk bottle in his hand and at the splintered wagon that was his backstop. Whiffs of snow swept down the street. December winds!

Through gusts of snow, a figure appeared. Bleeding from the left cheek and right leg, he was limping up the street toward Gordon, moaning with each step. With a shake of his head, Gordon woke up and realized that this was a fellow human being. Not a ghost. An old, injured man, determined to go up the hill past Gordon.

As the man approached, Gordon could see that his beard and eyebrows were badly singed. His left eye was closed and blood dripped from under the pinched lid. There was a gash in his left pant leg. As he passed, Gordon could hear his rasping, weak voice, mantra like, chanting the words, "Train station. Train station! Train Station!" Determined to get there—come hell or broken limbs.

"Maybe this fellow knows where it is," Gordon thought and he raised himself up. Taking up a position beside the older man, they hobbled down the street. Wanting to confirm his suspicions and trying to open up some conversation, Gordon asked his companion if the train station was up ahead.

No reply.

Gordon reached over, circled his arm around the man's shoulders. "Let me help you."

Unable to communicate, the gentleman simply gripped the sleeve of Gordon's tunic firmly. "Train Station!" he mumbled more quietly with each step. "Train Station."

They marched as one. The snow was blowing hard now. "Are you hurt bad, old man?" "Can you see with your good eye?" "Do you live nearby?" "Can I find you a warm place to rest?"

"Train station," were the only two words the man would say as they churned through slushy and muddy roads. Gordon was sweating with the effort of supporting his friend while dealing with his own wounded leg.

Ypres: Canadian Corps Trenches
Thursday, March 1, 1917, 2:30 p.m.

The paper was wrinkled, damp on the edges from his own sweat. He'd kept the letter in his right trouser pocket through the past few hours. Mud from the trench and blood from a wounded captain had soaked his pants. "Damn officers—they bleed like the rest of us."

The address was still legible and the handwriting was clearly hers. "Private Gordon Davis." The neat, squat lines could belong to no other.

Gordon tore the edge of the envelope, extracted the pages and then folded the envelope neatly into his first aid kit. "A bit of spare paper is always a useful tool in emergencies," said Whiskers during the last day of their training. "Never know when you'll need to write down vital information, send a message back to the line or pen a dying wish." This latter piece of advice proved to be bang on. How many promises had he scribbled out? Last testaments of forgotten men. "Tell my wife I love her." "Send my duffle to my father back home." "Give my son a hug from me!"

Holding Jo's pages in his hands, Gordon allowed his eyes to go out of focus for a moment, blurring the lines. He didn't want to know. Taking a deep breath, looking about the trench one last time, he forced his gaze back to the letter and read slowly, savouring every word.

> January 12, 1917
>
> Dear Gordon,
>
> I have long wanted to write and tell of great changes in my life, but not yet. Suffice it to say that my world is overturned and radically altered. I am delighted and I know you will be pleased for me, for us. It's all for the better. Really! At some distant point, hopefully not too far off, I'll be able to explain my recent fortune.
>
> Great are God's blessings. I had no idea about love until now.
>
> Dear me, that sounds so mysterious, but it isn't. When we meet face to face, then I'll reveal all.
>
> Remember your promise to wait for me, love me forever!
>
> How are you? Christmas has just passed. My favourite season of the year. The trees, the presents, and the sense of expectation—the firelight still lingers in my soul. Oh, it's magic! As I write with this merry tone, I know how miserable you must be. News of the trench warfare is just now coming to light. Last week Father interviewed two wounded veterans who described the rats and the lice. Surely, they

were exaggerating. If only half of what they said is true, you are most to be pitied.

I cannot believe how incredibly stupid the entire business seems from this side of the Atlantic. Have we lost all semblance of sanity? What ever happened to basic … Excuse me. I was about to launch into one of my sermons.

Terry, silly oaf, joined up last fall. You may not have known this. He couldn't resist the promise of glory and the chance to play in a military outfit. They fitted him with a rifle and assured him after basic training he would get his chance at the regimental band. Fat chance, I say! They have already shipped him off to France. No music in sight.

Now both my loves are in hell.

Did you receive the Christmas care package? It comes with my deepest wishes for your health and safety.

Father is strangely worried on your behalf. Each day or two he asks about you and waits as anxiously as I do for your letters. I believe he's smitten—do you have some undetectable potion that you use? Laced our morning tea with it, did you?

I wish there were a similar spell for protecting loved ones at a distance.

Here in Canada, the war cry continues. In an open air speech downtown, the prime minister promised more young blood for the Empire. Ridiculous. Even clergy are getting on the band wagon. Last month I heard one talking as if this was a "holy"

war. Father knew him. We are at special cathedral
mid-week vespers and this fellow, I think the name
was Haweye or such like, was unbearable. I would
have stood up and shouted him down if it had not
been for my bishop's restraining hand.

Speaking of holding, how I wish I could see you
and touch you, lie with you and hear your heartbeat again. To know the security of not leaving
your side!

Come back soon!

I'll write again soon. Be safe and watch for
your comrades.

Love, Jo

PS. You never mention friends. Have you made
any? (Or lost any for that matter?) What about this
rumour concerning the hospitality of the French
houses called *estaminets*? Filled with beautiful
women, they say. Stay away, you rascal!

PPS. I think I love you more now than ever. Soon
we'll be together forever!

"Merry Christmas to you too," murmured Gordon as he folded her
letter carefully and placed it reverently with the others in the folds of his
Bible—a sacred bundle. A rat scurried past as he flopped over into his
funk hole for a rest. A drip of water hung from a root on the ceiling of
his dugout.

She still loved him. That much was clear.

The letter sounded as though nothing had changed—at least as far
as their love was concerned. Was his drunken worry unfounded? While
the opening paragraph hinted at an ominous alteration in her life,
Gordon clung to her final sentiments, the promises of affection. Surely

she wouldn't play with him. Samuel was just a passing acquaintance, an old school chum. "That must be it, an old friend, a fancy. Nothing else!"

Drifting off to sleep he dreamt of the love she sent, the best Christmas present ever—even if it was two months late.

Sometimes words are enough.

Saint John: Centenary-Queen Square United Church
Tuesday, Nov. 17, 1992, 11:22 a.m.

The funeral service progresses from confessional prayer to the reading of Scripture.

Looking down at the Bible, I offer a standard introduction: "There are times when our words don't seem adequate to life's circumstances. Death is one such instance. Death makes us all feel inadequate, especially when confronted by a dying friend or family member." A couple of heads nod slightly as I speak. They're old enough to know the weaknesses of speech in times of trouble. Who hasn't been hurt by worn out clichés at the graveside? "He's gone to a better rest." "God just took her because she was so virtuous."

I say to myself, "This stuff is hogwash."

Opening the Bible slowly, "Let me read first from the prophet Isaiah, the fortieth chapter. In the close of that chapter, Isaiah's words speak directly to the aching heart, weary from grief:

> *Those that wait upon the Lord shall renew their strength;*
> *They shall mount up with wings as eagles,*
> *They shall run, and not be weary, they shall walk,*
> *and not faint. (Isaiah 40:31)*

"For those who are listening the message is simple: God will not forsake you. No matter how far down you go, the Almighty is beside you. Eventually, you will rise again, even after death."

I say, "This is the Word of the Lord."

"Thanks be to God," comes the scattered reply.

Vimy Ridge, France
Monday, April 9, 1917, 5:15 a.m.

"Pass the word!" The message was whispered down the line, "Fifteen minutes to zero hour." Gordon couldn't see the face that uttered the warning. He'd come up from the dank tunnels dug into the chalk. The fresh air was so good! Looking up, the moon was blacked out behind clouds. Completely dark.

The preparations for this battle had been meticulous. Nothing overlooked. Slightest details orchestrated. That meant that not even the light of a cigarette was permitted. "No cheap targets for Jerry," barked the lieutenant before darkness fell. No words, no signals, no tell-tale reflections, not a sound, no nothing. Just wait.

After the last seventy-two hours of waiting beneath a barrage of artillery fire, no one needed to be told. Each man was sticking closely to the rules.

Alas, in spite of careful precautions and several months of re-enacting their plans, it all came down to chance. No fool proof pattern, no way to avoid the shell with your name on it. In the trenches, death seemed so arbitrary. On the drive across no man's land, it took your mate in the small of the back, split him in two and left you standing without a scratch. Or standing watch, one moment your neighbour is lifting his head ever so slightly over protective sandbags on top of the trench wall, the next, he's down on the duckboards, blood dribbling from a neat hole in his forehead.

It wasn't just the uncertainty of dying, it was the obvious futility of so much of the killing that made trench warfare so frightening. Gordon had watched many attacks. He'd seen hundreds upon hundreds of men march to their death. At the Somme, thousands had been butchered by machine gun fire as they tried to cut past that German thick, tangled wire barrier. Scores were caught midway and crumpled into the wire only to be held upright by the barbs. They looked grotesquely pious as if kneeling down to pray. Never to rise.

Better not to dwell on it.

Gordon sighed and dutifully turned to the south, whispering the same message to his nearside companion, "Fifteen minutes to zero hour." There was a slight grunt, nervous and uncomfortable, as the phrase went down the line of anxious soldiers.

Silence again. No birds sang out.

For the hundredth time after waking, Gordon scratched at his left armpit. "Must be a whole colony of the buggers in there." When his company had been positioned for its final staging zone before the attack, he resisted the urge to scrape his underarms as long as he could. In the end, he could wait no longer, and his hand slowly, silently dug away at the blighters, attacking burrowing lice. Their bites were relentless and his hand dug away at them, as if he was powerless to stop it.

His comrades were going through the same nervous twitches. Lice were the great leveler. Officer or NCO, general or private, it didn't matter to them whose flesh they ate. Arms scratched up and down the line as they waited.

At five minutes to "over the top," they were ordered to crouch on the fire step, the last act before the real show began. Gordon ran down his instructions again. For the past three weeks, they had studied the terrain of the ridge from aerial photos and play-acted their advance over a practice terrain. They now knew the lay of land, and had memorized every indentation and molehill. His own company was to take the north flank. They were to advance north and east, past the wire, to secure and occupy the German forward trench. It sounded so sterile and simple, but there were live men waiting in that trench, not intending to allow themselves to be "occupied" nor "secured." Over our dead bodies!

Gordon tried not to imagine their faces. He'd seen too many Germans, slit open by bayonets, torn asunder by shrapnel. There was no pity for them. His compassion had long since died. Nevertheless, it was the history of each man that haunted him. This fellow with his head broken open had a mother, perhaps a lover or wife. That one, without arms or legs, was one of a circle of friends at the local bar in his home-town. They weren't monsters. They were just in the way.

In the twists that only combat can produce, Gordon had often attended to wounded Germans. When grey uniforms came back from a night raid, he was the one expected to patch up the tears in their bellies. Gordon made it a point never to look very long into their eyes, nor to read identification of any kind. Keep them nameless at least. Call them "the abdominal wound" or "the concussed skull," but don't call them human. It would blunt his resolve at moments like the present.

There were times when Gordon questioned his own cleverness. He had joined the medical corps because he hated fighting. Even as a child he would rather be beaten up than raise a fist against a bully. On the business end of a stretcher he saw the worst of it. His fighting fellows never had to look back at the wreckage they had created. None of them had to offer comfort to a man whose life fluids were draining out into the mire. Combatants didn't wait to contemplate the severed hands or slashed chests made during their bayonet-wielding madness.

Gordon saw it all, patched up what might be healed and waited while death stole the rest.

He now turned to look north again. No sign of his closest companion. He must be hunkered down waiting for the crash of thunder from our field guns, the signal to climb out of a relatively secure haven and fling your body into the arms of Lady Luck. Some men said they felt a great roar of energy during the last few seconds before an attack, as if their muscles were bursting with power. Others claimed their guts were churning up acid like a Mills bomb in a mud puddle. Still others rehearsed the dirty stories and macabre jokes they'd heard the night before, trying to take their minds off the grim prospect of charging enemy machine guns.

Gordon was one of these latter types, and, as he waited for the crash of the opening barrage, two stories came to mind. The first was a classic. It was Sam, a small, cigar-smoking labourer from Brantford who cornered the squad before lights out. "There's this young solider see, and he's cleaning out Fritz's trench when he comes upon a dugout. Now, he has a Mills bomb in his left hand and puts his right hand to his mouth and shouts, 'Anybody down there?' There's a brief pause, then a German voice shouts back, 'Nein.' 'Nine, eh?' says our Tommie. 'Well, you'll bloody well have to share this among the lot of you.' And then he chucks the bomb into the pit." A ring of laughter greeted Sam's story and a number of fellows went off to retell it to their friends.

Gordon's second joke was closer to the common language of the trenches: smut talk. It was crude jokes that were the *lingua franca* of the trenches. There was no friendship in the mud and murder of that war, not in the ordinary sense. It was a close kinship, one perhaps closer than blood would permit, but strangely indifferent at the same time. The close quarters meant community, but very few personal details were shared. Each man would get labelled for a particular quirk in his physical person or mental disposition and that mark was how he was known. "Big lips." "Hot blood." "Hairy pits." No one looked any closer than your nickname suggested. Consequently, the one mode of acceptable exchange, besides swear words, was the dirty joke, the raunchier, the better. Sharing lewd tales released the tension, helped laughter flow.

This tale was first told by Max, a New Brunswick farmer who obsessed about joining the Air Corps. Two nights ago while the company was eating its dinner of bully beef and biscuits, he launched into what for Gordon became one of the best, filthiest tales of the war. It was so good that he heard it repeated several times since, shared in other clutches of men as they waited for their battle to begin.

"There's this 'original' (someone who had come over to France with the original Canadian Expeditionary Force) and he's waiting outside his billet for the ration detail, and along comes this greenhorn, see. He's carrying a duckboard (the small platforms placed at the bottom of trenches). 'What you got there, son?' hollers the original. 'Why sir, it's a duckboard,' says the new recruit. 'I can see that. What's it for?' says the older man. The young pup replies, 'Well, I'm off to catch me some ducks....'

Just at that moment, flashes lit the sky interrupting Gordon's remembering. The roar of explosions ripped through the air.

"This is it!" shouted the captain down the line. "Over the top with the best of luck." The word was given and men lurched up and over sandbags. Would any of them survive? Gordon felt his knees pushing upward. He was now on the parapet, looking across into no man's land.

The front began to explode into a thousand showers as the creeping barrage landed its first shells.

The war had taught each side to work death to their best advantage. In this attack, the Canadian artillery was trying a new tactic: a rolling barrage. Rather than pounding an enemy position directly and then sending in the infantry shock troops, this morning the gunners were timing their range to move it forward 100 yards every three minutes, allowing the infantry to follow safely right behind the shell blasts and attack the enemy immediately after the protective wall of fire had passed. Before the Hun came out of their dugouts, the Tommies were in their faces. The theory was brilliant, but at Vimy the Germans were well placed in heavily protected bunkers that would withstand everything but a direct hit.

Gordon lurched forward, dreading, expecting the bark of machine guns coming from their flank. It came—almost as a response to his fears. Ahead, a few men fell to the ground gripping their legs. Gordon glanced back to be sure his comrades were following him and started in the direction of the downed soldiers. He had every intention of assisting them, but his heart froze. His instincts were screaming. Something was wrong, desperately wrong. A red-hot pain shot across his belly. As if cut in two, he lurched to the ground, holding his midriff.

"What's the word, soldier?" Gordon looked up into the questioning eyes of his sergeant, unable to speak, fear choking his throat.

Montreal: Mount Royal Park (Sisson Ridge)
Friday, March 24, 1916, 2:15 p.m.

Jo looked up into Gordon's face and smiled. This was her dream. Her hands played with his coat buttons. He was lying on his side, close to her in a pose only lovers could enjoy without blushing. "Let's see what's in here." She was now tugging. He giggled, feigning resistance. "Not now you silly, we're in public view for heaven's sake."

"This is a park for lovers."

"Lovers? How so?"

Johanna pointed to maple trees on the slopes. "They say that each one of those trees was planted by a couple."

"They? Any particular 'they' or just the generic 'they'?" Gordon smiled.

Johanna was adamant, "Silly, the 'they' are the gods of romance. Don't they teach you anything in theological college?"

"I'm not there yet."

"I forgot that." Johanna pushed him to his back. "Take my word for it. In this park, the maples are a living testament: 'Love never ends.' Each leaf is a promise that true love can never be lost."

Gordon laughed, "And I thought maples were for syrup."

"Unromantic Upper Canadian slanders!" She joined Gordon in laughter and then she began digging through his coat, tunic and shirt. "I'm not getting distracted by your protests and ignorance of love's poetry. This is our second-to-last day together and I want it all now." Her hand finally hit flesh and began to rub his skin, with delicate curiosity. "Mmm, feels good."

Gordon laughed, eased Johanna off his belly and tried to piece together his uniform and overcoat. "It's not seemly, you little wench." He had never been so delighted in physical touch, nor so intimidated. Of course Jo was the first to ever pay him serious attention, but that didn't seem to dawn on Gordon as a significant factor in his pleasure. "After all, I'm a member of his Majesty's Royal Guard. Not to be toyed with on a hillside." The smile in his voice, made Johanna persist in her ministrations. "You're just playing hard to get, you crusty moralist." With that she flopped back on his chest and began to run her hands down his stomach inside his coat, catching the belt buckle and wrestling it open. "You've listened too well to too many sermons on the evils of the flesh."

"Indeed," Gordon replied as he wiggled out from under her and straightened himself up to a sitting position. "The Reverend Hawthorne would regularly glare down upon us with lips pursed and spit out a warning against fornication. 'The Devil's own brew.'"

Johanna looked incredulous, "The Devil's what?"

"Brew, the Devil's brew. Sex was an intoxicant," Gordon answered. "He'd call it the 'liquor of lust.'"

Jo looked at his face and ran her fingers over his lips, playing. "Silly prude. I'll bet he just wanted to get some himself."

Gordon winced when he recalled his many visits to the confessional, the increasing intrusive interrogations into his sexual desires. And for a moment he turned serious. "I think he was the kind that liked little boys." It was almost a whisper.

"What?" Johanna had a nose like a hound when it came to the ill-treatment of little people. "Did he ever act on it?"

"Don't know." Gordon's tone was evasive.

Johanna could smell a rat. "What are you not telling me?" She searched his eyes. "Did he ...." She was certain of what she saw. "He tried to assault you, didn't he?"

"Once."

Johanna was thunderstruck and felt a towering anger explode. "That bastard. Did you tell your parents?"

"I was too ashamed." Gordon fiddled with the hem of his coat. Off in a distance he heard a mother call for her son. "I wasn't ... I mean ... I didn't know what to think or do. Father Hawthorne said it was part of the training—learning to exorcize the Devil's urges within me. It only happened once. Well actually, I think he was working up to it over time by prying into my private ... I mean my ... ah ... sexual life. He ... ah ... he asked me about masturbation. Told me how evil it was to touch myself. I guess I was too humiliated to ever mention it to anyone. I felt sick. No ... it was ... I felt dirty."

Johanna was silent. There were tears at the corners of her eyes— tears of rage and compassion mingled together. "That son of bitch. I'll tell my father. They should string him up by his balls. How dare he use his office to attack vulnerable boys!"

Gordon was unable to speak. Jo reached and caressed his face. "Is that why you're nervous about my touch?"

"I think so." Gordon still couldn't look her in the eye. "I want to reach out and hold you, but my mind is saying it's wrong." He rubbed a hand on her forearm. "You're the most desirable woman I can imagine. But I'm scared." Looking up to the sky he could feel water rolling down his checks. He tried to check its flow. He coughed and breathed deeply. Why did it hurt so much?

"It's always hard when a basic trust has been violated, isn't it?" Johanna had an unnerving ability to read Gordon's thoughts.

"Exactly!" He could say no more for his ability to speak from the heart was in an infantile stage. He marveled at Jo's easy access to the deepest currents in her soul.

As if making up her mind, Jo stood and stretched out her hand. "Let's go, Gordon."

He looked puzzled. "Go? Go where? We just arrived ..." He looked around at the sandwiches and cookies spread out on the quilt. "We haven't even begun to finish this meal and ...."

"Stop the stalling." Johanna was firm in her decision. "There's no time like the present to cure you of your sexual fear." Gordon continued to look confused.

She tugged at his hand. "I told you I had a plan. Well, it's time to put it into action. We came here to Sisson Ridge Park because it's just the right distance from home. Father has a synod meeting that, if I am not mistaken, has just begun. Since they're debating a motion to give women the right to vote in the election of the people's warden and other local ecclesiastical matters, I don't suspect it will be over very quickly. Terrance is off in Quebec City with his band, so the house is empty, and I intend to make love with you all afternoon. That is, if you're up to it." There was a wink in the final words and Gordon could feel his spirits rise.

"Up to it?" He laughed over his own terror and rose. "I'm a soldier of his ... a soldier—"

"Right, of his Majesty's Royal Guard."

Gordon laughed, "Royal and loyal!! We're always up for 'it.' In fact, we are trained to be prepared for all circumstances."

"Come along, then, Sir Lancelot," Jo was almost dragging him. "Let's see what our war bonds have accomplished by way of up-for-it training."

"Lay on, Macduff."

Johanna offered the response, "And damn'd be him that first cries, 'Hold enough!'" She put such a lurid emphasis on "hold," that they both fell into a spate of laughter—it carried them down the ridge, over many blocks to her waiting bed.

Vimy Ridge, France
Monday, April 9, 1917, 6:05 a.m.

"Get up, man!" Furtive hands were gripping his tunic, yanking so that his head bounced in and out of the mud several times. Water slipped inside his tin hat and soaked his hair. Try as he might, Gordon still couldn't move, as if his entire body was stricken by lockjaw. His hands gripped his stomach with a desperation he didn't know he possessed.

"You're not hit, Davis! Stop the faking and get the hell over to those wounded men." The flint hard strength of the sergeant was famous, and he literally threw Gordon to his feet. "Move your fucking feet!"

It was the fear of humiliation and punishment that kept Gordon's knees from buckling as he tried to paddle his feet forward. His hands still would not release his midriff, so he hobbled in the direction of his fallen mates. The growling sergeant went off in the direction of his disappearing company, and Gordon was left on his own to make his way toward the wounded.

Early morning mist, the smell of gunpowder and his own sweat filled his nostrils. Fear choked off any other thought. Had he been hit? Was he on his last legs? The pain was splitting him in two. He looked down at his jacket. There was no blood dripping from his fingers or down his leg. He couldn't feel any specific stabs of pain to indicate a bullet hole. But he must have been shot. Why else the immediate and breath-stealing flash of anguish?

After a few faltering steps Gordon fell at the side of a groaning soldier. His knee was burst open from a "dum-dum" bullet—the soft nosed variety that caused maximum internal damage on impact. His lower leg was dangling by the threads of tendons and a few shredded muscles.

Beyond pain, the young fellow was actually smiling, when Gordon drew close. "Looks like you've been hit too, mate," he said.

Gordon ignored the effort at conversation and took a closer look at the wounded knee. There was little to be done, but put a tourniquet on his thigh and wait for a stretcher to haul this guy back to the closest Casualty Clearing Station (CCS), where a surgeon could complete the amputation begun by an enemy bullet. Gordon finally looked up into the eyes of his patient. Wrapping a rag around the wounded leg, he asked, "Where you from, Tommy?"

Unlike Gordon's constant agony, this soldier's pain came and went. At this point the wounded man was stiff with a jolt of agony and so didn't respond except with grunts.

Gripping his side with his elbows, Gordon fiddled with the strings on his kit on his belt. Breathing deeply, trying to ignore the rising fear in his gut, he reached into his emergency bag for the flask. "Here, I'll give you something for the pain." Releasing his waist for a moment he used one hand to hoist the man's head slightly, he used the other to pour a few ounces of rum in the mouth open in silent torture. A few gulps and it went down.

A monstrous thrust of white pain cut off further comment, as Gordon fell to his stomach. Looking back to his own line, he saw his squad busy with a soldier hit almost on the brink of the jumping off trench. Obviously badly hit, they were trying to staunch a wound high up one thigh, close to the groin. Gordon shouted for a stretcher for his patient and then rolled over in pain, pulling his legs up into a foetal position.

Within a few minutes, his buddies responded to his pleas for help. They lifted the now unconscious soldier onto the canvas and began the quick crouch-like trot back to the communication trench and the dressing station.

"He can go straight to the CCS." Rising on his elbows, Gordon called after the receding backs. One arm went up in a wave to tell him that they had heard Gordon's command. Then he fell exhausted from the effort.

How long did he lie motionless? Hours? Days? In time, Gordon rolled over on his stomach and tried to rise again, push forward to his next fallen man. But fear again gripped his sides and senses. He couldn't move, couldn't think of looking for another broken body. He heard his own voice shout, "To hell with this mess. I can't take it."

So he lay still. "The pain will pass," he said to himself.

As he waited he saw wave after wave of soldiers pass him by. Tramping boots, all moving east. Every now and again, a few pairs would stumble west, dripping blood and pain in equal measure. Once an officer loomed over him and peered down, first in concern, then when he saw there was no apparent wound, in disgust. "What's up soldier? Lost your nerve?" A quick kick was administered to his side. Gordon lurched in anguish but was unable to reply. "Get up, coward!" The officer's face was turning red and he might had been tempted to use his side arm to propel Gordon to his feet, except that a fellow officer called him away to reinforce a sagging line further south.

"Coward!" The officer's word lingered in Gordon's mind. "So that's it." He'd heard of cases where men were physically crippled by their fear. Now, he was the same, branded as a coward, the worst stigma in the ranks. Spat upon. Gordon closed his eyes, wishing he could melt into the ground. It would be around the company in no time. "Gordie's a back-sliding yellow-belly!"

He tried breathing slowly, allowing his limbs to relax. It worked for a few minutes and then the searing agony would bite his side again and he could do nothing but writhe in pain. Could his mind create such a physical state? Was this how some of the poor souls who feared the battle actually felt? Were they driven to cut and run by the sheer suffering?

Twice more he tried to rise and help his wounded brothers and made it to his knees, but before he could manoeuvre his legs into a standing position he fainted.

He started talking out loud, berating his weakness. "Look at other guys. They keep marching into gunfire even though they've been hit. Look at you, you sorry excuse for a soldier. Paralysed by fear and on the first day of an assault for Christ's sake." Another stab of pain silenced his iron-fisted sermon. This time, he could hardly groan, it hit him so hard, robbing his chest of breathing space.

Montreal: 27 Sebastopol Street
Friday, March 24, 1917, 2:45 p.m.

His breath came in short spurts. He had never felt the tickling delight of another person's hand on the flat of his stomach. His penis ached with stiffness and he felt his back arch ever so slightly—pushing his skin closer to her wandering fingers. A moan escaped his lips unbidden. Jo's breath caressed his ear and he heard her whisper, "Relax, let yourself go."

Gordon wanted to do just that but his heart was tied in knots of doubts and apprehension. Was this right? Weren't they sinning? Why did something so evil feel so tender? He didn't want to hurt her and, heaven forbid, he certainly didn't want to be cast in the role of a seducer of young women. She would have to take the lead.

And Jo did. The moment they were inside her room, she gently closed the door and pushed Gordon toward her bed. "Lie down, silly. I'm going to undress you."

Gordon did as he was told and watched with rising delight as she unbuttoned the lower buttons of his khaki tunic one by one. She was in no rush, confident that the house would be theirs for several hours to come. With each button, came the slight rub of her fingers on his undershirt.

Cooing in a teasing fashion, Jo played with his lapels. "I love a soldier in uniform. So masculine. Actually, I think I love you more out of uniform." With that she took hold of his collar and deftly pried open the final clasp. She looked into his eyes, smiled and then kissed his lips ever so slightly and ran her hands down his sides, massaging his ribs, abdomen, stopping at the belt level for the moment.

"Sit up, private! That's an order!" she commanded in an officer's voice, and, as Gordon obeyed, she slid the tunic off his arms and flung it on the floor beside the bed. Before Gordon had time to complain, she whipped off his undershirt and there he was, bare-chested for her pleasure.

Her kisses began slowly at the neck, one on each side, tingling and fleeting.

Gordon, finally coming alive, began to grope with his hands, trying to find the button that held the top collar of her dress in place. "Not yet,"

Jo protested, pulling away slightly, "I'm next. But right now let me work on you."

The kissing continued, with hands paving the way. Her lips were like fire; each place they landed, Gordon could sense a new heat. He had no idea how sensitive his chest and stomach could be. Jo was working her way to his nipples. Biting each in turn with a gentleness that was followed by a brush of her tongue, it was almost too much.

Gordon could feel his control slipping and her mouth came down on the small hairs at the base of his rib cage. Another moan passed from his lips. It felt so good to travel beyond restraint and allow his feelings to flow naturally. "Oh, that feels so good."

Jo looked up, smiled again before she kissed him and ran her hands over his chest. It was the uncertainty of where she would stop and caress him more deeply that was exciting for Gordon. He was alternately holding his breath and groaning in delight.

"Do you like this?" Jo paused in her labours to check signals. "It's not too hard for you to bear?"

Gordon smiled. Ran his hands from her shoulders down her arms, "It's wonderful. I ... I don't want you to feel any ... what I mean is you don't have to do this if you don't want to. I mean I don't want to pressure you to."

"Don't want to? Where's your head, Gordon? Who is running this show right now? Do I look like a helpless, distressed damsel, pressured for sex by an overbearing black knight?"

"Hardly."

"Exactly! Just enjoy it." Her hands began to work his shoulders. "Roll over and I'll give you a back rub."

"I don't know if I can stand much more." But Gordon dutifully pivoted onto his stomach. His penis was harder than he could imagine. Pressing it now against the mattress, he felt it would explode. "Stay calm," he thought. "Think chaste thoughts—at least until the time comes." He closed his eyes and tried to relax his vibrating passions.

He could smell the sweetness of the ointment before it touched the small of his back. Lilac. "What's that?"

"Just a little oil to soften these stiff soldier muscles. My, my. This belt is too tight. Lift your hips!" Gordon followed her instructions and felt her hands creep around his waistband and unclasp his belt, unbutton his pants and pull gently to loosen their grip. "Better?"

"Much."

Oil-slicked hands began to crisscross his back, ploughing ripples in his skin, and then stretching it flat. Once he felt her fists pounding up and down his spine and then her hands danced down his sides. Gordon shifted away from her probing fingers. It was getting too close to tickling.

"Just relax," she purred. "I'm not tickling. This is supposed to be soothing, silly."

Alas, for Gordon, a novice in the playfulness of the bed, Jo's efforts had the exact opposite effect from relaxation. His desire rose with each sweep of her hand. His mouth seemed to be speaking a language of its own, murmurs, gurgles and grunts. He was being swept down a pathway he had never known, a journey beyond words, with pleasure as his only guide.

"Now, let me do your front." Jo eased up off his back while Gordon rolled onto his back. They looked at each other, smiling. Jo had hitched up her dress, revealing her knees and thighs. Leaning back slightly, she laid her hands on the two flaps of his trousers. Pulling gently, they fell open of their own accord.

The bulge under his shorts was now pushing into view, and Jo laughed with desire and delight. "Hello." Her right hand swept down and began to massage his erection. "Aren't we pleased to see me?"

"Ahhhh." Gordon was on the brink, his eyes closed while his hands reached up for her. Fingers desperate, touching her breasts ever so tentatively.

"Not yet, my dear."

Jo moved back into a squat on his hips as she began to rub oil on his chest. It was pungent, and, ever after, the fragrance of lilac would excite a tingling passion between his legs.

Tracing slow circles through his chest hair, around his nipples, down his abdomen and over his belly button, Jo's strokes came closer and closer to the seat of his passion. Moving back slightly, her hands slipped gently beneath the waistband of his underwear, still massaging slowly.

"Lift your hips." Gordon did, and with a swiftness that surprised him, Jo pulled his pants and shorts down to his knees. "We don't need this between us, do we?" Jo winked and laughed. Working off his socks and then his pant legs, finally off came his underwear and Gordon was naked.

"You have beautiful legs." And her hands began to move up his shins, over his knees, her left hand fell between his thighs and slid up slowly, stopping just short of its goal.

"I can't wait," she moaned. "Now it's my turn." She flopped down beside Gordon on the bed. "See what you can do."

Vimy Ridge, France
Monday, April 9, 1917, 4:17 p.m.

Two men crouched over Gordon's bent form. The sergeant turned to Major Ryan. "You see what you can do with Davis, sir. I can't get a word out of him. Looks like the blighter crumpled under enemy fire and crawled back here." They both looked at the fallen soldier with contempt in their eyes. The sergeant continued, "A pity. First time for him as far as I know." Gordon was twisted into a tight foetal position again, lying on the duckboards of the now empty jumping off trench. He was either asleep or unconscious.

Ryan suspected he was faking a wound. "This ain't the first time. I found this lousy excuse for a soldier lying drunk in a ditch some months back—a deserter if I ever met one." His punctuated his words with kicks to Gordon's side.

The battle was raging up on the ridge. The artillery barrage was thundering. Nothing decisive yet, but all reports were pointing in the right direction. He wanted to disbelieve it, but these Canucks might just pull off a victory and take Vimy before nightfall. The Brits and the French before them had tried to take this blasted ridge and failed miserably. Could these Canadians really be that good? The major was torn between a grudging pride and angry consternation. How could these colonials win such a strategic stronghold, when England's best had failed?

Setting aside his dismay, he gazed again at Gordon Davis. "Damn my luck! I'm at the top of this battle and instead I am stalled by some yellow-belly, who has stumbled downhill from Vimy." It grieved Ryan to be called back from the supervision of his section of the front to deal with a coward. "Like I say. This is the second time this bastard has tried to pull one over one me." He spat out his words. "Well you won't escape this time, Davis." He drew out his revolver and placed the muzzle against Gordon's temple.

The sergeant gasped, "Sir?"

Ryan looked up. "What?"

The sergeant was unsure how to protest. Sweat was beading up on his forehead.

Ryan shrugged. "Death is too good for you." Pulling the trigger, he heard a metallic click. The chamber was empty.

"Blast," he shook the revolver, "I must have fired all my rounds at Fritz."

Ryan was bleeding from a flesh wound above his wrist. His cap had been blown off in the first few minutes of the charge and he hadn't stopped running for the past eight hours. There was no time to hunt around for more bullets for his pistol.

"Tie him up and drag him back to our reserve trenches. We'll have to court martial him later. There's too much movement up ahead to waste time on this bloody fool now." Ryan turned to leave. "Oh, once he wakes up," Ryan gave a last kick to Gordon's head, "tell Chambers to take him over to divisional HQ and they'll fix his wagon, but good." He turned to leave when another thought struck him. "Once you've stowed this trash, you get back up to the front with as many rounds of ammunition as your sorry ass can carry and don't forget to find a box of bullets for this." He waved his revolver in the air. "Got that sergeant?"

Ryan hopped over the sandbags, ran in a crouch toward the fighting and quickly forgot Gordon Davis. It would be weeks before the incident came back to his mind. By then he was occupied with other pressing matters of his own.

The sergeant stooped closer down to look at Gordon carefully and wondered if this fellow really was a coward. His nerves were settling after the close encounter with Ryan's summary execution. "Never seen you run from a fight before, Gordie, my son. I wonder what ails you?" He took Gordon by the shoulders and shook him hard, but he was drifting somewhere beyond speech. The pain pushed him out of consciousness, his mind swimming in a fog of half-images. His body was lost in waves of anguish.

"Nothing I can do for this guy," the sergeant grunted, shaking his head in frustration. Then he straightened up, forgetting his height for the moment. A fatal error as a lone sniper still able to get a bead on the trenches below Vimy. The bullet entered the sergeant's spinal cord just below his shoulder blades and took a downward spin into his heart. He was dead before he hit the muddy sidewall of the trench.

Gordon was left to fend for himself, as the shadows lengthened on that, the greatest day in Canadian history.

Montreal: 27 Sebastopol Street
Friday, March 24, 1917, 2:46 p.m.

Jo had closed her eyes, waiting for Gordon to act. He had never felt so intimidated, having to fend for himself when he was so obviously unprepared. Had he known that the picnic on Sisson Ridge would end up at this juncture, he would have at least quizzed his mates.

Winter light played across the wall above Jo's head. Her printed dress flowed down over her knees, dusty pink roses with fine green threads for stems on an off-white background. A white belt gathered it at the waist before it flared out again toward her ankles.

She was a perfect picture of vitality, beauty and happiness, lying face up, eyes closed, a slight smile tracing across her lips and golden hair flowing over the pillow. Gordon would always keep this picture in his mind, his brightest memory of love. If he could only stop time. The vision passed and he set about keeping up his side of their passion.

He was a bit rough and clumsy at first, but he allowed his instinct to direct his fingers. It seemed his initial efforts were not too far off the mark. Jo moaned with every touch of his hand.

Trying to imitate her caresses, he marched his fingers over her dress, slowly, rubbing here and there. His hands danced a silken path down around her hips, paused and slid back up either side of her dress. Then sitting up, his hands began a dance on her stomach. He stayed clear of her breasts. Little did he know that his tentativeness in not touching an erotic zone was taken as teasing, all the more exciting to Jo. Purring with delight, she rubbed her heels against the quilt cover, the rough fabric in contrast to his light touch.

His fingers continued to trace circles over her stomach. After a few rounds, and uncertain where to go next, they stopped. She could feel his nervousness, even though her eyes were closed. "It's okay Gordon, I won't break if you touch me here." With that she took his hands in hers and placed them squarely on her breasts.

Electric current couldn't have been stronger than the jolt Gordon felt. He didn't know what to expect, but Jo's breasts were soft to his touch and even though the dress masked them, Gordon could feel two hard nipples beneath. If her hands hadn't been holding his, he would have withdrawn from such an intimate encounter, shocked, aroused and above all, uncertain. After the initial shock wore off, Gordon began to play.

Jo groaned her delight.

"Please, undo my dress." A whisper.

Gordon, fully alive and terribly aroused, leaned forward and kissed her earlobes. "If you like."

"I would like."

Trying to make each move count, he played with the buttons, gently brushed whatever he found beneath (mostly white satin) and kissed her cheeks, eyelids, lips each time a button gave way. The belt was easy and accompanied by a long passionate kiss on Jo's lips. Working down past her stomach, his hands came to rest between her knees. A gentle light caress along the inside of her thighs and Jo's hips began to move. For some time Gordon couldn't undo the last few buttons but left his hands moving where they were.

Watching Jo arch her back, moan gently and rock her head on the pillow was almost as powerful as being touched himself. He could feel her move her thighs into his grasp. Smiling, involuntary sounds came from her half-open mouth. Once her tongue licked her lips, as if tasting his most recent kiss.

Jo was on a crest of pleasure. Her hands, which had been gripping the bed cover at alternate moments of ecstasy, reached out, came down beside her hips and made their own journey over the valleys and mountains of her body, pausing for a moment on her breasts, and then moving up to her neck finally brushing through her hair into the pillows beyond.

"Don't stop, don't stop."

Gordon took her words as a command to continue the undressing process, so he quickly moved down, unfastening the last button and drawing each side of the dress apart.

Beneath the dress she was awash in frills and white. Magnificent.

Johanna sat up slightly, enough to allow the short-sleeved dress to fall off her shoulders. Slowly, she drew an arm from each sleeve, and raising her hips she drew the dress out from underneath in a smooth easy movement, suggestive and inviting. With a quick smile, she slid back down, ready from more tenderness.   Gordon was blushing, his mind spinning. He looked down at her feet. "Where are your shoes?"

"I threw them off long ago, silly."

Gordon began again with his marauding massage, up one leg and over her stomach, pause, down across the other shoulder, between her thighs, pause, and down to her toes. It was a lingering, painfully erotic waltz. Jo was moaning at every touch and unable to keep herself still. "Move quickly, Gordon, I want to feel your body against mine."

This entreaty left Gordon perplexed. He didn't know where to go from here. The dainty laces of a woman's undergarments were confounding. Sure he had seen his sisters half-dressed, at least when they younger—but his father had been very clear about boundaries. Bed sports, sexual matters, the private and personal were strictly prohibited as topics for discussion. Heavens, Gordon didn't even know what to call the under things Jo wore, let alone devise how to undress her any further.

Jo, alert to the pause in his touch, giggled, rolled off the bed gracefully. "Let me help you." As Gordon watched, his own passion throbbing, she undid her clasps, pulled on strings, unfastened loops and hoops and within seconds was nude before him.

For several moments they were naked to each other, he on the bed, she standing in the middle of room. Young, alive to all their desires, it was the calm before the tempest of their passions broke.

"Do you like what you see?" Jo was always able to put into words her emotional interests. She looked at him and delighted in his awkward innocence. She ran hands behind her neck, and shook her hair.

Gordon fumbled about for just the right superlative. "Yes ... I mean ... you're beyond words. You're a gift for the eyes."

Jo laughed, "Ever my poet." She reached out a hand. "You're not such a bad parcel yourself, Gordon Davis. Now dance with me."

Taking his hand, she pulled him to a stance beside her and then moved her body into his. He could feel the brush of her pubic hair against his thigh, her small delicate breasts pressed into his middle.

There were moans and sways. "Dance with me." She finally whispered, "Pretend we're still at Sisson Ridge. Naked in the sunlight." She hummed a few bars of a love song and then began to move.

Gordon couldn't follow the melody, but he had a natural grace and swayed with her about the room, his hands resting on the small of her back.

Johanna could feel the muscles of his chest pressing against her. As they danced, she allowed her hands to run down his back, curve around his thigh, over his buttocks.

His erection was hard and large; she ached to feel it inside her. She could sense her own body's readiness, the moist pleasure between her legs, the sun-washed desire that radiated from her heart and loins at the same time, rising to blank out any other feeling.

"Touch my breasts, fool! I need you!"

Gordon's hands crept around from their perch on her hips and slid up over her ribs and caught her breasts.

Dancing ceased. Johanna took a slight step back and watched as Gordon played lightly at first, and then more uncontrollably.

"Gentle, be gentle with them. Lick them, kiss them." She arched her back slightly, thrusting her nipples toward his waiting hands.

"Oh God, you're good, Gordon, touch me! Take me!"

Vimy Ridge, France
Monday, April 9, 1917, 7:15 p.m.

The general looked sternly at his men. "The enemy that we face on this ridge is good. No … they're fucking good. Word has it that German high command has kept its Bavarian regiments on the heights for years. Make no mistake, Jerry isn't going to give up this ridge without a hell of a fight."

Gordon's dreams came in brilliant flashes, pushing through the clouds of fear and frailty. At times, he thought he was awake to his surroundings. Other times he would drift into memories or daydreams. The current stage was the recollection of their first "pep" talk before the training began for the Vimy assault. Many more serious, put-the-fear-of-God-into-the-troops words from on high would follow, but this initial speech was the best.

Their commanding officer, General Currie, was warm, almost informal with his troops. In great contrast to Major Ryan who ruled by fear, Currie worked wonders with humour and understatement, mixed with a healthy dose of Canadian skepticism.

"This is no picnic at Hamilton Beach, no sir. You'll work your arse ends off and still might not make it to the top. The Brits tried it. The French had their go. Now it's up to us to get the job done. As Field Marshal Haig said to me last week, "Currie old chap, try your hand at it. Just march your Canadians up to the top of Vimy, will you?'"

His accent was perfect and as he looked down at the crowd, he caught many slight smiles. Outright laughter at the expense of a supreme commander was still a few wars away. Nevertheless, the rank and file enjoyed sarcasm, especially when aimed at the uptight British army.

"Any sorry son-of-a-lumberjack that starts up this godforsaken hill ain't coming back, except on a stretcher, or unless he has to take a piss."

Gordon's mind drifted to the present. He was able to open his eyes. Darkness was falling. The pain in his midsection had lessened considerably—almost gone. He was staring at the drooped end of a mud-soaked sandbag. They were piled from floor to parapet at this section of the trench. The smell of acrid slime met his nostrils.

The trenches around Vimy had been churned by countless artillery barrages. From their heights, the Germans reigned terror on each square inch of the Allied position. When the Canadians arrived in 1917, repairing or building the trench work was like digging corpses. Practically every shovelful of dirt contained some remnant of past combatants' valour—bits of uniform, old mess kits, shredded legs, heads and torsos half-eaten by rodents.

Some historians argued, half seriously, that the Canadians took Vimy because they didn't want to stay down in the valley with the rotting corpses of past battles.

Gordon couldn't see the source of the foul smell, but his expert nose decided it was a many-months-old victim of gas. Funny how you could pick out a useless detail like that in the fog of semi-consciousness. The searing pain was strangely absent, though his stomach ached from the hours of straining against it. He didn't dare move. It might come back.

Machine gun fire echoed in the distance. It was certainly further away than the German front line. Someone must have broken through to the ridge. It was impossible to tell from the activity in the trench whether his side was winning or losing. Mud-spattered boots, blood-soaked puttees ran past him in both directions. A few swear words accompanied their departure over the top. No one turned in his direction or paid any attention to the fallen stretcher-bearer at his feet. Like so many other casualties, his remains—whether living or dead, could wait until the shooting was finished.

Gordon finally awoke to his own predicament. Night would soon cover the trenches in thick ink. Finding help or being assisted by a passing soldier would become all that more cumbersome. Whatever felled him might come back. "Better to get it checked," he muttered. He wiggled his nose against the stench of the mud nearby which prompted him to try to move his toes. They did—right on command. His legs, fingers, feet all obeyed his wishes, so with care he rolled onto his knees and eased his head up. Gordon put a shaky hand out and touched the blood-soaked scalp of the dead sergeant. A pause. No stabs yet. The stabbing agony was gone. Like a splinter pulled from a festering wound, there was only a numb throbbing where the knife-edge pain had been.

Gordon waited, assuring himself that he would not be split in half again. He struggled to a crouch and began working his way back toward the medics. A company of men, faces blacked out for a night raid on the German defences, pressed him against the trench wall. He could feel the damp sandbags imprint his tunic with the slime of many days rain. Once they were passed, he fell back into his slow march toward safety. Debris was scattered about the duckboards, overcoats discarded at the last moment before the morning's charge, empty cans of bully beef, a few bits of rope. The clutter slowed his shuffling feet and increased his exhaustion.

It took several hours, a number of long rests and a pee break before Gordon arrived at the dressing station. It was crowded with blood and pain. Moans came from rows on rows of stretchers. Blankets covered the carnage and on each victim was a neat tag. Those who were beyond hope had a yellow one, indicating their status as non-entities, waiting for the grave. Those who needed help and had a chance of survival were given the blessed red flag. A ticket to Blighty and maybe a long and happy life.

Gordon flopped between a blood-stained stretcher and a large white box and sighed. He could go no further. The pain hit with full force. His abdomen was on fire. The exertion of his long crawl back had drained his energy. He opened his mouth. Nothing came out.

Dick Higgins, a new orderly assigned to the fifth battalion medical corps, looked up as Gordon sank down beside the box of amputated limbs. Dick's first thought was grotesque. "Maybe I should dump this one right into the box, save us the energy of cutting his off first." The long day had robbed him of any compassion. Each new patient was simply another decision: yellow or red? On closer inspection, Dick thought this new arrival looked different than most. The lack of blood or an obvious wound, made him stop for a moment. "Maybe a faker?" he said out loud.

Turning to find the doctor, he shouted out a coded message, "Yellow fever, Doc. I need an assessment." "Yellow fever" was their code for trench cowardice or shell-shock. No scientific study; they just knew that a certain percentage of their victims were knocked off the rails into dementia—who knew how long it would last?

The weary doctor turned slowly. Brent Woods had been cutting and sponging for twelve hours straight. He felt like a bloody fool, patching up broken bodies with little more than some gauze and bottle of whiskey. "What?" His patience was running low. "What now, Dick? I've got this fellow's gut half open—damn knife thrust—missed almost everything vital." The doctor muttered to himself, "Lucky sod."

"Sir?"

"What ... what is it?"

"Yellow fever," Dick replied, pointing at the semi-conscious Gordon who had inadvertently allowed his left arm to slide into the box of severed legs and arms.

"Give me a minute." Brent was not going to be rushed with this patient. Here was a chance to save at least one. "A few stitches will make the difference between life and death," he muttered. "God, I wish I had stayed back in Prescott—settled down to the family practice like my father asked." He grimaced as he tied off another suture and looked about for a nurse. "Hopkins," his eyes raked the lines of stretchers, "Hopkins, get me some more goddamn gauze." Hopkins left the side of a delirious corporal and brought the good doctor his gauze. "Barks like a bloody general," Hopkins said to the Red Cross-marked box of gauze, "and I'm his only private." She smiled at her own joke as she dutifully carried out his orders. Truth be known, he was actually a very gentle boss, but in the heat of battle he turned into a demanding tyrant. Fighting off the Grim Reaper turned Woods into a tiger and in that state everyone jumped to his demands without question.

Brent wiped his aching hands on a now red apron, and left the side of his most recent patient, satisfied with his work. The man would live, probably have nagging stomach pain through the rest of his days, but that was certainly better than occupying a space six-feet underground.

"Now, where's this yellow fever patient, Dick?" He was putting on his rough exterior, ready to shout down a whining coward and browbeat him back to some semblance of courage. He'd done it hundreds of times. His bloodied appearance and his finely tuned professional aggression usually had the cheaters out of his station and back to their companies.

"Over here," Dick winked. "Looks like he passed out."

Woods marched over and looked down at Gordon and immediately lost his severe demeanour. "This is Davis, best stretcher-bearer we've got. He's no faker, Dick! I've seen him dance through enemy fire, dragging back dozens of men. Who knows how many lives he's saved?"

Dick defended his first call. "No blood, no wounds. Just hugging his middle, like he's going to vomit. Sorry sir, he just looked ..."

"I'm not doubting your judgment. It just seems strange." Brent bent down and tried to unfold the bunched up legs that acted like a shield to Gordon's chest.

Gordon opened his eyes and tried to speak again. "Doctor —" The pain was drowning his words and he couldn't breathe. Sweat poured off his forehead.

Brent reached down between the legs and the stomach, feeling for the gash in the uniform that signaled a bullet entry. Nothing. He looked into Gordon's eyes and read the pain that was so obviously present. "Does it cut across your middle?"

Gordon nodded.

Brent felt the right side, a simple jab in the location he most suspected and Gordon crumpled in pain.

"Jesus Christ." Brent leapt to his feet and searched for his nurse, found her by a distant wall, slouched in fatigue. "Hopkins, clear that table. This man has a severe appendicitis. Let's just hope it hasn't ruptured." He motioned Dick to help. "Take his arms, I got the legs. Gently, now, every movement is like another bullet wound."

With care they lifted him across rows of wounded soldiers.

"It's a miracle he made it this far on his own." The doctor was constantly surprised by the endurance and courage of men in arms. "Tough as a pig's backside. With guys like him, it's no wonder we're taking the ridge."

Montreal: 27 Sebastopol Street
Friday, March 24, 1917, 4:10 p.m.

Gordon and Johanna sweated their way toward another climax. How many times had she felt her body surge toward ecstasy? She'd lost count. It was a rushing torrent of light and lust. Her hands gripped the small of his back and they rocked together.

"Wait for me," she moaned.

He looked down into her wondrous eyes, unable to speak.

How had they come this far? He recalled the rush of his hands over her body, the firm stomach, taut to his touch. His lips caressing her breasts, his tongue teasing her nipples. Who first made the move toward the bed? He couldn't recall. Maybe they fell together, side by side.

Then she had played with the hair of his chest, allowed her hands to tickle down the line of his stomach to his erect penis. His mind almost exploded as she began to rub her palm on its tip.

Slowly, gently, she pushed his erection down between her legs, allowed it to massage her into greater arousal.

She was oblivious to everything but his touch. Wanting to please him, wanting this first time to be better than her initial encounter, she whispered, "Feel good?"

Gordon moaned, "Yiss ... moorrr," something between yes and more.

Johanna knew the cry of pleasure and continued her play. His hand ran up and down her side, gently playing with her hip. Turning down between her thighs, he ran his forefinger along the lips of her vagina. The touch that set her burning.

"Now ... please ... come inside." With that she straddled his hips and thrust him between her legs. Tenderness was left behind as she rocked back onto her knees, feeling him move inside her, pushing backward and forward.

Her hands on his chest. His on her nipples. Eyes locked on each other as mouths opened in silent pleasure.

Gordon was consumed by heat and the fiery friction of her belly against his own.

Sounds he had never heard before ran from his mouth in a stream of delight, sounding like a split between agony and ecstasy.

Johanna's words were more distinguishable. "Oh, Gordon, oh yes ... please don't stop ... that's oh ... I love it ...."

Their first time, they came together in a rush of groping hands, and liquid desire. Gordon was beyond thought. Johanna was trembling with satisfaction, body and soul as one.

In time their breathing slowed, Jo lowered herself to his chest, kissed him lightly on the lips and rested her head on his shoulder. Gordon's hands moved up and down her spine, reassuring.

"Don't ever stop. I love it." Jo was ready to sleep. Maybe she did for a few minutes. How could some men be so gentle while others were so rough? Gordon was a magician with his hands.

Gordon's eyes were wide open. He had never felt his body rule his mind in that way before. The sensation went well beyond the physical. Perhaps it was her openness, vulnerability that touched him. Yet she was anything but helpless. She had shown him her heart just now and that was the kindest gift he had ever been given.

Were they in love? Gordon had no experience by which to judge. It felt right, as if their bodies had been made for each other even though he was so lumbering and clumsy and she so light and spring-like.

As if reading his mind, Jo moaned, "You're just right. We fit together. I was afraid we might be mismatched. But my old soul and your new one like each other." With that she began to play with his nipple, and the dance began all over again. "I take that back. You may have an old young soul."

"While yours is old, old?"

Johanna smiled. "Exactly!"

The shadows were lengthening on the wall when they fell into each other exhausted, wet and filled with their new-found passion.

"Can love stretch across the ocean, do you think?" Johanna was suddenly filled with deep sadness. The contentment ached for continuation and she knew he would be leaving. "Tell me you'll send all your love toward Montreal." She pulled back from his grasp and looked at his face, eyes closed, mouth open slightly.

"I will." Gordon swallowed, opened one eye and looked at her. "I will think of you always." He fumbled for something deeper, a way to touch her soul with the passion that stirred him. "I am not very bright … I don't know much about loving except that it is not ours to command. It comes unasked. Love like ours is a gift, not often given."

"I love you, Gordon Davis." She kissed his shoulder tenderly, knowing how hard it was for him to speak. "You're right. I don't know how or why this happened, except …." Johanna paused wondering how much to let out. There were insights she was always frightened to share lest she reveal too much, walk out on the limb that snaps. Her heart won out over her fear and she said, "Except that we have been meant for each other—two lights coming together after a long absence. Perhaps in another life we were lovers."

Gordon was puzzled. "What do you mean?" Inwardly, he could feel his mind resisting. It was too preposterous.

Jo's hand toyed with the hairs on his chest, a grin spread over her face. "There is a legend about great love." Gordon let out a chuckle. "Stay with me and don't laugh. You know I'm the brains of this outfit." She continued, "Love, the deep-rooted love—the one you yourself say is a gift given to only few — well, it doesn't die, even when those who share it have passed on. Love that has reached a level of intensity and truth becomes eternal, passing from one couple to the next generation, searching for the perfect pair to enjoy it again."

Gordon was skeptical, "Come now, Jo, do you think that it's true?"

"Of course," her hands gripped his face and she turned his eyes toward hers, intense and very serious. "Don't you feel it, the waves of contentment, the deep, almost knitting together of thoughts and instincts, knowing the other is open and alive, like we're flowing into one another."

"Yes, I felt that."

"Well, we're swimming in a river greater than ourselves. We've been touched by the love affair of some past glory. I can feel it, there's no going back now, Gordon. We've found each other ... no ... an ancient love has found us and won't let us go."

She rested her head on his shoulder again. "Even when you're in France, it shall bind us. We are not its master, but its servants."

This talk was beyond Gordon's imagination and he broke the spell with a practical thought, "When did you say your father is coming home?"

Saint John: Centenary-Queen Square United Church
Tuesday, Nov. 17, 1992, 11:23 a.m.

After a brief pause, I turn from the Hebraic mind to the Christian one. Not a great distance.

"The apostle Paul understood, perhaps better than any other disciple the vision of Isaiah. Paul was faced time and again with the question of death. 'Surely God has forsaken us,' Christians would ask him." I pause, to allow the consternation of past generations to sink in.

Then I conclude, "Nothing can separate us. God's love binds all beings into one and the love we share takes us over the grave."

Silence reigns in the sanctuary. My student intern has been listening. The stranger under the balcony is also attentive. I see her smile, but this time she's looking directly at me, no flinching or downcast eyes.

"The Word of the Lord."

"Thanks be to you, oh Christ!"

Montreal: A Café, two blocks from Thelma Lint's Gentlemen's Parlour
Friday, December 7, 1917, 7:25 p.m.

"Thank heavens I found you. I had no idea you hadn't heard of your father's passing." Cruikshank recovered quickly from his embarrassment. A twitch of guilt picked at his mind, but quickly he turned on his funeral charade. "Don't take this so hard, son." His hand reached over and touched Gordon's. "The Almighty has ways and means that are beyond our lowly minds."

"I am sure your father is resting in the arms of Jesus, comfortable in the knowledge that he fulfilled his life's calling." The suicide did confound that logic, but Cruikshank was not about to let life's idiosyncrasies interrupt his best sermon. "We must trust in God's overarching purposes. Recall what Martin Luther said, 'Be ye —'"

Gordon looked up abruptly. The cold cup of tea swirled in front of him. "Suicide? Did my father really take his own life? I can't believe it."

"Alas, my child, it is true."

Gordon choked down his tears. "But he was always so keen on living—telling his stories to the junior Sunday school."

Cruikshank smiled sweetly. "Only God knows."

"How did he ... I mean what ... oh God, my family. Did he ... I mean ... was it at ... Did he do it near the house or ...."

Cruikshank whispered, "You don't need to know, really it won't change anything —"

Gordon's eyes flashed, "You think I haven't seen death. I've had more than ten lifetimes full of it. Now, how did it happen?"

"I shouldn't say. I wasn't there. It was only my friend Father Hawthorne who told me—"

"How, damn it!"

Cruikshank could feel the fire building up. "In the upstairs washroom. He used his own shotgun, I understand. Tragic."

Gordon lowered his head and groaned. "Why? After all this .... Mother's death and now this! It just doesn't make sense. He always said he kept that gun for hunting."

"If it's any comfort, he left a note saying that he couldn't live without your mother and that he felt deep guilt—being unable to provide for her when she was sick. Feeling a failure, having 'let down his many children at church.' I imagine this last thought was thinking of what his suicide would say to his young charges in the church school."

Gordon could feel the tears running down his cheeks, the desperation of the last few days leaving him close to the edge of his emotions. "That's just like him—taking on everyone's woes as his own. Blaming himself for their failings. It wasn't his fault the family had no money for

Mother. Times were hard and we were lucky to have food on the table most weeks. Our neighbours were much worse off."

"A pity, I agree."

They sat silently for a long time, each in their own thoughts.

Gordon blurted out the fear that was gnawing at him. "It wasn't because I got accused of desertion?"

"Pardon?" Cruikshank looked up from his daydreams. "Desertion?"

"It was not proved. A big mistake really." Gordon felt shame rise in his face and felt the need to justify himself to his principal. "I was drunk and disorderly for sure, but I was no coward."

Cruikshank coughed with displeasure, "Well, no, there was no one who mentioned that in connection with your father's death."

"It's just that rumours get back here and people don't have all the facts—they don't know what it's like over in France." Gordon looked at his companion for some sympathetic response and seeing none he rushed on, "I don't think people could imagine the mud and lice, the constant killing."

"No, indeed."

Gordon began to blubber out his dismay and anguish. "It's beyond me. I can't stand proud again. Flanders is our worst nightmare. We march lockstep to an insane beat and no one has the power to stop it, this dance of death! We're caught in this storm, unable to change, not wanting to murder another human being again, but knowing that it's either him or me. So you harden your heart and grab your rifle. You know the war is killing more than men. It first attacks your soul."

The mention of a religious idea gave the principal his opening to bring this young fellow back to earth. "Souls are indeed injured in this conflict. I was reminded of it this morning. I was talking with Bishop Hinks and he mentioned your name. I believe you know him and ah … his daughter—Johanna I believe her name was. Well, my lord Hinks said that he …."

"Have you seen her?" Gordon's words were blurted out before he could refine them.

"Who?"

"Johanna."

"Who?" Cruikshank was being stubborn now that his comfort-to-the-grieving sermon was completely spoiled.

"Bishop Hinks' daughter, Johanna." Gordon's voice had an edge of urgency.

"The daughter? Heaven's no. The good bishop was just relating her recent trials. He hasn't seen her for a number of days. The news of war seemed to spark considerable anguish and she was beyond consolation. She was to take a trip to Halifax, for what purpose he didn't say. Maybe she went, but with the explosion and all, there's no news at all coming from the east. I wonder if she was caught in that terrible debacle."

Gordon's heart rose and sank at the same time. He had no realization that his hands were gripping the tablecloth, sending ripples through its length. "Do you know where the bishop is now? It's urgent that I speak with him. I went to his home earlier and couldn't find him."

"Yes ... well ... that makes perfect sense, my child." Cruikshank put a consoling hand on Gordon's. "There's a great meeting of bishops these past two weeks. A once-a-decade conclave—a "national synod" we call it—to deal with church matters. This one is focused on recent events in France, of course." The principal gave each word such weight, as if the ecclesial affairs were of ultimate importance to the war effort. He coughed slightly. "Yesterday, I was called to speak to them concerning the readiness of our students for overseas service." he smiled in recollec-tion, "I gave a rather good account of —"

"Where?"

"Where what, my son?"

"Where is the meeting?" Gordon's eyes were burning.

"Oh yes, well, at the cathedral of course."

Gordon was up from the table before the principal finished his directions. Flying out the door, he was unable to hear Cruikshank's final words. "But there's no one there right now, the meeting is adjourned for two hours more."

Seeing that his words were lost to the fleeing soldier he waved a hand of dismissal. "Go find your silly bishop. See if I care. Hinks is just a pompous know-it-all anyway. Has no patriotic zeal. That's his problem."

Looking for the waiter, Cruikshank's mind went to the evening of delight that he had planned for himself. "Waiter, a glass of red wine please." He snapped his fingers to punctuate his command. He would enjoy the delights of Montreal while he could. Toronto was so parochial and prudish.

A glass was pushed before him and he moved his teacup aside. He lifted the glass in both hands like a communion chalice. Reverently, slowly, he raised it to his lips and took a great gulp of wine. "Women have such keen minds for a man's transgressions." He laughed into his cupped hands as he thought of his wife and he waited for the alcohol to settle his nerves. Here in Canada's great European city, he was free to exercise his passions. Oh, it will be glorious. A quick rallying of the troops at the evening meeting and then off to ... where was it? Cruikshank pulled the slip of paper from his vest pocket and whispered the address and name—to remember them before he crushed the paper and set it in the ashbin by his table. "Thelma Lint's Gentlemen's Parlour." "How delicious!" he thought. "Nothing better for the soul than the odd desertion into the enemy territory of sin ...."

Cruikshank's head snapped to attention as he recalled a far-off conversation on desertion. Gordon Davis had featured in that discussion and so had Ryan. His political mind was leaping ahead to questions and strategies, and he jumped up from the table and rushed out to the street. "Where to find a blasted telegraph office at this time of night? This might be the chance for which he had so fervently prayed. I'll have to visit Thelma's later than expected."

Canadian National Rail Line: Three miles from Halifax
Thursday, December 6, 1917, 9:07 a.m.

Johanna struggled to her feet. The sudden screeching halt of the train had knocked her backwards down the aisle of the frigid rail car. She rubbed her hip where an armrest had poked her on the way down. "Damn trains. Why do we have such cattle cars when in Europe they are so civilized?" Cursing her luck for being crammed into a square box, in the rising storm of wind and cold, she paced back to her seat and flopped down, impatience showing for all to see.

She ached to arrive at the Halifax harbour. She had promised to be on the pier when Gordon arrived, and now it looked like she would be late. "Curse them to hell," she muttered. He would think she had forgotten. Looking down at her burden, she smiled in anticipation thinking, "He has no idea what I am bringing him, the gift of a lifetime." Dreaming of their encounter, she drifted off. The wings of her spirit taking flight towards her imminent reunion with Gordon.

A gruff voice brought her back into the stalled train. "Word is we're here for some time." The conductor was weaving through sprawled legs that crossed into the aisle. "Sorry about the delay folks. The dining car is serving up hot coffee and wonderful porridge, compliments of the Canadian National Railway." His singsong voice went further down the car. "Sorry, madam, I can't tell you when we're moving again." "No, sir, I won't be able to send any messages on; the telegraph seems to be out."

Johanna turned a sour face to the window. "What if he leaves without me?" She dismissed the thought immediately. He was too much in love. His letters were clear. He wanted her and he would wait for eternity until they were together again. He'd be there on the pier.

The young mother sitting opposite Johanna was fussing with her baby. "Now, Jacob, are you hungry again?" she purred softly. A few whimpers came in response, a reply that only a mother can interpret. "Okay. Lucky your meal comes with me wherever I go." The woman tugged at her dress and eased the child into position.

Johanna reached forward. "Let me help you." She draped a warming blanket over the woman's shoulders to cover the baby who was now eager to latch onto a breast and feed. The operation complete, the woman sighed to her baby, "There you go, honey." And then to Johanna, "Thank you, Madame. I appreciate your help and you being so weighted down yourself." A quick smile crossed her face before she looked under her blanket at the wonder that was feeding.

"He's a beautiful boy." Johanna's voice was soft. Then looking out the window she wondered aloud, "I wonder what has held us up?" It was a question asked to the wind and snow, and she didn't really expect a reply. But from behind her head, a deep voice offered an answer. "I was just down at the dining car." The male voice was quiet, not wanting to disturb the feeding child. "Appears there's been some sort of fire in the main station at Halifax. Held up traffic everywhere."

Johanna turned her head to see who had spoken. He had a wrinkled face, a thick white moustache and carefully trimmed beard. There was a faint smile in his eyes. "Sorry for you folk. This is hardly the place for children."

Johanna smiled in return. "We'll be fine."

The gentleman was about to turn back to his own business when a thought struck him. "Can I get you ladies a hot drink, perhaps some cocoa or tea?" Johanna was about to refuse when she realized that her limbs were a bit cold, even under her heavy coat. Tea would be soothing. "Yes thank you, a cup of tea would be reassuring." She turned to her benchmate. "Would you like some tea?" A gentle nod in the affirmative was the only answer and she relayed her request to the kind man. He left immediately for the dining car, pleased to be of service to damsels in distress, even at his advanced years.

They sat in silence for a time. The odd slurp and swizzle coming from under the blanket was the only sound to disturb their thoughts.

Before their "white knight" had returned with tea, the conductor walked back up the train. His mind was filled with emergency plans. "The food won't hold out much past noon," he thought. "Wonder where I can find a farm close enough to supply some eggs and milk, at least for the little ones." He looked down at Johanna and her companion. "Got to keep 'em well fed, at least."

Johanna looked up to catch the conductor's gaze and asked if there was any news about their delay. "A gentleman suggested that it was a fire in the main station that has all train traffic stalled. Is that so?" Her anxiety was showing.

The conductor was about to give his standard "I'm not in a position to say" reply, when something in this young woman's eyes caught his breath and silenced him. Brushing a strand of her hair out of her eyes, Johanna continued, "You see my fiancé (she liked the sound of that word), my fiancé is disembarking today. Pier Seven. He was wounded in France." She produced his most recent letter and pointed to the line where his destination and time of arrival had been scribbled. Repeating it word for word, she said, "Halifax Harbour, Pier Seven, December 6. That's today. Do you think we will be here long?"

The conductor bent down and whispered, "Ma'am, I can't say for sure, but the news isn't good. The last word we had from Halifax was that a ship was on fire. We were to stay clear. Since that message came, the lines went dead. Nothing coming in or going out. Whatever happened, I'm sure your young man will be all right." The conductor was about to pass on, but a twinge of sympathy slowed his departure. "I'll get the telegraph agent to send a message as soon as the lines are repaired. What's this young fellow's name?"

"Gordon Davis."

"Davis ... right. I'll check it out. Would you like something warm, tea perhaps?"

Johanna smiled, even though her heart was panicking. "Thank you, I believe a passenger has already seen to our needs."

"Good. I'll send word, if any news comes in." He continued up the car, passing out what assurance he could.

Johanna looked out the window. A slight skiff of snow formed on the gravel roadbed, faint warnings of the arriving storm. Where was Gordon? Had he been on the ship that was ablaze? Had it spread to the pier? What if he was trapped and she couldn't reach him? Why don't we get this train moving?

"Here's a little something for you ladies." The gentle voice was back with a tray, loaded with tea and a plate of scones. "I took the liberty of acquiring a few sweet buns for energy." Johanna was preoccupied, but her lips moved automatically and motioned to the vacant space, "Please, sit here and I'll hold the tray."

The stranger prepared the tea and when all were served, he observed, "Isn't hot tea glorious? I recall a time when I was waiting in a train station in Calcutta—years back, it was blazing outside—melt your best intentions it would. Anyway, a friend suggested we take a cup of hot tea and I didn't think it was ...."

As her companion continued his tale, Johanna's mind raced back to the harbour fire and could only think of the heat of the flames and her Gordon caught in them.

Saint John: The Buttress Home
Thursday, Sept 10, 1992, 8:45 p.m.

When I pulled the robes from my bag, Gordon shoved aside his cup of hot liquid. Coffee, tea? It was forgotten whatever it was. "What a glorious feast for the eyes, my child." Pastor Inkling was in fine form. I had brought along a black gown from the choir room and a preaching stole. He had asked if he might dress in his clerical best to receive communion. I had no Anglican vestments, but gathered the fanciest robes at the church and borrowed a few items from an Anglican colleague.

"Excellent." Gordon's skeptical hands stroked the satin hem of the gown. "It is important to meet one's Maker dressed appropriately, don't you think?"

I could feel a sermon coming on.

"Alas, my child, we have become such a shoddy band of reprobates in these past few years. I was telling the verger that our congregation has lost all sense of liturgical decorum, when, what should appear, but a choirboy without his proper jacket and tie. I ask you, friends," Gordon, a.k.a. Father Inkling, waved a rebuking hand in the air, "I ask you, how can we expect God to do right by us, if we don't have the common decency of dressing well for Him? It is important to meet one's Maker dressed appropriately," his hands rubbing the gown reverently, "with all one's buttons done and the hems in place."

"Father!" I interrupted.

"What, my son?" said in that clerical condescending tone.

"You said something about meeting your Maker. Twice now. Are you expecting to die soon?"

"Die …. Heaven's no. It's just a figure of speech. Don't they teach you anything in college these days?" Carefully inspecting my attire, noticing every thread and seam in my dress, he said, "From your appearance I must assume they don't."

"I came as quickly as I could after evening prayers. Sorry if I look tattered around the edges." (Truth is ... after forty-two years, clean I can do, but neat escapes me.)

"Indeed, well, you must put your back into it. Give your body the attention it is due. Another figure of speech. Did you notice?" he laughed.

I nod.

"Words are not just vowel sounds separated by consonants," he began, no doubt surveying the imaginary balcony of his church audience. "They are the vessels of our truth, the vehicles of our passions. Without words we are nothing."

"I ...ah...."

Father Inkling stopped me in midstream. "Don't interrupt! The problem with this generation is that they think they have the right to comment on everything. Bide your time and listen to your elders for a moment."

"I—"

He cut me off again sharply. "Stop pretending you have advice or knowledge that alludes you!"

A cough raked his shoulders, but I didn't move.

"As I was saying, our words are everything. Weigh them well! Use them carefully. Too many people count their speech as worthless. Betraying promises, playing fast and loose with loved ones. It is a shame." He looked at a distant point that I could not see.

"There was a time when words were costly. You stuck by them. Your whole sense of dignity was caught in keeping your word. Woe unto those who broke theirs."

The priestly voice fell silent, his eyes cast down. Whatever he saw was not pretty.

"Have you ever broken your word, Father?"

"What's that?"

"Broken your word?" He looked blank. I tried again. "Have you ever gone back on a promise, not kept your word?"

Inkling was tracking again, his eyes sharp with pain. "Alas, I have. The most heinous of crimes. I broke my troth when I trusted her too little." Whatever powerful image danced in his mind, he was not sharing it.

"Her?" I prompted.

He looked up, deep sadness in his face. "My church, dear child, my church. I believed too little, took my own opinions for gospel. She never stopped loving me, but I assumed she had. I went off like the prodigal, whoring in other lands and left her to fend for herself. I even cursed her and her seed."

"The church?" Gordon's images sounded out of focus, but his anguish was real.

"Indeed. Mother church is the foundation of us all, of all, of all. She touches us where no one else can ... befriends us when we are alone. She is all ...." His words dwindled away into another daydream and for a number of minutes he lived an ancient pain. Its furrows traced across his brow. Tears welled at the edges of his eyes. He let them fall onto his cheeks without caring.

The long silence was interrupted by an explosion. Gordon actually shouted, "I played her for a fool, I did. Lost all confidence in her. Thought her words were trash."

He spat out, "I was the one who was trash!" He trembled, on the verge of weeping and began to rock back and forth.

"Father," I rested my hand on his forearm. "I'm sure the church has forgiven you."

"I never had the chance to tell her," he mumbled.

"Tell her what?" I was trying to ease open the door of his suffering— let in the freshening breeze of grace.

"That I was sorry. That it was I who had betrayed our love. That it was I who was so unfaithful, unbelieving. That it was I who was the coward at the ridge, the yellow-bellied coward who couldn't live up to his own words."

"Surely, you are forgiven." I didn't know what to say beyond broad platitudes.

"It's too late. Don't you see? It's too late. I never got to tell her. Never offered her any explanation. Only saw ... only saw ... only saw ... once ...."

He was getting more agitated. I wondered about a shot of Valium and turned toward the door. Could the nurses hear me if I called? I didn't want to leave Gordon's side, and yet he definitely was working himself into a serious state.

"Only saw ... Only saw ... Only saw ... once." The words grew more angry and pronounced. "Only saw ... only saw ... only saw ... once."

I was about to leave his bedside when his tone changed, almost to a lullaby. "Only saw ... only saw ... only saw him once."

"Him?" I was not following Gordon's logic, but my interruption acted like a switch.

"Hymn?" Father Inkling, asked indignantly. "Why would you suggest we sing a hymn at this hour? This house of prayer is for silent reflection and adoration." His tone was winding up to clerical heights again. "Don't they teach you anything in college these days?" His preaching voice was back. "Life, my son, is like a puzzle. We're all looking for the missing pieces. Well, it is mother church that supplies them—meets all our needs in fact." He took a breath and then, as if for the first time, saw the vestments I was holding. "How glorious! What a feast for the eyes! Let me try them on. It is important to meet one's Maker dressed appropriately."

Whatever his betrayal, it was too deep to touch, at least in this session. I gently assisted him into the gown, preparing to meet his Maker. He pushed and pulled, fretting with feeble hands that could not find their way through the folds of cloth.

At one point in the struggle, I hit his Bible and sent it to the floor. A cascade of letters spilled onto the floor. Reaching to arrange his few belongings, I saw the most curious of his letters. Water-stained and mud-smudged, I have puzzled over its meaning many times since. Like all the rest it had no return address, but this one was the only one missing a date and a signature.

Gordon,

A quick word. A single one: Joy!

This is your lucky day. You don't know it yet, but it is. I am so happy for you that I have prepared a special present for you this Christmas. All

those wishes you sent into the heavens, they
are answered.

If anything is ever lost, you will find me. I know this
is the lasting truth of time together.

Santa Claus

PS. A serious note. If ever you can't find me, don't
look at the North Pole. Try Thelma Lint. She's
my matron saint now. Her address: 14 Aylmer
Street, Montreal

CHAPTER SIX

The Sermon

Priests … The sermon is degrading to the majestic flight of worship. It is a foul fowl. If this tired buzzard was not the sole responsibility of the priest, church elders would have killed it long ago.

K.R. Guard, *Sermons: Sickness unto Death*

Toronto: 20 Mountalan Ave.

Saturday, April 12, 2014, 7:30 a.m.

I woke with a start. Jack was crying in the next room. He'd been pounding on the bedroom door (which I had shut tight on my son's advice!) and was frantic. There's a sermon coming from his mother, if she ever finds out!

I hustle down the hallway as the phone on the hall table rings. Without thinking, I answer. "I am so sorry Rob, … I forgot to get up with Jack. He's crying now, but …."

"I'm not Rob, but on his behalf I wish you would take better care of little Jack!" Laughter followed.

"Who is this?" The doorknob would not open. Is it broken? Jack, hearing my voice, rekindled his pleas to be let out. "Patricia? Is this New Brunswick calling again?"

"Yes it is."

"It's Saturday. Did they outlaw weekends in the Maritimes?"

"I have to clear out this office completely. 'New broom sweeps clean!' And that sweeping goes all the way down to any dangling issues with files. It has taken quite a while to find you and we are under consider-able time pressures. If my successor takes this over, you may be in for years of wrangling. It wouldn't be beyond the new regime … it wouldn't be beyond them to demand back payment for your great-uncle's care. Best not let that happen, don't you agree?"

"Of course." The bloody knob was stuck. Jack is beside himself, thinking that I was intentionally punishing him. "Excuse me, Patricia." I set the phone down and speak through the door. "I'm trying. Jack! Don't cry! Papa needs a hammer." I pick the phone up again as I go in search of my hammer. "Sorry about this … a bit of household emergency … poor Jack."

Patricia laughed again. "I'd cry if I were Jack. Pastor, is there any chance you could get down here in the next day or two?"

"You serious?"

"Absolutely. Any chance at all?"

"Well, I have to preach on Sunday but I could leave after that … takes me about fourteen hours on the bike."

"You're fast!"

"A Goldwing, not a bicycle … My one vice. How is Monday morning?" I was rummaging around for a good claw hammer.

Patricia sounded relieved. "Great. Shall we say noon? I'll text you with the address. Good luck with Jack and that door, Grandpa!"

"Nice … thanks. Next time, I'll leave it open."

Montreal: Mont Royal Park (Sisson Ridge Park)
Monday, December 10, 1917, 9:37 a.m.

In the past twenty-four hours Gordon had grown up. He knew it … for certain. From a bumbling child, shackled by self-doubt to a bold coura-geous man. Others saw him that way, but now he knew it. Like a fog lifting, he could taste his stupidity in relating to Jo and could count the cost of his emotional cowardice.

The child was cast aside, as Gordon walked the path toward the city centre. A plan in his mind. A quick stop at a bank office, and he would be done.

The past evening's debacle still sharp in his mind. He went over the events again: the shouts of recriminations, the harsh lies and the panic in Jo's eyes—her horror and dismay. At the side of the sanctuary, the huddled, broken figure of her father, the bishop, slumped in shock. Gordon had sprinted from the building, not looking back, not heeding the shouts for him to stop. Even when that woman, the one who seemed to be a mother to Jo, tried to stop him, he'd brushed her aside, not breaking stride until he was hidden deep in the forest of Sisson Ridge Park. Their safe place ... only there was he alone.

Waking early, his resolve had not weakened. If anything, it was stronger.

Walking briskly, Gordon preached one last sermon to himself: "No more excuses. Time to live up to your promises and pay the piper." There was steel in his intentions. He was never as certain about anything as he was at that moment. "So this is it," he smiled and silenced his mind.

Montreal: Thelma Lint's Gentlemen's Parlour
Tuesday, June 26, 1917, 10:49 p.m.

"That's it? 'A horse in a bathtub.' You've got to be joking." Thelma began to howl with laughter, finally coughed, almost choked and had to sit up.

Hinks was enjoying his story. "I kid you not. Here we are. The congregation is hushed. All ears on the pulpit. The newly elected primate is about to utter his first words as the chief cleric of Church of England in Canada, representative of the Crown. How does he begin his sermon? Will we be singed by fire and brimstone? Or lifted from our seats in rapture?" Here Hinks screwed up his face in consternation, rubbing his chin.

Thelma held her sides—aching from laughter.

Hinks continued. "That's how he looked. What did he do ... he started deep breathing—from his toes, chest heaving. A sight!"

Thelma was confused, "Deep breathing ... I don't understand."

Hinks explained, "He wanted to look like the perplexed preacher, weighing mighty doctrines in the balance. The audience is now prepared for a pronouncement from Mount Sinai. The eleventh commandment or a new edition of the Beatitudes. Instead he clears his throat and says, 'The elevation to the Office of Primate, my friends, is similar to finding a horse in a bathtub, a once-in-a-lifetime experience.'"

Thelma burst out in guffaws, the bishop joining in her laughter. "I suppose it does sound a bit far-fetched, doesn't it?"

Thelma, still finding it hard to catch her breath, replied, "Want to know why I quit going to church?"

"I can't imagine!"

"It's not that it asks so much," Thelma was suddenly sincere in her dismay. "No, it asks so little. That's why I left when I was a teenager. Feeble banalities dressed up in imaginary clothes of substance. And these 'good' priests expect me to take them to my heart. 'Horse in the bathtub' hogwash!"

"Can I quote you?" Hinks kidded her.

Thelma laughed again. "Be my guest. I can hear it now. 'Friends, my mistress once said church is hogwash.'" On the last word, she tweaked his chest hairs.

"Plays well, but don't leave out the 'horse in the bathtub' part. It would please the primate to be quoted," Hinks sighed deeply. "My superior. Imagine. I am to be ruled by such a shallow man. He can't build a coherent argument about anything important ... even if it jumped out of his cassock and bit him on the nose."

Thelma looked incredulous. "Douglas, you don't mean to say this fool is now your boss?"

"Well, that's a bit basic. I don't fetch and carry for him. But he is my 'lord' as we say. He speaks for Canadian Anglicans ... at least as far as ecclesiastical matters go." Hinks sighed at his own predicament. "The church is beset by such sick ironies."

"But how can you stand it?" Thelma sighed and a new idea struck her. "You certainly wouldn't follow such a silly man. Didn't you say he was a war monger?"

"Yes." Hinks was deadly serious now. "That's the worst of it. The upper ranks of the ecclesia are filled with simpletons like our primate, the Right Reverend Cheesborough. Yes-men who praise Jesus and pass the ammunition." Hinks' cynicism spoke next, "It was really the fact that his brother-in-law is a General in the BEF in France that got him the nod. Nothing else." He rolled over on his stomach and rested his head on Thelma's luscious pillows. Closing his eyes, he continued, "Do you want to hear the entire sermon? I think I can recall most of it."

Thelma began to rub his back, not from duty but from a strange attraction to spiritual people, an attraction she would never admit having—especially to Douglas Hinks. "Please do. I wonder what other pearls of wisdom he might have. But roll over; I want to watch as you preach—adds so much!"

The bishop rolled onto his back. He was not a handsome man, not in the traditional sense. Thick and flowing salt and pepper hair, a jutting chin, high cheek bones—overall, a strong countenance. His green eyes could flash disapproval and laughter, switching from one to the other in a heartbeat. No flabbiness, all tight and muscular. Give him a horse and Stetson and he could easily have passed for a rugged prairie cowboy. That wild side was buried under his church propriety and a pair of thin spectacles. His body was acceptable to Thelma, even inviting, but it was his mind and spirit that touched her most. Hinks had a keen intellect, growing sharper with age. And his heart …. The good bishop was a complicated emotional being. There were times when his tenderness and understanding would take her breath away. And in the next instant he could be so pigheaded and smug that she could spit spikes.

"Go on," she prodded, giving his belly a loving brush. "Let's hear the whole thing." She rested against his chest, while her hands moved slowly massaging his thighs.

"Here goes." Hinks was enjoying the playfulness. Putting on the mock British accent of the new primate, assuming his pious air, he said, "The elevation to the Office of Primate, my friends, is similar to finding a horse in a bathtub. A once-in-a-lifetime experience. As I was saying to my wife just the other day, such a load of responsibility rests with this office, I was uncertain who among the synod of bishops is able to shoulder the weight. She assured me, 'God gives strength to those He calls.'"

Hinks paused with a chuckle. "I am certain that most of the audience was asking for the strength to listen to this drivel for the next ten minutes. That's what I'm certain of." The bishop thought for a moment.

"What did he do next? Ah, yes, his self-aggrandizement speech. 'Having been called out from among you, I assure you that I will work to the last drop of energy in the fulfilment of this high calling. I will run with perseverance the race that is set before me, as the apostle Paul said.' Then he gave us one of his down-the-end-of-his-nose stares. Long pregnant pause, and then he thunders: 'And you, what is your calling?' Here Cheesborough pointed at all of us with a sweeping finger." Hinks mimicked the gesture and Thelma began to laugh again. "'You … you … you.' He stabbed the air just so. 'Have you ever pondered that ponderous question? It is one of life's awesome tasks—the sorting out of the divine vocation to which we are called. Blessed are they who find theirs early in life.'"

Thelma mused, "I found mine early enough."

"Hmm." Hinks was smiling at Thelma's inviting nakedness. "I'm not sure our good primate would consider your work the calling he had in mind."

"What came next?"

"Next?" Hinks scratched his head in mock seriousness. "His personal testimony, of course. 'I recall that moment when our Maker called me. It was at church camp. I was but a small lad of ten when we held an evening prayer service down by the lake. The sun was setting, water rippled against the shoreline. We were singing "How Great Thou Art," when I felt my soul take flight like a dove, the heavens opened and a voice said, 'Feed my sheep.' From that day forward I knew that I was destined for the priesthood.'" Hinks threw his arms wide. Thelma had rolled off Hinks, laughing.

"Jesus himself couldn't do it better. Come to think of it, he did a tad bit worse. It's on to the Red Sea. Cheesborough continued, 'My calling was like standing before the waters that parted at God's command and I felt the hand of my Lord directing me to lead, to be a soldier for Christ—no matter the peril.'"

"Oh, stop." Thelma was holding her sides again. "Please, I think I'll throw up, if I laugh anymore."

"I can't stop; his sermon gets better. From the Exodus he went on to the Mount of Olives where he had a vision." Here Hinks stood up naked and took on a penitent air, folding his hands in a prayerful gesture. "Holy angels ministered unto him and he spoke with his dead mother who sent a divinely inspired message to her son. Marvelous stuff."

"And people listened?"

"Well ... not all, but most. It's the polite thing to do, and Anglicans worship propriety above God."

"You've said that before."

"Have I?"

"Yes ... but how can you sit through it?"

"With great difficulty." Hinks sat down on the bed beside Thelma and traced crosses down the length of her thigh. "I thought of making obscene gestures under my clerical gown or using my foot to tap out my disagreement in Morse code. The banality of preaching is sufferable, if it restricts itself to spiritual matters. What I find so offensive is how such mediocrity becomes hopelessly naive and dangerous when it turns to the world of politics." Hinks was no longer laughing. "He concluded this mess with a call, not to the altar, but to arms."

Thelma's voice lost its smile. "No!"

"It was most unsettling. 'My friends, there is no greater calling this day than the battle cry. Our Lord's empire is not of this world, I grant you, but God's cause is put to the test in Flanders. That is where the attack must be focused. I ask you if Christ's mission has ever been clearer. To arms! Strike down the foe. We are called, each one of us—men and women, young and old—to fight the Hun until he is utterly crushed. My mission as your primate is to strengthen our men at arms, for they are fighting in our Maker's ranks. Fight the good fight in Europe. How can we resist our God's pleas to confront Satan in his dark lair?'"

"Was that it?"

"Alas, no." Hinks thought before continuing. "His best piece of rhetoric was saved for the final punchline. A pity it was so evil, so utterly misleading. As he spoke his last sentences, he grabbed the standard that sits on the side of the chancel. Waving the Union Jack, he shouted out, 'Turn hell upside down and it will have "Made In Germany" written on the bottom. To arms, my friends, to arms! For God's sake, to arms!' He then led us in a rousing chorus of 'God Save the King.'"

Thelma shook her head, allowing her hair to caress his shoulders. "It's demonic."

"My dear, you speak the truth." Hinks twisted around to look at her. "Thirty years in the service of men's passions, not one single hour spent in the house of God as an adult and you know more about religion than most clerics learn in a lifetime of sermons."

She smiled. "I've spent more time with Christ's servants than you can imagine."

Hinks became silent. The mirth disappeared from his countenance. Thelma, ever watchful for the shifting moods of her "special" client, asked if anything was wrong.

Hinks mumbled something unintelligible.

"Speak up, damn you. What's the matter? Spit it out. Is it still Terry?"

Hinks sighed. "Oh, it's always Terrance. He never leaves me—haunts me."

Thelma tried again to smooth over the rough edges of his soul by massaging his shoulders and chest, leaning over him directly. "Now, lie still while I do my magic."

For a long while Douglas watched her face as she worked his cares away. "What a woman!" Feeling the tension leave his bones he asked lazily, "Why didn't we marry years ago?"

She answered his question immediately, but without rancour, "Because back then you were a self-centred bishop-wanna-be."

He ventured a compliment in return, "Thelma, you're the best woman I know."

She laughed, "And you've known so many. Really, Douglas, comparing me to the shriveled prunes that occupy your church pews is not high praise."

"The best I could do."

The clock in the hall chimed eleven o'clock. A voice from the first floor shouted out the hour and invited "guests" to prepare to leave.

Thelma looked at her beloved. "Time, gentlemen, please. Are you staying the night? If not, I'll have to ask you to leave along with all the other patrons."

Hinks wiggled further into the pillows. "Do you mind if I stay?"

"Never." Thelma was pleased. She was getting too old for the quick tussle and furtive departure of her men. "I'll fetch us some sherry and we can sit by the fire—like mom and dad waiting for the kids to come home—a domestic scene."

Seeing her delight, Hinks replied, "Please don't pull out all the stops on my account." A serious thought struck and was out of his mouth before he could stop it. "Talking about kids, could you care for Johanna's lover, if he ever comes by? I mean, if he were ever in trouble? You'd know how to handle him—keep him safe for my sake."

Thelma was on the edge of the bed, her mind halfway into her fireside fantasy when she turned back to face him. "I hope you don't think he'd ever want to cheat on Johanna with one of my girls."

"No, not really. He's just a bit naive and I picture him running into ... problems ... Maybe being shoved about by his fellows and dared into trying a prostitute. If he came here, you'd stop him."

"I'd do what I could." Thelma was good at promises, priding herself on her loyalty. "What's his name again?"

"Private Gordon Davis."

"Gordon Davis. Sounds simple enough." She stood up and stretched out a hand.

Taking it, he replied, "Something tells me he's nothing even close to simple. With Johanna at his side, my heart shudders at the complications of passion they could stir up. I want Johanna safe."

"I'll do my best, though none of us is safe. Do you honestly think he'll show up at my door?"

Hinks pondered the question long and hard and finally shook his head. "No, I suppose not. It was just a foolish notion."

Thelma smiled. "In times of war, everything gets a bit foolish."

Domestic issues are put aside, Thelma tugged on his arm. "Let's go. Come this way, dad, and sit by the fire." She motioned toward her sputtering remains of glowing coals.

Hinks looked at his hostess with renewed affection. "Will you marry me?"

"You don't mean that. Don't tease."

"Someday, I'm going to make good on it."

"Yes, and someday I'll be elected pope."

Montreal: Mount Royal Park (Sisson Ridge Park)
Saturday, March 25, 1916, 1:20 p.m.

"Marry you?" Johanna was shocked. "What brought that up?" They were strolling over their ridge. The air was sweet with the promise of spring and the beaten brown grass was still soggy with the recently melted winter snow.

"Well ... I ... I'm off to France in three days." Gordon was struggling to get his feelings in order, to sort through the jumble of passions. "I didn't want to leave without telling you how much you mean to me."

"So you ask me to marry you?"

"Well?"

Johanna stopped walking and faced him. Looking carefully. His eyes were so filled with light, fires just recently brought to full flame.

While a hopeless romantic, Jo had a strong practical side. "Why don't you just say it? 'You mean so much to me.' Easy!"

Gordon smiled. "Easy for you."

Johanna would not be put off. "No, it isn't any easier for me than it is for you. No, I will not marry you. We hardly know each other." She saw his hurt and tried to soften the blow. "I mean …. Yes! I believe our souls are truly meant for one another, but let's give this some time. Let me catch my breath."

Gordon felt the sting of rejection. He turned to look toward the city centre. "We've had time enough to become intimate."

Jo laughed, "We have indeed."

"So why won't you marry me?" Gordon's frustration was showing.

Johanna felt her anger rise rapidly. "Drop it, Gordon. You're spoiling what time we have left by pressing too hard. Everything will happen in due course." She tried to smile, but didn't have any feeling behind it. Touching his arm, she had the urge to move, to walk out her temper. "Let's just stroll along in silence for a time. Breathe!"

Gordon was in turmoil. He had never known such a burning desire mixed with confusion and hurt.

"You have plenty of time to wait. I'm about to march off to France."

"Don't I know it!" she snapped. "You'll be off to your bloody adventure and forget about me the moment the boat leaves the dock, while I'm stuck here with the blasted home fires and no one."

Gordon wasn't sure where to go. "It's not my fault."

Johanna exploded, "What does fault have to do with this? When you get frightened do you always run and hide like some sulking child?" That was close to the bone, and Johanna could see the injury in Gordon's eyes. "I am not blaming you for anything. You can't make love happen. It has its own reasons that we cannot control or understand. Just drop your selfish pushing."

"I don't know what to say. Your anger undoes me entirely."

"My anger does nothing. You choose to be undone. Now will you settle down and relax? Just breathe. What will be, will be."

Gordon walked on in silence. He could feel her hand on his arm and took that for a sign of their connectedness, but uncertainty still ruled his heart. He scuffed his feet on the grass. He could feel tears welling inside. Was he losing her already? His thick-headedness was always weighing him down. Each footstep became heavier than the last.

Johanna tried to lighten the mood. She let go of his proffered arm and spread hers wide and circled about slowly. "After yesterday, I feel light as a bird. Shut your eyes and drink it in."

Gordon tried to imitate her spirit, but felt the leaden weight of unworthiness drag him down when his eyelids closed. He was unworthy of her. She was a flame, while he was a wet rag. He could feel her energy, even now with his eyes closed. How could he ever match her spark? "Face it, Davis," he said to his miserable self, "she's beyond you, moving fast, and you're plodding along at a snail's pace. It's over. She admitted as much just now."

Gordon opened his eyes and gazed around the park. Sisson Ridge, the place of his triumph and now his humiliation. Simple. Here she touched his heart, and here she ran away from him. He wanted to run himself. Keep what shred of dignity he had left. Seeing a bench over the next rise, he admitted defeat. "I think I'd rather sit." He eased himself down and could feel the weight of France rising in his stomach.

Johanna wasn't listening—she was caught in her own joy. When she realized he was leaving her dream world, she shouted back at him, "You can't escape me. You'll have to stop sulking and grow up."

Gordon sighed, "I can't. Not quickly enough."

Johanna smiled and came back to sit at his side. "You will, and when you do, I'll still be there."

"Is that a promise?" Gordon could feel a glimmer of hope in the midst of his despair.

"A covenant, between you and me. I will wait for you. Like this bench: solid." To punctuate her promise, she kissed him gently on the lips. A light touch, but a clear message. "You can count on it, and what is the intervening time except an opportunity for each of us to grow in maturity?"

Gordon smiled, weakly. "I thought I had lost you just now." He took her hand in his. "My untried heart is plodding along while yours is flying. I can work out complicated mathematical equations and list arguments for the existence of God, but with love, I'm all over the map." He looked closely into her eyes. "Can you forgive a young soul lost in your sunshine? You burn so brightly; I keep thinking you'll leave this dull light called Gordon Davis."

"Never." She gave him a squeeze. "I'll be here and if you can't find me, ask my father. He'll know where I am."

"It's a deal then."

"A deal, partner."

Gordon spoke solemnly and Johanna laughed.

They sat in silence for another few minutes, lost in the joys and fears of the promise they had made.

Finally, Johanna broke the silence and rose. Taking his hands, she said, "Gordon, I have to go now and start Father's supper. I'm already overdue. Let's meet here tomorrow. Here … our bench!"

"You can count on me."

A final squeeze. "I know. That's one of your many great qualities. Here—tomorrow—after morning prayers, we'll spend the whole day together." And she was off at a trot.

"A deal!" he whispered as her figure disappeared behind a bend in the pathway.

Hamilton: St. Giles Anglican Church
Thursday, November 15, 1917, 8:43 p.m.

James should have knocked. But this would not wait. That was the deal he had always made with his priest. "I will never disturb you unless, it's a matter of life and death."

Thursday evening badminton had just ended. James loved to tell stories at his Sauble Beach and guide his school classes on Sunday morning, yet he never lost sight of young boys' love of sports.

James was the badminton coach. He didn't have much skill with a racquet, but his ability with boys was more than adequate. They loved his obvious sympathy and goodwill. Some who had lost fathers in the war looked upon James as their surrogate dad.

One of these boys, Brent Smith, started the nightmare of that Thursday night. His father had died recently, as fate would have it, marching downhill from Vimy Ridge. Stepped on an unexploded shell.

Brent had been a member of the church school since he was five, sung in the children's choir and was a regular helper for the priest. The Reverend Hawthorne praised him often and mentioned how helpful he was to James, his Sunday school teacher.

Perpetually happy, a kid with a permanent smile, Brent was always willing to do whatever was asked. On this Thursday night, he sat on the bench as if suffering from a severe headache, not showing any reaction to the game as it progressed. The best player was giving James a shellacking.

James looked over several times and wondered what had gotten into Brent. And when the final score was tallied, he sat down by the sullen boy.

"What's up Brent?"

No answer.

"Brent. It's James calling. You home?" Here James knocked on Brent's forehead to get his attention.

The young boy lifted his troubled eyes to gaze at James. "Can we talk?"

"Sure." James tried to sound nonchalant, but he could see there was a serious problem.

"Not here," Brent blurted. "Not here … in private."

"Right. Let's go into the kitchen. I am clean tuckered out." Once they were out of earshot of the other boys, he asked, "What is it, Brent? You look troubled. Is it your dad? Your work?"

He whispered. "It's kind of personal …. I was here at the church last night and I … I am so ashamed …."

That's how his long tale of abuse began. James was struck dumb. He couldn't believe it could happen on his watch. He listened, cried and offered what peace he could. James promised to talk with Brent's mother that very night, and Brent smiled for the first time that evening as he rose to go. That's exactly what he hoped his coach would say.

First James had to report it to his priest. Brent would only say some man had taken advantage of him. The sacredness and security of this church had been violated.

With that urgency, James ran to Father Hawthorne's office, quietly turned the handle and whispered in deference, "Pastor, I have a grave—"

James was shocked into silence. At the far side of the room, a young boy, his back to the office door, was standing naked before Reverend Hawthorne, who was kneeling … his hands running up and down the boy's legs. They were so intent on their congress that neither heard nor saw James standing slack jawed at the door.

In an instant, the pieces of Brent's story fell into place. It was Hawthorne who had abused him! James was stuck dumb, betrayed by the very man he had trusted. He backed up slowly and quietly and closed the door.

He had sent boys to Hawthorne to get help saying, "The priest is wise and will help you." His own son, Gordon, in fact!

James stumbled down the hallway, slumping down. What could he do? Had his beloved boys been …. How could he …. And Gordon? Had he been abused too? James was floating into chaos. With his wife so sick, each day he felt lost, drifting and hopeless. But this, this rocked him to his core.

His gut churned and he flopped over onto his knees and retched on the red brocade hall runner.

Saint John: Centenary-Queen Square United Church
Tuesday, Nov. 17, 1992, 11:25 a.m.

Time to preach. I offer a prayer to settle my nerves. "God, help me never to use my reason against the truth." Then my mind starts to wander.

I like the sermon most of any part in a worship service, finding it especially important in funerals. At the time of death, I don't want flowery promises of the sweet by-and-by, where the "spark" that was Gordon Davis will never lose its light. Straight talk is best. When we die, it all disappears. The unique embodiment that was Gordon is gone. The fatal tragedy of finite existence. It ends!

Looking down at my notes, I pause to recall Levan's rule #1: "When you get to the end of your sermon, stop!" There are always temptations brewing in the preacher to put a better flourish on the conclusion, carry on beyond the strength of your ideas. Better to keep it brief and to the point. Never off-the-cuff, my funeral sermon goes out word for word as I penned it.

> *"Gordon Davis was a puzzle to many of us. Sitting for close to seventy years a silent mute, and, then, only in the past few months, speaking in a cryptic tongue. We have trouble making any sense of his life. There isn't much to say. He went to war, came back and never spoke again.*
>
> *"Most claim—including all the medical officials who have ever touched his life—that he was a victim of prolonged battle fatigue. To be blunt, he was senile. End of story. Nothing else to report."*

I can feel their attention growing.

"Gordon was more than a blank slate. The longer we
spoke, it has been my privilege to listen to his voices—
that's right I said 'voices.' In recent times he had two
personae through which he greeted his visitors. Stop by his
bed in the morning and Captain Jims would greet you. In
the evening the sailor was replaced by Father Inkling, an
Anglican priest. The more I listened to these two figures,
the more I was convinced that he went silent for a reason.
His obdurate nature was not the result of psychological
trauma, but the final choice of a very ethical and coura-
geous man. There was a great secret he was hiding and he
took it to his grave."

Did I hear a gasp?

Looking about the room, I see little evidence of dismay until my gaze rests on the stranger. Her hand is on her mouth, and she obviously looks shocked. Does she know something I don't?

Neuville-Saint-Vaast, France
Monday, April 23, 1917, 3:12 a.m.

Major Ryan watched as rank on rank of soldiers fell into order, half-asleep. The order to "fall out" had caught everyone off guard. He had a little secret planned for these lazy Canucks, one they wouldn't forget. They thought he was only bluffing when he gave them the "You better not desert" sermon. This morning they'd see he meant business.

Even as he delighted in the clear message his early morning examples send, he was bothered by a loose thread dangling in his memory. He'd left it unattended. The past few weeks of both mopping up and report-ing of the victory at Vimy to his superiors had driven this detail from his mind. The niggling disquiet wouldn't leave him. Try as he might he couldn't bring it to his conscious mind.

Small matters were lost to Ryan, as he began the proceedings against private Francois Dubé.

"All companies are accounted for, sir." The regimental sergeant major barked out his report. The lines of men were silent, puzzled and angry.

Ryan could feel their hate and he was pleased. "Nothing like animosity and fear to keep a fighting man on his toes."

Ryan turned to his sergeant major. "Very good, Smith. Now let's get this march under way." With that he took the reins of the horse from his batman and mounted. Looking down at the columns of his regiment, he gave one last command. "Quick march, sergeant major. I don't want to keep the chaplain waiting." He laughed and rode off eastward, on the road toward the front lines.

"To the left, quick march!" The order was passed down the ranks, and the regiment, now well-trained to obey without pause, pivoted on left feet and began a swift half-walk, half-run.

Gordon was as puzzled as any, when this early morning procession began. Moving in full gear, with a corporal barking encouragement at your side, there was very little opportunity to exchange ideas of what was up. "The front line near Souchez." "Another attempt to take Bailleul." "Just a routine march." These were the suggestions. Between Gordon's hard breathing and the stitch in his side—the result of his recent operation—he just muttered, "Let's just get it over and get back to bed."

As they continued on their bleak morning march, an ambulance sped by. At this time of day and when there were no battles imminent, this was strange. But with sweat dripping in their faces and straps biting into shoulders, no one gave it more than a passing thought.

It seemed endless in the dark, but actually it was little less than an hour and the regiment was formed up again outside a small broken farmhouse. It was cold. An easterly wind had picked up and was whipping dust into their faces.

Ryan stood in the centre of a small courtyard while the ranks formed a U-shaped perimeter. The ambulance was off to one side. Its attendants were leaning against the fenders waiting for their next orders.

Once the regiment was silent and assembled, a nod from Ryan and the back door of the farmhouse opened. Gordon could hear a single low voice chanting and he recognized immediately the 23rd Psalm. "*The Lord is my shepherd I shall not want.*"

Out of the opened door, a stooped figure appeared silhouetted in the square frame, a portrait of fatigue. Behind him an Anglican voice continued the Psalm,

"He leads me beside still waters, he restores my soul."

The solitary figure, pushed forward by a squad of soldiers, was marched into the square, toward the open end of the formation of ranks. He walked slowly, feet dragging, the soldiers were smart stepping and efficient, untouched by the early morning air. The priest trailed behind all, his hands holding a prayer book, his eyes looking heavenward.

Gordon could feel a dreadful shadow steal across his heart. This is no play-acting. Something deadly was unfolding before their eyes. Ryan stood resolute and ramrod straight, eyes raking the ranks of soldiers. Gordon tried to shrink from his sight and disappear.

Ryan watched the accused move forward. He had caught this wretch running from battle, abandoning his Lewis gun, a deserter, whose cowardice had cost the lives of an entire company. There is no need for pity. This bastard is getting what he deserves.

"He leads me in paths of righteousness for his name's sake."

The escort marched the accused to the front, stood him alone, and then wheeled right. On command, a soldier stepped forward and wrapped a handkerchief around the condemned man's eyes and then stepped back into formation. As if trained for weeks, the firing squad moved as one, backwards, into a line facing the now-shrinking private, who knew his life was about to end, not in a glorious manner, but as a traitor to his comrades. The name Francois Dubé would be spat upon, ground into the mud.

Dubé could see nothing through his mask. He could hear boots marching and knew that his firing squad was turning to face him, their fingers itching to get it over. He could feel the knot tighten in his stomach. He wasn't a coward. He wanted to shout out his innocence, but he knew no one would listen ... not now. He'd been over the top more times than he could recall. Shown bravery often enough!

He could feel his legs growing weak. "It won't take too long now," he thought. He tried to keep his shoulders back. "Look brave, at least," he said to himself. It wasn't his fault he'd run from the machine gun position. His number one had been split in two by a grenade blast and the number two was impaled by the barrel of their machine gun as it exploded in their faces. He was getting out of harm's way when he ran straight into the arms of that bastard Ryan. The fact that the other mates in his machine gun crew had bought it, that their gun was now useless, that he was a sitting duck, that he had no means to cover his section's advance—even though he wanted to—these points were not noted in his quick trial. He wasn't a coward. It wasn't his fault. But damn it all, anyone who could have explained his actions was dead. Ryan was looking for a scapegoat, and Private Francois Dubé knew he was it. Bad luck.

Dubé tried to breathe deeply, take in the last shreds of any sensations before the bullets snuffed him out. He could feel sweat on his brow. God, help me not to piss my pants.

"Yea thou I walk through the valley of the shadow of death, I shall fear no evil."

Ryan was stone still. He could feel the shocked silence of his men. "This will teach them to obey me," he thought. "I am not going to be made a fool by these backwoods lumberjacks." He had personally coached the firing squad and was pleased to see their precision and professional manner. No flinching on their part.

The chaplain was whispering something to the accused, and Ryan grew impatient.

Dubé could feel the breath on his cheek below the blindfold. It had the faint odour of garlic. "My son, prepare your soul to meet your Maker, ask for forgiveness and the Lord will bless you and receive you into eternal life." The voice receded and Dubé wanted to scream, "Fuck you, Father. Blessing me to hell for something I didn't do." But his tongue was parched and his mouth wouldn't open. In his mind he promised, "Better not to give them the satisfaction."

Gordon shut his eyes.

This can't be happening. He had heard of the British and French punishing their own men, but surely Canadians were beyond this vindictive sport. They'd all done their damned best and had indeed been victorious where others had failed. Under his breath he whispered, "We took Vimy, for Christ's sake! Give the poor private some slack." Gordon clenched his fists. Did he have the guts to step out and protest? Ryan, the British bastard was making a show for their benefit. Rubbing their colonial noses in their inferiority and powerlessness.

"For thy rod and thy staff shall comfort me." The chaplain was stretching each word out, standing with hands clasped in a prayerful gesture, just to the right of the accused.

Ryan fumed. This was intolerable. The little priest would take all day. The major walked purposefully up to the cleric, as if it was part of the procedure and reclining his head toward his ear, commanded, "Get on with it, man. This is not one of your bloody sermons." His lips barely moving, he added, "If we don't shoot this coward soon, I'll have a bloody mutiny on my hands."

Gordon knew he was called to say something. Stop the madness. War was insanity enough without us turning on each other. His feet wanted to move, his heart was bursting with the need to put an end to this farce of military mania.

The priest rattled off the final lines of the Psalm quickly.

"You prepare a table before me in the presence of my enemies…. My cup runneth over. Surely goodness and mercy shall follow me all the days of my life and I shall dwell in the house of the lord forever."

Dubé closed his eyes. He allowed his arms go limp, tried to relax his stomach. It would soon be over.

"Ready."

The entire regiment seemed to have their eyes closed. They could hear the slap of hands on rifle butts as weapons were brought up to the firing position.

Dubé's mind went blank. From his left he heard a solitary voice ring out: "O Canada …" At first, it was a frail, bird-like squeak, but in the silence of the square it was deafening. It was Gordon Davis.

Dubé picked up the melody immediately, whispering, "Terre de nos aïeux …"

"Aim."

Gordon's sucked in deeply as his lungs burst with the next line, "True patriot love …"

The firing squad lost a shade of crisp attention. Several glanced around, wondering who was singing. The squad leader paused, not sure if this was part of the drill.

Gordon's single voice was joined, as if by common agreement, by the entire regiment thundering anger in each word, "In all thy sons command …"

Ryan barked out the last order, "Fire!"

Dubé's body fell backward by the impact of the bullets, two hit his heart, one his throat and the final one his forehead. The rest of the rifles had contained blanks. His body crumpled, silent in the dirt the farmyard.

The voices rose to louder heights, a mixture of French and English. "With glowing hearts we see thee rise." "Il sait porter la croix."

The melody grew in timbre and pride. The ranks were looking straight ahead, but in their minds they were glaring at Ryan, the bastard.

Ryan could feel the hairs on the back of his neck rise. Should he forbid them from singing this stupid national song? Blast the prick who started this! This little gesture of defiance was ruining the message of his execution.

Gordon was almost hoarse he sang so loudly. It was a fitting gesture, but it was well short of what he could have done. "You stink." He could hear his sister's recrimination again. Ryan wasn't the problem. In the end it was his timid soul that had betrayed him. Next time, if there was another one, he would not flinch from his duty, no matter what the cost.

Friday Nov. 16, 1917

Dear Gordon,

I don't know how to begin. My heart is weak and faint as I write and I know it is my lack of courage that stilled my pen in writing to you for so long.

Mother's gone. Today … or last night, in fact. I wish I could say it more gently. I rose to help Mother with her morning wash and found she had passed on to her reward during the night.

It was a shock for everyone and I imagine you feel now as we did—lost, empty, alone. We all thought that Father would be the first to go, since his health had been failing. Mother was always the rock. We expected she would last forever. The doctor was hopeful that she might recover. That was his last message. There has been so little money with Father sick and off work, that we called the physician only at great need. We thought Mum might be suffering from consumption, or overtiredness. The bedrest seemed to help her spirits and we all imagined after the rough bouts of the past few weeks that she'd slowly recover.

Not so.

We'll bury her in the St. Giles' Cemetery, the Reverend Hawthorne presiding. I went down to see him right away—he went on forever. He spoke so well of Mother. Even mentioned you—how you were such a delightful child to have in the vestry. That shocked Lil since she didn't even know you had gone to help him as a server. He said that Mother was the example for us all to follow, in a line with Mary the mother of Jesus, mild, meek and forbearing all things.

Truth be told and I am only telling you, I thought his remarks a bit over the top. Mum had her faults like everyone else. After he was done with her I thought we were going to bury a saint, a second Madonna, but not my mother.

Serves us right for putting up with his emptiness all these years. It comes back to haunt you. I just hope he does a better job at the funeral.

Eva wants the service to be, and I'm quoting, "angelically serene." Edna, always the sceptic, said we paid the priest too much if this is all he did. Will can't get back from the West but sent his best. It is all happening so quickly.

Father was unable to come down from his bed today. He just lay still and looked at the wall when I told him. Shock. He doesn't want to go to the funeral, said something about her being in heaven, not at some little human ceremony. A philosophical point lost on me. He's fighting some other demon .... I am not sure what, but it looks bad.

There were hosts of friends who stopped by the house. Many asked to be remembered to you and sent you their fond regards.

Remember Isabelle Langtree? She was your sweetheart in grade 10. She still hasn't found anyone and was clearly out to get the scoop on you. Interested? I told her you already had a flame, but I didn't know her name. I'm right aren't I? You moon over someone in your letters. I can tell. Is she French? Maybe you met a dashing young nurse who's stolen your heart. Do write and tell me. I want to know and I promise not to gossip about you. If you don't tell me something, I'll give Isabelle your address. She "dearly wants to talk with you." What a weasel!

It doesn't seem right to be joking in a letter of this kind. Black- edged and sombre—except that I know Mother would want you to laugh, to find as much joy as possible. She dearly loved you and her fondest wish was to see you safe home again. I guess that's what we all feel.

How long can this slaughter go on? The casualty figures are astounding. Almost all the families we know have suffered a loss.

Lil says to hurry up. She'll take this letter to the post with her other correspondence, if I've "stopped scribbling."

So I'm done. Stay well Gordon and come home soon. I am rushing off to get this into the mail tonight!

Love,
Mabel

PS. I do so miss our chats. I have no one to talk with now.

PPS. There's a new fellow down at the factory. I met him when I went down to pick up Dad's tools. "Bert" he calls himself. Nice looking fellow.

Montreal: Thelma Lint's Gentlemen's Parlour
Monday, June 19, 1916, 8:10 p.m.

"I have to talk with someone." Johanna paused, not certain how to continue. "Forgive the intrusion, but Father once mentioned that you had a good set of ears."

"Ears indeed! Is that what he said? My, my!" Thelma smiled. "Does your father know you are here?"

Johanna blushed, "Oh no. I ... ah ... found your address in his desk directory. I don't know who you are, though I can make a few guesses, but please don't turn me away because I am young and a bishop's daughter. I can be discrete and I have no one to talk to about women's things since ... ah ... my mother died. I've had to fend for ...."

They were standing on the front doorstep. Thelma had been passing the reception area when she heard her maid refusing entry to a pleading voice. She immediately recognized the name. Brushing the maid aside, Thelma took over the interview herself. She knew the public area of a bawdy house was no place for a mother/daughter chat.

"Look dear," she smiled as she thought of being some child's mother, "Why don't we go out for a stroll? The air is fresh on the mountain and we would have more privacy there."

Johanna face lit up. "Could we? That would be so kind of you."

Thelma laughed, "Think nothing of it. My services as counsellor are much more in demand than as bedmate these days anyway."

Johanna blushed at the reference to Thelma's profession, but was polite enough to say nothing.

"Oh dear, I can be blunt," Thelma giggled. "But you'll have to forgive that in me. I've a tough tongue that often wags too loosely before my mind reins it in." All the while she was talking, Thelma was sizing up her bishop's daughter, and on the surface, liked what she saw. Strong forehead, piercing, clear eyes and a hopeful, committed countenance. Yes, she could see why he was so proud of her. Out loud, she simply said, "Let me dress for a walk."

Johanna gripped her bag with both hands and held it close to her chest like a shield.

"Relax, dear, the walls won't bite you. This is a safe haven for women. I work very hard to keep it that way. Sit in the parlour, while I change my house clothes for something more fitting."

The parlour, Johanna noted, was arranged with excellent taste. None of the extravagant or garish flourishes one might expect in a whorehouse. No pots of opium or thick curtains with slumbering limbs sticking out underneath. Two burgundy wingbacks faced a marble fireplace. A merry little coal fire gave the room life and laughter. The side tables were arranged with precision, no clutter of useless ornaments. Wine glasses, a decanter of sherry, a few scattered books of poetry. Shelly and Wordsworth were favoured by the mistress of the house. The walls were covered with works of art, delicate flourishes of flowers, snow-swept street scenes. Like a gentle English garden, the room was pleasing to the eye and soothing to the soul.

Johanna sat down, and, taking a book at random from the coffee table, she was sure that she had made the right choice. Her hands opened it to a poem by Wordsworth, "Tintern Abbey." She found his description of an Almighty being more palatable than the countless sermons she had endured at the hands of Anglican prelates. The words cast a spell on her as she read,

> "Whose dwelling is the light of setting suns,
> And the round ocean and the living air.
> … A motion and a spirit, that impels
>
> All thinking things, all objects of thought,
> And rolls through all things."

Before she knew it, a half-an-hour had passed. The words carried her off, and she did not realize that Thelma had crept to the door of the parlour and had been examining her from a distance.

"She's got courage," Thelma thought, "that much is clear." There was a strange stirring in her gut, as she watched this young woman. "What was it?" she wondered. Johanna was attractive, to say the least. Her long hair was arranged in a fashion to highlight her sharp features. No curls to fuss up the natural cascade as it fell over her tiny shoulders. The dark eyebrows and the captivating eyes gave power to an otherwise unremarkable face. But her looks drew you closer, invited frankness and intimacy. There was little doubt that anyone who met Johanna Hinks would not soon forget her.

Inwardly she chuckled, "Douglas would never sire anything less than remarkable." A deliciously disquieting notion jumped to her mind. "What would a child between us have been like, Douglas, you and me? Much like this delicate creature here, no doubt." Sadness mixed with Thelma's admiration.

Montreal: Outside the Bank of Montreal
Monday, December 10, 1917, 3:13 p.m.

Gordon stood in the brisk breeze, looked left, then right. Either way the street was filled with pedestrians, crowds that would hide him. He had no plan. Just determination.

He looked down at his torn uniform, made sure there was no distinguishing mark, no telltale evidence of his unit, his name or rank. Nothing to give him away. All the badges, patches and stripes were gone … left in the snow in Halifax.

Next he checked his pockets. He wanted no stray papers left, nothing to give him away. Finding the few scraps of his notes for the previous evening's speech, he scrunched them into a small ball. This he held onto while he inspected his medical pouch. Sorting through the contents he pulled out some old wrappings, a snippet of gauze. These he threw, along with his crumpled notes, into a garbage bin at the door of the bank. Then he pulled out his Bible with the letters tucked behind the front leaf. Ah … the Bible … it had only his first name. No address. He looked at the letters for a long moment, running a loving hand gently, slowly over them. An onlooker might think Gordon had discovered a treasure map or a long-lost formula for human flight, such was his reverence for these small tokens.

Eventually, he put the Bible and letters back into his medical kit. If he was going to march off into obscurity, he'd at least have some record of where he had begun. He never noticed the fountain pen still stuck in his lapel pocket.

Gordon did a last check of his appearance, his pockets and his pouch. Nothing. He left no trace behind. He gave a nod of his head, as if saluting an invisible companion. The Gordon Davis, who stepped into the crowd of Notre Dame Street, turned left and disappeared, never to be seen again.

Montreal: Thelma Lint's Gentlemen's Parlour
Monday, June 19, 1916, 8:40 p.m.

Interrupting Johanna's reading, Thelma swept into the room, her walking clothes set to precision. "Well, I'm ready to meet the world."

Johanna looked up. Trying not to stare, but being drawn to her face, she nearly missed the side table as she set down the book. Thelma was magnetic, having about her an air of assurance and calm. Johanna noted the lines of her outfit were straight and neat, no babbles or bells. A plain uniform for a gentlewoman of her station, and, yet, the overall effect was remarkable. There was a colouring and zest for living that shone through the drabness of the clothing, making Thelma a woman able, even now in her forties, to turn most men's heads in ... in what? Lust? Longing? Respect?

Johanna was never slow to comment. "You're radiant." And then she stumbled about for an explanation. "I'm sorry, I don't mean to be frivolous, it's just that I can't recall seeing a woman with so much poise."

Thelma laughed to herself, "It is so easy to like people who make you laugh." To Johanna she simply admitted with an ironic smile, "I've had years of practice. Shall we go?"

Thelma led the way, held open the front door. "Poise, you say."

Johanna blushed for a second time. "I meant it honestly. You carry yourself as a queen."

Thelma now blushed. "Oh please, stop. My thick head can't take any more swelling." They reached the sidewalk at the bottom of her stairs and she looked up and down the street. "Shall we walk up toward the mountain? Sisson Ridge—isn't that what your mother called it?"

Confused, Johanna replied, "Yes. How did you ...."

"Your father is a friend, as well as customer. We share many stories. He's still in love with your mother and speaks of her little ways to me quite often." Johanna stopped walking and looked up into the face of her companion with wonder mixed with disquiet. Thelma touched her shoulder, "Does it shock you that your father is just a man with manly desires or that he shares his memories of his wife?"

Johanna coughed. "Both, I guess. I never thought much about his ...."

"Sexual side?" Thelma laughed. "We all have one." Johanna looked dismayed, so Thelma added, "If it helps, your father is still devoted to your mother and is the most considerate lover I have ever known. You have nothing to fear on his account." A pause and smile, to quiet her questions. "And, oh yes, he asked me to watch out for you if I ever had the chance, so I am delighted you came to call."

They fell into a gentle gait, and, for a considerable time, nothing was said. They enjoyed the bustle of the city as it moved around them. A door-to-door salesman pulled his wagon of knives toward Sherbrooke Street, ringing a relentless bell. A bakery wagon clattered off to the harbour for more flour.

As they approached the mountain summit, they passed two gentlemen walking arm-in-arm, puffing cigar smoke like steam engines climbing a steep grade. Both nodded toward Thelma and Johanna, as they marched passed, respect written on their faces.

Thelma smiled meekly and bowed her head slightly. Then once the men were passed, she looked at her companion. "You're pretty poised yourself, Johanna Hinks. Did you notice how those two men gazed at you?"

Johanna smiled. "They were looking at you, I am sure."

Thelma was not modest, and she was always clear with her girls. "Johanna you probably already know this, but I'll tell you anyway. You are strikingly beautiful. Not in the classic sense, but as a passionate flame—attractive, warm, and oh, so mysterious."

Johanna made to protest.

"Don't try to deny it. You are too intelligent not to know. You could have any man in this city that you wanted."

They walked up the steep grade toward the lookout and paused to enjoy the view. Johanna turned around to gaze upon the spires and smokestacks in the distance. "The man I want is no longer in this city."

"Oh yes, your father mentioned someone." Thelma walked tentatively through this emotional terrain. Not wanting to give too much away she offered a vague reply. "I believe he is a young private—"

"In the medical corps." Johanna completed Thelma's sentence and went on to paint Gordon's background. "He's not in favour of the war and certainly not off in search of glory. He intends to study for the priesthood. He's already been accepted into theological college, in Toronto." Johanna's voice was rising as she thrilled to tell someone about her love. "Born in Hamilton, his father is a bridge labourer and his mother's a farmer's daughter. He has a number of sisters who sound dreadfully ferocious. He has such beautiful full hair and his eyes ... oh, his eyes are like —"

"Slow down, child," Thelma cut into Johanna's rapture. "Let's start at the beginning. Why did you come to see me?"

Johanna swallowed and took a few heartbeats before she answered. A songbird (she could never tell them apart) sang out in a nearby maple tree. "I needed to talk to you about love."

"Love?" Thelma's smile curled the word around in her mouth and winked at Johanna. "Love, eh? That's a new one! Most people want to talk sex with me."

Johanna was surprised by the openness of her matron and delighted that she found Thelma so agreeable. "You know, my mother died a number of years ago, long before boys or romance were in my life, so I have never had the chance to talk with another woman about these things. I hope you don't mind, if I bend your ear with my questions."

"Bend away." Thelma was struck by the honour she had been given, and she ached, not for the first or the last time, over her lost career as a mother. "What about love?"

"Well," Johanna was uncertain. Now that the way was clear for her to ask, her heart didn't know where to begin. "Well ... ah ...."

Thelma was wise enough to coax her slightly. "There are no simple questions where love is concerned. Spit it out, and we'll rearrange your thoughts once they're all on the table."

Johanna started, "Why does it hurt so much?" The question was out before she could refine it, and, rather than retreat, she continued boldly. "I knew it was soft and delicate like rose petals. Endless sermons tell me love is strong as steel, able to withstand the assaults of the Devil himself. I've even heard people speak of it as a woolly blanket, but I didn't know it had prickles and stings."

"Stings?" Thelma mused. "In what way?"

"Well, there are the sharp pains of withdrawal. When I watched his boat leave, I felt like my stomach had been sliced open. I could hardly breathe. A horrible feeling yet delicious too. Can love be more than one thing at the same time?" Johanna went suddenly silent.

"And the prickles?" Thelma prompted.

"He's so bloody pushy at times. Then when I want him to stand tall, he seems to shrink. One moment I can't get enough of him, the next I want him to leave me alone, and, blast it all, he doesn't seem to have any idea which is which."

Thelma tried not to laugh, but a more apt description of love she could not imagine. "Alas, my dear, I believe you have been bitten—well and truly."

"Bitten?" Johanna was perplexed. "Is love like a snake bite?"

"Very."

"But surely, it is sweetness and light, the floating on clouds of ecstasy."

"And have you floated on those clouds?" Thelma was uncomfortable with such elusive imagery, but felt she might get closer to the problem if she played along.

"Oh, indeed. There were moments when he held me that I thought my arms could be wings, carrying us both off into eternity." A warning bell sounded. "Thelma, you won't tell my father any of this. He'd have my head if he knew I had ... well ... if ...."

Thelma finished her thought, "If you had slept with a man?"

"How did you know?"

"It's in your eyes."

"It is?" Johanna's hands went to her cheeks in dismay. "Do you think other people can see it?" She looked around quickly. "My father — can he?"

"Hush, Johanna," Thelma put a reassuring hand on her shoulder. "Sex is my profession. No one else will know and certainly not your father and not from my lips. You enjoyed lying with him?"

"Oh, it was heaven." Johanna looked at her surrogate mother. "Oh, I know it is supposed to be a duty. 'Close your eyes and think of England.' But it was so much more. I have never been swept into that world before. And when it was over, the hurt, the aching inside. Why is that?

When he left, I was with a dreadful solitude I didn't know was possible. How could that be, for I had just felt him so near? Am I crazy or selfish or kinked in my soul somehow?"

Obviously, these were not rhetorical questions, and Thelma beamed with delight and honest affection. Seeing the doubt in Johanna's eyes, she hastened to make herself clear. "I'm not laughing at you, but with you. Isn't love grand?"

Johanna let a thought grow in her mind. "Have you been in love? I mean have you felt this storm?"

"Yes, I have!" Thelma's mind wandered into her own private rooms. "There is a man ... but it's not ...," she looked for a word that would not give too much away, "it's not easy ... for him."

"My father," Johanna blurted out and then she blushed at being so forward. "You love my father. He is very fortunate to have you."

Thelma was silent but her gaze gave it away. She bowed her head, trying to hide her pain. "Isn't love grand?" She rubbed her hands together nervously. "Ain't it just."

There was a long silence. Johanna reached out this time and held Thelma's hand. "I won't tell him I know. He can be so pig-headed at times. Does he know how much you feel?"

"Oh, yes." Thelma looked up. "And he's as smitten as I. That I know. But that damned church—she's his real bride, and, until he lets her go, I'll always be his beloved mistress."

"He's a fool!"

Thelma smiled. "Thank you for the sentiment, but life and love get more complicated as we grow older. Trust me. I wouldn't have him leave his work—it would kill what we enjoy right now and ...." Thelma shook her head. "Listen to me going on about my woes. You came to see me. What was your question? 'Why does love hurt so much?'"

Johanna took it up again. "And it does hurt! You know that too."

Thelma looked off to the horizon. "Hurt ... yes. Well, love hurts because it is ...." Thelma groped around for a way to begin. "You've just felt ...." Her gaze slid from the sky to a park bench set in a grove of oak trees. "Let's sit for a moment."

They walked in silence to the bench and sat close.

"You see, Johanna, we all die. Damnable fact! And love is painful precisely because it opens us up to our finality. The unity you felt with this private ... what was his name again?"

"Gordon" Johanna whispered his name—reverence and longing mingled in the one word.

"Gordon. The unity you felt with Gordon is not going to last ..., at least not as we imagine. That's why it hurts—love is about letting go. Whether by death or break up, we lose its completeness. That makes it such a mixed emotion."

"But, surely, there is more." Johanna's pinched features were a portrait of pathos. "What if he is killed, if I never see him again?"

"Steady child," Thelma calmed her charge. "That union of body is not all—desirous and bountiful though it is at the time. Love grows deeper roots. We are fools if we only look upon the surface of things. There is a mystery to loving that transcends time and place."

"A mystery?"

"Yes, a mystery. Love's power is stronger than death. Once we have created love, or, should I say, once love is created between two beings, it has its own mind, so that little things like war cannot overcome it. It's a miracle ... love's a painful miracle and it will last well beyond your lifetime. Of that I am certain. And you will also feel great fear for what Gordon could do with your affection. Do you see?"

Johanna was deep in thought and made no reply.

Thelma patted her on the knee and rose from the bench. "Anyway that's my sermon for today. Except for one point."

Johanna rose with her. "What point?"

"Don't run from it, Johanna. If it is true and good, love will not die, because of separation or distance. The apostle Paul was right! Love can endure all things."

"How did you know about Paul's letters? I thought you had nothing to do with religion!"

"Oh, you'd be surprised what I've picked up on my travels," Thelma chuckled. "But he was right. Only the weak and sentimental will try to escape the pain of loving. There is no secure perch from which to fly when love lifts your wings. How's that for a flighty image! I can be so pathetic in poetry."

They both laughed, and then Thelma put on a serious front. "You have to take the risk, in spite of the suffering involved. In the end you'll see that it's worth it."

"But what if he dies?" Johanna pleaded.

"Would his death change the moments you have already enjoyed?"

"No, not really."

Thelma looked at Johanna. "Love isn't about forever, Johanna. It's about for always, but they're not the same thing."

"I don't follow. Didn't Paul say love lasts forever?"

Thelma smiled. "Well correct me if I'm wrong, but I think it was 'Love never ends.' But that doesn't mean its goal is countless days and nights of pleasure. Even one instant of true love can hold eternity with its grasp. Do you see?"

Johanna didn't. "No, I just want him back and safe, so we can enjoy old age together."

"I understand." Thelma looped her arm through Johanna's. "Let's walk around the top of the hill before we go back."

"Thelma, if I need your help again, may I call?"

"Anytime, day or night." The sun shone down on their passage, and Thelma knew in her heart that this was the closest she would ever come to motherhood.

"Close enough, I guess," she thought.

Saint John: Centenary-Queen Square United Church
Tuesday, Nov. 17, 1992, 11:25 a.m.

"Many of you were not close to Gordon, so you have little notion of what I mean by his 'secret.' You're here to pay your respects—honour what you do know of him, support me as well, perhaps."

Someone coughed.

Funeral homilies balance the essence of a person's life with the Gospel message of hope. It's a thin line between being too concrete, trivializing the Gospel by shaping it to one life, and being too broad, leaving the individual behind in a dust of religious slogans.

"Gordon's secret was about love. While I am unclear about the details, I know that he wandered the streets of Montreal for four days, just after the Halifax explosion. Something in those four days silenced him, and it is my guess that it was not the war or the disaster that robbed him of speech. It was deeper than shock and hatred, and the only possibility that makes sense is love. I know that sounds naive and perhaps far-fetched, but Gordon did give some hints of his anguish."

Saint John: The Buttress Home
Thursday, Sept 17, 1992, 9:15 a.m.

"The halyard, mate! Pull on the halyard." Captain Jims' face was purple with frustration.

"Where's the halyard?" I looked around the deck of his bed for anything that resembled a rope. Finding the coiled wire with the call button on it clipped to his bed sheet in case of emergency, I tried again. "This, Captain?"

"Aye, aye, hoist that mainsail or we'll lose the wind. Can't let those bastards beat us."

When I entered Gordon's room, his mind was in the middle of some momentous race. Before I had an opportunity to change into my sailor's garb, he was shouting orders, most of which sounded like Greek to me. "Bastards, Captain. Are they off the port bow?" I pointed right toward the room's only art—a print of Tom Thomson's "Northern Pines."

"Silly fool, where did they ever teach you nautical affairs? Port is that way." He pointed left. "And yes, if you look carefully, you'll see their sails rise on the swells. They've got a fair head start, but I've never lost a race yet." Looking at my idle hands, he shouted, "Pull that halyard! Damn you! I'm not about to lose because my crew is lazy and witless."

I made as if to pull mightily on the thick rope of his bed buzzer. "Hoisting the mainsail, Captain." I had no idea when it was fully deployed, but I watched Gordon for further orders.

"Slowly now, mate," Gordon was looking at the corner of the ceiling where our sail was, no doubt, rising. "Keep her going steady. That's got it. Tie her off and go forward."

I wound the slender coiled wire around the bedpost and sat at the head of his bed. He was stationed in his rocker, hands pressed on a tiller that looked very much like an armrest. Never having sailed in a race before, I needed more help. I tried to phrase my question so as to fit in with the plot. "The seas are rising, Captain, how much can our craft take? She's not that large."

The captain was concentrating on the distant sails of his competitors, but found time to reply. "Go away with you. This beauty has won many a race for me. A six-metre champion. She got more heart and soul than boats twice her size. Hasn't let me down yet."

At least now I knew how big our ship was ... not very. I wondered why we were racing at all. Maybe if I encouraged him a bit more. "Sir, we're gaining on them, I can see them clearly now."

"Hush, man," Gordon looked behind, "I'm trying to gauge the wind direction. Looks like it's shifting. We'll cut them off at the first turn, if this keeps up."

"Who are they, Captain?"

"The lowest form of bottom feeders that ever licked the ocean floor." Gordon's face went dark. "Cut your throat will they and smile in your face while they're doing it." Captain Jims spat on the floor. "Bastards!"

"Why are we racing them, if they are so rotten?"

My captain looked at me in disgust. "Where's your guts lad? This is not an idle race. It's a run for the final prize. Can't let them win without a fight. I'll pass the marker ahead of them, if I can only get this wind to help me." He pushed hard on his tiller and the rocker almost upset. "Wow, she's a devil, this sea."

Wherever we were, this was not a gentlemen's race. That was clear. He was steering for his life, after some very significant prize. I felt a tingling in my gut. Were we close to Gordon's secret?

"Move out on the gunnels, my lad. She's heeling too much."

I dutifully sat on the end of the bed.

"Further out. Hike right over the side, or we'll drag too much." He waved at the floor as if I was to sway off into thin air above it. Looking about for help, I grabbed his quilt, tied one end to the opposite bedpost and, grasping a corner, leaned out past the mattress. I wondered how long my stomach muscles could hold, hoping for a quick race.

The captain was peering from one side of the bed to the other, his gaze fixed and angry. "Damn spray. Can't see a blasted thing!"

My arms were stretched tight. I tried to penetrate deeper into his fantasy without disrupting it. "What's the prize? I hope all this work is worth it."

"Prize ... what prize? We're just trying to stay alive."

I pushed a little. "But there's got to be a goal besides racing."

He looked at me sideways. I was uncertain if it was the wind or my question. For a time, he was silent, sizing up his answer.

"Mate, we're not racing to lose, and I'll be sore put out if we do. The prize, the prize is seeing her smile again."

"Seeing whose smile?"

"The lady's." He offered his response definitively, as if there was no further discussion.

I decided to be cute. "So, is she frowning right now?"

"Keep your eye on that sail and lay off the wise-arse comments, or I'll have your guts for garters. Blast this wind." Captain Jims was growing more agitated. He shifted his tiller from left armrest to the right. Neither seemed to work as he wanted. "Bugger the waves." He wiped imaginary spray from his eyes. "Bring on the wind, you sea dog. Blow ...." His face was turning red with frustration. "Look at that!" He shouted angrily at the picture hanging over his neighbour's bed. "Those bastards have cheated again. Goddamn pious pricks, can't trust 'em for spitting. They'll stop at nothing to win. Smiling bastards."

"Who," I asked, "who are we racing?"

"Hounds of hell that pretend to be heaven-sent, that's who. Hang out there, mate, by the hairs of St. Joseph, we're catching them."

I didn't know if I could follow Gordon's twists of metaphor, and I wasn't sure he could either. I tried to get back to safe ground. "Begging your pardon, Captain. But I can't see their colours anymore.

What are their ships called again?" Maybe another tack would get me clearer answers.

"Well, the one in the lead right now is called Cruikshank. Bloody fool of a sailor. Got a smile like an eel and just as slippery." His voice was rising. "Then comes Hawthorne, another empty-headed bottom dweller. Can't trust him to be straight, even if he was stretched out for a week to dry. The worst son of sea serpent is Ryan. The first two would sell their own mothers to win. And the third, the third did sell us all, but to the Devil."

Here the Captain fell into an angry silence. After a pause, he spat three times on the floor and burst out in an explosion of fury, "But we'll beat 'em this time, those sorry sodding sinners." He was shouting now. "No mercy, no pussy-footing modesty." The Captain shook his fist at our opponents. "Hear that, you blighters? I'll take you down with me, if I have to. Leave you in my wash, like sunken waterlogged sea dogs. I won't sulk away this time nor take the blame for your wickedness. Damn you all to hell!" His final words were almost a scream, and I looked around to see if the nursing staff was running with a tranquilliser. Though I kept my place over the gunnels, I hoped they would arrive with something. "Must be on a bloody coffee break again."

Gordon fumed at the wind and I worried he would blow a blood vessel. His face was red; his knuckles were white from gripping in the armrests ferociously. I was about to let go of my rope, haul myself back on board and comfort our captain, when he started to relax. His gaze went fuzzy, I saw the sinews in his hands soften and the tautness of his forehead loosened, until he was a relaxed, elderly gentleman.

This race was over, and I had no idea if we won, if Gordon thought he had left his enemies in the backwash of his successful sailing. He went silent. I tried commenting on the gusty winds, the high seas, even asked if I could let down the mainsail. But he seemed indifferent to my queries, a senile, silent old man again.

I decided to leave. The captain had gone down below to his cabin for a rest, well-deserved. Placing a gentle hand on his shoulder I smiled. "Captain, you gave them a run for their money."

I had turned left at the entrance to his ward, heading for the stairs when I heard a crusty sailor's voice answer back, "By the grubby feet of St. Peter, I did. Indeed, I did."

Montreal: Christ Church Cathedral
Friday, November 30, 1917, 7:45 a.m.

"If we are to tread the path of St. Peter, friends, let there be no mistake. We are called, as he was, to the utmost in faithfulness. In spite of past betrayals and denials, we are now facing the ultimate test. 'Rise up, oh men of God, have done with lesser things. Give heart and soul and mind and strength, to serve the King of Kings.' The hymn speaks eloquently. Rise up, I say, Rise up!"

Cruikshank banged the pulpit, waking a few. He gazed down upon the rows of bishops present for the emergency debate, convened by their recently elected primate. The topic: to discuss the question of conscription. He suspected that they were far from committed. Many of the Quebec prelates were worried over rumblings of dissent in the French community. Western Ontario clerics were furious with what they saw as a soft approach to the question—allowing some citizens to evade the fate of military service, while others went obediently to do their duty.

A seasoned preacher, Cruikshank was not thrown off stride by several bishops who were reading their pew Bibles rather than heeding his words. He'd wake them up. Give him a week (which the primate had done), and he'd shake their minds awake. These lords of church had to endure a long day of sermons, similar to his own. A scattered few appeared more interested in the architecture. Cruikshank knew he would have to turn up the heat, if he expected to make a dent in their apathy.

A brief smile stole across his lips. He had just the trick to arouse their faith. They would wake up soon enough.

"I have a personal testimony to offer, the blood of my own veins, so to speak. For not one of us is exempt from the current battle." Here a few bored bishops straightened up, wondering what their preacher was proposing. "More on that in a moment." Cruikshank coughed and took a sip of water, all the while staring at his listeners. Most bishops had now turned, curiosity piqued, to listen to his sermon.

"Until recently, the ranks of the Canadian Corps have been replenished by the tide of courageous volunteers, eager to serve God and country. But alas, the foe is more vicious than initially expected. More troops are required for the final push onto Berlin. The unwilling, the lazy and the backslider, must be dragged into conscious action. It is no longer acceptable for us to see the flower of youth sacrificed while the idlers sit back, safe in Canada."

"Arise, my friends! Arise!"

Cruikshank was coming to end of his sermon. He had delivered a brief homily this morning. "Just a little inspiration for the debate to follow" was his instruction. He would have more time tomorrow to bend the ears of his peers. He would make his mark, foreshadowing his place among the lords of the church. A place he was determined to win through his unquenchable zeal for Christ and speaking prowess as a preacher.

"Friends, let not the past sacrifice of our children be in vain. Think well before you speak today, the fate of the Empire lies in the balance. Can the church stand on the sidelines in such a crisis?" He smiled and waved a hand at the surroundings, the well-sculpted ceiling and sparkling stained glass. "In this house of God, we are accustomed to prayer and meditation. Forgive me if I have been too political this morning, but it is a sign of times. Faith cannot be severed from its political consequences. Tomorrow morning, I will introduce a great soldier for Christ—the blood of my veins, I mentioned a moment ago. His testimony, both of his action at the front and his desire for victory will certainly inspire you where my feeble words have not."

Cruikshank smiled again. Ending with modesty gave his talk even greater punch. The bishops like humble servants, and Cruikshank was indeed prepared to play the role.

"Amen."

The preacher took his place beside the primate, who rested a hand on his arm in silent gratitude.

Saint John: Centenary-Queen Square United Church
Tuesday, Nov. 17, 1992, 11:26 a.m.

"Indeed, love expresses itself in many ways and can hurt us deeply. Hatred and animosity, as we witness between ethnic groups or mortal enemies, do not strike to the core of our being as much as love. We are not crippled by the violence of an enemy so much as the betrayal of a loved one."

"So it was with Gordon. From what I have pieced together, his long silence was the result of a broken promise, a broken promise he could not forgive."

"If only Gordon could hear again and believe in the message of the apostle Paul, 'Nothing can separate us from the love of our Maker.'" Is that not the lesson of Gordon's life? Neither death nor life can break the bond of forgiveness that binds us to the Creator of all life. Our task, and it is not easy, is to live our lives dependent on that everlasting forgiveness. No one can be perfect. The totally balanced life is an illusion. We all must throw ourselves on the goodwill and mercy of God and depend on God's gracious love. If only Gordon could have forgiven and known forgiveness. Perhaps he would have broken his silence much earlier."

Saint John: The Buttress Home
Thursday, Sept 24, 1992, 7:25 p.m.

"I am unworthy to be called thy son." Gordon (a.k.a. Father Inkling) was reciting the story of the prodigal son, one of his favourites. He enjoyed telling me Bible parables. "Mark me child, Jesus said 'unworthy,' and indeed all God's sons and daughters are unworthy. This one, particularly, for he had taken all he had been given and wasted it."

Father Inkling stared at me directly. His sermon voice at full throttle, I could feel my guilt creep over me. It had been another poor day at the church. I missed two appointments because they hadn't been written in my datebook: one with Mary Sanderson, a grieving widow whose husband had died after a lengthy illness. I wanted to see her and bring some measure of comfort. Now I had my own foolish, broken promise to contend with first. The second, a shut-in, Marilyn, who had waited faithfully with a hot cup of tea ready for the knock at her door. Damn it all, anyway!

Besides my lapses in memory, I had quarreled again with Mary at the office. It wasn't serious—we were at odds over the arrangement of this week's flowers—but it left a sour taste. Several cups of coffee and a few feeble jokes couldn't dispel the hard feelings. Double damn it!

I hadn't had time for dinner, and I was feeling testy when I arrived for my visit with Gordon. "Maybe the good priest will grant me absolution." I was wrong. He was in his condemning mode.

"We are all sinners," he boomed. "'But alas, I am the worst,' said the prodigal son. He knew the pain, not just of betraying his father, but even more so of betraying himself."

"How do you know that, Father?"

"Because I have lived it, my child." He offered this confession with complete assurance. His lips were clamped shut, and a determined look was growing in his eyes.

Without prompting he continued, "I broke a promise with the most important person there is."

"God?"

"No, my son, myself. I broke a promise to myself."

Saint John: Centenary-Queen Square United Church
Tuesday, Nov. 17, 1992, 11:27 a.m.

"Is there a moral in my sermon, some inkling of insight we can take way? If there is, it is simply this: Don't wait to extend your hand in friendship, don't hesitate to send the card of sympathy. Put out your offer of forgiveness as soon as possible. Love extravagantly. For the crucial moment passes and then fades and all our efforts cannot bring it back. As with death, the chance is snatched from our grasp.

"Thanks be to God that each day is a new moment in which to live anew the message of forgiveness, each hour an opportunity to love again. Even the grave cannot block the next sunrise."

The church is hushed. It was a feeble sermon. Not my best. Nevertheless, I feel a rising spirit within me. God works that way. Even with our poorest efforts, forces move, gravity loses and a burden is lifted, if ever so slightly. Perhaps Gordon himself can now find rest.

CHAPTER SEVEN

The Great Prayer
of Thanksgiving

Once my prayer life was peaceful. Alas, no longer! It is now a
battleground, an invitation to grapple with the Devil, hand-to-hand
combat ... Too much praying is sentimental trivia offered by black-
robed lightweights.

Grab Satan by the throat, go for the juggler or leave the entire practice alone!

A. Gus Stine, *The Heart's Wrest: Prayer in the Modern Context*

Montmagny, Quebec
Sunday, April 13, 2014, 8:39 p.m.

Blasted rain.

I hit the kill switch and flick out the Goldwing's kickstand. My
gloves are soaked. I stand up, hoist a leg over the seat and look about
the rest stop. Thank God for awnings over gas pumps. It's now coming
down in sheets. It had been building for the past thirty miles. While the
cold was bad, it wouldn't defeat me. But riding though a rainstorm at
night ... that was tough going.

Luckily there were only a few cars on the highway. Pulling off my
wet gloves I fiddle with the gas tank lock, wondering how much more I
could do tonight. My joints were stiff. The energy to fight the rain was
dipping low.

"Don't push it, old boy," I said out loud, mimicking my oldest son's advice, when he wished me well before I took off. He has such a great heart, genuinely concerned about his aging father. Sweet, really!

Little did he know! I grab the nozzle for super octane and start to fill.

Four weeks ago, I'd had my second hernia repaired. Took more digging about than the surgeon had expected. He warned me against physical exertion. "Take it easy for a month, at least!" I didn't mention the motorcycle and he didn't ask .... I imagine he wouldn't have advised a 14-hour bike ride as good therapy. "Just don't strain too hard. No heavy lifting."

"Right! I'll take it easy." And I had every intention of not straining "things."

As I fill the tank, I wonder about rain. I had hoped to get as far as Rivière-du- Loup, tonight ... within striking distance of Fredericton.

My heart is a bit low. Rain does that. I go in to pay for the gas, pick up a premixed milkshake and sit down to wait out the rain, tired to the bone and yet also frantic to start again!

Halifax, North Train Station
Thursday, December 6, 1917, 3:35 p.m.

After spending nearly six hours searching frantically for Jo, hoping against hope to find her, when he walked through the glass and rubble of the train station, he prayed he wouldn't. "Dear God, not here. Let her not be here." It was obvious that not a single living being had survived. Whatever had caused the blast—U-boat torpedo or secret German weapon—it had had devastating power. The entire structure had crumpled like a deck of cards, crushing everything and everyone beneath its weight. Ten-inch steel girders were twisted and broken like twigs. The roof of glass and brick had fallen flat. Any survivors of the initial crash of the building were pinned down by the debris, only to be overwhelmed by thick smoke.

Bodies were everywhere, crushed and contorted. Fire crews had arrived soon after the blast. They jumped from their wagons and stood stunned. The captain of the fire brigade finally mumbled, "Looks like a bloody battlefield. Let's go, boys. There's nothing here for us. Let the army get this lot out, when there's more time." The fire brigade quit that graveyard in search of the living.

After the fire crews left, only a few stragglers had returned to the train station. Mid-morning snow had drifted into open eyes and gaping mouths of the dead. Corpses lay undisturbed. When Gordon arrived, no voice of greeting, no human touch reached him. What was left of the south wall had scorch marks where the fire had been fiercest.

Walking through this disaster zone was haunting work, going from body to body, looking for, yet not wanting to find, Jo's bright eyes. The old man whose single-minded hobbling had directed them to this place had reached the charred front step of the train station and collapsed, as if on cue. Crushed in spirit, Gordon watched as his life ebbed away—heartbroken. There was no focus to his eyes, no hint of what his purpose might be. Nothing. Each time he returned from his own search, he asked the same question in a new way: "Old man, who are you looking for?" "Can I help you find her?" "Is it a son?" There was no response. The man was slumped and unmoving.

Gordon made several trips around the rubble, looking right and left as he climbed over metal and brick: scattered luggage, a few telltale uniforms, men's twisted legs and women's coats. These latter finds were the worst. He would have to turn each face to the light long enough to ensure that it wasn't Jo. There were eyes sliced open with glass, jaws broken by brick, throats slashed by steel. How many families had lost a mother, a daughter? He felt his resolve weakening. How long could he keep prying into the death dance of strangers? Only his yearning to know for sure that Jo was safe pushed him to the next heap of clothing.

Two hours of grisly work, and Gordon was finally through the entire structure. His hands were covered in other people's blood. He gave up. No Jo. She hadn't made it to the station. He was uncertain whether to be thankful or dismayed.

There seemed no point in waiting there. As he made his way back toward the old man, a splash of blue caught his eye. As he approached it, a shiver went down his back. At his feet, he caught sight of a discarded woman's cape. Was it Jo's? It was delicate enough. Could it be that she ran for her life, leaving this behind? Tentatively, he reached down and lifted the garment fearful of what he might find. Nothing. He slung the garment over his shoulders.

Taking a last look around the collapsed structure, Gordon came to the front entrance and found his companion. "Old man." He shook his voiceless friend. "Old man, let's go." But the crouched figure fell over at his touch. Gordon felt for a pulse and knew he was gone. Lost to suffering.

Tears welled in Gordon's eyes; he stumbled toward a mangled wrought iron bench by what had been the entrance, slumped down and wept. Not for the old man. Well, maybe for him a bit ... more for useless, cruel death that surrounded him. There was no purpose. As bloody and foolish as the battleground appeared, at least Flanders had an objective, a strategic hill, the hoped for breakthrough that would end the war. What meaning was here? Nothing. Slaughter with no point. Hell. Grief poured out that he could no longer stop. Fury and anguish mixed together.

Gordon wanted to be free, lost, to suffer no longer. His cold fingers grasped his uniform and ripped off the insignia on his chest and arms bands—smearing blood everywhere. He screamed, "No more orders. No more death. No more." He yanked off his dog tags and reverently, purposefully, placed them on what was left of the bench ... laying down his sword in defeat. Then the cloth patches followed. It took several minutes for his anger to subside, leaving a vacant place in his soul. He stood, weakened by fatigue and grief. Gordon looked down at a small pile of torn cloth and looked up and shouted to heaven. "No war. No more!"

What now?

Gordon was completely lost. He stretched to his full height, felt again the stiffness of his leg and wondered which way to go. His gaze passed down the tracks and saw an answer to his confusion. Boxcars were moving slowly, ever so slowly. He had no idea where it was going, but it was living, it was order in the chaos.

Unthinking, he stumbled toward it, no plan, no desire. Just to get away, get away from the chaos that was rocking Halifax.

Montreal: Thelma Lint's Gentlemen's Parlour
Sunday, August 6, 1916, 11:35 a.m.

"Of course you can stay." Thelma motioned for Jo to sit in her favourite wingback chair. "I won't have you go anywhere else."

"But Father," Jo was close to tears, "Father will want to send me to my aunt's house in Sackville. He's been insistent that as the war rations tighten I should go back to the family farm. But I couldn't stand to be …."

"That far off!" Thelma viewed her young protégé with kind eyes. "You think Gordon might come back, and you don't want to miss him."

"Exactly!" Johanna was so pleased to talk with someone who understood her so well; she never gave a second thought to why Thelma could read her mind so well. Jo was just relieved Thelma could. "Father is so stubborn." Here she sighed deeply. "He says that the war will go on forever, and, if Gordon does come back, it won't be for quite a while, and, if he were to come back, we'd have plenty of notice. But I don't believe him, and I knew you would understand. I can't leave—not now."

Thelma agreed. "You had best be where he thinks you'll be. Douglas can be dense about matters of the heart and so naive about the army. Just last week a whole regiment of wounded amputees arrived on the dock. No one knew they were coming. Nothing was prepared."

Tears began to flow down Jo's cheeks at the mention of amputees. "I can't stand waiting," she hissed—anger, frustration and fear mixed together. "I hate waiting, I hate war. I just want my Gordon back, safe and whole." A long pause as she wiped away the tears that wouldn't stop. "Oh God, if he's not whole what will I do?" Here Jo looked to her mentor. "Am I shameless to want him whole, when so many … so many come back missing limbs?"

Thelma moved forward, crouched by Johanna's chair, gently touched her cheek, and whispered, "There's no shame in wanting what was. None at all. But if he is wounded, that isn't the end—his beauty, as you well know and, as your father attests, is his inner strength."

"My father?" Jo smiled quickly, "Who would have thought?"

"He likes him very much and said he had considerable intellectual courage."

"He'd never admit it to me, though, would he?" Jo tried to breathe slowly, as Thelma had taught her. "Calms the nerves." But it wasn't working. The harder she tried to slow down, the shorter came her breath. She could feel nothing but the heavy weight around her heart and thought she was suffocating. Without warning the heaves began. Deep sobs of distress and grief—for lost love, for a lost childhood. The strong young woman collapsed. "Oh help, Thelma," she blurted between the sobs.

"Hush now, dear, let it all out." Thelma held Jo closely. "Cry for all the broken dreams of this godforsaken war. Cry as long as you need ... your tears are safe with me."

For many minutes they swayed back and forth saying nothing. When the practical, controlled Jo awoke, she moaned, "Oh ... what will Father say?"

"You leave him to me." Thelma stroked her hair. "I'll make it all right."

"But," Jo looked up into Thelma's eyes, "but he would never stand for me to stay here. I mean, I'm a bishop's daughter and I ... He doesn't even know that I came here this morning. I lied, claiming I was going to Holy Trinity for worship. He'll ...."

"You leave him to me," Thelma laughed. She could feel the mother lion coming out in her voice. No one would hurt her child—not even Douglas. Not even Gordon. "I have a few powers of persuasion."

They rocked in silence again—this time more contentedly. Jo was melting into the secure arms of another woman, feeling for the first time in ages that she was secure, that someone else would protect her and "make it all right." Thelma was marveling at how easily she had adopted Jo as her own daughter. "Damn that Douglas! He'll pay dearly if he pushes this child away," she thought.

"Thelma," Johanna's voice was muffled in the trim of Thelma's dress. "I wish you were my mother."

Thelma smiled, a broad, contented grin. "Do you?"

"Yes," Johanna paused, "You'd know what to do with ... with ...."

Thelma pulled away far enough to look into Johanna's eyes. "With what? What is it?" And then seeing the answer in Jo's eyes, she swallowed, smiled again and asked the simple question, "When?"

Fredericton, New Brunswick: The City Motel
Monday April 14, 2014, 3:07 a.m.

Made it. I can hardly lift my leg over the seat. I stretched, rubbed my stiff legs and said a quick prayer of thanksgiving for a safe arrival. Now for bed. I'm exhausted. A warm bed summoned. Patricia Patterson and the promise of mysteries solved. They can wait for my body to catch up.

Montreal: Christ Church Cathedral
Saturday, December 8, 1917, 9:45 p.m.

Cruikshank was shouting into the phone as if the volume would carry his words to Quebec City. "Look, we'll pay dearly if you don't get back here.... I know you're busy ... well ... yes ...." A look of consternation raced across his face. "No, he's here! Of course, I'm sure .... I had tea with him last night.... That's right." Cruikshank listened for some time and then interrupted. "A fascinating history lesson, but, right now I'm not interested in reliving Vimy Ridge .... We're very close, but the momentum is slipping. We have to strike soon. One bishop, the Bishop of Montreal—very influential—is having Davis speak at tomorrow's midday service. Wants us to hear first-hand about, in his words, "the mindless slaughter." He's chosen Davis as his spokesman. Yes. It will be a disaster if we don't undermine his address .... That's why we need you here to contradict him. Call him a coward—that sort of thing .... Of course it's important! Damn it, Ryan, you owe me!"

Cruikshank was fuming as he held the earpiece at a distance. Ryan's military bark had not caught up with the innovations in technology. "Ryan, listen! Stop your jabbering for once. I know what's at stake here and you don't." He hadn't meant to be so blunt with his ally, but the synod was slipping from his grasp. Each time Hinks took the pulpit, more minds turned against his holy war proposal. A few more days and he'd lose the project entirely. Cruikshank turned his thoughts back to

Ryan. "Yes, ... crush him! You'll get your chance to accuse the bugger in public—like you wanted. Why you couldn't find him out in France, I'll never know .... All right, it was confusing. I grant you that .... Right. But what about some planning now, old chap? No more whining. What can we do?"

A long silence ensued as the principal listened to his instructions. "Right, I have it all in my head. Thank you. Now, don't waste time. Get on the next train. Yes, I know it's the overnight express. Just get here."

Hanging up with a good deal more force that he intended, Cruikshank stormed out of the cathedral looking for fresh air and relief from the strain of his day. Maybe one more visit to the "parlour." He smiled to himself as his steps took him up toward the mountain. With Lieutenant Colonel Ryan on the train to Montreal, the good principal's political prospects looked good—the best.

Three miles from Halifax: Canadian National Railroad Tracks
Thursday, December 6, 1917, 4:15 p.m.

The train lurched backward. Johanna opened her eyes, a smile fading from her lips. She had been dreaming of Gordon again. It was *the* fantasy, now imprinted on her mind as reality, of their joyful reunion. His hands grasping her waist, while she smothered him in kisses and then standing back to watch the smile dawn across his face. She could feel his strong shoulders under her hands and knew that she was safe, never to be separated again from the one who made life worth living. She would then unburden her soul, and he would know all her secrets.

How often had she drifted into this delicious scene over the past twenty-four hours? Fredericton Junction, Saint John, Moncton, Sackville, Truro. As each station platform receded, she wanted to shout out her excitement. Instead, she had closed her eyes to be embraced yet again by the man she was calling her fiancé to anyone who asked.

"I'm off to Halifax to meet my fiancé, a returning soldier."

"Really?"

"He was wounded in Passchendaele."

The name meant nothing to most people but they were polite. "I hope not seriously, my dear. What unit was he with?"

"He … my fiancé was in the medical corps. He was at Vimy Ridge."

"Indeed!" Now that was a place name everyone knew. "Really, did he help take the ridge, this fiancé of yours?" Who wasn't looking for a hero?

"Fiancé!" Johanna said it with pride, firm and resolute, rolling the word over her tongue, expecting a voice, her father's perhaps or some unrecognized friend of the family, to deny it. None did. Strangers all smiled their understanding. "Of course." How could the glow in her eyes be anything other than pent-up, soon-to-be-released, love? They would sigh and dream of the time when such passion once visited their own lives.

Johanna drifted in and out of sleep. At one point, she saw Gordon clearly on a battlefield, bullets flying about his head. He was reaching toward her saying, "Help me!" She woke with a start. Peering drearily outside, the scene had not changed, had it? There was the rough hillside, the hayfield shorn closely and the wagon wheel resting against the cedar rail fence. How long had they been sitting here? Six or seven hours? Snow was now falling and a north wind was whipping it up into white clouds, so, that, at times, the pastoral scene disappeared.

After a few moments, she fell back to sleep. The dream had changed and this time she was stretching her hand out to him as they walked along a distant shore. Sunlight cut across their path, when he suddenly fell in his tracks. A lurch of the train brought Johanna back to reality with a start and she peered out the window for the thousandth time.

Johanna shivered from the cold. Frost was building on the cracks between the floorboards. Her foot warmer was cold. She pulled the blanket further up her body, adjusted her skirt under it and looked about the small section of train that had become her home. All was quiet. No baby sounds awakened slumbering passengers.

The sudden jolt signaled that the train was finally moving, if ever so slowly. At last! They'd be off to Halifax. Johanna sat up in anticipation, but then realized with horror and dismay that they were not going forward.

A gruff voice broke the solitude. "Folks, folks, I have important news. As you can see we are moving again, but, alas, we're bound for Montreal."

It was the conductor. Straddling the aisle and hoisting himself up to his full six feet, Fred tried to sound self-assured. Disappointing passengers was always his nightmare, especially train loads of vets' wives all steaming to get to their dockside reunion with loved and lost ones. Every minute's delay was sticking needles in their eyes.

The conductor had taken a stand a few yards to the rear of Johanna's seat, so she could hear his general announcement quite well. "I am sorry to disturb you, ladies and gentleman, but, ..." Fred fumbled with the twenty-years-of-service gold watch fob he had dragged from his vest pocket. "Look, I am real sorry for you women who want to get to see your menfolk, but we've been ordered to retrace our steps back the way we came. You will be asked to disembark at your point of embarkation. There will be no exceptions."

A number of cries of disappointment rose up. "What's happened? Can't we get off and walk?" Fred used his best authoritative voice to calm jangled nerves as he offered explanation. "As you can see, there's a snowstorm brewing, and we have to clear the tracks for a few emergency trains making their way to Halifax." A forest of upraised hands shot up, and Fred took each question in turn.

"No, it's too late to try to reach the city, the best I can do is let you off in Truro, but I can't guarantee any transport to Halifax. ...Yes. It seems there has been some kind of disaster. ... That's right. I don't know what happened exactly. ... Thank you for the offer, but the last thing you want to do is go to a city that is blacked-out or burned up or blown apart. Who knows what you would find? ... I can't say how bad it is. But I'm afraid it might be very serious. The word I have was not clear, but it appears that this snowstorm and the courage of the dispatcher in the Halifax station may have saved us all from grave danger. ... The best I can say is that there has been a tremendous explosion. 'Fire raining from the sky' was how they put it."

This final picture silenced the voices struggling to be heard. Fred played his trump card. "Friends, I know you'd all like to help out, but the prime minster himself is racing toward the city as we speak. He needs a clear track to get through. The best we can offer right now is our prayers."

Murmurs of assent all round. Some folk nodded and a few, being religious, seemed to take his advice to heart, crossed themselves, bowed their heads and started their spiritual efforts immediately.

Johanna caught the conductor by the coattail as he made his way past and asked her only question, "Are there many casualties?"

Her deep blue eyes held the conductor, who wanted to get back to his warm cubicle and his emergency rum ration. "I'm not certain, missy, but there may be thousands. It didn't sound good." Fred saw the dark spectre of doubt flash across her countenance and tried to ease the pain. "But it's too soon to tell." He made to leave, unable to find other comforting words to offer.

Johanna held firmly to his coat. "No word yet of any disembarking soldiers? I … I am going wild with uncertainty."

The conductor recalled their earlier conversation and knelt down to whisper in her ear. This real news was not for general consumption, not yet. "I am sorry Miss. I tried to ask about your man, but the lines are taken up with more vital messages. Seems that the entire north end of the city has been wiped out—not a house, church or factory left standing. Hundreds of people buried alive, I'm told. Hundreds more burned. The hospitals are overflowing with the wounded. It sounds like a hellish mess. I am not one to lose heart, but if your fellow was coming to the north end of the harbour, he's probably not in good shape. I heard there was a tidal wave that swept away several piers and the fires took care of the rest." He spoke in a level, fatherly tone. "Now, I imagine it's better for you to go back to Montreal. You can't do much more than the authorities are already doing. The military will get in touch, when they've sorted it out." He patted her arm in paternal way.

"He's not my man, sir," Johanna's eyes flashed. "He's my fiancé, and I'll be damned if I return to Montreal to sit like a polite patient matron while my beloved is perishing—no matter how hellish it is." She was hurt, frightened and, above all else, angry. She could feel a towering fury building as she thought of this futile war and the possibility that the most precious person to her had been sacrificed for a useless, pig-headed cause.

Fred straightened up, a bit affronted by this diminutive tiger. "In that case, you'll have to detrain at Truro and catch the next passenger back into Halifax, but with this storm and the emergency trains taking priority, you'll be a week waiting." "Young people!" he thought. "They burn with a fire that only ignorance can fuel."

Johanna made ready her escape. If Truro was her next stop, she would waste no time getting off the train. But she had no intention of waiting for the next available seat. A freight car, the prime minister's coach, anything would do. As she bundled up her possessions, she ground her teeth. Nothing would stop her.

Her hands moved quickly, stuffing sweaters and shoes back into her carpetbag.

The train was gaining speed now. The click-click of the wheels set a rapid cadence. They passed through a tunnel and the sudden darkness caught her unaware. She stopped her furtive packing, and, in an uncustomary way, her mind went to prayer. "Heavenly Father, God of all, please save him. Keep him alive, until I can come to him." Johanna had a very open manner with her Maker. "Okay, you're right. I haven't called at your door too often of late, but you are never far from my thoughts, and you have promised to keep me and mine forever. I'm calling in that promise now. I won't ask for another thing in my lifetime, if you grant me a reunion with my love."

The train left the darkened tunnel suddenly and light flooded her compartment. "Message received," she thought.

No sooner had the train left the shadow of the tunnel than it ground to a halt on a siding. Wheels screeched and the cars joggled to a stop. For a time, Jo could hear nothing but the hissing of steam from the brakes and the subdued chatter of passengers. Then there came the sound of an approaching train. It woke Jo to her chance and she leapt up with her belongings, slogged her way to the exit and before she could think of what was going to happen to her, stepped down from the footplate of her train and stepped across the rails, watching for the light of the on-coming train. When it came into view, it turned out to be a ragtag freight—several empty cars filled with rail riders. No hope there. Besides it was going in the wrong direction … away from Halifax. It was moving too quickly for Jo to get information or ask a question. One unshaven man blew a lecherous kiss. Ugly brute. Jo shouted her scorn, "Save it for your honey, sweetheart!"

Nothing for it, Jo began to walk toward Halifax. Turning once she saw her passenger train leaving the siding as it retraced its steps back toward Truro and safety. She bent her shoulders into the wind and trudged toward her destiny.

"Where was he?" She spat her question into the drifting snow and began to doubt if her prayers had been answered. As the frost bit into her fingers, she mumbled, "Maybe this wasn't such a bright idea after all."

Saint John: Centenary-Queen Square United Church
Tuesday, Nov. 17, 1992, 11:27 a.m.

The sermon concluded, I move behind the table for our prayers. That's when it struck me. Why not have bidding prayer? A bit unconventional in a funeral service, but perhaps more fitting than it might first appear.

It was a spur of the moment idea. That made me suspicious. Levan's rule #6: "Beware of good ideas that 'just come to you.' They're often disasters." Nevertheless, I thought a little informality would not ruin the flow. I invited the gathered community to participate.

"Friends, we're an intimate gathering today, and most of you had only a passing acquaintance with Gordon Davis. At this point in the service, you may wish to offer a special prayer of Thanksgiving. During the prayer, when I invite other petitions, stand at your place, suggest the name of someone to be remembered before our Creator God."

Joan Simmons, one of nurses, looked at her partner and smiled. Mary, my secretary, would mention her brother in England who had just died.

The Prayer Book entitled this section of the funeral service, "The Great Prayer of Thanksgiving," and, indeed, it is great if length is any measure of grandeur. I had planned to read the entire prayer, but given my spur of the moment gesture, that didn't make sense. Skip the last few paragraphs and lead people directly into the bidding prayer.

"Friends, I will read a few verses offering thanksgiving for Gordon's life and conclude with: 'Lord in your mercy,' and I will ask you to respond, 'Hear our prayer.' This pattern can be repeated after each petition."

There is a slight shuffling of feet. Two orderlies lean forward, cupping their heads in their hands. The undertakers at the back bow their heads. I hear a police siren in the distance and a heavy truck shifting through several gears making its way up Wentworth Street. Life continues even though Gordon does not.

"Let us pray." I pause. It's time to take a breath, feel the hurt and the loss and try to put our helplessness before death into words.

"Dear God ... lover of every life, look down upon us as we offer our farewells ...."

I imagine Gordon had said his farewells long before I met him.

Montreal: Bank of Montreal, Office of Accounts Manager Mr J. Tompkins
Monday, December 10, 1917, 10:47 a.m.

Even at the beginning of the week, John Tompkins could feel his frustration rising. He was already running late—a cardinal sin in his banker's heart that cherished punctuality above all else. His boss, the vice president of investments, wanted a full rundown on his current account allocations. "Immediately," the memo stated bluntly. Two clients, who had made appointments for "first thing Monday morning," were cooling their heels in the hall. Tompkins had already proffered tea and comfortable chairs, apologized for the delay and introduced a colleague, who could handle their affairs. He then retreated to his office to dash down a few more lines on the demanded report for his superior.

The vice-president of investments was not to see the report that morning. No sooner seated than an insistent soldier hammered on his office door, gave his name and Tompkins had his secretary fetch the file. As usual, he offered a hospitable beverage and the assistance of a fellow banker, but there had been no question of anyone else. He would "wait as long as it takes."

Looking over the file, Tompkins groaned. This would not be a simple matter. The stipulations and regulations were complex. He looked through the neat painted letters on his glass door and watched his new customer. Apart from the torn uniform and darkened eyes, there was a certain resigned, stone-faced countenance. A man with a mission and a mad one at that. Suicide, maybe? Handsome in a rugged sense, a bit of a wild beast lurking just below the surface. "Too many bent creatures coming out of that Flanders slaughterhouse," Tompkins shook his head and mused over the fate of so many vets.

For the hundredth time that day he thought about his own son, "missing in action" at Vimy Ridge. There had been several official apologies for the military's inability to offer more details, but their words didn't help. Eventually a medal was sent by post, "Henry J. Tompkins" printed neatly on the back. He had "returned it to sender" with a crisp retort: "I'd rather have my son back."

Tompkins closed the door on his grief, sighed and rose from his desk. Motioning through the glass door, he ushered Davis into the leather chair facing his desk.

"Mr. ... Davis ... this account is a bit peculiar." Tompkins looked up into the distressed, bloodshot eyes of his client. "The cash is held in trust and of course is available to you, but it will take several days for the transfer of funds to be complete. I would imagine that we will require a letter from your college stating ..."

Gordon smiled ever so slightly. "It's not cash I want."

"I see. I apologize. I just assumed that you were here to get the financial means to ... how can I be of assistance?" Tompkins had been sure it was cash grab. This soldier's tattered uniform and unshaven face gave all the signs of a shell-shocked desperado. He'd pegged Gordon as someone looking for beer money to drown in.

"I was given to believe," Gordon tried to give his voice the confidence that he had lost the night before, "I was given to believe that the funds could be transferred to a third party of my choosing."

Tompkins, a bit surprised, surveyed the stipulations of the trust. Flipping through several pages, he finally located the pertinent line and read it clearly. "Yes here it is in point seven: 'The trustee (that's you, Mr. Davis) shall have the right upon receipt of the trust, to designate a third party or parties to be the recipient of the accumulated assets of the trust." Tompkins looked up and smiled, wondering how any soldier that looked as badly as this one, could think through financial concerns, especially complex matters of a third party bequest. "You have someone in mind, do you?"

Gordon sat silently, lost in his own thought.

Tompkins coughed and repeated his question. "Ah ... Mr. Davis ... did you have someone in mind to be named as a beneficiary of this account?"

No response. It appeared to Tompkins that Mr. Davis was weighing his options carefully.

To fill the gap in their conversation, Tompkins read the general instructions outlined in the preamble. "It does state here—are you following me?" He looked up wanting to see if Davis was understanding his words. It appeared he did so. Gordon nodded his head. "He's alive then," thought Tompkins. Out loud he continued, "As I was saying. It does state in the preamble to your great-uncle's bequest, that you are to receive full control over the account the moment you register for theological training. I see that we do indeed have a letter from your college indicating that you have been accepted into their program." Leafing through the file, Tompkins extracted a single page. "Signed by a Principal Cruikshank, I see."

Gordon let out a short bitter laugh.

Tompkins was too busy with administrivia to detect the scorn in his client's voice. "So that, duly noted, allows you full control over the funds with the one curious stipulation. Should you ever take your own life, the remainder of the account would revert to the college from which you received your original acceptance." He looked from the file to Davis. "Does put a twist in things." Secretly, he thought that given this young man's obvious disheveled and distracted condition, suicide wasn't far from his thoughts.

Davis was certainly awake now. "Can I designate such a third party now?"

Tompkins read through the introduction again. "Ah … I believe … yes … It does appear … ah … that you have that right. Yes."

"Let's do it, then."

Tompkins was not about to rush. He hadn't made it into the manager's chair by rushing into agreements. He wanted some advice from Frank in "Wills and Trusts" before he signed off on this case, especially given the obvious distress of this Gordon Davis. "Yes, well, we can do that of course, … but I will need some proof of identification and a few hours to draw up the papers." He looked down at his desk calendar. Can you come back this afternoon? At 3:00 p.m. perhaps?"

"This afternoon?" Gordon wanted the business over and done. "Can't it be done while I wait?"

"Three o'clock will be soonest I can I have it completed." Tompkins now knew he was right to stall. "You may want to think on this a bit. Giving away your inheritance is a major step, and, while battle does change our outlook, you're a young strapping fellow, and you will certainly have needs for," Tompkins looked down at the ledger listing the account's assets, "… needs for what is indeed a considerable fortune. Giving this sum of money to a third party should not be done lightly. You might split the assets … set some aside for your future …."

Gordon was silent.

Tompkins, noting the religious tenor of the trust added, "A few prayers might be in keeping with your great-uncle's wishes."

Gordon stood, "Prayers are useless for those who lose faith." He turned slowly to the door. His feet were lead weights and his heart was turning blank. Somehow, he'd have to find the energy to wait. "I'll sit in your waiting room until three o'clock, if you don't mind." After that, he could sleep and say farewell to the world.

Tompkins shut the door, gave a quick glance toward Mr. Davis and determined to do right by this soldier. They would transfer the money, of course, but he had the discretion to manage the account and so he would split assets. Tompkins would slice off a good portion of the inheritance, so that Gordon Davis would have a nest egg when he surfaced from his war-weary frenzy. It wasn't following his client's instructions, not strictly speaking, but it was wartime and people learned to bend the rules to make the senseless make sense. Tompkins thought of his own son … wishing someone had had a similar power to save him from his best intentions, when he signed up to this bloody war and charged up that bloody hill!

He made the appropriate notations and fixed his own signature to a draft his secretary would polish into a legally binding transfer document. Looking into the outer office, Tompkins examined his now patiently waiting client. Gordon Davis. From what height had he fallen?

On an impulse, Tompkins rose and went to the door, opened it and called out to his client. "Ah. Mr. Davis … did you," Tompkins coughed slightly, "… I mean were you at Vimy Ridge, by any chance?" He coughed again. Nervous.

Gordon looked up, "I was, … though I didn't see much action."

Tompkins pressed him, "Was it … I mean … I lost my son on the first day. I, ah, I … you didn't know him perhaps … Henry Tompkins? He was with the infantry …"

Gordon shook his head, spoke slowly … words well-chosen. "I was with the medical corps. The day is a blur to me now … can't say as I recall any Henrys … but I am sorry, so sorry, for your loss."

Tompkins was about to respond with the usual "thank you," when he looked more carefully into Mr. Davis' eyes. He saw a sympathy he had never known before. It was the look of a man who knew pain and who cared. It took his breath away. Sincere, and genuine. A tear fell down his cheek. "With this man," he thought, "I can cry without shame. There is no shame in being hurt by the war, being unable to 'hold it together,' as so many of his family and friends expressed it. Davis knew his grief first-hand.

Tompkins smiled his gratitude and offered, "They say the battle was horrendous. Like nothing we have ever seen."

Gordon paused and remembered the waiting for the action to start. "It was the waiting that killed you."

Vimy Ridge, France
Saturday, April 7, 1917, 3:12 a.m.

"It's the waiting that kills me."

Gordon, whose mind was focused on his carving, turned to his left, "What's that, Frank?"

"I said, it's the bloody waiting that is fucking killing me." Frank spat to the ground. "Can't we get out of this stinking cave and do something useful like getting ourselves killed." Several others down the line chuckled. Frank was a comedian, the new boy on the squad and had yet to see any action. He had no idea.

Waiting was a soldier's first job, and, while it was deathly dull, it was a far better place than being sliced open by machine gun fire.

"You'll want to watch what you ask for." Gordon turned back to his carving. "You might just get it. 'Dead,' I mean."

They had been in the chalk tunnels for almost three days, waiting for the order to attack. Food rations and latrine duty were their only interruptions. Gordon had no idea, actually, if it was day or night. They slept in shifts, when the company commander ordered lights out.

To pass the time, Gordon had decided to carve a maple leaf in the chalk by his head. Kept his mind off the coming battle. Like many in his circle, he wondered what they were doing. The Canadian corps was set to take on a well-fortified German position that the French and British armies had been unable to capture.

It was often made clear by superior officers, seconded to them by the British, that very little was expected of the Canadians. Their job on Vimy was to distract the enemy's focus from the major attack to take place further south. No one expected anything better than a "good effort" (code in World War I for a high casualty count) from the Canadians. Just die well. Period. Vimy was beyond anyone's reach.

Was it defiance or boredom? But to pass the time and to build his strength of heart, Gordon chiseled the red maple leaf, his shoulder badge, into the white chalk wall of his cave.

When complete, he blew away the dust, fingered the edges of his design and wondered how many maple leaves would fall, never to rise again in the battle that loomed ahead.

Hamilton: 75 Barton Street
Saturday, November 17, 1917, 9:24 p.m.

James Davis hefted the butt of his well-oiled shotgun to his shoulder and looked down the sights.

How could he have been so blind?

He was sitting alone in the locked washroom on the second floor of his small house. Most of his neighbours still had outdoor plumbing, but, with all his young daughters, his wife had insisted that he build them proper, modern facilities.

And he'd done it all himself. Looking idly around the small room, he noted the odd carpentry mistake, a cracked tile, the slightly out-of-level sink. He could see it all from where he sat on the toilet. "Glorious!" "Great design!" "So convenient!" His family had been lavish in praise when the work was done. It meant nothing to him now.

His mind was not held by the washroom. Rather, it went back to the nightmare he'd been living over the past few days. He could hear Brent's plaintive voice. "It began on the 'special retreat vigils.' When the church worship leaders took us off." James remembered. The Reverend Hawthorne regularly took his new communicants class up to James' cottage at Sauble Beach. There would be five or six men, the two wardens and a selection of elders.

"At my cottage ... what happened?" James had felt a knot tightening in his stomach as he tried to unlock Brent's pain.

Brent was slouched on a kitchen stool, his eyes downcast. "Father Hawthorne, he would set us all up separately. Each night a different boy. We'd be set up by the fireplace while everyone else was allowed to sleep. A 'vigil' he called it."

"A 'vigil' ... yes he told me about that ...." James wasn't sure where they were headed. "What ... what did you do on your vigil night?"

"I am so ashamed." Brent stared blankly at the stacked dinner plates on the kitchen shelves.

"There's nothing to be ...." James stopped talking when he saw Brent's tears, now streaming down his cheeks. "There is no shame here, Brent. You are a great lad, everyone's favourite."

"That's what Hawthorne told me, too!" Irony dripped from his words. Brent had suddenly burst into a loud voice. His lack of respect for the priest was raw and bitter. "He would blindfold us, so that we couldn't see anything. We were to stay standing all night long as devotion to God. 'A prayer,' he called it. He would make us take off our clothes and stand in our underwear, again as a sign of devotion. And then, somewhere in the middle of the vigil, I felt a man come into the room and pull down my underwear ... he began to ... to touch me down there." Brent was now back to a whisper. "It was ... I was so ... it lasted for just a short time, but I was ... was so frightened!" Brent paused, recalling the nightmare of his vigil. He wiped tears from his face and concluded, "I never knew who it was ... and I was too ... too ashamed to say anything." Here he looked at James, "But I can't bury it any longer. It happened three years back, but ... but I can't sleep and I ...."

James felt like he'd been sucker punched. His head was swimming. "You don't know who it was? Really? Did he hurt you?"

Brent mumbled, "I never wanted to find out. He didn't do anything except touch me until I was ... I was ... you know ... hard."

James didn't know what to say. He had never heard or even thought about abuse of his students. After a long pause, "Who?" was all he could say.

"Don't know, sir. During the day they all looked so pious and pleasing."

Brent looked at his badminton coach, remembered his great stories of courage and faith and decided he owed the old man the truth. He spoke softly again, "Sir ... James ... did you ever wonder why so many young men from our church have signed up for overseas service?"

"Loyalty, I suppose," James replied. His hand rubbed the back of his neck, an involuntary gesture, a sign of agitation.

"Yes ... that's true, they wanted to get over there and whip the Hun's backside. But they were also running away from someone close to home whose hands were far too interested in little boys' private parts."

"Who?" James whispered again. "Someone here in the church!"

"Someone ... yes." Brent was silent for moment, caught by remorse and guilt. "I should have said something, warned the younger lads ... I just jumped at my chance to leave. Then the army turned me down .... Bad luck, I guess. Anyway it's over, and I don't want to say more against the church elders. But someone should know." Brent bowed his head. "Right now, I can't sleep and my mom is all worried, thinking I am going crazy ... and ... well she's right. Wants me to see a doctor, but I just don't know how to tell her what really happened." Shame silenced him.

James was rooted to the spot, so stunned he didn't even notice that his companion had gone silent. "All the boys???" he finally asked.

Brent looked at the floor tiles, making no response.

James went right over to stand close at his side. "Come, son! Tell me at least that much. All the boys???"

Brent nodded and more tears came to his eyes.

"Look Brent ... I ... ah ... I'll come with you to talk to your mom. You wait outside the front door of the church. I'll be right with you."

Once Brent had left, James went to Hawthorne's office to report an abuser in their church, only to discover it was the priest himself.

For how many years had he steered his best students toward Hawthorne's office. Told them ... gone so far as to guarantee their safety. All the while he was enjoying ... indulging his .... James was as good as an accomplice and he knew he couldn't live with the guilt.

James fidgeted with the trigger of his shotgun and thought about how he'd do it as he looked about the washroom. "Is this it, then?"

Hamilton: St. Giles' Church
Sunday, Feb. 27, 1916, 10:55 a.m.

The Reverend Hawthorne was enjoying this part of the service, indulging in a bit of theatrics, when he turned to the prayers for the faithful. Tears were in his eyes, as he spoke of the sacrifice and courage. As the war progressed, the list of newly enlisted young men had grown exponentially, so that now he needed at least three minutes to get through the names. He was proud of the sacrifices his parish was making. Reading out the names, he held the Union Jack high and as he finished, he waved it slowly back and forth. A lovely flourish. To give greater glory to the service of young men, he had highlighted the names of fresh enlistments in the weekly bulletin. This special mention was a way to drive home the message of their importance.

Later on, in the prayers of petition and thanksgiving, he would list the names of those who had made the supreme sacrifice, or who had been wounded in the service of their God and King. Alas, that list was growing longer, too. And, at that point, he would again take the flag and lower it slowly to the floor.

His bishop would be pleased with his efforts on behalf of the Empire. Principal Cruikshank, had made a special visit to St. Gile's to offer his personal congratulations, and whispered about the deanship of the cathedral. "Perhaps Hawthorne was interested? If these numbers continue to climb, well, who knows how far you will go. The bishop is always turning to me for suggestions of up and coming church leaders." No promises, but, … More recruits from his parish and the Hamilton area in general, and he had more chances at advancement. Who knows, maybe even a mitre was in his destiny?

Hawthorne was a wily cleric, and, when it came to finding ways to advance his cause, he was an expert. No one seemed to mind these additions to his Sunday morning office. Besides the weekly reading of the two lists, Hawthorne had designated the last Sunday of the month as "Farewell and Godspeed" Sunday in which all the new men in uniform were presented to the congregation, then commissioned to take their part in the great battle in France.

This morning was a special "Farewell" ceremony because young Davis was one of the men being honoured. Hawthorne was loath to see him go. There had been so much promise in their most recent "confession." The boy was so innocent that he was sure to break down soon and become a "devotee" of the parish priest. Too late now.

Hawthorne had enjoyed the ministrations of a dozen or so such "devotees" over the past few years. He liked to think of them as his own secret society. They had all joined his club willingly, some with pleasure, others with grudging curiosity. None went away abused or hurt. It was all innocent stuff really, a little mutual masturbation, some pleasant evenings of fondling and fun.

Always discrete, Hawthorne never allowed his evening "devotionals" to side-track his ministry. Only the retreat "vigils" were risky. Otherwise, they were unspoken dalliances, a sop to his sensuality. Careful to pick lone rangers, boys with few friends or outside contacts, he didn't want gangs showing up at his door. Likewise, he chose young men whose parents were poor, often on the fringe of the church, so that, if anything ever did come to light (and it never did), his word would be believed above these marginal backsliders. Davis had been an exception to this last rule. "A bit of a chance, since his father is so devout," he mumbled to his conscience, "but what's life without a little risk?"

And to give the Devil his due, Hawthorne was very generous to his "devotees," lavishing on them not just his wisdom, but also some measure of his wealth. To be truthful, his wife's wealth, but that was of little consequence, now that they had been married for twenty-three years. "What's yours is mine and what's mine is my own," he often chuckled. There had been pen and paper sets, inscribed Bibles, a few tailor-made jackets. Nothing too much. Don't want to call attention to myself. But enough to keep their little mouths shut.

As one devotee grew tired of the games, another was groomed. Gordon had been the last in a long succession of devotees, and he was certainly the most handsome and intellectually challenging.

All these images of delight passed through Hawthorne's head, as he droned down the list of valiant names, men off to seek glory. He pondered his own fate. With Davis going to war, there would be little opportunity for private confessions. That would be a great loss. Compared to the road sweepers and factory hands Hawthorne had schooled in his private classes, Davis was an Adonis, a prize, dare one say "a pearl, of great price." All things must end. Davis never really got to begin. Who knows, he might never have agreed to anything, he was still too fresh to predict.

"Now with Davis leaving," the priest mused, "I'll have to enjoy a little celibacy. It wouldn't hurt. If this one new recruit adds to the mounting rewards I am reaping with the church hierarchy, then so be it." Hawthorne was calculating, if nothing else. But even then, he was eyeing the congregation picking out a few new young faces.

"... the name of the Father, the Son and the Holy Spirit. Amen."

As Hawthorne looked out into the assembled throng, he smiled broadly. The Sunday crowds were growing as the war continued. "Keep the battles coming! It fills the pews." He chose his highest of clerical voices. "Into God's hands we commit these our brothers, for safekeeping. May the Almighty shine down upon them." He could see a number of the parents of the names he had listed, they smiled or nodded their approval. "Play to the audience," is what he had told young Davis, but Hawthorne suspected his words were wasted. Doesn't seem capable of any guile.

Nevertheless, Hawthorne took his own advice to heart when it came to war mongering. He was first to posture himself as the perfect patriot. Had he not joined a reserve unit as chaplain the moment war was declared? He did his stint in boot camp and specialty training exercises, right there with the men. He was viewed by many as the very paradigm of dedication and imperial loyalty!

Now, he would wish his young recruits a fond farewell. He came in front of the table and spoke his prayer with eyes open and head held high. "Friends we are here today, not just to praise God, but to dedicate to his purposes this month's group of young men who have chosen to serve their Saviour in the fields of France. Allow me to introduce to you a very hearty band of Christians, marching as to war." Hawthorne motioned to the string of uniforms in the front pew. They came forward and faced the congregation.

"Here is Jacob Ashfield, son of our deacon's warden." Jacob took a step forward and allowed the priest to rest a warm hand on his shoulder. Hawthorne passed him a personally signed copy of the New Testament. "Take this Bible into battle," Hawthorne said with great unction, "Keep it close to your heart and know that your church and your God stand with you." Jacob received the book with reverence and stepped back.

"Sam Edgar, a long-time member of the junior choir. Sam when did you grow to be so tall?" The congregation laughed, as Sam stepped up to the priest. Again the hand was on his shoulder. The church community saw such physical gestures as evidence of the priest's compassion. He was not a stuck-up cleric, but down-to-earth. Hawthorne smiled. "Sam, I'm proud of you, really I am." Sam nodded as he received his Bible. There was a shadow that no one but the most astute could have seen in Sam's eyes. He had been one of Hawthorne "devotees"— Gordon's predecessor. Still confused about what it all meant, the army was one way to get out of this man's clutches. "Thank you, sir," he whispered.

"Gordon Davis."

Hawthorne turned to see his young target come forward. "Ladies and gentlemen, it grieves me to say farewell to Gordon, for he has been training with me toward the priesthood. We wish you Godspeed, Gordon, and may you return to accept the invitation you have received to enter Wycliffe College." Here the priest broke from all decorum and began to clap—slowly the congregation joined in. A solider and a priest—it could hardly get any better.

The sending forth of St. Giles' men took ten minutes and the priest revelled in the ceremony. Gordon was buried in conflicting emotions. He felt the crosscurrents of shame, pride, anger and doubt, as he watched Hawthorne go through the motions of affection and dedication.

When the service was over, Gordon hurried from the sanctuary, deposited the New Testament in his mother's hands, with a lame excuse that he couldn't find room in his kit. The family walked as one from the church and headed home for a special dinner.

It would be Gordon's last dinner on Barton Street in Hamilton, though no one was aware of it. His mother patted a seat beside her, when they gathered at the table. "Sit here, Gordie. One last time." Gordon obeyed. "Wasn't that a lovely send off from the priest today? I was so proud of you. He seems to have taken a special interest in your advancement. I'm sure when you get back, he'll help you out."

Gordon smiled. He could think of no reply. The air was thick with feelings and sorrow. Down the line of his sisters, he could feel the anxiety. Would he really return? He could think of no meaningful answer, but, not wanting the silence to linger on, he blurted out: "Let's give thanks."

James took up the cue. "Sure, I almost forgot. Let us pray ..."

Neuville-Saint-Vaast, France
Monday, April 30, 1917, 3:00 p.m.

It had been almost two years since Ryan had first met Cruikshank. After they joined in a secret conspiracy, in Toronto, and now again on this current tour of the front lines, Ryan was getting used to the old codger's tricks. He knew exactly what the old man was doing—building up his image as a fighter, the priest for the people. He never missed a chance to shake hands with the men in the trenches or offer a prayer for their survival. You had to hand it to this cleric. He was not foppish or foolish. Not like the British chaplains. Cruikshank spoke the men's language and gave as good as he got.

"Let's pray, men," the principal said. "There's no time like the present to get your sorry souls ready to meet your Maker, if he'd have any of you." General laughter greeted his frank talk. "Oh God of the Lewis gun and Mills bomb, put strength in our arms and resolution in our hearts as we stand firm for our faith this and every day. Keep us facing forward to meet the enemy with courage assured that your hand guides us. If we should fall, take us up, dear God, take us up and bring us safe at last into the loving arms of paradise. Give comfort to those we left behind in Canada and if it is your will, see us safely back to our 'true north strong and free.' For it is for freedom and truth that we fight. In your name we ask it. Amen."

There was a scattering of "Amens" through the cluster of soldiers. Cruikshank smiled at the raised faces. "That was my clerical voice, but in my patriotic one, I say, 'Give 'em bloody hell.'" General backslapping and applause met this candid show of belligerence. They liked the old man very much. As they dispersed, he could hear them muttering how they'd carry the 'bloody hell' to Fritz next chance they got.

Ryan steered Cruikshank down a communication trench. "Very impressive, Doctor."

"I aim to please," Cruikshank laughed. "I find it so strange that in sermons I say exactly the same thing and no one cares. Put a 'let us pray' before it, and the whole world stops to listen."

They were wending their way past several dugouts, the purposes of which Cruikshank could only imagine. Foul smells arose from every corner and try as he might to cover his nose with a handkerchief, the potent stench got through.

Ryan noticed his friend's struggle with amusement. "You won't block it out, you know. It seeps into everything. Sometimes I think the gas masks make it worse." Laughing, he began to nudge his way into the lead. "Let me walk ahead. The next patch of trenches is badly damaged. It helps to have a feel where the solid ground lies."

Cruikshank demurred. "A sound piece of advice I've always tried to follow." He bowed in mock subservience, "Lead on, O King Eternal."

They passed a number of rough timber chambers, where a few sparse lights were shining, a dressing station out of which came the most desperate smells yet and then into the Major's "headquarters." Thirty rough steps down, a few twists behind large tree trunks holding up the ceiling and they were at his dugout level.

"It ain't much, but it's home." Cruikshank looked around. It was indeed a dismal abode. Water dripped from the ceiling of split logs. Sandbags covered with mildew formed walls, and, at their base, a yellow, putrid liquid oozed onto the floor. Light came from a single candle hanging in a tin can punched with holes. A table with three good legs and one which looked like a broken rifle butt, sat in the middle of the room. In one corner was a bucket for nightly duties, in another was a heap of discarded bully beef tins. Sleeping was crude. Two large boards were propped on a line of sandbags. Cruikshank could hear the skittering of rodents in the shadows. It was hard to remain calm, but his iron will quelled the retching sensation in his stomach.

Ryan was enjoying his guest's discomfort. "You're the one who asked to see it like it is. Welcome to hell, Dr. Cruikshank."

Cruikshank could only acknowledge Ryan's humour with a curt nod. He looked about for someplace to sit and finally lowered himself down onto the "cot."

Ryan wasn't finished. "Of course, this is your five-star accommodation. Thirty feet down—able to withstand everything but a direct hit. Indoor plumbing and secure floor." He stamped once to illustrate its strength and sent mud squirting up between the floorboards and a few splotches splattered on the cleric's crisply pressed trench coat. "Excuse me, sir," Ryan wiped the spots off Cruikshank's uniform with a dirty handkerchief. "I'll have the valet send it out for cleaning."

"Enough," Cruikshank was not about to allow this mockery to continue. "You've made your point. I wasn't prepared for it to be this bad. It's a wonder any human being can stay sane in this mess. Why don't you clean it up?"

Ryan flared. "Because the bloody Germans have such a nasty habit of blowing it to bits just as we finish sweeping the floor and washing the walls." He pulled down the box he used as a seat. Placing it by the table he continued, "This is war, Father. The place where you send all those willing feet who scamper to your office door in nice clean, respectable Toronto. They end up here, trying to keep warm, hoping they won't drown in the slime or get buried in a wall of mud. Half of them get trench foot. Last week one stupid fellow lost all his toes because of it. Not a pretty sight." He waved a hand at his surroundings. "Welcome to hell on earth."

"Stop!" Cruikshank glared. "I get the point. Now can we get down to business? I have a train to catch in three hours and don't want to stay out here any longer than is absolutely necessary."

"Right." Ryan had enjoyed rubbing the priest's nose in his own naiveté, but, on command, he was all business. Now that I have seen my share of battles—Vimy being the best example of Canadian valour, I'm in good shape to push for more enlistments. I hear they've slowed of late."

"Bloody pacifists and Frenchies in Quebec. They've stirred up a hornet's nest of animosity against the war." Cruikshank looked down at his hands. "I thought we could contain it, but the feeling is spreading across the country. I hear slurs against the King, and many folk wonder when or if we can ever hope for victory. It looks like conscription is our only hope."

Ryan smiled. "There's goes your knighthood, my friend."

"Not so fast." Cruikshank had not yet played his trump card. "The government still needs the church to sanction its efforts, conscription or not. Men won't go gladly if they don't feel the support of their trusted institutions."

"True."

"Let's do a quick summary of my side of our bargain." Cruikshank pulled out a small notebook. "The Anglican Church of Canada has supplied the army with 67,549 recruits—at least by my unofficial tally."

"Unofficial?" Ryan chuckled. "Sounds damn accurate to me."

"I keep in constant touch with all my parish priests, past students from the college who owe me favours. They're doing the spade work in their own area. I'd say we've kept up pretty well in terms of recruiting, especially when you compare us to other churches or service clubs."

Ryan knew too well how the Anglicans were doing. It was a well-known fact in recruiting circles that this one colonial church, among all those in the Empire, was singular in its zeal for the war effort. "And I kept my side of the bargain by trumpeting your success to my superiors." He pointed to the pips on the lapel of Cruikshank's khaki jacket. "You didn't get that colonel's rank for praying and preaching. And I arranged for you to come here. I'd say we're been about even in keeping up our promises to each other."

Cruikshank nodded. "Agreed. Now for the final stroke. As I mentioned in our past meetings, if we are to get the church's approval for a holy war, we'll need a strong primate."

"You said in your last letter that you'd found one?"

Cruikshank smiled. "I have. He's well-bred, has gone to all the right schools, knows the old boys' network like the back of his hand and has been privy to a number of very important scandals—not implicated, but close enough to be pressured according to my wishes." An evil chuckle escaped the principal's lips. "Just enough to push him in the right direction."

"What's his name?"

"Cheesborough."

"Do I know him?"

Cruikshank thought for a moment. "No, I don't think ... wait a minute. Yes. He was at the Governor General's ball two years ago when you were present. Tall fellow, clean-shaven, long nose and small spectacles."

Ryan tried to recall the night. "Can't say as I recall. No matter. He'll do our bidding you say?"

The cleric smiled. "Do you know how many hours I've spent manoeuvring this buffoon into place? He may be dumb about the finer points of Christian theology, but he's no fool when it comes to politics. He knows what I've done for him, and he'll do what we ask when the time comes."

"And when will that be?" Ryan took out a cigarette from his jacket pocket. "Want one?"

Cruikshank declined. "Soon."

"'Soon' may not be soon enough for Prime Minster Borden and the others. There's an election coming up and they need strong support for their policies, especially conscription, if they expect this war to end well. I think we'll lose without more and better-trained reinforcements. The quicker we can get the church to publish its unqualified support, the better."

Cruikshank agreed. "Here's my plan."

Mockingly Ryan asked, "You have a plan? Why didn't I think of that?"

"Will you stop that and listen?" Cruikshank sat up straight and laid out his idea. "We're holding a special convocation of all Canadian bishops—first few weeks of next December. It will be in Montreal, and it will be a decisive meeting, for it will be the first our new primate will attend."

"He'll be in place?"

"He'll be elected when we gather in Montreal, but this synod will be his first real public appearance. Our man will be in power. I've gone over this with you before." Cruikshank shook his head in dismay. "So when he calls this gathering together, it will be the perfect time to push for a holy war declaration. Just prior to the election, hand-in-glove with Borden's plans. We'll strike a decisive blow."

"But will the good bishops agree? One man you can control, but an entire room full of clerics?" Ryan was dubious.

"Yes, well, you're right. They're an independent lot, but I have a secret weapon."

"What's that?" Ryan loved secrets and weapons.

"You."

"Me?" The major looked blank. "What have I got to offer?"

It was Cruikshank's turn to be pleased with the dismay of his comrade. "You're perfect. British-born, strong military background, deeply religious …."

"I haven't set foot in a church in twenty years."

Cruikshank ignored his protest. "Like I say, deeply religious. A war hero. You will be able to persuade those old farts that this war needs their full support."

"How will I do that?"

"Regale them with stories of Vimy Ridge. Help them to feel the courage, the grit of our fighting men. Tell them we've received more V.C.s than any other force our size. I'll supply you with a few pithy theological references. They'll eat you up."

Ryan grimaced, "That's what I'm afraid of."

"You look the part so well. Young, dashing." Cruikshank actually rose in his place, seeing himself announcing this young hero to the tired and overweight bishops. "My lords, here is the paragon of virtue and courage, a commander of Canadians, pleading for your most necessary support."

Ryan, whose imagination was just as active as Cruikshank's when it came to scenes of glory in which he was featured, agreed that it would be grand. "So all I have to do is get myself back to Canada for December."

"Yes, the first two weeks."

Ryan ran his hands through his wavy hair. "It can be arranged. I heard rumours that we might be back in Flanders again before the winter sets in. There's to be a big push in the Ypres salient or at least so I'm told. But I should be out of that mess by the first of November and able to ask for leave to do some home-front recruiting." He smiled when he imagined his superiors receiving his request. "They never balk at me going back for more men. We're losing them so fast here. If we don't keep up a strong program, there won't be anyone on either side to fight each other. And wouldn't that be a pity?"

Cruikshank didn't mind Ryan's cynicism when it was directed at politicians or even the church, but he found it hard to listen when his doubts about the necessity of the war were stirred up. Trying to take his mind off that dark prospect, he looked across the room at the stack of empty tins. "Have you any food? I'm famished."

Ryan winked. "Room service is on the way."

"Room service?"

Ryan laughed. "My batman is bringing us sherry and sandwiches— compliments of the divisional CO. It seems you're quite an important man now that you have a real rank in this backwoods army."

Cruikshank just grinned. He noticed that his left hand had been scratching his trouser leg for some time. "What is the matter with this material? It scratches like the dickens," he muttered more to himself than Ryan.

Ryan laughed, "You've been invaded, Reverend. The little blighters have found your Anglican flesh to their liking."

"Blighters?"

The major explained. "Lice. They're everywhere in these trenches. Can't keep them off you, not with a dozen baths a day."

"What do I do about them?"

"Learn to live and let live and then find a delousing station when you head for England. Do some chatting in the mean time!"

"What has 'chatting' to do with bugs? I don't want to talk to the little beasts. I want to kill them!"

Ryan smiled. "Chatting is burning out the lice and fleas from uniforms."

Cruikshank continued to scratch vigorously. "If I have only a few minutes left in this infested land, it will be too long."

A conspiratorial silence fell between them. The distant crunch of mortar explosions could be heard. A persistent drip was landing in the pile of opened tins, making a troublesome melody as it fell into the discarded lids. Ryan was puffing gently on his cigarette, contented, knowing that his career was moving upward as it was destined to do. "Next year I'll be a colonel, if I play my cards right," he dreamed. "From there it's a simple step and a hop to a general's seat … If the war lasts long enough, that is!"

Cruikshank looked to fill the silence, cover his hunger with words. "Say, you haven't run into a medical man here, Gordon Davis by name?"

"Gordon Davis." Ryan turned the name over in his mind. "It rings a bell. But why?"

"He's a student of mine. Good-looking chap. I believe he's a stretcher-bearer."

"Davis." Ryan's brow was furrowed. "That's it —bloody hell! I knew there was one more out there." He stood up and searched for a pen in his pant pocket. "Damn-it-all if my memory isn't going." Ryan whipped out his regimental notebook. "Davis … now I have you!"

Cruikshank looked at his friend, puzzled by the sense of urgency that fired his words. "What's the matter? Has he done something wrong?"

"Your precious student is bloody deserter. At Vimy no less! Wouldn't follow up the attack, just lay on the ground pretending to be sick." Ryan scribbled his notes. "I'll fix his wagon, right smartly."

Cruikshank, surprised, responded, "Dear me, was it that serious?"

Ryan's lips went tight. "Serious enough to warrant a court martial. I shot one coward in battle and had another deserter shot by firing squad later. But Davis, I missed him—forgot 'til now. Can't have weak livers running from battle, can we?"

Cruikshank was almost sorry he'd brought up Gordon's name, but he agreed in a weak voice, "I suppose not."

"Cheer up, old chap. Not all our children are heroes. Some just can't cut it. I'll find your Gordon Davis for you. It may take a few weeks, but I'll get him and then send him back home … in a box."

Cruikshank winced, "Oh dear, that harsh are we?"

"It's a bloody war, but someone has to fight it." Ryan turned as he heard the footsteps of his batman bringing lunch. "Ah, it looks like dinner is served."

Montreal,
April 17, 1917

Dearest Gordon,

It has been nine weeks now since you wrote last.
Well, that was when I got your last letter. No doubt,
you've written more, but nothing has arrived. I am
lost without your news. Each morning I rise and
pray to God for your safety. "Please don't let him
be hurt. Keep him safe." A little mantra. Whenever
I have time during the day watching the children in
the park or kneading bread dough in the kitchen, I
repeat it. It's more for my sake, than for God's.

I haven't grown suddenly evangelical—all this
praying. There is just nowhere else to turn. I am
so frightened for you. Actually, I did find one
soulmate, and in the strangest of places. Her name
is Thelma Lint and she is in the same line of work
as Mary of Magdalene. Can you imagine? It's
hard to credit, but Father knows her and mentioned
in passing that she listens well. So without his
knowledge or permission I looked her up and it
turns out she's a very cultured woman, able to
discuss everything from Renoir to Rauschenbusch,
and with both wit and wisdom. She's been a great
help. Whenever I am distressed, feeling like you
are too far away, I make my way to Thelma Lint's
Gentlemen's Parlour.

She's always home and always ready to listen.

I imagine she would help you too if you ever can't
find me.

How are you? The papers here are still trying to make the war sound glorious and victorious. But if it is going so well, why is it going on so long and why do we seem to continue to battle over patches of ground that just the other week we took "decisively from the wretched foe."

The editorials are calling Vimy Ridge our day of independence. When we broke free from the British yoke. I don't know how that is, but strangely I do sense a greater pride in the country. We're no longer a wart on the backside of the British Empire after all! We can win a battle that the motherland could not! The King can no longer claim we are simply at his beck and call. We won the ridge that they themselves failed to capture. Don't you find it curious that we fight a German enemy to free ourselves from an overbearing parent and that we do all this on French soil? The irony of history astounds me.

And yet since that battle, it seems like all the news is downhill from Vimy.

Home life is not changing fast enough for me. My Lord the Bishop is sufferable enough, but I strain against the implications of his friends that I am his maidservant; that the only thing distinguishing a woman from a table leg is our ability to cook and clean. There's talk of giving women the vote, but that won't change much really. Casting a ballot once every four years will do little to change the misconceptions men cultivate to justify the suppression of their women while making for their own, unmerited advancement.

There. I've said it. I've given you my best argument
for the freedom of women. Now fire right back. Let
me hear your argument against my ideas. Don't
spare me at all.

Oh how I long for one of our jarring debates, the
kind that made you purple with rage. I love you
when you're angry. You turn so strong and handsome. But I love you when you're weak and beaten
too. Your gentle voice and tender touch—oh where
are they when I need them?—the soft tones of your
heart played out through your fingertips.

Do you recall the afternoon when we lay together
on the ridge and then found ourselves back in my
room? I have never felt such a delicate touch. It was
both erotic and comforting at the same time.

I would give anything to walk over to Sisson Ridge
Park now and find you waiting for me as you did
that night before you left for the front. It will live
in my memory always as the high point of our
romance. A touchstone for many more encounters
to come. Please keep it sacred in your heart and
know that if we are ever separated again, you'll
find me at our bench waiting. That's where I'll
be found.

Enough mushy talk. When shall I see you?

Here's a wild idea. Can I travel to France to meet
you? Imagine. I could be waiting in the feather
bed of one of those inns we women hear so much
about. A hot bath, a bottle of wine—can we swing
it? Father says it's out of the question and it's his
cussedness that makes me try all the harder to
figure out how I could achieve it.

I'll write with more details if any fall my way.

All my love,
Jo

PS. I'm not afraid. I know you'll come back to me.

Saint John: Centenary-Queen Square United Church
Tuesday, Nov. 17, 1992, 11:28 a.m.

> "... look down upon us, we who are in mourning for
> the loss of a dear friend and loyal companion, Gordon
> Davis ... It is at times of death that we feel most vul-
> nerable and small."

Leaving the script, I enter into the petition portion of the long
prayer with a frankness that I imagine Captain Jims would enjoy. Father
Inkling would be horrified—on the surface, at least.

"Let's be open, God. We see no purpose in dying. Why did you
ordain that all things must perish?"

At this point I give the words a break—Levan's rule #13: "Silence is
the best punctuation to wisdom." After a long pause, I get back to work.

> "Nevertheless, God of our fathers and mothers, we
> turn to you in our grief and ask for your healing pres-
> ence in our lives. For the many who are living separate
> from loved ones—relationships broken through dis-
> tance or death, we ask your comfort and compassion.
> Lord in your mercy."

There is a weak and confused reply. "Hear our prayer."

This takes practice. We can't expect a loud chorus from a dozen
voices in a sanctuary which seats 1100. Another few petitions and we'll
have it down.

> "Creator God, you are our beginning and ending.
> From you we came, to you we go. We ask for your
> guiding hand for those on the journey ..."

Montreal
April 21, 1917

Gordon,

Oh God, how the journey of a day changes your
life forever.

Your letter about Terry arrived today, hours after
the official telegram. And you were right. The army
message told us nothing. Father was crushed. I've
never seen him collapse—did he faint, or his heart
stop? He slumped into the chair by the parlour
door, grasping the yellow sheet that announced
Terry's death. I thought he was dead. No tears, no
great cry of dereliction. Just silence, the kind that
spells the end. You can imagine my fright. I patted
his hand, clutched him to me and rocked for ages.
No sound. Suddenly he cried out—screamed,
really. And at first that felt better. We were both
weeping, but with each sob, I could sense that he
was growing weaker. I thought I was losing him.
He went pale. He began with a whisper, "What
happened to my son?" But then he got louder,
"What happened to my son?" In the end he was
shouting, "WHAT HAPPENED TO MY SON?" And I
thought his heart would break and give out. When
his fury was spent, I could feel him drifting, his eyes
went blank and his hands grew cold.

A horrible hour—one I do not wish to
endure again.

Then as we read your note, it was like food for
a starving man: it brought him back. Here was
something, a scene, an explanation to the tragedy.
A word. Call me crazy, but I believe Father

survived because of your compassion—I mean this with all my heart. It was your understanding and caring that pulled him back from the brink. You may have saved many men at the front. I suspect you have, though you never boast. Well, know this Gordon Davis: you also saved an old, crusty Anglican bishop back here in Montreal—as surely as if you had dragged him from the mud and mire of no man's land. I owe you so much.

I will run to post this now. I want to thank you right away. After a few more hours of mourning, Father suddenly ran out.

Oh I miss you—these one-sided conversations are so unsatisfying. But it's all I have. I feel closer to you when I get down my writing paper and pen. So in my sadness I reach out to you. Do you understand?

Keep us in your prayers. We will survive this, but not easily and not as before. Terry was our anchor in a strange way—in his crazy music and cynical voice we found such a love of life. Gone now.

I love you all the more. You are my only brother now as well as my lover. Does that sound weird—so be it. Terry was my flesh and blood. I stand alone, but for you.

Your final words will remain with me always: "For now I am overwhelmed with gratitude for his sacrifice and sorrow for his passing." We were all overwhelmed by his courage.

Keep well,
Jo

PS. As you pray for me, so I pray for you.

Saint John: Centenary-Queen Square United Church
Tuesday, Nov. 17, 1992, 11:29 a.m.

> "Lord in your mercy, Hear our prayer.
>
> "Now if there are any who wish to express their grief,
> please do so now …."

The first is always the most difficult. No one wants to go first. Once one person speaks, the floodgates open and everyone discovers a burden they yearn to lay down.

Right on cue, Brian, my student, steps up. I suppose that is what I admire about him most—his courage to speak his heart at times, when it would be so easy to stay silent. "God of my waking hours," he coughs. This is not easy. "God of my sleeping nights, I lift up to you my family, our broken bonds, the deep silences that still exist between my brother and father. And …." He stops. I know he's thinking about his own breaking marriage. His spouse refused to come to this Maritime city for the eight-month internship. "And comfort the weary and confused. Lord in your mercy."

"Hear our prayer."

Mary is next—straightforward and no nonsense. "God be with my brother." There's an awkward silence. I add for her, "Lord in your mercy."

"Hear our prayer."

Then Joan Simmons asks for help with the staff of the home. My loyal honour guard pray lovingly for their pastor. They have no idea how much I appreciate their simple acts of caring.

I am about to let it go, bring a conclusion to our when a small voice pipes up. "Gordon's life reached so much further than he ever knew. God be with all his children. Lord in your mercy."

"Hear our prayer."

CHAPTER EIGHT
The Lord's Prayer

I have no Lord. Away with your man-ipulating words. If there is God
in the universe, She is my *Mother* of deep desire and my *Crone* of
compassion ... not my male overlord. Certainly not my father!

... Let's get rid of the "Lord" in the Lord's Prayer.

I make no apology. Go ahead and howl, you denizens of church courts.
Get the "Lord" out or there is no place in your circle for women.

N. M. Clung, *Never Apologize! Howling down the Sanctified Spirits*

Montreal,
Monday July 10, 1916

Dearest Gordon:

Can you forgive me? I started to draw up your
birthday card and then realized it would never
arrive in time. When you receive this card, July will
be a memory. Please know that I was thinking of
you on your day.

Montreal was all a bustle with the preparation
for our Dominion Day parade. Father enlisted me
to organize the Anglican "army." To make a real
show, I got every parish to send a troop of kids and
their leaders. Imagine finding the ribbons for 500

kids, looking after snacks ... Listen to me ... what I
go through is nothing compared to you. Just put my
whining down to impatience. I want you home. I
want to kiss you and hold you.

Now sit down somewhere before you read
any more of this letter. I have a serious matter
to discuss.

Are you seated?

Good ... here's my proposition. Will you
marry me?

I know it's convention to wait for the man to do
the asking and, if I recall, you did just that when
we were together in March. I turned you aside
... perhaps too brusquely. Was I cruel? Did you
doubt me? Yourself? I am so sorry.

But that is past. I now repent of my former reluc-
tance and take my turn at proposing.

Take a deep breath. Focus on me!

Gordon Davis, I ask in all sincerity and with my
whole heart, "Will you consent to marry a poor
woman who loves you more than she can bear,
who wouldn't live another hour without you if she
could help it?"

Don't answer right away. Think it over ... write
when you can.

I love you with all my heart.

Jo

PS. I swear you'll never recognize me now that I have cut my hair.

Fredericton, New Brunswick: Isaac's Way Restaurant
Monday, April 14, 2014, 11:45 a.m.

I had assumed we'd be in her office. How will I recognize her? Don't important meetings happen with polished desktops and fountain pens? Surely, when estates are transferred there are imposing filing cabinets, hushed voices and well-arranged file folders with "sign here" sticky notes protruding out the open side.

Instead, once I called Patricia, she offered lunch. Without thinking I suggested Isaac's Way, "my unofficial office." At least that's what the owner told me. Jason greeted me with open arms, ushered me to my usual table, asked if I would like the wine list and if I was waiting for Scott, my usual partner.

"No. Scott's off fighting crime in Moncton. No, today it's a stranger. A lawyer-type bureaucrat from the province. You may know her. Patricia Patterson?"

Jason paused, "... tall and blond?"

"I have no idea." I smiled, looked around and realized how comforting it was to be back. "Just bring me the usual red. God, it's good to see you!"

Jason hurried off for the wine, saying he'd watch for a lawyer-type and send her my way.

"I'm married," I called after him.

"That's what they all say."

Montreal, Thelma Lint's Gentlemen's Parlour
Saturday, April 21, 1917, 11:35 a.m.

"That's what they all say!" Standing outside a third floor room, Thelma smiled as she spoke with the new girl. "They all claim to love you ... You'll get used to it." She opened the girl's door and gave her a friendly pat on the shoulder. "Don't take it personally ... now rest."

It was Saturday afternoon. Her Gentlemen's Parlour was quiet. Most men, gentle or not, were busy. Very few were looking for the services of a bedmate. That suited the matron just fine.

Not a tough taskmistress, Thelma wanted to give her girls something more than protection. So each Saturday morning, once their personal chores were complete, she'd line them up—much like drill sergeant—and scowl a bit and lecture them on saving their money ("a penny saved is a penny earned"). Then she'd fuss over the details of their dresses, and, after holding them in suspense for a minute, she'd finally relent. It was her gift—allowing her girls a few hours of freedom on a weekend afternoon. "Get on with it then. Go out and breathe deeply," she would say, pressing a few bills into the hand of each. "Be back by three sharp!"

Off they went, some with curious expectation—maybe they would meet some nice young man. Others would buy a few treats at Ogilvy's Department store. A few, jaded by the tough lessons of the street, took Thelma's gift and saved it with the rest of their stash—against the time when the men stopped coming to their door. It happened to everyone at some point. Thelma was never dismayed by either the frivolous girls or the cynical ones. Each one had their reasons for what they did.

Running a hand along the third floor balcony rail, she was debating whether to supervise the cleaning staff or return to the sensual novel she was reading—the main character was such a handsome, dashing ....

"Thelma!" A harried voice broke into her daydream. "Thelma, please … please." Hurried footsteps on the stairs below. Thelma rushed down to the second floor.

Grace was bending the turn in the flight of stairs to the second floor landing, a duster in one her hand, the other waving in the air, pleading, "Thelma, come quickly, there's a man on our front step. He's dead!"

Thelma had been ready for a pushy patron, someone needing sex "Right Now!" A meddlesome youth wanting to sneak a peek perhaps! A merchant with an overdue bill. But a dead man? Never before.

"Grace don't make a fuss. The last thing I want is a crowd at the front door. Where, exactly, is this dead man?"

"On the porch ma'am, slouched on the bench." Grace was regaining her composure. "I've seen him before I think." There was hesitation in her voice—not wanting to intrude on the matron's private affairs.

Thelma who was already halfway down to the front door, whirled around. "Before?"

"Yes ma'am. He was here not so long ago. The gentleman with the ... ah ..." here Grace whispered, "... with the cross. I believe you asked me to address him as ... 'My Lord.'" Her matron turned visibly ashen and nearly slumped against the banister. "Ma'am? Can I get you ... something ..." She reached out a steadying hand.

Thelma recovered quickly. "No ... nothing." She flashed a faint smile and ran briskly down to the door. Fear, as well as apprehension dogging each step.

Thelma would have conceded that she was fond of Hinks. Douglas had been her most steady "customer" over the last five years and one of a few that she kept after she had grown too old for the game. She might even have admitted that she loved *her* bishop. There had been times when she had wished he had broken his bloody vows to mother church and proposed something more permanent between them. He joked of it often enough. But as Thelma passed through the front door and saw her lover slouched on the wrought iron bench, her heart cried out in terror. A revelation! Who could have known, least of all Thelma, that this silly prelate meant more to her than life itself? Her hand jumped to her heart, stilling her nerves. "He can't leave me," she whispered.

Falling to her knees beside him, her fingers traced the outline of his face. "Douglas," she cried, "Douglas, don't leave me!" Nothing. He was gone. Tears welled up in her eyes and she laid her head on his chest, arms around his neck—checking his heart. Frantic. "Don't leave me." Did she hear a heartbeat? "Douglas, you silly man, don't you do this to me ... to us!" She looked up on the last word and searched his countenance for any signs of life. "Please ... please ... don't leave me." It was almost a whimper.

As if returning from a trance, the blank eyes regained their focus, and Hinks looked into her face. "Not likely, my girl." He began to laugh.

Then slowly his laughter turned to cries until he was weeping uncontrollably, shoulders shaking.

Thelma held on and moved with him, but her mind was racing. "What is it?"

No response.

"You can tell me. That's why you came." Here she held his face in her two hands and forced him to look into her eyes. "That's why you came. To tell me! What has happened? Is it Johanna?"

Hinks made no response, but his eyes said, "No." His sobs subsided and he wiped his eyes with his sleeve.

And then Thelma guessed. "Oh, my God, not Terry!"

Hinks broke down again. One hand covered the tears that flowed freely now, while the second held up a crumpled telegram.

"Oh, Douglas … No!" Reading the terse lines, Thelma felt as if she was losing a piece of herself. Terry! They'd never met. But in her lover's loss, she could feel her own. How was that? Terry was just a few typed syllables on this piece of paper, and yet, if someone had cut off her left hand, it would have been less agony. Tears were streaming down her cheeks, falling over her open lips. No words came out of her half-opened mouth.

Hinks left off masking his weeping and looked at her. Seeing Thelma's pain, he knew then he had been such a fool for many years. Here was his soulmate, his solace—not any bloody church prayer or silly sacred pronouncement. Let the Lord be damned. Here is my sacrament and my salvation. These things he saw in a flash, but he only said, "Can I stay?"

Thelma got to her feet and nodded. Taking his hands. "That's why you came. You're always welcome here." She was about to add that this was his "home" after all, but she could see in his eyes that he knew that already. "Besides," she thought, "When he was desperate, I was his first thought." While it wasn't official—not a public declaration, she could think of no greater testimony to their marriage than their shared grief. Not legal, but more than enough.

Silently, she offered her own prayer "Mother of God, we long for love all our lives, and, when we get it, why does it hurt so much? You do bless us in bizarre ways. Our Father indeed!"

Saint John: Centenary-Queen Square United Church
Tuesday, Nov. 17, 1992, 11:22 a.m.

Did I choke on my words? I must have. There was a silence where the Lord's Prayer should have been, a scratch in my throat where an invitation to join me in the "Our Father" belonged.

What possible meaning could the stranger have—naming Gordon's children in a prayer of petition? What children? Where are they? He had none. Maybe she meant all of us—survivors of the war.

The congregation didn't pick up on her prayer. But, after all, this is a funeral, not a court of law. No affidavits or cross-examinations allowed. So he had children. So what? Don't we all?

My gaze slides to the balcony where the stranger sits, head bowed. Willing her to look up, she shifts in her seat and casts a glance in my direction. Did she read my mind? There's the wisp of a smile on her lips. She knows what she's done and is obviously pleased. If she can discern my thoughts from afar, I can do the same. She's here with a message to deliver. That much is evident. The little bombshell in her prayer was just for openers. There's more to tell, some dark secrets perhaps and ... yes ... something filled with light too.

Why not just walk down the side aisle to the stranger? Right now! Is she expecting that? Willing me to break my priestly stride? How delicious it would be to flaunt convention and get her story right away. I push away temptation. People are waiting; a few coughs punctuate the air.

"Let us join all our prayers into one, as we pray to our Mother, our strong protector on earth, and to Our Father who art in heaven ..."

Montreal,
Friday August 27, 1916

Dear Gordon:

I haven't heard from you yet ... did you get my
last message. I know it fashionable to keep your
partner waiting ... not to rush into things. But it's
been over a month and no response.

How miserable we are when there is no news!
Everyone thinks the worst of course. Our daily trek
to read the casualty lists doesn't help much. Last
week, I walked with Jennifer Fergus. You don't
know her, but she's a school friend. She lost her
husband! I sat with her for hours, trying to make
sense of her loss. She has three small kids. No
family. I wonder what will become of her. Father
arranged for a farm family in Alberta to care for
her and her children ... at least that will give them
food and shelter. They leave today.

When things like that happen I want to scream.
This war is an unbelievable nightmare.

And then I remember. "You're in it, living it. And I
go cold with fear ... taking everything in the course
of a day ...the way the door knocker sounds,
the toll of bell ... as mysterious omens that you
are gone.

But my spirit and yours are tied. I would know if
you were hurt or killed. So far no strange stirrings
in that regard.

So you are alive ... I'm sure ... and with all my will
and strength I will continue to storm the gates of
heaven with pleas for your safekeeping.

Must go now, we're seeing Jennifer to the train.

My prayers are always with you.

Jo

PS. Each night when I recite the Lord's prayer with
Father I can't get the image out of mind that I am
talking to you ... the "our father" of our children
... I just hope that you "aren't in heaven."

Montreal: Thelma Lint's Gentlemen's Parlour
Saturday, December 8, 1917, 11:45 P.M.

Cruikshank took the steps two-at-a-time and lifted the door knocker.
This was going to be a delightful evening ... made all the more enjoyable
by the fact that he was close to victory.

Hanging up from Ryan, Cruickshank had been halfway up the
mountain to Thelma's Parlour when he realized he hadn't confirmed
the importance of the telegram with Ryan himself. Hadn't even mentioned it. It took him a further two hours to track down the Lieutenant
Colonel, caught him just before he boarded the train for Montreal. They
re-considered their strategy. The importance of Terrance Hinks was
assessed. They both agreed it could be the deciding factor if used properly. Cruikshank agreed to relay a message to Hawthorne, who would
drop the bombshell of Terrance's cowardice.

Hanging up again, Cruikshank took a few minutes to find
Hawthorne and relay the new plans. He was now satisfied. Nothing
could go wrong. All his players were in place. They'd been given their
cues. Hinks and Davis would be a one-two punch, neither knowing
what hit them.

Waiting for the door to open, Cruikshank began to whistle. This was
it. He smiled to himself. He was on the road to glory. He stuffed his
scarf into his pocket, took off his gloves and got ready for a night of
pleasure. The door opened slightly. Grace bid him enter.

As he walked into the vestibule, he caught sight of another patron
ascending the stairs. It was Hinks, of all people!

In a flash Cruikshank saw a golden opportunity. He would not confront the bishop in a house of ill-repute. No, that would be too vulgar

and useless since there was no audience. "Right," the principal thought, "better to wait until tomorrow, when he's mid-sermon ...."

Cruikshank, not wanting to be compromised himself, put on a penitent air and said to the maid "Excuse me miss ... I ... ah ... I was following a bishop, Bishop Hinks .... I found this scarf." He produced his own scarf from his pocket and offered it to Grace. I thought it might belong to him and well ... I couldn't catch him on account of the weather so I followed him here and ... I assume this is his club. I'm a stranger in Montreal ..."

Taking the scarf, Grace interrupted, "Thank you sir, I will make sure the bishop gets it." She began to close the door.

Cruikshank made to go, then turned as if a thought had just occurred to him. "Bless me, I didn't say thank you ... what's you name, Miss?"

"Grace" she replied and shut and bolted the door firmly.

"Well, thank you, Grace," he said to the locked door. "Grace, indeed," grinned Cruikshank as he walked off toward another house that could service his needs. "Hinks, you're a dead man."

Passchendaele, France
Tuesday, October 9, 1917, 4:45 a.m.

"How about a prayer, Padre ... for some men about to be dead?"

Gordon turned to look at the speaker. He was the second man over, a new recruit—fresh from Bay Street no doubt. There were a few chuckles down the line, as men soured by months of trenches and tedium laughed about asking for God's blessings.

The padre, Josh Ferguson, took a breath. Gazing at the closest faces he wondered what he could say that would possibly make any difference.

Pre-dawn chills kept everyone on edge.

The rain had halted for a brief spell and Josh could hear heavy breathing—tension eating into every soul. The winter was pressing fast and everyone could smell the stench of previous battles rising from the pre-dawn breeze blowing south across the killing fields. Each man wondered if he would soon join the heap of fallen comrades—blasted, broken, severed, skewered. They shivered and shrugged. Once you're dead, it didn't matter how it happened.

"Men," the sharp voice of their captain broke into their thoughts and silenced the padre for the moment. "Books" they called him. When he was free of battle, he spent his time reading. "We're in for it, this time." Books pulled no punches. His voice was no more than whisper, but he had the authority of one who had seen it all. "Every goddamn German fit to fire a rifle is waiting on the other side of this muddy mess. Make no mistake. They're fucking good. Broke every army we've brought up so far: The French, the British, even the Aussies. You'll see their dead filling every pothole and shell crater you crawl into. The very best of the Allied forces has fumbled the ball right here." A few grunts and an expletive punctuated Books' words.

"So ..." Books let his words slide out slowly. "So your King has called upon his brave Canucks to pull off another Vimy and drive the Hun back. Apparently, we have a reputation for victory, even though we're just field hands and farmers."

A few chuckles—Books had been at Vimy, deserved the Cross for bravery, many said. He knew the business end of a bayonet. His men would follow him into hell at the blink of an eye. He'd earned his men's respect through bravery and cool command under battle. It was men like Books that had turned a bumbling band of citizen volunteers into the finest attack force of the war. "So we don't want to disappoint our monarch—not to mention our prime minister—God bless his furry back side." More laughter.

"Seriously," Books looked about and prayed his own silent prayer for their safety. "....We're in for the fight of our lives. This battlefield has to be worst I've ever seen. Shit and slime. So keep sharp and stay low. Follow the plan, watch your flanks and when all else fails, stand firm. Don't give a goddamn inch, and, if you have to use your bare hands (rumour had it that Books had done just that at Vimy Ridge), go for their fucking juggler!"

Books could hear a few fists slapping against open hands. Men were pumping up their courage. Muscles flexing, anger building. "Good," he thought, "They'll need every ounce of both, if they are going to survive this shit hole." To the troops he said, "One more thing. Any man who gets dead without my permission will be court martialed." Tension-filled guffaws. "Padre—she's all yours."

Josh was a Methodist from Saskatchewan, and, unlike any of his predecessors in the regiment, he was not disposed to pompous preening. He knew each man by name and held many of their "notes home" in case they should fall. Perhaps as much as his captain, he was aware that this was not a Sunday school picnic. Sitting with his colleagues from other countries at a chaplains' meeting held three weeks previously, he had heard the horror stories of the mud and murder surrounding Passchendaele.

Barely twenty-six, fresh from seminary in Edmonton, he had no fancy talk prepared, no scripted call to arms. His long suit was his honesty and his conviction that God walked by every soul in need, a constant guide and comfort.

"Men," the pastor looked around. "I'm scared shitless. I'm not a fancy preacher and I don't spend much time on my knees. But I'll give you what I've got. Jesus comforted his followers when they were without defenses. He offered them a simple prayer. Let's whisper it together. 'Our Father who art in heaven ...'"

Soldiers joined in quietly, each man knowing it might be his last chance to speak with the Almighty, on this side of the grave at any rate.

Montreal: Thelma Lint's Gentlemen's Parlour
Tuesday, August 8, 1916, 3:42 p.m.

Thelma turned on her lover with a vehemence that only deep affection could produce. "Our father in heaven! Douglas, you can be the most pigheaded, blind fool of a ... of a bishop!" Stung by the words, Hinks rose quickly from Thelma's arms and stood by the window, his nightshirt open down his chest.

"I don't care what you say about me. Insult me if you like, she's not staying here. My sister's home in Sackville is better for a woman in her condition."

"What?" Thelma was breathing flames.

"Don't get that look on your face." Hinks hadn't turned, but he could picture Thelma—the frown on her brow, the tight, closed lips and the piercing eyes—there was no fire to equal her "I've got a cause" look.

Still without turning, Hinks continued. "I have to think of her future. All these years without a mother have left her naive in the ways of the world. A season down in the Maritimes with a real matron will bring her so much."

Thelma smarted at the slur: "real." As if her offer to shepherd the child was "unreal." She swallowed the hurt and asked evenly, "What, Douglas, is her condition? Exactly?" The last word came out with a bit too much of an edge, but Thelma never apologized for her passion.

Hinks turned a half-measure and cast Thelma a quizzical glance. "Why her youth of course. She's infatuated with this Gordon chap—mooning over him. They're betrothed … did it by mail … silly notion. She needs to see the big picture, get some distance."

"Dear … she's not …"

"I know what you're going to say," Hinks interrupted. He wasn't really listening—except to his own voice. He turned back to face the window. "She's not going to get over him while he's at war and you're right. This love of hers is bordering on nostalgia." He turned, studied the floorboards that stretched out from under her bedside rug, trying to make Thelma see his point. "It's not real. She's so young, hasn't seen enough of life … A few seasons in another home might dispel her …" Here he glanced at Thelma. "I mean she's …" Hinks stopped. The lightning in her eyes was fiercer than he'd ever seen there before.

"She's pregnant!" Thelma blurted out. "Can't you see anything? Your daughter is carrying Gordon's baby!" It was as if her words froze Hinks; his mouth half-open, eyes wide. His hands caught mid-gesture making a point that was now lost, were chilled to stone.

A chasm opened between them. Had she gone too far, presumed too much? She reached a hand into the space separating them—like a lifeline. He stood stiff—unmoving. She might as well have been invisible.

"Douglas … speak to me!"

"Pregnant?" The single word slipped out. Anger flickered in his eyes. His body crumpled onto the window seat.

"Yes!" Thelma rose, crossed the distance between them and sat beside him.

"Davis is the father?" A whisper, doubting, frightened.

"Yes."

"The bastard. I'll kill him." Fists crashed into each other.

"Not if you want to see your daughter again, you won't." Thelma touched his arm, tried to pull apart his clenched fists.

Hinks felt his fury exploding. "Leave me go, Thelma. You knew this, and you did nothing? She's all I have, and now she'll be …. How can I explain this to …?" Hinks slid away from her touch. "How could you … how could you betray me like this … You did nothing!"

Thelma was not about to be wrongfully accused. "Nothing? I am doing exactly what I should do, right now. I am telling a bull-headed, blind father about the love of his daughter. If he would only forget himself and listen, he'd see that she is a grown woman who loves a man with a folly and depth that is astounding. She is utterly overjoyed."

"Nonsense! She's a child and I'll be blamed for her … her state!"

"Douglas Hinks, I love you, but there are times when you can be such an arrogant ass! Johanna is her own woman. She wants this child and fully intends to marry Gordon Davis and make her life with him."

Hinks waved him away. "Pah … a simpleton!"

Thelma fired right back. "A simpleton? You yourself said he had great courage. The brightest student Wycliffe College had ever seen. Is that not so?"

"Yes. Yes … I said that …" The bishop sighed as his anger began to drain away, being replaced rapidly by a deep fatigue.

Thelma moved closer and held him. "It isn't what you expected, no white bridal gown, no fancy wedding. But they will build a good life together. Don't ask me how I know this, but I can feel that they are exceptional couple."

"Pregnant?"

"Yes."

"When … when is the baby due?"

"December." Thelma ran her hands through his hair, the way he always liked. It had become her signal to him to come to bed. "Late December."

They sat together, swaying slightly. Many minutes passed in silence. Hinks, eyes wide open, searched the pattern of the throw rug at his feet for wisdom. Thelma, comforting, inviting, gentle.

Finally, Hinks looked into her playful eyes. It would be all right, somehow. In response to the invitation of her caresses he winked. "Not yet. I have things to think out. Will you help me?"

"Of course," Thelma felt a warm glow burst in her heart, the thrill of being a confidante.

Hinks was running the knuckle of his index finger across his lips—a sign he was thinking deeply. "Why are you telling me this and not Johanna?" A look of shock crossed his face as he realized what he had asked. "Did she tell you? ... Of course she did! Then she knows that you and I are ... that you are a ...."

Thelma laughed at her lover's consternation. "She didn't actually use the word 'whore' but yes, she knows what I do and why you come here. Don't look so foul. Johanna's much more mature than you think. She's actually quite happy for us—that I have you and that you are not alone and yes ... she told me about her baby. She asked me to tell you and to persuade you to let her stay here with me."

Hinks "That's impossible." He withdrew her hands from his hair. "She needs family. All the more so now."

It was Thelma's turn for fury. "Douglas, she doesn't want to go to your silly sister's." The words were almost barked. "She wants to stay here, in my home. Do you know why? Do you, you silly old man? Because she's got family right here!" Thelma clapped an open hand over her heart. "Right here! A mother who loves her no matter what mess she gets into." There, it was said! Thelma had claimed her territory. More evenly, she continued, "Those were her words, Douglas, not mine. And by your God, if you turn her away, Douglas Hinks, you'll never warm my bed again."

Hinks raised an eyebrow. "Is that a threat?"

"No, a promise!" Thelma couldn't help a smile from creeping into her voice.

Hinks was running to keep up with the revelations of the past minute. And it wasn't his daughter's pregnancy that caused his mind to stumble, but Thelma's she-bear declaration of loyalty. And to his daughter? An officious inner voice boomed, "How dare you presume to take her mother's place." But a deeper wisdom whispered, "How dare you not?"

"She loves you, Douglas. Please don't mess this up with silly male pride."

Thelma knew his thoughts all too well. Hinks laughed, "… I was about to do just that, but then a little angel stilled my tongue. Instead, let me apologize to you, my dear, for my insults." As he spoke Hinks took her hands. "And may I extend a profound word of gratitude to my daughter's new mother. Heaven knows she needs one. Did she actually call you family?"

.   "'I wish you were my mother.' Those were her words—among others."

Hinks frowned. "You'll keep her safe?"

"Of course!"

"Maybe this is the best place for her. She'll certainly not lack for helping hands."

"Come to bed, Douglas, we'll work this out."

"Not yet. I'm still thinking …. Do you have any of that sherry left? I'm awake now. Will you join me in the sitting room?"

Thelma was always eager. She slipped on a dressing gown. "A man after my own heart." Going into the next room, arms linked.

Hinks laughed. "Oh, I'll be after your body soon enough."

Thelma remembered a final piece of information. "One last request. Johanna doesn't want Gordon to know … about the baby, I mean. She has her own reasons."

"What?" Hinks stopped in his tracks.

"Please. She wants to surprise him …."

Hinks moved toward the living room fireplace. "Well, Mother … what do you think?"

Passchendaele, France
Tuesday, October 9, 1917, 12:15 p.m.

"Gordie, what do you think?" Books spoke quietly. They were the only two left. Crawling across mud holes filed with bloated corpses, they'd seen their assault waves cut to shreds. Now they were crouched several dozen yards from a pillbox blocking any forward movement. The enemy was still well supplied—endlessly, it seemed—for their machine gun fire swept over the Allied position with relentless fury. A crossfire killing field.

Gordon had been a few steps behind the first attack "over the top." Except there had been no "top" to go over. The trenches had long since disappeared into the sludge of water, clay and blood. His company had simply leapt from their funk holes, casting aside the pieces of tin they'd used to keep of the rain. And with rifle in hand these brave souls slipped and slid toward the enemy guns.

In places, the water was up to their waist and movement forward was more like a slow dance. Shoulders twisting and turning the only visible movement; each man trying to hold his weapons above the slime. Each step churned up the mud, sometimes releasing a foul stench or dislodging a scrap of uniform, a severed limb. After weeks of wading through this quagmire to prepare for battle, the men were exhausted and then ordered to fight in it?

It was slaughter.

Gordon had been overwhelmed almost before the first shot. Men fell like straw before the German guns. Blood spurted from tunics. Bodies flew into the air at every shell burst. Many were dead before they hit the ground. The wounded shouted for help.

Gordon paused by each fallen soldier, assessed the damage and gave his medical attention to the ones who had any hope. Bandages staunched the flow, gauze wrapped split heads. He whispered as ever, "We'll have you right as rain, as soon as the offensive pushes further ahead."

"Pushes ahead." What a silly notion. Every inch of that quagmire was captured at a dirge-like pace. Gordon slid from one causality to another until he discovered that he had run out of bodies. The Hun fire was still spitting flame, but he could find no other members of his company. They'd all fallen.

If it wasn't so frightening, he might have laughed. The perfect ironic twist of battle, the medic finds himself at the head of the advance! There was nothing to do but wait.

It was as the second wave of assault troops met him that he picked up with Books. The captain had seen the medic lying in a shell crater and motioned for him to follow. Shrugging off his doubt and fear, Gordon had belly-flopped over to the movement of soldiers spread out behind their leader. They pushed on toward the enemy.

Was it hours or minutes later that he found himself alone with Books? The screams of dying men, the thunder strokes of artillery fire were a blur—stretching seconds into an eternity. Their company had hardly lurched forward when a previously silent German machine gun on their left flank opened up the gates of hell. Men dropped by the score. Books led a small assault on the machine gun nest and soon it went silent.

Gordon slogged forward and met his blood-spattered captain coming back from the attack. Alone. Turning, Gordon noticed that he, too, was on his own … again. They huddled in the mud, shivered and took deep breaths.

"Gordie, what do you think?"

Gordon was almost numb, but Books' words brought him back to life. "It's these pillboxes, Captain. They're mowing down every wave." They both flopped onto their stomachs to take stock of their predicament.

"Right you are. We'll have to take them out." Books looked around. "I guess it's you and me. Got any ammo?"

Gordon tried to smile. "Sir, I'm a non-combatant, remember? Don't carry a weapon …."

Books wasn't listening. "Take these three Mills Bombs and chuck them into the front of that pillbox to the left—try to draw the fire from this segment of the front. While the guns are aimed your way, I'll take out the pillbox to the right—it's the key to our forward advance."

"Chuck it, sir?"

Books looked more closely at Gordon, expecting to see cowardice and was pleased to see the clear look of dedication. "Chuck it! Haven't you ever played ball, Davis?" Books smiled outwardly, but thinking, "This is lunacy!" Aloud he said, "Get close. Lob it into front slit—slither up and get the job done—make noise, get the whole line to shoot your way. I'm counting on you."

Had Gordon been off-duty behind the lines with his buddies and this kind of manoeuvre had been suggested, it would have been met with laughter. "Right, Davis … be a good chap. Run out there will you! Get those snipers, a machine gun crew or two and every other blessed Hun in the German army to shoot at you, while I make a single-handed, frontal assault on a fortified enemy position."

"Do what?" Gordon asked again.

Books was already planning his moves. He stopped and turned to Gordon. "Lob it. Like you're tossing a slow pitch into home plate. Just lob it in the front door."

"Yes, sir, … lob it," Gordon gritted his teeth. "Easy … just lob it in … maybe I could ask for their help. I'm sure the Germans will oblige." Taking the bombs, he rolled onto his stomach and began his crawl into hell.

Books was impressed, very impressed. He'd seen many strong men buckle. "This Gordon fellow," he thought, "has got more courage than an entire company." Aloud, he whispered, "Gordie???"

Gordon looked back at his captain. "Yes, sir?"

"Don't stand up!"

Montreal: Mount Royal Park (Sisson Ridge Park)
Monday, March 27, 1916, 8:47 p.m.

Gordon was standing alone in the shadows near the entrance to Sisson Ridge Park, his shoulder touching a maple tree trunk. He shifted the heavy army issue blanket. It was getting cold again. A south wind off the river carried a crisp chill up the mountain.

He'd been waiting an hour. Jo was late. His mind began to play its normal tricks. *Maybe she's thought better of coming to see me. Finally decided I'm not worth the risk. It's all been too fast. She's not coming.*

He traced the designs of bark on the maple tree beside him. Fingers finding groves, rough outcroppings and ridges. He wondered how many other forgotten lovers had waited beside this tree, etching their worries into its bark.

"You going to carve our initials into that tree?"

He'd been so intent on his imaginary jilted lovers he hadn't noticed her approach. Her voice startled him so that he almost dropped the blanket.

"Just get my name right. I don't want future generations to be mistaken. 'JH loves GD,'" Jo laughed.

Gordon joined in, "I could put a heart around it—with an arrow piercing both sides. Just so there'd be no doubt."

"I like the arrow ... yes." Jo smiled "Sorry to be late. Father was fussing again about his churches—wouldn't let me get the dishes done."

Gordon was beaming. He didn't care at all about her excuse—just that she was now present. "No need to apologize." He grinned. "I knew you'd arrive—sooner or later. What else does an army lout have to do on a Monday night anyway?"

"Come here you big hunk." Jo pulled at Gordon's arm, directing their steps onto the path. "You thought I wouldn't be coming." She peered sideways at her man.

Gordon shrugged. "No."

Jo felt the tentativeness in his voice and held his gaze. "Liar! You were worried. Don't ever lie to me, Gordon Davis."

Gordon made to reply, but she cut him off, "You can break a promise, even betray me, but never, never lie to me." She looked down, paused to rid her voice of the stern tenor and said more evenly, "Did you honestly think I would abandon you—after all we've done this past week ...?"

Gordon cut across her thoughts. "It's been so quick and ... I'm such a ... I just thought you might find someone better. I wasn't sure you ...."

Jo stopped, turned to Gordon and planted a long and passionate kiss on his lips. She drew away and searched his eyes. "Are you sure, now?"

Gordon blushed slightly. "I'm sorry, Jo ... I've never been here before ... in love ... I mean ....I am such a young soul. I feel like I'm learning to walk all over again and bumping into every obstacle in sight. Can you ...." He paused, looking off toward the horizon.

"Can I what?" Jo's hand drew his gaze back to meet her eyes. "Can I what?"

Gordon took a deep breath. He wanted to ask if she would be able tolerate such a clumsy lover and be patient when his fears took him into despair, but all that came out was: "Can you wait until I come back? Really?"

"Of course I can ... I've told you that before ... many ...."

"... Many times .... Yes, I know. It's just that the war may drag on for longer than we imagine." Standing still, Gordon chewed on his bottom lip, shamed by her vehemence, a bit embarrassed by his own uncertainty. Was it his unfaithfulness he feared, more than hers? Perhaps he was the one who lacked the strength to wait?

Jo saw repentance in his countenance and stepped close to whisper in his ear. "This is our last night together. We're in our sanctuary—Sisson Ridge—if you come over that next rise with me, out of sight of this path, I will make love to you as I promised ... but right now kiss me ... long and well, you fool. It will have to last us for many months." Her arms folded around his shoulders. They were lost to this world in an embrace that took them out of time into a realm which knew not death nor separation nor war.

Halifax: North Train Station
Thursday, December 6, 1917, 7:35 p.m.

As Jo walked down the tracks into the city, the distant fires grew larger. Soon they cast a faint light on twisted beams and broken glass that had been the north end of the Halifax. Grotesque shadows danced across the snow.

It had taken many hours, halting often, but Jo finally arrived in the midst of the shambles that had once been the train station. At the sight of so much destruction, she could feel her weary soul crash. She set down her burdens and crumpled to her knees. Hot tears flowed over her cheeks.

For a time, she crouched in the snow, eyes closed. She had heard of such destruction but had never visited it first-hand. On her solitary walk along the tracks into what remained of the north end of Halifax she had seen too much: blasted houses and broken bodies.

The hardship of the wounded was difficult, but what struck her to the bone was the creeping and ever increasing sense of chaos. Every step took her further into that nightmare—no order, no control, no sense of purpose. Just mindless, cruel devastation.

Shutting her eyes tightly, Jo waited, hoping for the nightmare to end. Someone would turn on the bedroom light, tuck her in and comfort her. "It's okay, dear." Jo cried out for help—but none came. She longed to wake and find the blood wiped away, the bricks placed back into walls.

Opening her eyes, Jo saw there was no reprieve. Death was real, and Gordon was missing.

A house across the street suddenly burst into flames ... one more victim to the day's tragedy.

In her desperation she prayed, "Dear Father in heaven ... bring it back. Bring back the beauty, bring back the compassion, and bring back my love." It was nothing more than a whisper in an ocean of shrieks, but somehow her Creator heard and offered a small coincidence as condolence.

Jo looked about for comfort, saw what was left of bench, trudged toward it and sat down. Rest ... not their bench, of course, but familiar none the less. Her hands reached out to steady herself and her right hand fell upon a small chain. Without thinking, her fingers closed over it and drew into the dim light of the fires across the street.

Jo had never been concerned with military paraphernalia, but she knew enough that the small silver cross was a military identification tag. She's seen one around Gordon's neck on the delicious occasions when they had held each other.

As if on command, or perhaps it was the recollection of the fire she shared with Gordon, an explosion closer to the harbour shed a burst of light on the collapsed station. For an instant, she could read the name on the reverse side of the tag: Pte. G. H. Davis. It was a flash and then the semi-twilight gloom closed in again. Had she seen correctly? Could it be possible that she had found him—or at least evidence of his survival?

Then Jo went cold—could he be here—trapped in the mesh of bent steel. A frantic fear gripped her. Jo rose to her feet and began to stumble about the debris, calling his name. Her voice echoed in the chill air. No greeting came back. Beginning in the immediate vicinity of where she had found the tag, Jo repeated the ghoulish search that Gordon had completed only hours before, rolling over each body, now stiff with frost, searching open eyes and gaping mouths—hoping not to find what she so desperately wanted to see—a task made all the more gruelling, since, in the creeping darkness, she had to come within inches of each contorted face.

After an hour, she could bear it no longer. Her heart told her he wasn't here. Stopping to let her heart speak, she was certain he was still alive. She could picture him in this place—heartbroken and close to a frenzy, as she was—and then glancing down the ribbons of steel leading away from the destroyed station, Jo knew. She knew what Gordon had done. Not finding her in the station, he had headed toward Montreal. There could be no other explanation. That is what her love would have driven her to do, had she been in his place.

Shaking her head, she smiled. "I am in the very place where he was … at the wrong end of the tracks." With a queer lightness of heart, she lifted her belongs and started off back west. "It's Montreal or bust." Did she whistle—impossible to say. Later she tried to remember, but for the time she was too tired to take account of anything more than placing one plodding foot in front of the other.

Ahead on the track she heard a train whistle. "Perhaps I can hitch a ride back the way I came." Her feet started to run.

Passchendaele, France
Tuesday, October 9, 1917, 1:13 p.m.

Gordon lay in the shadows of a great shell hole. Close to the Germans now. He could even hear their grunts and curses. He wished he'd studied the language in school.

It had taken over half-an-hour to belly walk his way toward the pillbox Books wanted him to "take out."

Battle takes forever, and yet it also moves more rapidly than any can imagine. There's no time for reflection. Logic is absent. It is only in hindsight one finds a pattern to the events. At this instant, Gordon wasn't thinking at all. He was a breathing, crawling soldier, waiting for his chance.

And, as if on command, the firing stopped. Maybe the crew was reloading or the gun was jammed. Either way, this was Gordon's chance. Throwing caution to the wind, he jumped to the top of his shell hole and threw a Mills Bomb straight through the gun port of the pillbox.

A shot rang out. Gordon was whipped backwards into the muck, and then a deafening explosion knocked him senseless.

A fountain of churned up slime and wooden debris was the last sight Gordon remembered.

His war was now officially over.

Montreal: Christ Church Cathedral
Saturday, December 8, 1917, 7:49 p.m.

The narthex was dimly lit. Several groups of black-robed prelates were moving silently into the sanctuary. The late night session was about to resume. Hinks was secluded in a corner, deep in conversation with a priest serving the Rosemere parish. It was the same story—a divided flock, some favouring conscription, others opposed. He was about to query the young man about his personal views, when a hand grabbed his shoulder with considerable desperation. Whirling with resentment, Hinks was stunned.

His lips went dry, and he was unable to speak.

"Sir. My Lord ..." Gordon was so tired he could hardly say a word. Since leaving Cruikshank the night before, he had gotten himself thoroughly lost, finally sleeping in a deserted doorstep in the east end of the city. It had taken all day to find his way back to the cathedral—many false starts along the way. Whenever he asked about a cathedral, most inhabitants pointed him toward the Catholic one on Dominion Square.

"Sir ..." Gordon tried again. "I'm Gordon ... Gordon Davis .... I just got in from Halifax."

Hinks was still stunned.

Gordon looked down at his tattered uniform, "Please forgive my interruption, but I am beside myself. Have you seen Johanna? She promised to meet me on the dock and there was an explosion and ..."

Hinks went white. "She left several days ago ... she went off to meet *you* as she promised. My God what happened? Are you sure you didn't miss her ... she was so determined to get to the dock in time to greet you."

Gordon hesitated. "It's a war zone. Impossible to say anything for certain, but I looked for twelve hours before hopping a freight here."

Hinks' mind was racing. "She left on the 5th with ..."

"With Samuel ..." Gordon finished his sentence. "I know all about him."

"Do you?" Hinks raised a curious eyebrow. "Then you'll know that she's not a free agent. I suspect she never made it to the city."

Gordon started to feel signs of some relief—even the mention of Samuel couldn't dampen it entirely. "The trains were all stopped. They wouldn't allow any to enter the city after the explosion. I passed a half-dozen sitting on the sidings between Halifax and Truro. Could she possibly be safe ...?" His heart was apprehensive. Hope had seemed such a distant possibility for the past three days.

Hinks tried to sound reassuring. He needed to be sure. He'd lost one son to this bloody war, he couldn't even visit the prospect of losing his daughter. "She'll be fine. Probably caught on one of those trains then."

Gordon sighed. "If only I could believe that."

"Believe it, Gordon. I think I would know if there was a problem."

Gordon wasn't so easily persuaded. He was unable to focus, had to tell his story to someone. Was he speaking too quickly, too loudly? He couldn't tell, didn't care. "I've been looking everywhere—ever since the disaster at Halifax—so many bodies, so many lost people. She wasn't there like she said she would be. Took a train here and began again. I even went to a whorehouse—the one she said I might find her in emergencies, … but she wasn't …."

Hinks interrupted Gordon. "You've been to Thelma Lint's?"

Gordon tried to concentrate on the bishop's words. "Thelma Lint's … I don't know the name … a house up the hill from here. Was it really a whorehouse?"

A few heads turned toward Hinks and this vagrant. No doubt they were wondering why he would be speaking with a vagabond stranger. The session was about to begin, and Hinks was first to speak. What business could he have with such a ragged and dangerous looking vagrant?

Hinks took Gordon by the arm and led him outside. "Let's speak privately." Closing the door behind them, Jo's father turned to his companion and looked deeply into his eyes—seeing there the weight of grief and despair. "Don't give up, Gordon, she'll come back when she doesn't find you in Halifax. I am certain. She's not lost to you … just hang on for a few days."

"A few days …." Gordon repeated Hinks' words. "She's not lost??" He was coming back to the land of the living. "My Lord, I … I have seen so much … I don't know if I can hold on much longer…. The war has cut out my courage."

"Nonsense." Hinks was a firm believer in the cold-shower approach to human strife. "Wake up and pull yourself together. Straighten up!" It was a command.

Gordon, long habituated to obey, pulled his shoulders back. "Yes, sir." Hinks wasn't finished. "How is your strength? Private!"

"Fair to middling, … sir." Gordon tried to come to attention, arms at his sides, face forward.

Hinks faced his recruit and barked, "She'll come back! Repeat after me. 'She'll come back!'"

"She'll come back."

Hinks smiled briefly. "Again!"

"She'll come back!"

"Louder."

Gordon shouted, "She'll come back!!"

"Good." In a flash, Hinks had an idea. He pulled Gordon away from his erect posture to take a stroll down the lane beside the cathedral. "Gordon, she'll be back in a day, two at the most. In the meantime, I need your help."

"Me sir?" Gordon looked at Hinks with growing mental energy. "Me? What could I possibly …?"

Hinks had his doubts—great ideas were always laced with danger. "I am in the middle of a great church battle—perhaps the fight of my life. Your principal, Cruikshank," Hinks pronounced the word as if it was a curse, "He wants to twist this country into a nation of warmongers. He's forced a vote on wanting the church to declare a holy war."

"Holy war?" Gordon wasn't following.

"A holy war. Cruikshank is asking the Anglican Church to pronounce on this conflict—calling it the will of God that we defeat the Germans. He thinks he'll bring the church more fully into the Allied cause—possibly persuade the Anglican Church worldwide to follow suit. Can you imagine what that would mean?"

"No." Gordon was trying to picture the battle of France with religious overtones.

"…. It would multiply the horror a hundred-fold …."

"Would it?" Gordon gave the bishop a close look and stopped walking, "My Lord, I …."

"Gordon will you stop calling me that? A simple 'Douglas' is more than sufficient. I am not your Lord … closer to being your father."

"Douglas," Gordon began again. "I don't want to contradict you, but there is very little that could make that mess any worse. With all due respect … you haven't been there. It is a hell that can barely be imagined. I could tell stories that you would never credit." For ten minutes he recounted some of the horror of Passchendaele.

Hinks listened, too startled to speak.

Gordon concluded, "In the trenches there is no virtue or glory. Adding the word 'holy' to that slaughter would not make a whit of difference. Men would still butcher each other with the same evil cynicism .... It is out of control. Any church body that blesses the war is either out of touch with reality or incredibly stupid."

Hinks smiled broadly. "Here's what I need, Gordon. I need you to say exactly that ...what you just explained about battle, but to the crowd inside." Here he motioned toward the cathedral door.

Gordon looked puzzled. "Again? Okay. Any church that ...."

"No, no, ...not here." Hinks took Gordon's arm again. "Let's keep walking. I want you to speak to the entire congress. Tomorrow. I have a right to address the cathedral congregation during the regular Sunday service. Tomorrow, I want you to take my place and tell people what it is really like."

"Sir ..., ah I mean, Douglas, is that wise?" Gordon was uncertain. "They wouldn't understand."

Hinks was more and more certain of his plan. "Give them more credit for comprehension. Just tell them what you saw—talk about the misery, your friends, the battles—whatever you like. If you speak clearly, they'll get the point."

Gordon stopped and looked up to the sky. Silently, he thought back to the many torn and twisted faces. How do you capture a generation's anguish in a few words?

Hinks was wondering if Gordon was praying, lost in his despair or thinking it through.

"I'll do it, Douglas." Gordon sighed. "I'll do it for you ... and for Jo. Not because I think it will make a difference."

"Good ... great!" Hinks began to walk toward the front entrance again. "Come along, Gordon ... I need to make an announcement about your speech—then we can go get you a hot bath, some clean clothes and a warm meal."

"The bath and meal sound good." But I won't change these clothes— they're my uniform—it's how most face their death in Flanders—no shining buttons or well-pressed trousers.

Hinks paused, "Indeed!" He led Gordon into the church, just in time to stand at the pulpit to explain how he would introduce a solider from the front to the Sunday morning community. "A courageous man, the best eyewitness we could want. He will open our eyes … and our hearts. A brilliant scholar, candidate for the ministry from St. Giles, in Hamilton … a great man."

Standing in the shadows at the back of sanctuary, ashamed of his disheveled state, Gordon listened and wondered to whom Hinks was referring.

Hamilton: 75 Barton St.
Saturday, November 17, 1917, 9:54 p.m.

James saw them all … the circles of boys he had taken under his wing. They were happy lads, ready for mischief as much as any, but also polite when he told his stories and courteous when he raised church matters. Now those same faces were accusing him. They haunted his steps.

After the initial encounter with Brent, James tried to tell himself that it didn't happen or that Brent was exaggerating things. He was always doing that when he was younger, puffing himself up in front of the older boys. James started to check out the scandal with others. Nothing scientific, just a random question, when he met them on the street. Nothing too probing. If they wanted to fill in the blanks, they could. "So … ah, have you seen Reverend Hawthorne lately? I understand he's being asking after you …."

Each response confirmed Brent's story. There would be snarls or grunts. One called him "loose-fingered." "He liked little boys too much." Jesse Hall, made a full confession. His need to talk had apparently been building, and, when James opened the door, he barged right in.

"He didn't do not'in hurting-like, Mr. Davis." Jesse pulled his companion away from the market stall where they had met. "I mean, it were not like he broke me arm or smacked me about. I agreed to it … sort of."

James pushed as gently as he could. "What did he do?"

Jesse replied softly, guilt quietening his voice, "It were at your country place, where you told us those wonderful stories. When it came time to

change into our swimming gear, the reverend would always wait in the change house and watch us boys undress. When they all left ... and I was the only one left ... well ... he would say I was special ... 'his angel' ... and then ... well ... I try to forget what happened next and ... well, when it was over he told me not to tell anyone. 'It would be our secret.' I was especially warned not to tell *you*, sir."

James' mind was in a fog of anger. How could he have been so dolt-headed not to see it? He looked back over the years and saw Hawthorne's hand resting on the bare knees of his boys as they sat in a circle listening to a Bible story. He never even imagined what it meant. "The bastard, ... the low, underhanded shit. How dare he do that at my place? ... A betrayal." James didn't realize he'd been talking out loud. His rage was building, "In my very home .... How can I ... how can I face anyone again?"

Jesse wanted to help his old Sunday school teacher, so he tried to explain. "But it weren't often there at the lake. He did more in his study ... his 'special study sessions' was what he called our meetings."

"Study sessions. Of all the ...."

Jesse tried another tack, "But he gave me nice stuff, Mr. James. I wouldn't want to say anything about him ... not out loud like. I just try to forget." Jesse shook the older man's hand, wished him well and left him standing alone in his misery.

There was no way to pretend it away. Hawthorne had used him, played him for a fool, all the while abusing the very children he had been asked to guide. And ... he had drawn James into his filth.

James turned on his heel, rubbing his hands together roughly, trying to clean the dirt he felt must surely be showing on them. His steps took him unerringly to Bartonworth's General Store where he bought a box of shells for his shotgun.

"A little late for birds, ain't it, James?" old man Bartonworth asked as he passed over the box.

James only grunted. Not any bird, he thought. There was just one particular buzzard he wanted to shoot.

The church door was locked. Hawthorne must be away.

James took his shells home and went upstairs. The house was quiet. All the girls were out at the YMCA dance. He locked himself in the bathroom and had been playing with the trigger, looking down the sights, opening and shutting the muzzle, all the while trying to sort through his shame and remorse. He wept for each loss of innocence, but his deepest distress arose when his gaze fell upon the bright features of his son Gordon.

Hawthorne did ask James if he could start his special study classes with Gordon. He'd been had! The pain was too great.

James slowly reached down into his right pocket, leaning slightly to the left as his fingers found the box of ammunition.

Straightening up, he read every word on the box carefully, as if examining a sacred relic, looking for evidence of its authenticity. Then he opened the shotgun gently, selected two shells from the box and slid them neatly into the barrel. He snapped the muzzle shut with a snap.

"Enough stalling," he said as he put the butt up against the bathtub's claw leg and shoved the muzzle into his mouth. His left hand gripped the barrel. James stretched his right arm out to full length, so his fingers could reach the trigger.

Now!

Passchendaele, France
Tuesday, October 9, 1917, 7:13 p.m.

Books looked down at the unconscious medic. Darkness was falling and he wiped the mud from his tunic and face. "Bloody marvelous ... he's still alive. I have never seen a man do a more courageous thing." Here Books looked around the circle of men who had stumbled back to the reserve trenches with their wounded burden. "Any of you see it?" There were blank stares all round. "See what?" one asked.

Books' enthusiasm was not dampened a bit. "What ... why how he took out a pillbox all by himself, that's what. You see how far we came today ... Davis here made it happen ... did what half the British army was unable to do ... broke the bloody gridlock of bunkers on the rise by the town."

There was wall-to-wall disbelief. "He's only a stretcher carrier." "What'd he use ... a roll of gauze?" "Bloody unlikely!"

Books turned aside their remarks with the sweep of his hand. "You weren't there; you didn't know what it was like ... Only the two of us left from our first two attack waves."

"Right. Well hero or not, he'll bleed out if we don't get his ruptured leg back to a clearing station."

Books was all business again, "Right, take him back ... I'm off to write this up. Be careful with my friend here. I'm going to be recommending his sorry ass for a Cross. That may be famous cargo you're carrying."

The troops smiled and carted Gordon off.

Books began his crouched walk back to his forward position, and it was just as he turned down the fire trench that his luck finally ran out. A direct hit from a German mortar buried him alive in mud. When they finally dug him out three days later, his hand was still grasping a blank report form. The account of Davis' valour was never written.

Montreal,

Thursday November 30th, All Saints' Day, 1916

Gordon I haven't written in two days. Did you miss me?

I have no idea if these notes all get through. There's been nothing from you in over a month. So I just keep writing my letters in the hope that they will be delivered to you somehow.

Today's will be a short note. I have to get off to the cathedral for a special service of mourning for the fallen. We seem to be having them every week now. Today we're remembering two school chums and a cousin of mine. Blasted war.

Did I tell you Terrance has signed up? I might have mentioned it before. I can never remember from

one letter to the next what I have said. He's a
bloody fool ... all smiles and bravado. You'd think
he was off to a summer concert.

Just watch out for him if he ever gets close. He's all
the brother I have.

I have to go ... I love you. I love you.

I'll be here when you come home ... so make
it soon.

Jo

Saint John: The Buttress Home
Tuesday, October 13, 1992, 9:55 a.m.

"Just push me off the end of a boat, a skiff, a sloop, row boat ... even
a god-forsaken fishing trawler would do." Captain Jims was turning
purple. "Just do it, mate!"

I had made the terrible mistake of suggesting that, when his end
came, the captain could find a fine resting place in our church cemetery.

"Landlubber ... never! The sea's the place for old sailors!"

"Think of the people who would come to see you."

"Never."

Argue as I might, Captain Jims was adamant. He wanted a burial
at sea and made me call the funeral director to make the arrangements.
"Right now ... before the tide turns."

So I had found a wheelchair and together we had sailed off in search
of a phone. Once I had old man Ferguson on the line, Captain Jims took
over. He grabbed the mouthpiece and shouted his instructions, as if he
was calling from one fog-locked ship to another. "St. Martin's will do
just fine .... You go see a lobsterman down there by name of Woods,
Peter Woods. He'll see to everything. I want her done quick and quiet-
like. No hangers-on, no fuss."

With that last command, Captain Jims handed the phone back to me. "Here, you talk to him." The funeral director was asking how an ancient vet would know who was fishing lobster down in the bay, and I had no answer. A few days inquiring, Ferguson called me back to inform me that it turned out that there was indeed a Peter Woods in St. Martin's *and* he had a boat *and* he would be willing to perform the service ... for a fee of course.

At the time, a burial at sea seemed a little far-fetched.

I tried suggesting alternatives to my seafaring friend. But Captain Jims would have none of it. "Don't fail me, boy," were his last words when I took my leave.

"No sir, Captain."

Montreal: Bank of Montreal, Office of Accounts Manager Mr. J. Tompkins
Monday, December 10, 1917, 3:10 p.m.

"I was worried I might fail you, Mr. Davis, in arranging your affairs, but I believe we have all the documents in order and ready for signatures." Tompkins held out the polished fountain pen given to him by his bride on the day of their wedding. "Sign here, please, Mr. Davis." Tompkins finger indicated a line on the second page of the document.

It had taken two hours to clear the legal niceties. Tompkins was still fuming over how long he had to wait. The original instructions seemed clear enough. But the company's lawyers had run on about why anyone would give away so much money. "Is there something we don't know?" Their reticence had taken Tompkins by surprise. It was like the money was a personal asset. Why should they care about this young fellow's motives? Once he signed, there was no more obligation on the bank's part. The money was given to a third party.

Tompkins didn't tell anyone about the split of the assets and how he had created a separate blind account with a considerable slice of the bequest still in Davis' name. He knew he would be fired if it ever came to light, but he was sure Davis would be coming back next week, next month, penniless and penitent. Then there would be a bit of a reprieve. A nest egg to start over.

Officially, the lawyers said, "Davis could come back and complain all he liked. But if he signs, there would be no grounds for an appeal." Tompkins had added the final piece of the puzzle that calmed the legal minds. "There's little risk of this man ever coming back to his senses. Besides, this Ms. Hinks, whoever she is, will most likely leave the account right where it is."

No loss, no fuss.

Gordon's head was spinning. Lack of food, no doubt. He was having trouble focusing. His hand was shaking as he clutched the pen, looking for a line that wasn't moving.

Guiding his hand toward the correct spot on the page, Tompkins said. "Are you quite sure you wish to transfer your trust fund, Mr. Davis."

Gordon's blank eyes looked up. "Pardon me?"

The banker took Gordon's response as evidence of hesitation and so he put on his most authoritative tone. "Sir, you don't have to sign this right now. I can keep the paperwork. Set it aside until you are certain. Given your … your recent experience at the … ah … the front I would advise you to take your time. Are you sure?"

Gordon grunted. "Have you seen Flanders?"

Tompkins whispered, "No. I haven't …."

"With all due respect … then you don't know much, do you? I'm sure. I'm sure of this as I am of anything. Now if you'll guide me please—I am tired and want to get this over with. Which line again?"

"Here, sir." Tompkins pointed, waiting in silence as Gordon slowly traced out his signature. It wasn't usually his style to get personal, but Gordon's reference to France brought back the businessman's heartache. "Tell me about Vimy ….You saw it, sir?"

"Yes. I saw Vimy."

Tompkins sighed. "As I said, I … ah … I lost my Henry, my son, there." It was the first time he used the past tense—relegating his son to a yesterday that would never turn into a today. As he spoke, he could feel a door close. The pain was stored away in a dark closet and his face took on a sharper, tighter resolution.

Even in his distress, Gordon was not lost to the subtle suffering of others. In a monotone, he replied, "We lost many sons on that blasted slope." His signature finished, he looked up.

Tompkins pressed. "What happened?"

Gordon's mind went back to those dark days and he continued, as if in trance—his voice all the more frightening for its absolute lack of emotion, "Every life lost at Vimy was a brave tragedy. I saw them fall—the best lads this country has ever produced ..." Shaking his head, Gordon came back to reality. "Your son wasn't lost in vain, sir ... whatever else you might think ... I am so sorry ... One of the fiercest battles I have seen. People say our country came alive on that ridge. I was ... ah ... knocked out early in the assault ... but I think it's true. We all felt a special pride after Vimy, a pride that wasn't there before. In that case, sir, your son's death was an important step in building this country." With no further comment, Gordon rose and walked out of Tompkins' office. Not looking back, not hearing the quiet "Thank you," which the banker whispered to Gordon's receding figure.

It was only several minutes later that Tompkins realized he was missing his fountain pen. After a thorough search of his desk he realized that he had allowed Private Davis to walk off with it. He scanned the cover sheet of the file and discovered that Davis had no current address nor any other reference to a parental home. "Damn!" he cursed. "Betsy (his secretary) will have my head."

Montreal: Thelma Lint's Gentlemen's Parlour
Sunday, December 9, 1917, 9:42 a.m.

"He's been here? He's alive?" Johanna was too exhausted to show much more than relief, though she could feel weight lifting from her heart. "Did he say where he was going? Maybe I could still catch him."

"He was here, but ... can you forgive me ... my maid didn't tell me ...." Thelma turned to the upstairs maid who was waiting patiently at the door and asked her to find Sally. "Fetch Sally to explain herself .... She should be in the kitchen preparing lunch." Thelma looked back at Jo and then added, "And have the cook send up a hot cup of tea and some of those breakfast biscuits."

Jo could feel a wave of fatigue crashing over her, she slouched in her chair, willing herself to relax, knowing that Thelma would take care of her. "Samuel's finally sleeping. Like me, he was up all night. But … I should get him …."

"Let him sleep." Thelma looked closely at her charge. "You've been through hell, Jo. That much is obvious. I only heard of the explosion yesterday. Then it was only much later that Sally let it drop that she'd turned away a soldier at our door. She was on duty and claims he looked and acted like a vagrant. So she sent him packing. I was busy with one of Celine's rougher clients."

"What will we do?" A whimper. "How will we find him now?"

Thelma had been in the world too long to despair easily. "There's always a way. We'll find him, don't you fret."

"But …."

"But nothing …. He's not gone far. This is where he knows you live. He'll surface."

"Dear God, I hope so." Jo looked down at her lap and then up at Thelma. "Speaking of God, where is my father … he'll be purple with anger."

"He's down the street at some large and important church meeting— at the cathedral. He was here last night, came in after his meeting was finished … so tired he didn't say more than good-night. Likewise, this morning … seemed greatly preoccupied. So he just dressed and left. He must be fretting terribly over you."

There was a knock at the door, and Thelma opened it. Sally stood waiting to be invited in, a tray of tea and sandwiches in her hands

Thelma motioned her forward. "Sally, do you recall telling me that a vagrant, a soldier came to our door asking for Jo? "

"Yes, ma'am," Sally replied quickly, "He were wearing a woman's cloak with blood all over it and so on …."

Thelma interrupted, "And he asked for Jo?"

"Yes ma'am."

And you didn't say anything to me about it because ...?" Thelma could feel her anger rising.

Sally felt the accusation in Thelma's question and so began to rationalize her dismissal of Gordon. "He were no one special, and, when he asked for Jo I thought he was trouble ... Jo couldn't handle him ... didn't need to be bothered with ... well ... he were a hobo and I thought we don't take his type round here ... so I just sent him packing ... It were Jo's safety I was thinking of most ...."

Thelma could read between the lines. Sally was vindictive, perhaps a bit jealous of Jo's life. However, keeping her voice even, she asked, "And when was this?"

Sally looked blank. "Ah .... I guess during the rainstorm. He came to the door all soaked like."

Thelma continued her cross-examination. "Did he say where he was staying or where he was going?"

Sally lowered her head and closed her eyes. Her intuition told her she was in trouble. She had better come up with something. She tried to picture that night again—his sad appearance, pleading voice. "There were letters. He were holding letters. I remember that much. But .... I don't know as he mentioned any address ... No nothing ... terrible set on seeing Jo he was ..." Sally looked at her mistress hopefully—sensing that her curt actions may have cost her the job. "I was just trying to protect ...."

"Yes, yes ... just trying to protect Jo. You said that already ... anything else?"

"No, ma'am."

Thelma sighed, took the loaded tray from her maid and turned back to comfort Jo. "Please close the door behind me ... quietly."

Sally had her hand on the brass knob when a small bit of information came to her. Catching Thelma's sleeve, she blurted it out. "Now I remember, Ma'am ... he did mention going to see her father ... that's pretty clear. He said as he'd been looking for him, and I wouldn't be surprised if he were bent on that—meeting the father, I mean."

Thelma brightened. "Well done, Sally, thank you .... You may go."

Sally smiled. Perhaps she had saved her job after all.

Jo was sitting bolt upright, her face blazing with hope. "It was him?"

"I think so." Thelma set the tray down by Jo. "Probably was Gordo and he's off to find your father."

"My father." Jo smiled weakly. "I left without warning. Leaving him a note saying I'd be back on the 7th and that I was off to Halifax."

Thelma smiled in return. "Don't you fuss over Douglas! I'll send Sally off with a message to the good bishop. Now let me help you with those sodden rags." Have some tea while I arrange it."

"I have to see Gordon"

Thelma put up a warning hand. "You have to rest and regroup first. To the tub …."

After dispatching Sally, Thelma worked her matronly magic on Jo. For years now she had practiced the art of soothing frayed nerves—it came with the territory. Jo was whisked off to a bath laced with rosewater. New clothes were found, her hair was washed, combed and set. She had a bite to eat, a sip of tea.

Even while she was being brought back to life, Jo's heart was racing. She couldn't sit still. "Now, … can we go?" came out every other minute.

Thelma was firm … made sure her charge was well nourished, properly attired and settled. Finally, she relented. "Okay. Let's go find him."

Jo was up in a flash, hugging Thelma. "Thank you … thank you … Oh, thank you. No one could have a better mother."

"Don't say that too loudly, especially since we're going to find him in church with your father. Wouldn't do to disturb the saintly church matrons with any scandals about your father, now would it?"

"Samuel?" Jo turned to find him.

"He's with the girls. They'll keep him busy while we go off to find Gordon."

Saint John: The Buttress Home
Monday, October 19, 1992, 8:50 p.m.

"You girls go home, now." Father Inkling sneered at my ministry student. It was Brian's ponytail that was the cause of his caustic dismissal. I didn't usually bring guests to see Gordon, but Brian had specifically asked. He'd heard all the stories and wanted to see the genuine article. Everything had gone swimmingly, until Brian had turned to fetch the Bible and the Sacrament from Gordon's night table. It was at that point that his hair—the full flowing extent of it— swept into view.

We all were accustomed to the ponytail—a minister with long hair. The congregation took a deep breath, assured itself by saying that at least he wasn't gay and went on with its work. So I was caught flat-footed by Gordon's response. "What do you take me for? Don't let that sissy near me. I'll not have the great sacrament defiled by a … a … man who parades around like a woman. The shame." His face was growing crimson and his voice rose with every word. "And you …" Father Inkling turned a wagging finger in my direction. "You … you traitor! Betrayal! I am surrounded by betrayal."

"Gordon," I sat down in his chair drawing it close. "Gordon there's no betrayal here. I brought a friend along. Brian is a student—he studied across from your Alma Mater. He is as you were once, and he wanted to …."

It didn't help a whit. Gordon stormed on "I was never a student … not like him." He almost spat out his disgust. "I've seen them before. Get all chummy and then wait 'til you're softened up and they pounce … no mercy."

"Them? Who is them?"

The priest was in a rant that I couldn't penetrate. "They play you up, pretending to be your friend, a kind mentor. It starts with little pats on the shoulder, then a lingering hand and then when your back is turned they thrust in the knife—so easily, so kindly. It's the wily friends that will cut you as soon as look at you that you must watch."

I could see that Gordon was working himself up—it seemed to be happening more of late. "Gordon … Father Inkling," I pleaded, "Let us pray … this is not the time for recrimination. May we not find mercy and forgiveness in the Lord's presence?"

"Pah!" Gordon brushed aside my suggestions and started again. "You girls go home. And you call yourselves priests!"

Brian was watching this exchange, mouth opening and closing. For once he was speechless, trying to think how to intervene, to slow down the growing storm. He finally hit on the Lord's Prayer. It came out of his mouth before he could think. "Our Father who art in heaven, Hallowed be thy name."

Like flicking a switch, the red-faced Gordon slumped into the meek prelate and joined the words, "Thy kingdom come, thy will be done … on earth as it is in heaven."

I was surprised by his outbursts and equally intrigued by the quick reversal from anger to piety, but I added my voice to the chorus. "Give us this day our daily bread." The words worked on their own accord. My mind was running over the past few minutes. Had Gordon been betrayed—was it his friends who had hurt him so badly? Was this a bit of history?

"For thine is the kingdom and the power and the glory, for ever and ever."

Brian and I left. I never met the good Father Inkling again. "Amen."

Saint John: Centenary-Queen Square United Church
Tuesday, Nov. 17, 1992, 11:25 a.m.

"Now to the one who can keep us from falling …" Jude 24

"… Remember that God is always with us."

Protestant funerals are brief. With the conclusion of the Lord's Prayer and a final benediction, the service is over. All that remains is the committal—not in the cemetery, of course, but according to the plans of Captain Jims.

I close off the service with a brief explanation:

"Friends, Gordon requested, just before he died, to be buried at sea, and so we will be driving to St. Martin's immediately after this service. I have arranged for a second limousine to be on hand, if any of you would wish to come to the seaside. We will be travelling out beyond into the harbour although the ceremony will be brief. We will reconvene then on the wharf by the lighthouse at 12:45 p.m. Thank you … thank you all for your love and support of Gordon for so many years and of me in the past few days. God grant us all peace and joy in believing. Go now in peace and in much love to live fully this precious and fleeting gift we call life."

As I walked out to the front door, I tried to steady my heart and steel my composure for the greetings from friends, all the while fighting down my fear of the rollicking and rolling ride that awaited me within the hour.

O joy! A fishing boat, on the Fundy coast, a weighted coffin and a few parting words.

CHAPTER NINE

The Committal

Rule one: At the graveside, keep the hounds at bay! Death is no time
for slothful performance ... priests and pastors everywhere, I say:
"Take charge. Do your job. Stand boldly in the valley of the shadow.
Tweak Satan's beard. Chain up the dogs of fear. Your job at the cemetery is to hold back the chaos and squelch the demons."

A.B. Lard, *Funeral Pyres and Hell's Fire,*
Spiritual Warfare at the Graveside.

Montreal: Bank of Montreal,
Office of Accounts Manager, Mr J. Tompkins
Monday, December 10, 1917, 7:35 p.m.

It was late. Too late to work, too early to sleep. Tompkins knew his
wife was waiting at home, but he couldn't leave the office. Not yet. The
memory of Pte. Davis was still troubling him. How could a man, so lost
and hurt, also be so gentle and kind?

He told himself he had done the right thing. The bequest was
divided carefully with a nest egg set aside for Mr. Davis, should he ever
look for it. A safety deposit box was ordered which Tompkins paid for
out of his own pocket. He placed the file verifying Gordon's requests
and stipulating the amount that had been held back for his use should
he ever need it in the box. Tompkins slipped the key to the deposit box
into an envelope with the beneficiary documents to be sent to the name
and address Gordon had provided. He added a simple penned note.

"Dear Ms. Hinks. Gordon Davis asked me to undertake the enclosed transactions. He wanted you to have everything. I have no idea where he is living or indeed if he has a forwarding address. It seemed he wanted to disappear. He left without giving any other instructions. I have no way knowing if he will contact you or me again. Should you meet him, could you please ask him to return my fountain pen? It has special significance for me ... a gift from my wife on our wedding day. You'll know it's mine for it is inscribed: "Love bears all things and believes all things."

Thank you ... I am most appreciative, J. Tompkins.

Tompkins rocked back in his chair for a moment. Thought about his wife, how much they had lost, and then sealed the letter to be sent the following day. Closing the safety deposit box, he set it aside to be returned to the vault by the night manager.

Bay of Fundy, New Brunswick:
2 miles south of St. Martin's Lighthouse
Tuesday, Nov. 17, 1992, 1:35 p.m.

The lobster trawler rocks with each swell as the captain attempts to keep it stationary. Huddled under a small canopy at the back of the cabin are the undertaker—old man Ferguson came out himself, his assistant, the captain of the boat, the stranger from the church, a couple of nurses from the Buttress Home and me.

We're all staring at the coffin resting where lobster traps normally sit. Like a mute Greek chorus, we stand, waiting and watching. Hoping for what? Could someone begin?

No one moves.

The water laps the hull, wind whistles through the cluster of antennae fixed to the cab's roof. The sun peeks out from behind a dark cloud and bathes our faces in heat and light.

Ferguson coughs.

All that was Gordon Davis, all the secrets of his insanity and reasons for his wanderings, will all sink below the rising tides of the Bay of Fundy. I am struck by the finality of it all. What is left of his thoughts? What will remain of his actions? He'll leave a handful of vague memories. But once the few who cared to know him are gone, what then? No one will raise a glass in his honour, or recall how he told this joke or that story. He won't be listed on any church memorial plaques. No sombre priest will read his name during Remembrance Day services. They won't even notice his absence at the Buttress Home for the Aged. Gordon is gone …. that's it.

And what of me? Death will stalk me too. A day will come when I will go out to the cemetery with a similar group of onlookers as those crowded beside me now. And after a few holy words are spoken, they will return to their cars, but I will not.

A second cough from Ferguson and a gentle nudge wakes me. With resolute steps, I walk to Gordon's coffin, run a hand over the grey muslin and sigh. "This is it then, Gordon," I whisper. I begin an appropriate Scripture reading for burial at sea. "This Psalm is traditionally read at burials at sea and speaks directly about Gordon's life.

> *I will keep watch over my tongue … will muzzle my mouth when the wicked are around. I was as silent as a mute person; I said nothing, not even something good, and my distress deepened. My heart within me became incensed … the fire burned. Then I spoke out….*
>
> *Surely every person at their best is a puff of wind. In fact, people walk around as shadows. They busy themselves for nothing, heaping up possessions …. How long, Lord, will I wait expectantly? I have placed my hope in you. Deliver me from all my offences, and do not let fools scorn me …. (Psalm 39)*

"God of the depths and heights of all creation, receive into your care this brother here departed … faithful in life, faithful in death …."

Fredericton, New Brunswick: Isaac's Way Restaurant
Monday, April 14, 2014, 11:55 a.m.

I needn't have worried. I recognized Patricia Patterson the instant I saw her approaching. I'd been studying the art display on the far wall and she waltzed into my line of sight. A stately, very fashionable pinstripe suit. She was all business, with a no-fuss manner. She had said she was retiring, but unless she was enjoying freedom 45, she looked much more youthful than her actual age. Blond hair, cut short. A round, pleasing face. Very intelligent eyes. In one hand she held a small briefcase, with the other she unconsciously checked the front of her suit jacket. Turning, her eyes met mine.

I waved. I needn't have.

Without hesitation she strode to my table. I stood. She sat. We shook hands and she smile and said, "Christopher, thank heavens we are alone. I have good news and bad. Which would you like first?"

Without thinking I opted for the "good" news.

In response she slid two envelopes across the table.

Montreal: Christ Church Cathedral
Sunday, December 9, 1917, 10:55 a.m.

"In the name of the Father and Son and Holy Ghost ... help me to speak faithfully now ... and always." Gordon coughed quietly and ended his prayer with a simple "Amen."

He looked up and tried to smile. He was standing in the centre of the chancel, an ornate eagle lectern to his right and a fancifully carved oak chair to his left. He glanced about. It was a holy space designed to exalt creation: a vaulted roof with a rainbow of colours accenting the ceiling sconces and mouldings; the polished slate floor reflecting every scuffle; ancient stained glass windows filtered all the rays of the sun, transforming them into biblical scenes of sorrow and joy.

Gordon was not used to public speaking so it was with greater effort that he looked directly at the crowd. He smiled slightly. They were hushed, shoehorned into every space in every pew and spilling back into the narthex. Apparently, Gordon was a big deal. No one wanted to miss a word of what this disheveled soldier would say.

Bishop Hinks stood at his side, silent.

Gordon coughed again.

Hinks turned to Gordon, rested a hand on his shoulder and said in a low voice, "Don't be afraid. Speak the truth as you saw it!"

Gordon smiled back and turning to the audience.

"Friends ... I hope I can call you that ... friends .... It is such a rich word: 'Friends.' You may take yours for granted, not even notice that they surround you. I was like that. My friends were an optional diversion on the journey, companions to be taken up and cast off as needed. Friends. As a soldier I have lost all of mine ... friends that is. None now live. I ... ah ... I live with their ghosts. I swore to each that I would not forget them. Sometimes they heard me and were content—their dying eyes holding me to my promise. Other times they were already dead, and so my pledge of remembrance was an oath to myself."

"Bishop Hinks," Gordon turned to him and smiled broadly. "Bishop Hinks asked if I would speak to you today of my experiences of war. I will not extoll the glory of battle or the triumph of victory. I want simply to hold up before you the faces of my friends. Let their lives and the manner of their deaths speak to you of war. In the final analysis, war is not about combat, tactics or strategies. It is an endless and tragic litany of lost lives like these I will name."

"There was Bob ... I don't know his last name ... we all just called him Bob ... have no idea even if that's his real name. Big hulking fellow from Peterborough, Ontario, loved to tell us tall tales, the marvels of his hometown. Had a sweetheart back home, waiting for him. His brother went missing at Vimy. Bob could eat a can of bully beef faster than any man in the unit. Shot across the eyes by a German sniper. He never knew what took him."

"And Jack, the sniper of our unit. He had a mouth like a sewer and a heart of gold. He could hit a button on a German tunic at 100 yards. Gruff and taciturn, he was like the rock of Gibraltar for all new recruits. Taught us how to keep alive, and stay well. Jack's gun jammed just as a German wave came across no man's land. Had nothing but his hands to defend himself. Took a bayonet in his gut, died three days later. I have no idea where Jack came from or whom he left behind. All I know is he left a big hole in our courage."

"And how about John?" Gordon smiled recalling John's face and continued, "John was a great party animal. Small, but strong. He could pack away more booze than anyone in the unit and you'd never know. Would just as soon sing a bawdy song as fight. On leave behind the forward trenches, John would scout out the best billet, scrounge up some music ... a troop of singers, a few instruments or, in one case, a gramophone. 'Music is the lifeblood of this army,' he would shout. He set us at ease, when we were waiting for an attack, by whistling a ditty. John was lost in the first wave at Vimy. Direct hit from a German mortar. Nothing left to bury. We called him 'Daddy Caruso.'"

"Then ... Max, a trickster ... 'Max the mouth,' we'd call him. Max knew more dirty jokes than anyone else in the regiment. We'd have contests to see who could better him ... 'joke battles' we called them. He never lost. Max must have a family somewhere in the Maritimes, because he received the most exotic care packages—dulse (that's a purple seaweed), smoked ham, nut cakes. Last time I saw Max he was leaping up from the firing trench at Passchendaele. No one saw him after that. I guess he was buried in the mud."

Gordon had been speaking so frankly and fondly of his mates that he had no idea of the power of his words. The audience was transfixed. A number had tears in their eyes. The humour made the pictures all the more poignant. They began to see war as a collage of wounded faces.

"There was Francois Dubé. I never knew him personally. Someone said he was called 'iron fist' because of the way he could hold tight to a Lewis gun ... that's a machine gun. He came from this city. Montreal. Lived over near St.-Henri I think. He was ... ah ... caught ... running back to our lines during the assault on Vimy .... Our own commander Ryan had him shot at dawn for desertion. I was there. He didn't deserve it. My sergeant said he was a brave man caught with no way to protect himself. So he ran. War is not pretty and certainly not too careful about fine distinctions between prudence and cowardice."

Audible gasps could be heard throughout the sanctuary.

Gordon continued stating the facts with thundering clarity. "I lost three mates in my stretcher company at Passchendaele. Gary, the one we called 'moose-breath.' He was from a funny little place in New

Brunswick called 'Riley Brook.' Marty from Rimbey, Alberta. Marty said he once road his horse through the town barber shop. And Val … a French-speaking buddy from Quebec City. Val couldn't put together a complete English sentence. He had one stalk phrase for everything: 'Thank you very please.'"

Here a few chuckles broke out. Gordon continued, "Val had a nice dad who would send letters almost every day and a fiancé who sent kisses to all the men in Val's unit. Nice. I lost all three of those guys in the first minute of the battle—machine guns from our right flank cut them in half. It took double the time to gather up all the parts."

Gordon looked down at the floor, trying to recall other faces and names. "There was Belch … never knew his real name, but you can imagine what he was famous for. Died of gangrene that set in after he cut his foot on a broken bottle. Ah … Frank the fart … again a pretty clear picture of him. His sister would write to him every Sunday, praying for his soul, and, from where we stood, Frank could use all the prayers he could get. Went missing at Vimy. Oh, yes, there were the three brothers: Jesse, Josh and Al. Jesse died of the fever and trench rot. Josh was lost to a German sniper and Al went missing on a night raid … never found him. A shame they all went. Their dad will be lost without his boys to work the farm in Kindersley!"

"Oh, yes, there was Terry." Gordon was so tied up in the recounting of the sorrows of his friends that he was into his next description before he realized who was standing beside him. Ah … I … ah," he glanced sideways and saw the grief in Hinks' eyes, but the bishop gave a nod of his dead for Gordon to continue.

At that moment there came a bustling at the back of the church as a uniformed officer strode into the church … exuding power. He was followed by a flank of MP's. Heads turned, but Gordon kept going "There was Terry, Terry Hinks … the son of our Bishop of Montreal … I never met him until I was called to drag him from no man's land. He was badly …."

Silently a side door opened, and Thelma and Johanna crept into the sanctuary. They whispered to each other and took a seat by the east transept. Hinks looked down and saw his daughter and lover and smiled ever so slightly in their direction. Johanna was beaming at Gordon, but Gordon's mind and gaze was fixed on the Lieutenant Colonel who was marching down the aisle. "Terry was badly hurt, but he had been a valiant soldier who gave his …."

Gordon never finished his sentence. Lieutenant Colonel Ryan pointed toward Davis, barked out a command, "Seize that man," and watched as the MP's ran forward, took hold of Gordon and began to strong arm him down the aisle toward their commanding officer. Ryan, now taking command of the audience announced, "I am arresting Gordon Davis on charges of gross cowardice, desertion of duty, dereliction of duty and insubordination. He will be court martialed under my authority."

Gordon made to protest. "I haven't finished … I want to …."

Ryan had been expecting trouble, he came prepared. "Gag that man, corporal." And in a flash Gordon was silenced.

A female voice rang out from Ryan's left, "Unhand him … Gordon … Gordon, please …"

Gordon heard the voice and turned, but as he struggled to free himself, the corporal, suspecting his charge might try to bolt, give him a quick clout with his rifle butt and knocked the prisoner senseless.

Ryan snapped, "No need for violence. March this worthless man out of here."

Hinks watched in growing horror and finally found his voice. "This is a house of God, a sanctuary and under my authority. How dare you barge in here and seize this man! He was—"

Ryan cut Hinks off and shouted, "He was a coward … Silence, old man! I have all the authority I need in this uniform. The man's a deserter and will be punished."

Here Cruikshank leapt up in his seat. "Let the officer do his duty."

Hawthorne rang out from the other side of the church. "I can't believe it … but, if the army says he's a deserter, who are we to question army intelligence?"

Johanna continued shouting Gordon's name. She struggled to make her way through the pews to where he was being dragged off.

"Army intelligence," Hinks spat out his derision. "There's an oxymoron. The man is guiltless. Gordon Davis is one of the most ...."

Ryan again cut Hinks' protests, "My Lord, let me do my duty .... Any further interference in this matter will require me to question your loyalty and to interrogate all your acquaintances ...." Here Ryan made a point of looking directly at Thelma Lint and back to the bishop, "... and who knows what sins I might uncover?" The threat was clear and Hinks went dead silent.

Thelma was reeling. How could Ryan have known about their relationship?

Cruikshank smiled to himself. "Ryan played that superbly. We'll have Hinks where we want him before the day is through."

The crowd was deathly still, not knowing whom to believe or what to do. Ryan stood in the centre of their silence ... allowing his personal power to impress itself upon them. Slowly he turned on his heels and walked out of the sanctuary, following his company of men who were dragging Gordon, none too tenderly, along with them.

Stunned silence.

With the click of the back door, the crowd erupted. Angry voices, doubting voices, questioning, berating, blustering voices. The church was a mad house. Hinks stood at the front alone, silent. Such was the confusion of the crowd that no one noticed the tears in his eyes, tears that poured down his cheeks as he gazed at Thelma. She watched him from her place and knew that he was weeping from guilt over keeping silent, from his own sense of cowardice and vulnerability. Her heart ached for her knight in shining armour, for he had just discovered he was frail and fallen. She mouthed the words, "I love you," and stood her ground proudly.

Montreal: Thelma Lint's Gentlemen's Parlour
Monday, December 10, 1917, 9:58 a.m.

Jo had been up early, walking with Samuel, trying to shake her deep anxiety. Replaying and replaying the last night's events—trying to piece together some pattern to what had happened. She longed to find a way to salvage Gordon's virtue and their love, but it seemed impossible.

Long after he had fallen asleep she continued walking. It had been torture watching her fiancé stumble through his written speech. It hadn't sounded like him at all. And his appearance …. He was obviously broken and beaten. He looked close to death and had clearly contracted a monstrous cold in his throat.

He had also been clear. No mincing of his words.

Gordon had denied their love … publicly … hadn't he? Jo tried again to think of his exact words. "I love no one." It was hard to recall all he said. His cough had been so persistent nearing the end of his speech, that she could barely piece together his phrases. What came next??? "I who went to Thelma Lint's to find my heart's desire. I am part of Hawthorne's circle of boys. I am a coward, a deserter. I have lost my faith. I broke my promise. I don't love any woman. I am not engaged." Yes … he had said it plainly and yet Johanna was unwilling to let it go. To Thelma it sounded like rejection … even to her father, who was inclined to trust Gordon more than she had imagined. It was a clear message. "He's not the same man," Hinks had offered earlier that night. "The war has taken away the Gordon we knew and left a beaten, broken wretch in his place."

But Johanna thought otherwise. What if it was a puzzle? For several minutes she beat out a path in the carpet trying to think what kind of clue might help her unravel Gordon's secret message. What if he was being forced to say something against his will? … What if … Johanna stopped dead in her tracks. "Oh my God! That's it!" She ran to Thelma's room, knocked urgently and passed Samuel to Thelma almost before the door was open. "Here … take Samuel …. I have worked it out …. Gordon still loves me. I know he does … I'm off to find him."

Thelma tried to slow Johanna down, "Please child, not so fast … what are you saying?"

Johanna was not about to be stopped now that she had discovered the truth. "I can't talk now …. I'll explain all when I get back here with Gordon."

"But," Thelma protested, "You don't know where he is … no one does. The military police have been searching all night no doubt …. If anyone has him, they do."

"I know he's not with the military. I just know. He's waiting at Sisson Ridge Park." With those words Johanna literally ran down the stairs and flew out the door. If she had stayed a second longer at Thelma's door, she might have noticed her father rising from bed to intervene.

Thelma closed the door and smiled at Hinks, "Well, Douglas … this is how it starts. One minute you're a parent and the next you're a babysitter."

Fredericton: Isaac's Way Restaurant
Monday, April 14, 2014, 11:57 a.m.

Turning the first envelope over in my hand, it's empty save for a small object lodged at one end. I looked up at Patricia. "May I open it?"

"We found it in a safety deposit box that belonged to Gordon Davis. You are listed as next-of-kin. So as far as the law is concerned," she spoke with authority, "you are the owner of that safety deposit box. Whatever is in these envelopes is your property."

The waiter brought my shiraz. Patricia asked for coffee.

I took up the first envelope slowly and tore open one end. Turning it sideways, a silver necklace fell out. An ornate Greek cross with a crown on the upper portion of the upright and a maple leaf on each of the other three arms. On the back, a bold inscription: 02698 Pte. G. H. Davis. Ironic! The Canadian government had chosen what was known as the "peaceful cross" or "square" cross as its symbol for the Canadian Expeditionary Force.

Gordon. My great-uncle. Final proof.

"That obviously once belonged to your uncle Gordon Davis. We have every reason to believe this is the same man 'Gordon' whom you buried in Saint John!"

I sat in the restaurant and turned the ID tag over and over in my fingers. Could it be that simple? My hand was trembling as I reached for the second envelope.

Montreal: Military Detention Block, Dorchester Armouries
Sunday, December 9, 1917, 3:40 p.m.

Ryan left Davis shackled to a chair—hands and legs both. He was trembling from the cold as he sat alone in the complete darkness of the isolation cell. Several hours before, the lieutenant colonel had banged open the door with an abruptness designed to make even the most stalwart soldier feel small and vulnerable.

Gordon looked up, but the sudden light caused him to lower his head shading his eyes. Did he cower a bit in his chair?

"What happened at Vimy, Davis? You get chicken? Run out on your buddies?" Ryan had done his homework and had pieced together the fragments of his notes coming up with a complete picture of Private Gordon Davis. "You yellow-bellied slob …. We'll make you pay."

Gordon had no idea where to begin. "I wasn't running. I was cut down by a—"

"By an attack of appendicitis …." Ryan approached and shouted in Davis's ear, "I read the bloody doctor's report. A load of shit. He just covered your sorry ass."

"It's true, ah … I was …." Gordon tried to inject certainty into his voice, but his fatigue made his words sound weak. "I did have an infected …."

Ryan cut him off. "Shut up, scum. This is not a conversation. I've just spoken to my superiors and we've agreed on a full-blown trial for you, Davis. Every sorry detail will be front-page news. You will be Canada's poster boy for cowardice. The military will roast you alive. The public will spit on your picture and all your pretty friends in the church will disown you."

Gordon tried to rally. "I have no friends anywhere …. I'm alone."

"Don't fuss with me, boy." Here Ryan kicked Gordon's chair out from under him and he fell with a crash to the floor. "Asshole! We know about your pretty little tart … and her bleeding heart father, Bishop Hinks. We also have the goods on his yellow-bellied son Terrance. Oh, and don't forget the whorehouse mother …. We'll expose them all. Your little girlfriend first of all!"

"No!" Gordon moaned. There was blood in his mouth. "No, it would kill her."

"Her?" Ryan's lips spat it out as if it were slime. "Her? I don't give a shit about 'her.' This is war, boy! Plenty of casualties!"

"No!" Gordon cried. "No, not her ... please ... I beg you leave her out of this."

Ryan crouched down beside his victim. "Oh yes ... yes," he whispered quietly. "She'll be smeared with your disgrace and that of her brother. The whole lot of them will all be dragged through the mud because of you. Oh, we have dirt on all of them. Thelma Lint's a whore and pimp ....Even your pretty Bishop Hinks ... Our good Dr. Cruikshank caught him visiting at Thelma Lint's brothel. And your Johanna ... with her Samuel ... need I say more!"

"No ... please ... take me, do what you want to me ... but not the others. Leave them out of it." Gordon struggled to roll over so he could look at Ryan but the lieutenant colonel put his riding boot firmly on the chair leg and held Davis in place.

"Brave words from a coward," Ryan laughed. "I'm afraid there's nothing I can do. It's out of my hands now ...." He whirled around quickly and went to the door.

"Please," Gordon pleaded.

"Grovel all you like; I can't do a thing to help low-life like you." Here Ryan laughed loudly and turned back to face Gordon. "You know, Davis .... it would have been better for you and your friends if you had disappeared in battle. Now they'll suffer your dishonour forever. Ta ta." Ryan grasped the cell door and was about to pull it shut when Gordon cried out.

"No ... wait ..." Gordon moaned, "I'll do anything you ask .... Say anything you want ... just keep my friends out of it."

Ryan smiled to himself. "Men are so weak and predictable," he thought. "All right," he said aloud, "maybe I can do something to avoid a scandal ... if ... if ...." He pretended to be weighing many factors. "Let's see ...." Long pause. "If you ... if you go back to that church meeting and ... and ... ah, if you say what I tell you ...."

"I'll do anything."

Ryan walked back to his prisoner, crouched down close and said softly, "That's right ... you will and when I'm through ... you'll beg for death ... but for now, you'll start by telling that church crowd exactly what I want them to hear."

Ryan left Gordon alone on the floor to ponder his fate.

Alone.

Montreal: The Corner of Rushbrooke and Charlevoix Streets,
Monday, December 10, 1917, 5:37 p.m.

Gordon had no plan. He hadn't designed anything quite as elaborate as a disappearance. His mental fatigue and spiritual exhaustion had taken over hours back. He wandered aimlessly, not heading for nor avoiding any landmark or street address. "Just don't think," he'd said to himself. "Stop thinking."

For the past 25 minutes he had stood motionless at the corner of two unfamiliar streets. Not knowing or caring what he would do.

It was perhaps his motionless state that first alerted a Montreal beat cop, Robert Wallace, that he had a problem case. A torn uniform was not news. Even a uniform standing alone on street corner. No big deal. But a uniformed man, not moving, covered in mud and blood, that was problem. Robert lost no time calling for some help to detain this stranger. "You never know ... Sarge ... One of these loonies from the war ... seeing a cop ... hell, he might go crazy. And this one's a big bruiser."

When backup arrived, Robert led his posse toward the still motionless man. They approached carefully, not taking any chances. A few had their nightsticks ready for action.

It was all over before it began. The dangerous stranger went limp at the touch of Wallace's hand on his shoulder. He seemed unable to speak. His eyes were blank.

"Another one," cursed Robert ... "Third one this month. Shell-shocked out of their minds, these guys are. 'Flanders disease.' Poor buggers. Better ship him off to the Douglas Hospital for assessment. They'll know where to send him."

Unwittingly, the police officer had given Gordon his script, a script he would follow diligently for more than seventy years. "Just keep silent," he said to himself. "Don't think anything, don't look like you know what's happening and people will assume you're out of your tree. No questions, no inquiries, no isolation chambers, no torture, no fuss."

So simple: death by silence.

> Montreal
> Monday, October 14, 1916 Thanksgiving Day
>
> Dear Gordon:
>
> You've been so silent ... but now ... I got your note and you accept! What a burden has lifted from my heart. I feel like shouting. I'll wait 'til the house is empty. Please know that I can hardly contain my joy ... we will grow old together and share so many things.
>
> I can hardly believe your words on the page. "We are to be married." I could jump out of my skin. This is such a blessed and bright Thanksgiving Day. I will always remember it.
>
> I love you ... and now I will call you my husband-to-be.
>
> I am with you always, husband-to-be!
>
> Still no word from Terrance. We think he made it to France, but apart from that ... nothing. How my soul is tortured over what could happen to him. If he was wounded ... or killed ... it would be the end of me. It would be like a piece of me had been cut out.

But you ... you my fiancé (isn't that delicious word).
I'll say it again. You, my fiancé, you will never
leave me ...

If you were shot ... well, I think our love would keep
us connected somehow. Remember what we said
about our love? It is one of the "great" loves that
we enjoy and we shall never be lost to each other
because of it. How fortunate we are.

This Thanksgiving we are entertaining a crowd as
per usual. Father has taken it into his head to be
benevolent to the poor of the street, so our table
will be ringed by strangers—the lame, blamed and
shamed. We had to order a second turkey from
an Anglican parishioner in the eastern townships.
Fresh and plucked ... I am to be the chef.

Those two birds and mountains of potatoes await
me ... I had better get off to the kitchen.

In the meantime, ... Just know that I love you.

Jo

Montreal: Military Detention Block, Dorchester Armouries
Sunday, December 9, 1917, 6:40 p.m.

Hawthorne stepped gingerly into the isolation cell, his black robe neatly
in place, Bible under his arm. He wanted to fulfil his errand and escape.
He was both disgusted and frightened by Gordon's condition.

"Gordon," he squeaked.

Gordon, who had finally managed to roll over, was lying on the
back of the chair, his hands still bound by shackles. He closed his eyes.
"Get out!"

Hawthorne tried his pastor voice, "My son, I just wanted ..."

Gordon snapped, "Don't you 'my son' me ... you little gutter slug."
His eyes flashed thunder. "Just get out."

Hawthorne was shocked and stepped back involuntarily. His priestly
decorum was too well-fixed to be shaken by angry shouts. "I am not
going to take up much of your time ... Just wanted to deliver a note from
your mom. I've had it in my Bible for some time ... got it one Sunday
after service from your sister, and we ... I mean ... I said I would deliver
it to you if I ever saw you. Your sister thought I might ... well, being
connected to the church and the military and all ..." Hawthorne took a
note from his Bible and held it out at arm's length.

Gordon looked up, saw the note and laughed. "What am I supposed
do ... my hands are tied, ... or did you miss that small point?"

Hawthorne was uncertain, "I ... ah ... I can just leave it here then."
He placed it on the floor close to Gordon's legs. "Maybe the guard will
open it for you later ... or I could do it ... if ...."

Gordon's temper broke, "You've done your duty ... now ...
bugger off!"

Hawthorne made as to speak, but the glaring anger of Gordon's
voice silenced his tongue and he left the way he came, silently and
deeply troubled.

Fredericton: Isaac's Way Restaurant
Monday, April 14, 2014, 11:56 a.m.

"Before you open that second letter, I want you to understand all that I
have discovered." Patricia Patterson had no small talk. I was expecting a
slow descent into our business. A few confirming questions, a comment
on the ride to Fredericton. Something to establish a relationship.
Nothing. Down to business.

Patricia was speaking quickly, assuming I would keep up. "Your
great-uncle Gordon Davis was a wealthy man. I think I told you that."
Swinging her briefcase onto the table between us, she opened it and
withdrew several files. "Indeed it appears he had a considerable estate.
But strangely, it was largely hidden, even from him, I believe. It was only
found recently, when I checked his name against the bank-closed back

files. A routine step that we now do, but it was missed somehow at his death. Perhaps they had no real ability to cross-reference at that time. Thank God for the internet." Here Patricia, paused and apologized, "I am sorry, I did not mean to swear ...."

"It's okay," I said, "I say it all the time."

Patricia relaxed slightly. "Yes ... well ... Our first clue ... we found a bank account that has been dormant since 1917 in Gordon's name. The residual of an even larger estate that he somehow transferred to a third party. Johanna Hinks? Do you know that name?"

"Well ... not exactly. Gordon's letters ... many of them were signed by a 'Jo.' Maybe that's her." I looked out the window, the Beaverbrook Hotel was shining in the midday sun. "Did she stay in touch or ...."

"It appears she was not familiar with this account. No evidence of any interaction of any kind from anyone. The money just sat there and grew year-by-year. A well-managed nest egg, it appears. You can thank a certain Mr. Tompkins of the Bank of Montreal for your good fortune. He looked after the portfolio personally for what looks like his entire career. Took it through the depression without losing a penny and then cashed in big-time in the forties. But he is the only agent on file. Apparently, he paid personally for the deposit box associated with the account."

"Tompkins? Don't know that name. I assume you've asked about him."

"Died back in the seventies." Patricia consulted a second file. "No explanation of his personal attention to this account. Must have had something to do with the war. Perhaps he saw Gordon as a patriot to be helped. There we have it!"

"At Gordon's funeral," I looked at Patricia carefully, "there was a stranger .... I can't recall her name. We only talked for a few minutes on the boat after the committal at sea. She told me quite a tale about her grandmother and the man she claimed was her grandfather and maybe my great-uncle. She was going to get back to me with details ... said she had some leads. I've been trying to remember her name .... I think she would be next-of-kin and deserving of this inheritance."

Patricia consulted her file, "Heather?"

"That's it!" I snap my fingers. "Tall lovely woman. Heather Davis ... did you ...."

"Died in early 1993, a fluke accident." Patricia consulted her file again. "Well ... a murder actually. She was in the bank where we found the safety deposit box and was mortally wounded in a failed bank robbery."

"Maybe she was going to open the safety deposit box ...."

"Her death basically made that lead go cold."

"Probably why I never heard from her after." I looked at Patricia's file. "Is that it, then? All the surprises?" It sounded like a complaint. "Sorry. I don't mean to sound churlish. I guess I was expecting something ... not sure what but ... but something more startling." I sighed, "I spent 14 hours on a bike last night playing with different scenarios."

Patricia was not to be put off. "There is more, Christopher. On further inquiry, we discovered last week that a safety deposit box had been opened in conjunction with this account in early December of 1992. I petitioned the bank and had it opened and the contents sent to me. It contained information on the bank account and the two envelopes which you now have ...."

A brief pause, I took up the second ... and held it to the light.

Montreal: Military Detention Block, Dorchester Armouries
Sunday, December 9, 1917, 7:50 p.m.

No bread, pitiful little water, complete darkness.

Gordon was still lying on the floor. His legs were numb and his fingers tingled.

Ryan pushed the door open ... again with a great bang. A sergeant walked behind him with a small table and chair. Together they lifted Gordon to a sitting position, placed the table in front of him.

Ryan took his chair from his underling and sat down facing Davis.

"Okay, Davis, here's the deal." He looked closely at Gordon's blinking eyes. "You with me?"

Gordon nodded.

"Good," Ryan took a deep breath. "Good ... now I am only going to say this once, so you had better think sharp and pay attention." Ryan paused for a beat, looking closely at Davis again and assured himself that his prisoner was tracking. "Here's how you can keep your friends out of the news and avoid having their dirty linen aired in public. You will be taken back to that church meeting and you will be allowed to finish your speech ... except, this time, you will read a statement that I have prepared." Here Ryan took a single folded sheet from his inner pocket, unfolded it, and laid it in front of Gordon. "It's a simple declaration of your guilt as a deserter, and your sincere request that the people hearing you will endorse the 'Holy War' proposition of Dr. Cruikshank. It concludes with an affirmation of the importance of the homeland war effort and of your undying loyalty to the Allied cause. Simple ... do it as it's written, and your friends will be spared. Stray from it, and I'll crucify them and you. Don't add a single thing, not a syllable more or less. You with me Davis?"

Gordon managed a single word, "Yes."

"Yes what?"

"Yes ... sir"

"That's better." Ryan's thin lips smiled malevolently, "You will appear repentant—because you have seen the error of your ways."

"Yes, sir," Gordon spoke quietly.

"And when you are done your little speech, you will be taken back here and I will decide how to get rid of you. ... Are we clear, soldier?"

"Yes, sir."

"Good ... very good. Now the sergeant here will take off your shackles and we'll give you a few minutes to collect your thoughts." Ryan rose from the chair and leaned so close to Gordon he could smell his prisoner's foul breath, "Don't mess with me, Davis, or I'll have your balls for breakfast...." Straightening up, he noticed the opened envelope on the floor, and he looked at it closely "... someone send you a love letter? O yes, Hawthorne said he was bringing you some mail." Turning it over Ryan saw Gordon's sister's name and address. "Who's this ... 'Mabel Davis' ... your mom? No? I think it must be your sister. Won't she be happy to know there's a coward in the family." He threw the note on the table. "... Well, pack it away quickly ... we're almost ready to go!"

Ryan left the room quickly and had no idea that the letter he had just given to Gordon would be his undoing.

Once the sergeant was gone and his hands were free, he tore open the letter. He was too tired to cry, but he read of his father's painful burden, recognized at once its deeper meaning and what he would do about it. A slow smile touched his lips as he devised a way to protect Jo, her father … and bring his enemies to justice.

Hamilton
Thursday Nov. 15, 1917

Dear Gordon:

I am weak now. It's time. Tonight I think. I'll get Lil to send this before I sleep.

Oh how I wished I could see you before … before I die … There! I said it. I am dying and there seems to be nothing that I, nor the Lord can do to stop it. I am so sorry to leave you … but I know your sisters will take my place and welcome you back to Barton Street and our family circle.

Please don't fret on my account.

Gordon, I have no wise words to leave with you. I will rely on all the good advice I have given you over the years and trust you will find your own pathway to truth. Be true to yourself and all will be well. You may not know it now, but we all saw greatness in your soul …

Alas, writing does tire me out and so I feel I must end soon. Mabel said she would make sure you get this note … how … I will leave that up to her.

There is one thing you can do for me. Try to cheer up your father if you can … by letter or in person

when you return. Tonight he came home from
church in a terrible mood. I have never seen him
so dejected. Just keeps muttering about the church
and letting down his boys. I think I even heard him
swear and curse. So unlike him. When I asked,
all he would say is that's it's nothing for me to
worry about. But he is deeply worried. Mentioned
Reverend Hawthorne twice and none too politely.
Maybe you know what he's talking about. Please
help him. I sense anger in his heart and perhaps
even some guilt … I can't figure it out. I'll have to
leave that one to you.

You know that I will always love you and will never
leave your side.

Mother

Montreal: Christ Church Cathedral
Sunday, December 9, 1917, 8:35 p.m.

"I am a coward and a deserter." Gordon's hands were shaking as he read
the prepared statement. He held the papers on his Bible … they had at
least not taken away his letters and Bible. These he now gripped tightly
… to steady his nerves.

The crowd at the church was stone silent. Many were shocked and
some were confused, but all listened intently. "I have lost faith with my
brothers in arms and I am ashamed of how I ran from the battle, letting
them and my country down. I no longer deserve to be called a soldier."

Gordon heard a gasp from Jo, who was sitting near the back of the
church with her father and Thelma.

"I broke my promise, and I am deeply sorry for being such a coward
and turncoat." Gordon coughed and somewhere in the silence of
sanctuary a voice muttered "Shame," but Gordon ignored it and kept
on reading. "This morning I am speaking out of my own humiliation.
Kindly disregard the disparaging remarks I made about the war. After

reflection, I want to proclaim that there can be no more noble a cause than the current conflict. The forces of righteousness are in mortal combat with the forces of evil."

Gordon coughed several times and continued, "I urge you to support Dr. Cruikshank's proposal to declare this conflict a Holy War. (Another cough.) It is the most virtuous of ventures. If our church were to stand firm in the faith and acknowledge openly and proudly that in this battle God's will is written on the hearts of all Allied commanders and soldiers who raise arms against to foe ... then truly we could count ourselves as blessed." Gordon had to stop for a moment to clear his throat. He coughed several times and paused to catch his breath.

Gordon looked to his side and saw Ryan standing at attention, his eyes boring into his prisoner, willing him to finish the speech.

"It is God's will that keeps our solders strong. The church can do its part for the war by strengthening our resolve through a declaration of Holy War. Please ... I am a lost soul ... a coward. I love no man (Gordon coughed again) and no one could ever love me ... not now." Again someone in the audience uttered, "Shame!"

Cruikshank, who was sitting in the front pew beside Hawthorne, was beaming. "This was too good to be true," he thought. "We'll sweep the synod after this."

"Yes, the war is our God's way of bringing us to our knees and pointing our hearts toward the light, toward Flanders and the coming Kingdom of God." Gordon choked for a moment and then began again. "I stand before you convinced of this message. But disregard me ... see me as the result of our country's lack of resolve. I am a product of our weak soul. The church needs to put backbone into our community's faith in the army. Please don't let people like me ruin your picture of our fighting sons. I deserve your pity; they deserve your praise."

Ryan stepped forward. Now that the speech was finished he smiled down at Cruickshank and Hawthorne and approached Davis, hoping to escort him from the stage.

But Gordon was not finished. He coughed twice and said. "I have a further confession to make. I ... ah ... I am the basest of creatures for not only am I a coward," here Gordon turned his head and coughed

into his hand, "but I am also a licentious beast, seeking out sexual grati-
fication wherever I can find it. For the last few nights I have visited a
whorehouse. Yes. Dr. Cruikshank can verify this. He saw Bishop Hinks
at Thelma Lint's gentlemen's parlour. But the good bishop was there
trying to fetch me, save me in fact. It was I who went to Thelma Lint's to
find my heart's desire." Gordon coughed again. "But worse, I have been
part of a sexual circle of young lads both in the army and at home. You
see ... I don't love any woman, wouldn't get engaged to be married ever."

Here Ryan's eyes narrowed. He could smell trouble ... why was this
lazy coward going on ... and about relationships and sex??? He made to
grab Gordon and drag him off, but Cruikshank, who was caught up in
his victory, stood up to protest.

The principal waved a restraining hand at Ryan and winked, "Please
let him finish his confession ... it will be good for his mortal soul ... he's
obviously quite sick in body as well as spirit, so let him get it all out and
be done." Cruikshank sat down, believing he had put the final nail in
Hinks' coffin.

Gordon smiled, "Thank you, sir." Here a spate of coughing kept
Gordon from speaking for several seconds. "I was ... I am part of a
circle of boys who enjoyed each other ..." Gordon coughed again. "We
met through the church ... It was Reverend Hawthorne's circle of
boys. He taught us the Bible." Here Gordon lifted up his well-thumbed
Scriptures. "He taught us ... everything …. He came to know us very
well." Gordon coughed again and Ryan had had enough. He took Davis
by the arm and began to lead him to the side door of the sanctuary.

There was deep hush on the crowd. The footsteps of the officer and
his prisoner rang out like hammer blows. As they walked, Ryan whispered to Gordon, "You'll pay for this ... you'll bloody well pay."

They were at the door when a deep and loud voice called out, "Let
Davis stay for a moment please. I have further questions to put to him."

Ryan turned, still holding onto his victim. "What questions?" he
asked, frustration in every syllable.

Bishop Hinks spoke as he walked down the centre aisle of the
church. "Questions about what he just said. Did he mean to suggest
that our good and loyal servant ... the Reverend Hawthorne has been

interfering with little boys ... Surely not. I demand that this cowardly man Davis come forward and explain himself."

Ryan was not about to be ordered about by a prelate. For a moment he dropped his grip on Davis and strode into the middle of the chancel. "How dare you order me about! This man," and here he pointed to Gordon Davis or, rather, where Gordon Davis had been. Once Ryan had released his grip and addressed Hinks, Gordon had quietly slipped through the side door.

Vanished.

"Guards," Ryan shouted, "Guards! After that man."

The guards, who had been standing at the back of the church, ran down the main aisle to do his bidding. They had hardly started through the sanctuary, when a woman backed out of her seat and knocked several of the front-runners to their knees. The rest of the company was bustling about trying to get by the obstacle of their fallen comrades. Thelma had years of practice dealing with rambunctious men. "This is fun," she thought as she continued to trip and confound the MPs.

"Guards," Ryan shouted.

Hinks smiled and said to Ryan, "Alas, Colonel, you are not in charge here. God is!" And then in his best Anglican voice, he declared in a loud voice. "I have my own questions to put to my friend Reverend Hawthorne ...."

Bay of Fundy, New Brunswick:
2 miles south of St. Martin's Lighthouse
Tuesday, Nov. 17, 1992, 1:45 p.m.

Completing the prayer, we moved into the burial at sea ritual. Nodding to the undertakers, I said solemnly:

We now commit to Almighty God our shipmate, Gordon Davis, sending his body to the depth's and into God's safe keeping.

Ferguson and his assistant stepped forward, lifting the bow-facing end of Gordon's coffin ever so slightly. It was heavy, so I concluded quickly. "May the sea take back all that was once hers. May the Creator of Earth and sky and sea take Gordon to his final rest. Earth to earth, ashes to ashes, dust to dust."

They hefted the plywood platform and tipped it up dramatically. The oil we had painted lavishly on the underside of the coffin worked its magic. Gordon slipped quietly into the water. Lead weights and a few strategic air holes did their duty. After a few bobbing, bubbling sounds, the coffin sank beneath the waves and was gone.

"Let us pray:

Support us, all the day long of this troublous life, until the shadows lengthen and the evening comes, the busy world is hushed, the fever of life is over and our work is done. Then, Lord, in your mercy grant us a safe lodging, a holy rest, and peace at the last.

We trust in God's great mercy that as our brother departs this earth, he will know the love of his Creator and we trust in God's great mercy that when our time comes, we, too, shall know the blessedness of eternal rest and life everlasting."

Heads bowed.

"And may the peace of God which passes our understanding keep our hearts and minds in the knowledge and love of God, this day and always. Amen."

There was a scattering of "Amens." The boat rocked slightly to port, the wind picked up and howled through our little circle of mourners.

It's done!

I sighed inwardly, closed the service book and stepped out of the wind into the shelter of the cabin.

The woman, the stranger, smiled and uttered a word of thanks. She wiped a tear from her eye.

Instinctively I reached out a hand, "Are you all right?"

She smiled and said honestly, "No ... I ... No ... it's a long story."

Smiling, I led her to a bench and said, "We've got time."

"All right," she sighed. "Forgive me, I haven't introduced myself. My name is Heather Davis. I believe you just buried my grandfather .... I don't really know. It's all so crazy, ...but we have nothing really to go on. I never met this Gordon but even the idea that he might be my grandfather makes me cry. You see I have no family left. But my dad once said to me ..."

Saint John: Veterans Hospital, Ward B,
Friday, December 3, 1937, 10:15 a.m.

Opening the oak doors of the Saint John's Veteran's Hospital, Samuel could smell neglect in the air. They were all the same—these warehouses for the war's lost boys. How many had he visited? A dozen, closer to two.

A grey haired receptionist greeted him with a smile, "Can I help you?" Everyone offered help, but none could. He was looking for a father that quite obviously did not exist.

"Ah ...thank you," Samuel responded. "I am here to visit my father ... well, at least ... to try to find him."

"Excuse me?" A questioning gaze ... the same look he had met whenever he began his story.

"It's a long story, but my father went missing during the war."

"Ah ... but this is a hospital. Surely Veterans Affairs has records of all men missing in action, and I think ...."

A janitor came through the frosted doors at the right side of the foyer, set down a bucket and began to mop up the mud and slush tracked in from the day's snowstorm. "Damn salt," he muttered.

The receptionist interrupted her examination for a moment and eyed the janitor with suspicion. Then she continued, "We would not be able to help you with combat casualties. As I said, the Department of War or Veterans Affairs might be a better bet."

Samuel tried to explain, "Yes ... well that's the point. They lost him. 'Unavailable for discharge' is all that's in his record. I believe he went missing in Montreal sometime in early December 1917 and maybe … just maybe he was so shell-shocked that he was shipped to a medical facility."

Now the pity would come and as if on cue, the receptionist offered some. "I am sorry. What a sad tale, son. But I don't believe we have anyone here who would fit that description. All our vets are from the Maritimes … I don't think we can help …."

The janitor looked up from his pail. "What a bout 'Gaga Gordon?'" He had been listening and was free with his opinions. "Gordon's been here longer than anyone and no one knows where he's from."

The receptionist was about to dismiss this silly suggestion when Samuel interjected, "Gordon? His name is Gordon?"

"Yes … ah … as far as we know … he's somewhat of a mystery."

"May I …. May I see him?" Samuel asked slowly … not wanting to get his hopes up.

"Well, this is highly irregular and I don't know if …." The receptionist started to shuffle her papers, sorting through her thoughts and excuses.

The janitor, seeing the chance to avoid the drudgery of his work, didn't wait for permission, but simply offered, "I'll take you down to see him … don't believe he's ever had any visitors, so this will be a first for him." Off he went without a backward glance and Samuel followed along behind. As they walked down white- washed corridors, Samuel lectured himself to stay calm. Not to hope too much. Over the disappointing weeks of this trip, he had a thick skin over his hope. "Expect to find another war-torn stranger," he told himself. "What else could this Gordon be?"

The whole search-for-my-dad trip had been a frustratingly futile exercise. Maybe he'd write it up some day as his "looking for roots." Samuel's dream was set on journalism and his mind began to shape the article he would write for the *Montreal Gazette* or the *Toronto Star*. It would start with a list of expenses: train fare, hotels, café food. He'd then progress to the cost to his soul: false hope, disappointment. He'd been on the road now for seven weeks.

The janitor led the way to the very end of the corridor and down two flights of stairs. Over his shoulder he explained, "Hospital authorities put Gordon down here. 'More peaceful,' they say. But I think they just want him out of their sight. Can't be cured. Can't speak ... bit of a failure in their eyes, I reckon." He opened a basement door and directly opposite was a patient's room. A single bed with a single occupant. At the end of the bed a single word "Gordon."

"So here he is ... our 'Gaga Gordon.'" The janitor went to the bedside, touched Gordon on his cheek gently and shouted, "Got a guest to see you ... you old moose hide ... don't talk his head off." Looking down he saw Gordon's Bible on the floor. He picked it up, shoved some papers and letters back in place and put it on the bedside table where it always waited, unused, beside the fountain pen which was his only other possession. "Someone knocked off your Bible, did they? No one cares anymore! More's the pity." With a loving touch to Gordon's hand and nod to this new visitor, the janitor left.

Samuel looked down at a complete stranger. Not a flicker of recognition, not the mysterious tug he always thought would happen when he met his true father.

Nothing. Blank eyes, dank smell.

Samuel went into his routine. "My name is Samuel Davis and I have been searching for my father who was ... ah, lost in the Great War ... in Montreal." Samuel stopped waiting for a response.

None came.

"I was hoping that you might be .... Can you tell me where you were born or where you were stationed during the war .... Anything?"

Gordon lay still, eyes staring straight ahead. He watched the young fellow through a fog of jumbled thoughts. For years now he had trained his mind not to think, his heart not to feel. He had been so efficient in his training to numbness that he could now not connect his thoughts together easily. Rather than whole phrases, his conscious world was a series of snapshots: young blond-haired man, nice face, mouth moving, words, words, words. Lost. War, Montreal, Johanna, father. Like a drowning man, he was struggling to come back to the surface, to rise above the flood of words to make sense of it. It was such a mess.

Samuel tried once more, "My mother, Johanna Hinks, told me that my father was a very brave man, that he had suffered a terrible betrayal and that I ... that we never met ... but now that I am older I wanted to find him … if he is still alive …. Mom said he was a man of great promise."

Samuel's words seem futile, so he let them trail away. His eyes began to wander around the room. There were no pictures on the walls, no mementos on the bureau, no signs of any distinctive life at all. The only trace of a human touch was the Bible on the night-stand and the jumble of crinkled papers tucked into his pages.

Gordon did not move. He'd woven such a web of insanity around his true self that he couldn't make his way back to reality—it was like rowing in mud. More words came his way to confuse him. Father, Brave, Betray, Promise."

Samuel could see that it was hopeless. If this fellow is my dad, he'd never be able to admit it. "Well … thank … you for your time …. I am sorry to have bothered you. You're not my dad are you?"

With that Samuel beat a quick retreat, almost running out of the room as if to evade another avalanche of disappointment.

If Samuel had stayed a moment longer and taken time to look into that dog- eared bible, he would have seen his mother's handwritten notes. Or if he had waited seventeen minutes for Gordon to respond to his question, he would have heard a parched singular word come from Gordon's lips: "Son."

Montreal: Mount Royal Park (Sisson Ridge Park)
Friday, December 10, 1937, 12:47 p.m.

"I didn't find him, Mom." Samuel kicked a clump of snow on the path where they were walking.

"No?"

"No …." Samuel laughed to hide his disappointment. "How many hospitals and old age homes did I visit on my quest for my roots? I counted them ….thirty-four, thrity-four chances to find my dad and no luck."

Johanna stepped closer to her son, put her hand through his arm and walked with him closely for a good while before she spoke. "Perhaps it's better that you didn't find him. I mean ... I don't believe he wants to be found."

"Why ... why not?" Samuel asked quietly. "I'm his son."

Johanna thought for a bit, looked up to the grey slate sky. "He has his reasons ... reasons that we cannot tell. I trust him to know what was right."

Samuel was not to be put off so easily. "Isn't it right for a father to want to be with his son? Isn't it right for a man to want to help his wife and child?"

Johanna stopped and took a step back from her son. "He did help ...."

Samuel looked at his mother, "How?" The word was dripping with scorn. "How did he even lift a finger to help?"

Johanna could feel her anger building. "Samuel." After all these years she still came to Gordon's defence. "Samuel, you don't know what you're talking about."

Samuel looked skeptical, "I know I don't have a father, that he didn't even have the courtesy to leave me a forwarding address ... that he didn't ...."

"Samuel," Johanna cut across him sharply. "Samuel, how do you suppose we have survived all these years after your grandfather died? How do you think we can afford for you to travel and go to the best schools ...."

"I always supposed it was Grandad's estate."

"We lost that at the beginning of the Depression ... he had invested unwisely. When he died he had nothing ... just a few pieces of art."

"But ... then ... how?" Samuel was scratching his head with a mittened hand.

"It was your father," Johanna sighed. "I never wanted to tell you this but before your dad disappeared, he signed his entire fortune over to me."

"What?"

Johanna smiled slightly. "It was a considerable sum, and, taking your Aunt Thelma's advice, I invested in real estate and we've done very well by it."

Samuel looked confused. "He did that for you?"

"For us, Samuel, for us. I don't know how I know this, but I believe Gordon arranged his disappearance for reasons that only he can tell. But that he did it intentionally and in a way to provide for me ... and for you ... Of that, I am certain." Johanna stepped closer and gave her son a quick kiss on the cheek. "He did love you ... more than you will ever know."

Samuel was silent. To redeem himself he mentioned the one bit of information from his trip that he thought worthy of note. "I did find one interesting 'Gordon' in Saint John, New Brunswick ... of all places."

Johanna's heart jumped .... She couldn't tell why, but her soul was crying out, "This is the one." "Really?" she tried to sound non-committal ... How many times had she tried in the early years to find her lover? "What did you think of him?"

Samuel laughed. "He was old, half-dead, and living in the basement of this second-rate hospital with no real regime of treatment as far as I could see."

"Really?" Johanna tried to breathe slowly. "And why do you think he was ...what did you say ..."interesting?""

Oh nothing ... just he seemed so lost ... so pathetic .... That's all."

"And did he have any identifying marks, papers or personal effects?"

Samuel thought for a moment ... "No, just an empty room."

"Oh ... I see ...." Johanna's heart began to slow down." She took her son's arm again and steered him down the pathway. "I love this park."

"But ... now I remember." Samuel brightened, "He did have a Bible ... stuffed with papers." He turned to look at his mother. "I don't suppose it means anything. It was on his nightstand."

Johanna held back her excitement, "A Bible you say?"

"Stuffed with letters, bits and scraps of paper ... and a pen ... that's right, there was a fountain pen, too."

"Really?" Johanna smiled inwardly and thought to herself, "It's him then! He had a Bible when she last saw him at the cathedral." She began to walk more quickly. There was lightness in her step, the sun shone on her soul. She'd found him ... finally.

"But I don't think it was him ... he was too ... too old." Samuel made this final pronouncement and began to think of his upcoming term at university.

Johanna started to whistle.

"You're suddenly in a cheery mood. What's made you so happy?"

Johanna lied. "Just having you home makes me happy." He was alive ... breathing the same air ... that was enough for Johanna—to know he was still living. Enough. If her fiancé has chosen seclusion and solitude, so be it.

So be it!

Montreal
Thursday, October 31st, 1916, All Hallows Eve

Dear Gordon:

This is the evening of ghosts and spirits and goblins. And ghosts are haunting me. Every night I sleep with you. Did you know that? Your body is close and I can feel your gentle touch. When I am waking I see your reflection in the mirrors of my room—there you are naked again, touching me ... Oh how I wish my ghosts would become real. To have you back again.

There was a moment a few weeks back when I heard you cry out. It was more like a daydream voice. A single phrase "I'll have you right as rain." I don't know who you were meaning ... was it me ... or someone I love ... I asked myself why you would say such a simple thing. "Right as rain ... is rain particularly 'right'? Anyway I now have it ringing around in my mind ..."I'll have you right as rain."

I'm still basking in the glow of our coming marriage. It changes so much in my life to know that we will be together forever.

You'll notice that I am sure you are coming back … I know this beyond any doubt. Last night, in fit of fancy I went outside and shouted "No" to death and war that threaten to take you. "No … you shall not have him for he is mine." Am I crazy yet?

So keep your head down, watch out for your friends, let your compassion be your guide and trust in your courage.

I'm off to prepare cookies for the little kiddies who come down our street this time of year. Better to feed them treats than have them play tricks. (Last year they took apart our neighbour's wagon and reassembled it on his garage roof!)

Know that you are never far from my thoughts and that I am with you always. And remember that I have said "no" to any harm coming your way.

Jo

PS. Father says "Hello" and wishes you a good Christmas.

Bay of Fundy: St. Martin's Harbour
Tuesday, Nov. 17, 1992, 2:03 p.m.

Heather had been talking for fifteen minutes without a break. I sat transfixed … she was filling in so many of the blank spaces of Gordon's life: his regrets, the battles he thought he had lost, the shame, his deep love and despair.

"So you see they never had a chance to talk ... My grandmother went after him as he scurried from the cathedral, but she never found him. He just slipped away into the late-night fog. That's what she said. When my dad was old enough, he too went looking for him. My grandmother told me of a long train trip he took to visiting every Vets hospital in eastern Canada. But nothing came of it.

"Your dad didn't tell you this himself?"

"My father was killed on Juno Beach, June 6, 1944. My mother never got over the shock and she died of heart failure a year later. So it was my grandmother Johanna who raised me."

"Johanna?' I looked closely—her sharp eyes, intelligent manner. "You wouldn't know if your grandmother ever called herself "Jo?"

Heather thought for a moment. "No one ever called her that. She used to say she disliked nicknames." She smiled at a memory, "Once she told me to hold my tongue if I couldn't think of a person's proper name. She was a great stickler for particulars ... my grandmother."

"You loved her very much," the words were out of my mouth and I regretted my intrusion. "Excuse me, I didn't mean to pry."

Heather laughed easily, "Not at all ... that's just the kind of forthright talk she enjoyed. Never held back her feelings. And when she sniffed injustice ... thunderbolts have less energy."

"She sounds delightful."

"She was the best of women." Heather looked to the horizon across the bay and then turned to face me directly. "There was once when I thought she would tell me the whole story ...."

"The whole story?"

"Yes, the real romantic story." Heather touched my hand. "How my father came to be .... My grandmother wasn't married. She gave birth alone. What it was like in her day to be pregnant out of wedlock. How she suffered the gossip, why she never found another man. Whether she loved only this 'Gordon' fellow. I would have given anything to know."

"She never said anything?" I tried not to push but wanted to know more.

"Nothing except she loved him and he had his reasons."

Thinking back over Gordon's wandering tales, I had to agree. "He had his reasons for certain, but they are certainly more of mystery to me than anything."

It was Heather's turn to look closely at me. She liked what she saw. "You know more about Gordon and my grandmother …. I can see it in your eyes. Tell me …."

The boat bumped against the dock and I fell into Heather's surprising grasp. I tried to pull myself back, but our eyes locked. A message passed between us … a connection, a hint of something deeper. Then the moment passed. Sitting upright, I began my side of the story. "Gordon … the one I know from Saint John? What I know about him has been pieced together through two voices—a sea captain and a priest. Both were burdened by a sense of having betrayed someone or something … a promise of some kind …"

As I spoke, I could feel tears welling up again so I looked away to the horizon, trying to get a grip on my emotions. Heather took my hand and squeezed.

Montreal: Christ Church Cathedral
Sunday, December 9, 1917, 9:13 p.m.

Ryan was purple with rage as his men struggled to get to the front and out the side door where Gordon had fled. He kept shouting orders no one followed. A young woman swept past him and out the same door Gordon had exited, but he paid no attention to her. He was trying to command his troops. Eventually they got around the obstruction of the woman in the main aisle and ran to do their master's bidding. Ryan followed them out into the night, still shouting about their prospects in the army, if they didn't recapture the prisoner.

Hinks, who had not left the centre of the chancel, held the floor and asked again his question. "Reverend Hawthorne, did I just hear a young soldier suggest that you had mistreated young men given into your care?"

Cruikshank was on his feet immediately, "Preposterous. You little weasel, you are twisting these proceedings to avoid your own sorry behaviour. You are nothing but a ..."

Hawthorne who was deathly white, slowly stood and walked to the front, by Hinks. He went straight to the pulpit. The deliberateness of his actions stilled all voices. Hawthorne opened up the Bible on the stand, spread its pages smooth and made to offer a sermon. The congregation watched in awe, wondering what he would say.

"I am innocent," he began, "of any wrongdoing. I have never ... never done anything but serve my church and my God. These ... these lies that Gordon Davis just uttered are words of a coward, and indeed of grief. His father committed suicide just recently and I fear it has been too much for him. We can only ask our God to forgive him for—"

"Ask God to forgive you first." It was a stage whisper, no more. Hinks was uncertain if it was just his imagination, until he looked out in the audience and saw a slight man getting to his feet. "Ask God to forgive your sorry soul, Mr. Hawthorne."

Cruikshank whirled around and tried to shout down this new speaker, "Hush man ... let the priest make his statement for it is true and right and he has such virtue ...." But something in the young man's demeanour told the principal that he was not to be deterred and that something quite monstrous was about to happen. Cruikshank could feel it ... the chilling calm before a tremendous thunderclap.

The young man stood tall, took a deep breath and said plainly, "My name is Brent Smith and just by chance my employer, *The Toronto Star*, sent me to cover this meeting. I had no idea that it was ... that I would be...." Brent cleared his throat. "Ah .... Let me say this clearly. My name is Brent Smith and I was in Reverend Hawthorne's 'special communicants class' ... the one he held in his vestry. It always began with touching. Innocent hands resting on my knee, but before the hour was out, I was naked before him and he would have to play games with his hair while he ... ah ... touched me .... It was ... it was awful." Brent coughed, paused for a moment, suppressing the memories, and then continued. "The Reverend said I was his 'special gift,' a gift from heaven. He called our sessions 'prayer sessions' and told me to say nothing to anyone. At first I believed him. I trusted him. I was too young to know any different. 'It was our secret,' he said. 'I shouldn't tell my parents what we did.'"

Brent coughed again and stopped for a moment to find his bearings. Ryan had slipped back into the church the way he came and was about to shout about the devilry of the assembly for letting his victim escape, when he caught the drift of the debate and went stone silent.

Brent continued, "It wasn't until later that I discovered he had done it to so many others ... including Gordon Davis here .... We were all too young to know what to do. We went along but we hated it ... and some of us just ran away. We just ...."

Hawthorne tried to shout this man down, "Lies, lies ... the forked tongue of the devil ...."

Hinks took over and commanded Hawthorne to "Be still ... this is my cathedral and you be silent." Then turning to Brent, he said, "Go on."

"I have nothing more to say ... except I wish I had spoken up sooner .... I tried to run ... most of the young men in our church did the same ... went off to war to avoid his filthy fingers. I must say ... I am dismayed. I came here to report on the church that I love. And since arriving at this meeting, I have been harangued by speaker after speaker on how my church and my priest are examples of the great things that should happen all across this country. It was only Gordon's speech last night that made any sense. Well ... if you want to recruit men on account of them being frightened of the roaming hands of their reverend ... well, you go right ahead."

A great buzz went round the crowd. Cruikshank, who had been standing through this entire exchange, looked up at Hawthorne, saw the truth of his crimes in his eyes, and sank into his seat.

Hinks saw his chance and took it. "In the light of these revelations I suspect it is premature to consider declaring this present conflict a 'Holy War.' There is far too much scandal to be uncovered in this matter to consider any further motions at this time."

There were no objections. Hinks dismissed the community with a blessing.

Ryan ... who had seen his plans crash to dust in less than a minute, left quietly by the same side door he had entered. "Bloody fops ... the whole lot of them. Stupid of me to get involved with church-goers. They're not only lunatics, they're faggots." Ryan stepped lively along the dark sidewalk. "Thank God I didn't press that Davis chap too hard ... let the silly bastard run ... God ... with superiors like Hawthorne and Cruikshank, I'd be running too." Lieutenant Colonel Ryan stormed off into the mist and fog of the Montreal night, an almost hero. His career had hit its high point. In two months he would die, a victim of an unfortunate mix of too much alcohol, black ice and the St. Lawrence River.

Hinks watched the defeat of his enemies and felt no triumph. It was a despicable display of the church at its worst. He wanted to vomit. Having dismissed the crowd, he walked slowly down the main aisle, tucked his cross into the breast pocket of his vest and finding, Thelma, took her arm.

Walking slowly out of the sanctuary he felt like a burden had been lifted ... not a burden of guilt but one of false hope. He no longer had reason to pretend about his church. It was as bad as he had feared. There was nothing more to do. Turning to Thelma he asked quietly, "Will you marry me?"

Thelma smiled. "Never!"

Bay of Fundy: St. Martin's Harbour
Tuesday, Nov. 17, 1992, 2:13 p.m.

The deckhands had long since left the boat. The undertaker was gathering up his ropes and winches, carpets and papers. Heather rose, thanked me for my time and promised to stay in touch. She had some leads she wanted to track down. A letter perhaps?

"Keep safe," was all I said as I watched her walk off the wharf. Somehow I felt I was losing a close friend or ... a relative.

Fredericton: Isaac's Way Restaurant
Monday, April 14, 2014, 12:01 p.m.

For five minutes I had sat in silence, looking at the second envelope, turning it over and over in my hands. Could I, should I open it? It was full. Unlike the first, it had a note on the outside. "For the Reverend

Chris: Here's the note I mentioned. My grandmother gave me this just before she died and asked me to keep it safe, pass it on to her Gordon's next of kin. Heather"

"Looks like she intended for you to have it," Patricia interrupted my thoughts. "She kept it safe … too bad she never was able to deliver it."

Slowly I opened the letter and pulled out a smaller worn, well-worn envelope. I looked down at this letter and could hardly believe what I was holding. There was nothing on the outside of this envelope but his name: "Gordon Davis." From what I could recall, it was definitely the same hand that had written the other eleven "Jo" letters Gordon had kept in his Bible.

I ran a hand over it slowly and then took a corner and ripped it open gently. Extracting a single sheet of paper, I began to read.

Friday August 6th, 1982 Hiroshima Day

Dear Gordon:

If you read this, I am dead. I haven't many days left … this blasted cancer takes me down step-by-relentless-step. God I hate it … the betrayal by my own body.

Are you dead too … I dread to think it, but I may be writing to your memory and addressing a relative. Whatever, I am not ashamed of my feelings and too old to take offence. Besides, my words are for you and if you are in another realm I trust our Maker to ensure that you get a chance to read these thoughts of mine before I pass on to join you wherever that might be.

Enough metaphysics.

I will leave this note with our granddaughter … yes … we had a child and he had a daughter. We had a son, Samuel … I know my father mentioned him to you, though no one ever completely explained who he was ...

I still love you. Of all the others twinges of affection that I have felt for other men, even for my father or Thelma ... they are but shadows of that deep love we knew. Remember true love comes only to a few in each generation and then migrates on into the next ... we were fortunate to have had our piece of that adventure.

O, I tried to find you ... wrote notes everywhere, thinking I could revive you from wherever you had hidden. Then I began to see that you were not to be found because you willed it. This was your last act of courage. Were you doing it for me? I think so. To protect me from some evil. I wish you hadn't. I wish you had let me make that decision.

Thank you for the money, by the way ... it saved my life and that of my father ... He always raised a glass in your honour on your birthday. He was so proud of you ... as was I. A Mr. Tompkins kept us informed regularly about your bequest ... oh, he wants his pen back by the way. So we toasted Mr. Tompkins too!

After you left the church, Cruikshank and Hawthorne discredited themselves. For one awful night I thought you meant it when you said that didn't love me and then I started to put together your puzzle ... it was the coughing wasn't it? Every time you coughed it was like a signal that you didn't believe what you were saying. I know that now ... clever ... too clever by half, in fact.

And Samuel? He was a great man ... the Second War took him. Damn war takes all good men ... but his spirit lives on in his daughter. They are both you ... I wish you could see them as I do. They shine in every fibre of their being with your spirit of generosity and courage. My, my! There are times when I start to cry when I think of them, for I see you walking in their skin.

I must go now. I will love you into eternity. O, yes ... Samuel did find you. He never knew it and I never told him that the un-talking man in a bed in Saint John was his father. I wouldn't betray you that way. Did you know him when he came in the door? Were you really a vegetable? I flatter myself that it was all an act, that you knew who he was, but you didn't speak, saving me from some dreadful truth ... to protect me ... To keep a promise maybe ...

Forgive me if I betrayed you in any way and with my whole heart I forgive you ... Our timing was never the best was it—me going one way on the train while you went the other. But we met for a time and in that week I knew the meaning of "joy." That was our story, an ancient and eternal story! Love!

Bless you and bless my granddaughter if you can. She is as much you as me.

Love,
Jo

Fredericton: Isaac's Way Restaurant
Monday, April 14, 2014, 12:36 p.m.

"I didn't tell you the 'bad' news." Patricia took a swallow of her coffee. "It is as I expected … the provincial government is claiming back expenses against this account. Now that we have established Gordon's estate, they are charging $2,376,457 against it."

"What?" I was hardly listening … reading and re-reading the last few lines.

"The bad news," Patricia continued, "is that your uncle's estate now only has $375.21 left in it. I am sorry …" She pulled forms from her briefcase to sign.

I reached into a coat pocket and withdrew a fountain pen engraved with "Love believes all things, bears all things" and signed where she asked. At last she handed me a cheque for $375.21. "That's it."

"Perfect," I replied. "Just enough for the gas home." I went back to the note and didn't notice her leaving. Who cares about money? I had my uncle back!

Finally, I stood up and looked about, foolishly thinking I should make a speech or raise a toast. In the end I paid the bill and left. In a state of confusion, I checked my pockets, found my bike key, looked around a city that had been my home and walked back to my Goldwing. Still confused, feeling a deep sorrow and yet, finally complete.

Trying to regain some reverent dignity, I slowly folded the letter, slipped it into my inside suit pocket, collected my thoughts, pulled out my iPhone and dialed my Ellen.

When I heard her voice, I started right in, surprised at my own excitement, "Hi Love, you'll never guess what a story I have to tell …"

The End

ABOUT THE AUTHOR

Christopher Levan, pastor, professor, and parent, has spent a lifetime working with words. His day job is in a church and his life's vocation is as a "repairer of dreams," helping others to achieve their goals and ambitions. Whether in a university classroom or a Cuban village, his gifts of enthusiasm and energy are conveyed by vibrant words that move hearts and turn heads. A baker, biker, and tour guide when not writing or helping others, Christopher dreams of crafting the right turn of phrase to change the world. He resides in Toronto, Canada with his wife, Ellen.

Lightning Source UK Ltd.
Milton Keynes UK
UKOW03f0401090217
293936UK00002B/511/P